THE DARK TIDE

Simon McCleave is a best-selling crime novelist. His first book, *The Snowdonia Killings*, was released in January 2020 and soon became an Amazon bestseller, reaching No.1 in the UK Chart and selling over 200,000 copies. His eight subsequent novels in the DI Ruth Hunter Snowdonia series have all ranked in the Amazon top 20 and he has sold over a million books worldwide.

Before he was an author, Simon worked as a script editor at the BBC and a producer at Channel 4 before working as a story analyst in Los Angeles. He then became a script writer, writing on series such as *Silent Witness*, *Murder In Suburbia*, *Teachers*, *The Bill*, *Eastenders* and many more. His Channel 4 film *Out of the Game* was critically acclaimed and described as 'an unflinching portrayal of male friendship' by *Time Out*.

Simon lives in North Wales with his wife and two children.

www.simonmccleave.com

THE
DARK
TIDE

SIMON McCLEAVE

avon.

Published by AVON
A division of HarperCollins*Publishers*
1 London Bridge Street
London SE1 9GF

www.harpercollins.co.uk

HarperCollins*Publishers*
1st Floor, Watermarque Building, Ringsend Road
Dublin 4, Ireland

A Paperback Original 2022
2

First published in Great Britain by HarperCollins*Publishers* 2022

A catalogue copy of this book is available from the British Library.

ISBN: 978-0-00-852482-1

Typeset in Sabon Lt Std by Palimpsest Book Production Limited,
Falkirk, Stirlingshire

Printed and bound in the UK using 100% Renewable Electricity at CPI
Group (UK) Ltd

MIX
Paper from
responsible sources
FSC™ C007454

This book is produced from independently certified FSC™ paper
to ensure responsible forest management.

For more information visit: www.harpercollins.co.uk/green

For Nicola

ANGLESEY

There is a word in Welsh that has no exact translation into English – Hiraeth. It is best defined as the bond you feel with a place – a mixture of pride, homesickness and a determination to return. Most people that have visited Anglesey leave with an understanding of Hiraeth.

Prologue

West Manchester, 12 August 2018

Detective Inspector Laura Hart of the Greater Manchester Police – or 'the GMP' – sat quietly in the back of an Armed Response Vehicle as it drove slowly out from behind the disused petrol station where it had been hidden for the last ten minutes. It turned left and headed towards Brannings Warehouse on the Central Park Trading Estate, situated to the west of Manchester.

She was sharing the stuffy vehicle with four Armed Response Officers – AROs – in full combat equipment. Within the police, AROs were referred to as 'shots', and they were clad in black helmets, Perspex goggles, balaclavas, Kevlar bulletproof vests and Heckler & Koch G36C assault rifles. The G36C carried a 100 round C-Mag drum magazine and fired at the deadly rate of 750 rounds per minute. In an operation like this, the AROs needed more firepower than the 9mm pistols or carbines that they usually carried. They weren't going to take any risks today.

As the armoured BMW X5 slowed, Laura reached up to hold on to the leather strap that hung from the car roof, to keep her balance. She could feel the adrenaline surging through her body. She felt agitated and highly alert. Her Kevlar bulletproof vest was heavy as it bounced against her shoulders. As always, it was way too big. She was a diminutive 5' 4", which meant even the smallest vest, with its heavy armour plating, jolted around her body and left scratches and bruises.

Why can't they make a vest that fits me? It's not as though I'm an elf, is it? she thought dryly to herself.

If wearing a vest had been a rare occurrence, she might not have minded. But because of the escalation in the number of armed gangs in Manchester, she was permanently putting one on. Part of her found it annoying, as she had never received as much as a scratch while on these operations. The other part of her thought of her kids: Jake, aged eight, and Rosie, fifteen.

There can always be a first time, she told herself. *You're not bloody immortal.*

Laura was forty-three years old, blonde, with arched brows that framed her large, expressive chestnut eyes. She wore a permanent expression of reassurance, whether it was on a police operation like today, or holding the hand of her son as he walked along the top of a high wall.

The inside of the ARV was silent except for the crackle of the Tetra police radio and the mumbled voice of Gold Command giving the driver instructions. It smelt of gun oil, male sweat and stale cigarettes. Looking over at the young ARO next to her, she got a waft of his chewing gum as he stared at the floor, readying himself for the operation.

As he scratched his dark beard, he sensed her gaze and looked up at her. 'You okay, ma'am?' He had a thick Yorkshire accent.

Laura nodded. 'Never better,' she replied sardonically. Her accent had a trace of North Wales.

2

He grinned. 'Just keep behind us, eh? We don't want you having to use that thing,' he said protectively and then gestured to the Glock 19 pistol in the holster on her belt.

She smiled back at him. Neither did she. It might have fifteen bullets in it, but she had never fired a gun in over twenty years as a police officer – other than at the police firing range.

She glanced back to the road behind where another ARV BMW followed them.

Today was *Operation Solar*. A reliable Covert Human Intelligence Source – the over-complicated Police vernacular for a snout, a grass or an informant – had identified the disused Brannings Warehouse as a major drugs factory for the Fallowfield Hill Gang, a notorious and powerful Organised Crime Group in South Manchester. The gang's formation and roots went back as far as the early seventies, and they had been part of the eruption of gang warfare in the nineties that saw over three hundred shootings in five years – the UK tabloid press had renamed Manchester 'Gunchester' at the time. However, the gang had become nervous and volatile after the arrest of their two leaders, Lee Jennings and Tyrone Amis, for a drive-by shooting at the funeral of a member of the Doddington Gang. Manchester CID had intel that the gang members they were on their way to intercept, who were running the manufacture of crack cocaine, were heavily armed.

The driver spoke into the radio. 'Gold Command, Gold Command. Sierra Oscar five, are you receiving, over?'

Gold Command, the officer in charge of *Operation Solar*, was Superintendent Ian Butterfield. He would be watching the operation in the warm safety of West Didsbury nick, via remote cameras placed in the ARV and the helmet of the lead ARO, Sergeant Phillips. Laura didn't rate Butterfield as an on-the-ground copper. He was a political animal, more

3

interested in schmoozing and working his way up the career ladder. He had no interest in straightforward police work as his time and energy were spent dropping poison into people's ears and watching his back in case there was a knife headed for it. And that made him a dangerous liability on operations like this.

'Gold Command to Sierra Oscar five. Receiving, go ahead. Over,' Gold Command acknowledged.

'Sierra Oscar five. We have arrived at the target destination. Out,' replied the driver. 'Stand by.'

Laura unclipped her seatbelt and opened the door.

Phew! It's even hotter outside than in the ARV.

Getting out slowly, she gazed up at the concrete warehouse. A few of the windows on the first floor were boarded up and covered in red graffiti. It looked dilapidated and abandoned, no doubt the reason why it had been chosen for a covert drugs factory.

She clicked her radio on and spoke. 'Five-three to Gold Command, we are approaching target location, over.'

In their well-rehearsed technique, the AROs fanned out and moved swiftly towards the flank wall of the warehouse in total silence.

It was going to be CQC once they were inside – Close Quarter Combat, which entailed moving quickly through a series of rooms and corridors until the suspects were captured or nullified.

A rusty, graffitied sheet of aluminium that covered a doorway shook noisily in the wind as if warning the gang of their presence. Two black birds, possibly ravens, flew from behind the doorway and up into the air, eventually resting on the filthy guttering above, where they squawked and chattered loudly.

She heard the faint sound of a police siren in the distance. It had become the incessant backdrop to many parts of Manchester in recent years.

4

It's very quiet, she thought. *Too quiet, maybe?*

There was a whoosh as the wind picked up again, and a discarded can of Coke rattled and skittered boisterously across the concrete ground beside her.

She felt uneasy.

Glancing to her right, she saw the AROs fan out further as they moved into position, crouching low against the building. They weren't going any further until everything was secure. Three of them reached to their belts and took out G60 stun grenades.

There was a sudden glint of light as a window on the first floor moved slightly and caught the sunlight in its glass.

What was that?

Her heart now pounded against her chest.

Was someone watching them from inside? Did they already know they were there?

How could they know we were coming?

Her pulse quickened as she approached the derelict doorway that had been covered by the rattling aluminium sheet.

She listened for a moment.

It really is too quiet, she thought.

Moving back, she peered through the smeared glass of a downstairs window to see nothing but an empty shell of a room. Not a single movement to indicate anyone was inside.

Maybe the intel had been wrong? It wouldn't have been the first time they turned up to find that a gang had been tipped off and cleared out. It had become a worrying pattern. CID was full of rumours about a leak. Was one of her fellow officers really bent and taking money to keep the OCGs one step ahead of them?

Taking a breath to calm her nerves, she glanced back at the AROs, who still hunkered down by the wall. One of them shook his head to show he hadn't seen anything either.

5

Looks like we're going in.

She clicked her radio on as she took a few steps away from the warehouse and glanced up at the first floor again.

'Gold Command, Gold Command from five-three. Over.'

'Gold Command. Receiving. Over.'

'Five-six. I'm at the target location, but we have no visual on suspects. Entry team is in final assault position, over.'

'Gold Command. Received. Proceed with caution—'

CRACK! CRACK! CRACK! CRACK!

Before she could react, bullets hit the ground beside her foot, throwing dust and dirt into the air.

Jesus!

The burst of automatic gunfire was deafening. All the firearms used by the GMP were configured to not fire on semi-automatic, so the sound of the automatic gunfire was particularly frightening to the police officers because they knew it couldn't be them firing.

They were under enemy fire.

Laura flinched and jumped backwards. She glanced up at a window where a man in a balaclava held some kind of assault rifle to his shoulder. Another flash from the gun's muzzle and she dived for cover.

CRACK! CRACK! CRACK!

Bloody hell. They did know we were coming.

The air above her exploded like an ear-piercing fireworks display.

Move! Move! You're a sitting bloody duck, Laura.

She crawled across the grimy concrete towards the cover of the warehouse wall.

Jesus H Christ.

CRACK! CRACK! BANG!

Shouting, glass breaking, a yell.

An ARO appeared beside her and shouted, 'You okay, ma'am?'

'Yeah, just about!' she gasped over the din. Her breathing was shallow, her heart thumping, but she didn't think she'd suffered more than a bruised knee and grazed palms from diving to the floor.

'Right, ma'am, I need to get you back to the ARV. Come with me, I've got you covered!' shouted the ARO as he grabbed her bulletproof vest and yanked her away from the wall. He wasn't really giving her much choice in the matter.

The sound of gunfire was ear-splitting as they sprinted across the ground to safety behind the ARV.

A bullet zipped over her head.

'Thanks,' Laura said, hitting the ground behind the vehicle.

The bullets from the gang members inside the warehouse hammered into the ARV's bodywork with a series of loud, frightening metallic thuds that rocked the vehicle.

Jesus! Please let me get out of here alive today.

The faces of her children flashed through her mind and she winced at another burst of gunfire. 'Gold Command from five-six. Code Zero! Code Zero! Officers under fire! I repeat, officers under fire!' she yelled into her radio.

The air was full of thunderous noise and the smell of cordite.

The ARO opened the back door of the BMW. 'Ma'am, we need to get out of here. We're outnumbered.'

Her radio crackled. 'Gold Command to five-six, we have reports of two uniformed officers inside the target location, over.'

What did he say?

'Can you repeat, over?' she hollered. The noise of gunfire made it hard to hear anything.

'Repeat, we have reports of two uniformed officers inside your target location, over.'

What the hell are they talking about? How could two uniformed police officers be inside the warehouse?

7

As the AROs retreated and scuttled back towards their ARVs, the gunfire from the warehouse started to subside a little.

'Five-six received. Why weren't we told this intel earlier, over?' she growled. It was information that would have changed their whole approach to the operation and their attempt to storm the warehouse.

'Five-six, apparently there was a delay somewhere in Dispatch, over.'

Well, that's not bloody good enough, she thought. *Those officers could have been killed if we'd gone in with all guns blazing.*

'Do we have any more details on the officers inside, over?' she asked, fighting to keep the anger out of her voice. Her ears were ringing incessantly.

'Gold Command to five-six. Officers' names are PC Sam Hart and PC Louise McDonald. They were on a routine call-out when they entered the target premises, over. We believe we now have a hostage situation, over.'

Laura felt sick at the news as she mumbled, 'Gold Command, received.'

An ARO pushed her into the back of the car and slammed the door behind her.

The side window exploded, showering them in glass.

'Let's go!' an ARO yelled.

Panic threatened to overwhelm her as the ARV started to pull away.

'Stop the car!' she yelled. Her head was spinning with what she had just been told.

The ARV slammed on its brakes, throwing everyone forward sharply.

As Laura grasped the handle as if to open the vehicle door, an ARO stretched out his gloved hand to stop her. 'Ma'am, we need to get out of here or we're going to get killed.'

She looked at him pleadingly and said, 'I need to get out. Please.'

Another bullet hammered into the chassis of the vehicle with a deadly thud.

'Why?' the ARV asked, looking completely baffled.

'PC Sam Hart is my husband,' Laura explained, her whole body now stiff with terror.

'If you go out there, you'll die,' the ARV shouted over more gunfire. 'And if we sit here any longer, there will be casualties. We'll have to come back for him.'

Laura nodded and closed her eyes. Her overwhelming instinct was to go and save Sam, but she knew the ARO was right.

'Go! Go! Go!' the ARO yelled.

The ARV lurched away from the warehouse, but Laura didn't really notice.

Chapter 1

Laura had set her alarm for just before dawn. It was late June – the summer solstice – so that meant 4.45 a.m. She didn't mind. She rarely slept properly anymore.

In a dozy, fumbling haze, she got out of bed and put on her swimsuit, woollen hat, hoodie and trackies, and tiptoed through the still, sleepy darkness of the house. Looking at her reflection in the hall mirror, she pulled her wavy blonde hair back into a ponytail.

Elvis, their three-year-old Mountain Mastiff – a Bernese Mountain and English Mastiff mix – turned his big brown eyes towards her from where he lay in his basket by the back door. Elvis was a beautiful caramel colour with a black and white muzzle. Not only was he a big softie with the kids, he was also a great guard dog as he was enormous, and his deep, thundering bark would make it clear to burglars that it wasn't just a designer cockapoo standing behind the front door.

'Come on, Elvis,' she whispered as they slipped out of the kitchen door and into the darkness.

The beach was within walking distance and she let Elvis off the lead almost immediately. He trotted over to the grass verge and sniffed like his life depended on it.

On the journey down, she gazed up at the sky, which still twinkled with stars, then looked low towards the north-east. She read that Venus and the waning crescent moon, which were only nine degrees apart, would be visible, and to her delight, they were. For a moment, she imagined what it might be like to look back at herself from the moon's surface. There was such relief to realise she would be just another indistinguishable speck on the surface of a tiny planet. If only she could keep that perspective throughout the day.

She undressed on the vast, empty beach, the only sounds the rhythmic whoosh of the waves and buffeting moan of the wind. The air was pregnant with the familiar salty fragrance of the sea. To the left was the endless span of wind-scoured coastal land that stretched to the north. A rugged kiss where the grey rocks met the indigo waves of early morning, as if they were playing a game where neither worried about who would win. Below the tide line, the rocks were festooned with swathes of glistening, dark green seaweed.

She and Jake, her eleven-year-old son, had recently explored the rocks, which were covered in exquisite crystalline flecks. There were many V-shaped ravines containing screes of colourful stones and small pools of seawater. Crannies that were filled with flowers: pink thrift, mauve mallow and white sea campions. At certain places, the water had worn the rocks into holes, like tiny, secret caves, and a stunning arched bridge of rock. Standing on the bridge, she and Jake had watched the violent force which the powerful waves generated within such a confined space. The noise and sheer energy had been thrilling and scary.

To the right was the long, dune-backed sweep of white

sand that dusted this part of the island. Elvis settled himself down and lay by her clothes, as he did on mornings like this.

She padded down the beach, realising that somehow the flat, wet sand that she dug her toes into had become her natural habitat.

A wave raced towards her feet and covered them as she waded in. Soft ribbons of birch-coloured oarweed, the local kelp seaweed, gently curled around her toes and then disappeared as the wave receded.

Across the icy water that now lapped at her calves were the dark, colourless shadows of the Snowdonia mountains on the Welsh mainland. It was only three miles across the narrow strip of sea. Yet, because of there being two tidal pulls, the Strait was a lethal mixture of powerful undercurrents and whirlpools.

Come in, Laura, you can do it, came the encouraging refrain from her reluctant mind.

Steeling herself for a second, she dived into the freezing water. Fully submerged, her whole body sparked, and she broke the surface with a tremendous gasp. It was like nature's defibrillator, shocking her back to life. Endorphins raced through her neural pathways and found their way to her brain, bringing exhilaration. All the pain, frustration and grief had been blasted away. She felt saved, reborn.

It's good to be alive, she thought.

Now dressed, Laura traipsed through the sand dunes with Elvis at her side. Her legs had that satisfying ache she got after exercise. The rising sun burnt a strip of orange across the horizon, and the air felt several degrees warmer than when she'd arrived forty minutes earlier.

A figure appeared out of the dunes in front of her and startled her.

It was Gareth. Or Detective Inspector Gareth Williams, to give him his full title.

'Christ, Gareth! You scared me!' She laughed a little too hard.

He pulled an apologetic face. 'Sorry. I was miles away.'

Crouching down to calm Elvis, she looked up at Gareth. In his early fifties, he was tall and muscular, with dark, hooded eyes and a shaved head. She definitely fancied him.

'How is it?' he asked, gesturing to the sea. He wore a grey hoodie and was carrying a sports bag, which she assumed contained his swimming gear and a towel. It had been Gareth who suggested she get involved in the early morning cold-water swimming club, the Bluetits.

'Colder than I thought it was going to be,' she admitted.

'Given the state of my head, that might be a good thing,' he said with a rueful smile.

'Hangover?' she asked.

'Either that or someone played football with my head last night,' he joked.

'That bad?' She snorted. 'Full-fat Coke and bacon seem to work for me.'

'Thanks for the tip.'

A couple seconds of silence followed before Gareth leant down to give Elvis a stroke. 'And who's this?'

'Elvis.'

'Elvis! Brilliant!' He chortled. 'He's beautiful, isn't he?'

'Yeah, he's a big softie.'

'I had a dog once. I called him Shark,' Gareth joked. 'Bit of a nightmare when I took him for walks on the beach.'

Laura groaned and rolled her eyes. 'Gareth, that is terrible.'

He grinned. 'Hey, it's dawn, so it's the best joke I've got.'

Their eyes met again. There was something reassuring, even soothing, about the way his soft brown eyes just rested on her.

14

'I didn't know you came down here on your own,' she said, fumbling for the right thing to say. 'I mean, I thought you only did the Saturday morning thing?'

'I haven't swum solo for ages,' Gareth explained. 'But I quite like having company. I think I have to be in the right frame of mind to come on my own.'

'Or seriously hungover?'

He laughed. 'Yeah. That too.'

'Hey, let me know you're coming next time and I'll meet you here,' she suggested and wondered if she was being too forward. 'I mean, if you want?'

'That would be great,' he said with a nod and a smile. 'I'd really like that.'

'You need to promise not to laugh at the noises I make getting in the water,' she said with a grin. 'I can be a bit of wimp.'

'Yeah, well, I sound like a ten-year-old girl being attacked by a wasp when I get in, so you're in good company,' he quipped.

She laughed and then caught his eye for a second longer than felt appropriate. There was definitely an attraction between them. She could feel it.

'I'd better go and drag the kids out of bed,' she said. 'Enjoy your dip.'

'Thanks,' he said, looking directly at her. 'I'm going to hold you to that morning swim.'

'Good.'

Turning to go, she walked away with an extra spring in her step as she clicked her fingers to beckon Elvis.

Does swimming together count as an actual date? she wondered. She felt a little tingle of excitement.

Two hours later, Laura's eyes flickered open slowly. She blinked as she felt the warmth of a tongue running down

15

her body, over her breasts, rounding her belly button and heading further south.

Straightening her back, she took a breath in anticipation. A soft hand guided her legs open gently.

She moaned.

'Sam, Sam, what are you doing to me? We've got to go to work,' she said, but she wasn't the sort of wife to offer too much resistance to her husband's morning attention.

His breath was hot against her neck and he bit her gently, and then with increasing force. He whispered in her ear and goosebumps shivered down her spine.

Then she felt the weight of him on top of her. This would be the perfect way to start the day.

As she wriggled in anticipation and moved the duvet away from her face to look at him, Laura realised that the hand and tongue had vanished.

Was I dreaming? Really? How is that fair? said the grumbling voice inside her head.

Reaching out her left hand, she could feel that the other side of the bed was cold and empty. An overwhelming sense of disappointment descended.

Sod it.

When she thought of her husband, Sam, she always imagined his face first. His strong majestic forehead, dark thick eyebrows and deep blue eyes. When she first met him, her sister said he looked like the film star Paul Newman. She couldn't see it herself – she thought he was more along the lines of Oasis frontman Liam Gallagher. She thought of the tiny lines around his eyes that made them twinkle, like he knew something she didn't. Or the flick of his eyebrow just before he said something sharp and witty. Because that was Sam. Sharp and witty. And if he said nothing, she would give him her usual quizzical look and ask, *What are you thinking, Sam?* Always a dangerous question in a marriage that had lasted over twenty years. Did she really want to know what he was thinking? Not those transient thoughts about what he might pick up for tea, questions for that night's parents' evening or whether there was enough petrol in the car to get to work. No, the deep, dark questions about life, its meaning and its future.

'You'd better get out of bed,' said a voice she recognised.

Sitting up on her elbows, she glanced over and saw that Sam had dressed for work and sat cross-legged in an old armchair on the other side of the room. He had an inner stillness that she found incredibly sexy. Other men his age were balls of nervous or awkward energy, weighed down by the stresses of middle age. But not Sam. He was a constable in the Manchester Met Police and he walked into rooms like a cowboy. Her cowboy, thank you very much.

'Were you just sitting there, watching me sleep?' she asked him with a knowing smile.

He smirked. 'Yes.' His accent contained a trace of Leeds, where he was born and brought up. Yet he was anything but the dour Yorkshireman.

'And you know that's creepy?'

He shrugged. 'You always say that, but there are wives who might think it's cute, or even romantic.'

'Not me, buster,' she joked, shaking her head with a grin. 'First, it's the watching you sleep. Then it's the demands to know where I've been. Then a tracker in the car. Finally it becomes stalking, divorce and a restraining order.'

'Bloody hell, love!' Sam chuckled. 'At least your career as a police officer hasn't darkened your view of the world.'

'I prefer it that way.'

The sunlight from outside had started to prod through the frail curtains. It was going to be another glorious day on the Isle of Anglesey.

Anglesey. A beautiful, historic island off the north-west

17

coast of Wales. With Holy Island to its west, and Puffin Island to its south, Anglesey had 260 square miles of stunning mountains, lakes and beaches. An island steeped in the folk-lore of druids, Arthurian legend and dark tales of Roman and Viking invasion. Laura had travelled the world and yet found Anglesey to be a unique place with a character and mood all of its own. More importantly, their kids, Rosie and Jake, loved it and the move allowed them a new start with a chance to lay some of the ghosts of the past to rest.

Laura and Sam had first met when they both worked as uniformed officers in West Didsbury in Manchester in the late 1990s. They connected over their dry and inappropriate sense of humour and love of music and film. On their second date, she played him the whole of Nick Drake's *Five Leaves Left* album as they smoked a spliff. When Sam got up to go, she made him listen to her favourite Velvet Underground song, *Sunday Morning,* telling him they could listen to it again while having breakfast.

Within four months, they had moved into a tiny flat in north-east Manchester, five miles from where they worked as their Sarge had told them to keep a decent distance from where they worked as coppers. You didn't want to be popping into your local for a pint, only to bump into someone you'd nicked the week before. It could still happen, but it was far less likely.

The first two years of living together were a blissful mix of working hard and playing hard. Sam's genuine passion lay within 'on the ground' local community policing. He had a real knack for winning the trust of locals, and an ability to communicate with and listen to everyone. From commu-nity leaders to the disenfranchised teenagers on the streets who felt that dealing drugs was their only option for a better life, Sam had time for everyone.

In contrast, Laura had wanted to be a detective ever since

she developed an early teen girl-crush on Christine Cagney, a scrappy, feisty NYPD female detective in the eighties television show *Cagney & Lacey*. The show was way ahead of its time, featuring nuanced storylines about date rape, abortion and working mothers. The two female protagonists were in control of their own cases and were rarely rescued by their male colleagues. They were brave and gave as good as they got, with a repertoire of acidic one-line put-downs. On top of all that, Christine Cagney was attractive, with a great eighties blonde hairstyle, the gravelly voice of a smoker, a complex love life and a slight drink problem. Growing up in a tiny village in Anglesey, Laura found everything in life relatively boring and mundane, so Christine Cagney became the perfect role model for someone looking to lead a colourful and interesting life as a young woman. So, Laura had resolved to become a detective.

Swinging her feet over the side of the bed, she stretched her arms towards the ceiling.

God, that feels better.

'I love the shape of your back,' Sam purred.

Grabbing a cream cotton dressing gown from the back of the door, she smiled. 'You always said that.'

'It's perfect,' he insisted. 'You're perfect.'

'Why, thank you,' she said in a jokey voice. Compliments, even from Sam, made her feel uncomfortable.

'Where did you disappear to at the crack of dawn?' he asked her.

'I went swimming. It was beautiful. But then I cheated and crawled back into bed and fell asleep. That's not really the idea.'

'You swam on your own?' He sounded suspicious.

She laughed. 'Yes, on my own.' Why was he being so weird about it? It wasn't as if it was the first time she'd been swimming at dawn.

19

'I'll come with you next time,' he promised.

His comment stopped her in her tracks for a moment. She knew that he'd never come with her.

'What are you after?' She laughed as she headed for the en-suite bathroom.

'Nothing,' Sam said with a shrug. 'Although your spaghetti carbonara and a blow job wouldn't go amiss when I get back from work.'

She rolled her eyes, realising that a tear had appeared. 'That's what I always loved about you. You always made me laugh.'

As she wiped the tear from her face with the cuff of her dressing gown, she looked back at the old armchair, which was empty.

She would have given anything to have Sam sitting there right now. Anything. Everything.

But Constable Samuel Edward Hart had been killed while on active duty in West Manchester three years earlier.

Chapter 2

Detective Inspector Gareth Williams yawned, stretched his back and then finished his second strong coffee of the morning. Despite a thundering hangover, he'd arrived at the CID office at Beaumaris Police Station just after seven. He had started the day with a swim in the icy sea and bumped into Laura Hart – or *Lovely Laura,* as he called her in his own internal dialogue. They had arranged to go for an early morning swim together one morning, and he couldn't wait. She had been on his mind for months now. She was attractive, intelligent and confident.

He glanced at his watch. Only 7.30 a.m. As far as he was concerned, the perfect time of the day. First, he could get on with his work uninterrupted. Second, in the peace and quiet of the early morning, he had time to think about the cases he was working on with a sharp clarity. No phones, no meetings and no petty arguments about overtime or budget cuts.

The top button of his cobalt-coloured shirt was already undone, shirt sleeves rolled up and his navy-coloured tie unravelled on the desk. The shelves in his office carried the obligatory family photos, although he had removed any trace of Nell. They now mainly featured his teenage nephew and niece, Charlie and Fran. Gareth's brother, Rob, lived in Hong Kong and made a fortune working for the Bank of America. He was happily married to a Kiwi called Aleida, had two healthy kids and a penthouse that looked over the harbour. Rob was officially a *jammy wanker*, but he was happy for his brother. They spoke at least once a week, usually about rugby, and shared a love of obscure eighties bands such as The Associates and Talk Talk.

On the rest of the shelves, there was the usual senior officer memorabilia. Framed commendations. A couple of newspaper cuttings. And, of course, his pride and joy – a signed photo of the Grand Slam winning Welsh Rugby team from 2012.

There were seven police stations on Anglesey: Holyhead, Amlwch, Benllech, Menai Bridge, Gogledd Cymru, Rhosneigr and Beaumaris, which was one of the smallest. With a population of seventy thousand, Anglesey had a relatively low crime rate, although Holyhead, the UK's major port for Ireland, brought in its fair share of problems from across the Irish Sea because, until recently, the port was perceived to be an easy entry point for gangs involved in human trafficking and drug smuggling. There had been attempts in recent months to address that and tighten security, which had helped. However, a darker, more menacing problem had appeared on their radar. With Merseyside less than eighty miles away, Anglesey Police were beginning to see various county lines operations on the island. And extreme violence was the inevitable by-product of county lines operations, as gangs fought out turf wars. It was a worrying trend.

Born and bred in Beaumaris, Gareth saw little reason to spread his wings beyond the island of his birth. A brief spell at the University of Aberystwyth had been cut short by a keen interest in rugby, drinking and girls. His degree in psychology became an unwelcome distraction to everything else on campus, and at the end of his second year, he was told not to bother coming back. A fight and an incident with a fire extinguisher had then nearly resulted in his arrest, which would have put paid to his real ambition in life: to become a police officer and eventually a detective.

Pushing two paracetamol from a blister pack, Gareth took a large mouthful of 'full-fat' Coca-Cola and swallowed them down. His raid on a fresh bottle of Jameson's whiskey the night before was driven by pride, self-pity and anger. His wife, Nell, was having an affair and he could do nothing about it. Last night, they had finally agreed their marriage was over and they needed to get a divorce.

Was he surprised? Of course not. They'd both known it was coming for a long time. There had been a terrible inevitability about the affair and their split that they'd ignored for years. Doing little to dispel the stereotype of the hard-drinking detective who worked long hours, Gareth had allowed Nell to play the part of his long-suffering wife. And then Andrew Leith, with his twinkly brown eyes and salt-and-pepper hair, took over the headship at St Cuthbert's Primary School where Nell worked – and that was that. Nell was ten years younger than Gareth and he wondered if the attentions of the forty-year-old Leith had proved too much to ignore.

Gareth knew there were more divorced and separated detectives than happily married ones. A cliché that proved the rule.

It wasn't just the hours they worked. It was the way that what they did and saw on a daily basis gnawed into their very being. As a defence against that gnawing destruction, detectives became increasingly detached, unemotional and morose. Civilians didn't get it, which explained why the older coppers got, the more they stuck to their own.

When it came to Nell, Gareth knew he had it coming.

23

If you neglected your wife, ignored her pleas to work less and spend more time together, then infidelity became the inevitable result. He might as well have packed her an overnight bag, given her a lift to Leith's house and left her with a pat on the back and an encouraging '*Fill your boots, Nell*'. It had got to the point where Nell was spending increasing amounts of time away from their home. He no longer bothered to ask where she was going or where she'd been.

Now it was just a matter of time before the documents were signed and it came legally to its inexorable conclusion. It still made him sad as they had been so happy once.

Logging on to the crime report system, Gareth tried to ignore those thoughts and focus on work – he could see that his file was full of updates. It was all local volume crime. Burglary, theft, fraud and a Friday night punch-up outside the pub at closing time. Sometimes there was a report of a missing person or an alleged sex offence.

He spotted a note in a dark red font that the local coroner needed the file back for a non-suspicious death. It was routine stuff. The computer fan's whirring seemed louder than usual – but maybe that was just his delicate head. By his calculations, he had fifteen live crimes to have a look at.

'Boss, I've got some intel from the National Crime Agency on that OCG we're looking at,' a voice said, breaking his train of thought.

It was Detective Sergeant Declan Flaherty, a thick-set Irishman in his early forties who had been part of the Beaumaris CID team for nearly fifteen years. His bearded face was chubby, his mouth full but a little lopsided and his eyes dark green and thoughtful. He always had a look of wariness about him, which could quickly change into a smile of amused friendliness when he felt happy or relaxed.

Gareth liked Declan and his no-nonsense attitude to

policing. It wasn't that Declan broke or even bent the rules. It was that he could apply common sense when it was needed. There were others who would get bogged down in procedure and the policy of modern policing, often losing the actual focus of an investigation.

'Anything interesting?' Gareth asked as he turned in his chair to look at his colleague.

'Seems that our operation up at Holyhead has rattled them,' Declan explained as he rubbed his chin. 'A DCI on Merseyside has an informant who reckons they're gonna try a softer target on Anglesey to get the gear in.'

He was talking about a drug shipment. These days it was usually heroin or crack cocaine, although seizures of Ecstasy pills and marijuana weren't unheard of.

Gareth wasn't surprised. Anglesey Police had stepped up security at Holyhead in the last year with some impressive results. In October 2020, cocaine with a street value of £6 million had been seized as part of an investigation involving Anglesey Police, the NCA and the Police Service of Northern Ireland. They'd discovered over 83kg of cocaine concealed in packages hidden within a lorry load of refrigerated goods.

Gareth scratched his scalp and asked, 'Any indication of where?'

Declan arched a meaningful eyebrow. 'He mentioned the beach or pier at Beaumaris.'

'What?' Gareth gave him a quizzical look. 'That's news to us. So, he thinks they're coming in by boat then?'

Declan nodded. 'Sounds like it.'

'Any idea when?'

Declan pulled a face. 'He thought it would be early this week, boss.'

'What? Shit!' Gareth said. The intel left him uneasy. They'd spent the last month tying up the loose ends of a series of local burglaries and so he had been looking forward to a week of mundane paperwork and minimal stress. 'How reliable is this CHIS?'

'DCI in Merseyside is an old mate of mine,' Declan explained. 'He reckons he's legit.'

'Bollocks!' Gareth mumbled as he sat forward in his chair. It wasn't good news. 'Nothing more specific than early this week?'

Declan shook his head. 'No, boss. Not yet.'

The busy pier or beach at Beaumaris would certainly provide a fairly innocuous place to land a small shipment of drugs if no one was looking out for it.

Gareth smoothed his hand over his shaved head, which he was prone to do when under pressure. 'What have we got down at the pier these days?'

'They still run the boat trips out to Puffin Island and the Menai Strait. Get the odd private charter,' Declan replied. 'There's that new company with a nine-metre RIB that takes out people wanting to see seals and dolphins. Plus fishing charters.'

'Oh, good.' Gareth pulled a sarcastic face. 'So, there are dozens of tourists getting on and off boats on the pier, never mind those sitting on the beach?'

'From what I can remember, there are boats coming and going around that area all day,' Declan informed him.

'Shit!' Gareth muttered as he ran through the logistics of intercepting a boat full of drugs, manned by criminals, in an area full of tourists. 'Thanks, Declan. Let me know as soon as you hear anything else.'

Michael Cole took another £15 bag of crack cocaine and put it with the others. Even though he wore a face mask, he could still smell the freshly produced drug as its thick, pungent stench was like burnt plastic and nail polish remover. His hands were getting sweaty inside the blue latex gloves, but

26

there was no way he was taking them off. The bizzies had had his prints on record since he was twelve, when he and his brother Callum stole a Vauxhall Cavalier in the Old Swan part of Liverpool and then crashed it into some railings.

Michael could see that the large black Puma sports bag in the centre of the living-room table was nearly full. £100,000 worth of crack cocaine and heroin cut, weighed and bagged.

Michael's brother, Callum, or Inks as he was sometimes known because of the multitude of tattoos on his body, peered down at the mobile phone in his hand. He was tall, well built and generally had an easy-going nature. However, when he was under pressure, he became spiteful and vindictive, wearing a frown that dragged his dark eyebrows together and a pronounced pout like that of a sulky child.

'Anything?' Michael asked nervously in his thick Scouse accent. Today's drop was a big opportunity and this time they were going by boat.

'Nah,' Callum replied, shaking his head. 'Any time now though. Don't worry, lad.'

A junior member of the notorious Croxteth Crew, based in Liverpool L12, Michael had just turned seventeen. Callum was twenty. Their mother had died when Michael was only three and they had been in and out of care since their dad went to prison seven years earlier.

They lived in a small flat just off Stonebridge Lane, Croxteth, which they shared with Paul Griffin, or Red, as he was known because of his ginger hair and patchy beard. Michael was terrified of Red, who had served time for assault and manslaughter. Red, in his late twenties, definitely had a screw loose, and he enjoyed dishing out beatings to low-level street dealers. Michael knew Red didn't like him and only tolerated him because of his brother.

Putting the last two bags of crack cocaine into the sports

bag, Michael zipped it up and then lifted it to check its weight.

'Perfect, lad.'

Today, they were transporting the drugs by boat from the Princes' Dock in Liverpool. From there, the plan was to take a nine-metre RIB speedboat along the ninety-mile stretch of water along the coast of North Wales to Anglesey.

They didn't know the exact location of the drop yet. It was safer that way.

The Croxteth Crew had been running county lines drug operations – trafficking drugs from major cities into rural areas and small towns – into Wales and Anglesey for several years now, but the North Wales Police were getting wise to their operation and had started intercepting runners carrying drugs on trains and cars with Merseyside registered plates. The Croxteth Crew had lost over £75,000 worth of product in recent months and transporting their drugs by boat seemed the safer option.

Michael strolled over to the kitchen and grabbed a cold beer from the fridge, which made a weird shuddering noise every time it opened. The sink was full of washing up and a half a packet of spaghetti lay opened by the cooker. Callum had attempted to cook food the night before but ultimately decided it was safer to go down the chippy. A mismatch of chairs sat around a wobbly round table whose surface was patterned with brown circles from endless mugs of tea. At its centre, an ashtray filled with the remnants of last night's spliffs. The tired plaster walls were spotted with random shapes indicating where photos once hung and above the sink was a Premier League football pull-out from a tabloid newspaper with a guide to the current season's schedule.

'You two queers finished yet?' asked a gravelly voice in a thick Scouse accent.

It was Red. His blue eyes were narrowed. His skin was

28

pockmarked with a swathe of depressed scars, evidence of terrible teenage acne, and he had the stature of a middleweight boxer – tough, muscular, but also lithe and quick.

Michael's stomach clenched a little, as it always did when Red entered the room. Red was violent, volatile and completely unpredictable. Michael had once seen Red throw one of the young 'runners' from a balcony at Primrose Court Housing Estate in Huyton because he thought he had stolen money. It turned out Red was mistaken, but he didn't care. In fact, he thought it was hilarious that the runner fractured his spine, shattered his pelvis and broke two legs because of the error. '*Fuck the little rat*' was his response to finding out the boy needed to spend the next four months in Broadgreen Hospital.

Michael opened his can of beer, took a swig and felt the bubbles fizz in his throat. He needed a bevvy before they left, to 'take the edge off'. He gestured to the bag. 'All done, mate.'

The word *mate* stuck uncomfortably on his lips. Red wasn't his mate. The only time they ever bonded was when Michael taught Red the lyrics to a Liverpool football chant about their striker, Mo Salah, set to the old-fashioned tune of 'You Are My Sunshine'.

> *Mohamed Salah, a gift from Allah,*
> *He came from Roma to Liverpool.*
> *He's always scoring, it's almost boring.*
> *So please don't take Mohamed away.*

Red thought it was brilliant and could often be heard belting it out in the shower.

'Where we dropping this then?' Callum asked. 'Holyhead?'

'Nah.' Red shook his head as he slumped down on the sofa and farted loudly. 'Bizzies are all over Holyhead these days. Fucking Paddies trying to get their gear over on the ferries from Dublin. They've ruined it for everyone.'

Callum looked over with a grin. 'Got a joke for you two. This Irishman, Paddy, goes into a pub and orders himself seven shots of whiskey and a pint of Guinness. The barman lines up the shots and goes to pour the Guinness. By the time he comes back with it, all the shots of whiskey are gone. "*Bloody hell, you drank those fast, didn't you?*" he says. "*So would you if you had what I have,*" this Paddy says. "*What's that then?*" the barman asks. Paddy reaches into his pocket, puts a coin down on the bar and says "*50p*".'

Red roared with laughter, a little too much for Michael's liking, and then there were a few seconds of silence.

'So, where we going then, Red?' Michael asked him uncertainly. He didn't like the idea of heading off with no idea of their actual destination.

Red was still grinning at the joke and rolling a cigarette. He suddenly fixed Michael with a suspicious stare for a few uncomfortable seconds. 'What's it to you, lad?'

Michael forced a thin smile as he drank more beer. He shrugged. 'Just wondering, that's all.'

'What you *wondering* for?' Red asked.

'No reason,' Michael replied, his pulse quickening. 'It doesn't matter.'

Red stared at him for a few more seconds. 'But it does matter. Cos you just asked me.'

Michael's stomach tightened. Red could be like a dog with a bone when he was in this kind of mood. 'I was just asking, Red. Don't worry about it.'

'But I am worried about it *now*,' Red snarled, getting up from the sofa with the rolled cigarette in his hand. He lit the cigarette, took a long, deep drag and blew the smoke from his nostrils towards Michael. 'Why do *you* want to know?'

Michael braced himself in case Red decided to physically attack him.

Callum looked over. 'Red?' he said in an effort to distract him.

'Shut up,' Red barked.

Michael was now stuck for an answer. 'I just wondered, that's all. It's nothing.'

'But it's not nothing. You meeting your faggot boyfriend there?'

Michael felt sick. He didn't want to end up on the end of one of Red's senseless beatings. 'No.'

'Or maybe you've got someone to tell?'

Michael shook his head, but he was shaky. What was Red implying? That he was a grass?

'No. Of course not,' Michael insisted, aware that the tone of his voice had gone up a little.

There were a few seconds of tense silence.

'Yeah, well, leave it to the grown-ups to worry about where we're going, eh?' Red sneered as he took out his mobile phone and peered at the screen.

The tension in the room dissipated as if it had been released in a relaxing exhale.

Michael felt his tense muscles ease as he and Callum exchanged a look.

Jesus Christ! What the hell was that all about?

Michael then glanced at the owl kitchen clock up on the wall. Nearly eight a.m.

'Beaumaris?' Red mumbled, looking at his phone and frowning. 'I think that's how you say it?'

'Eh?' Callum asked.

Red pointed to his phone as he got up from the sofa. 'We're making the drop at the beach in some place called Beaumaris on the south of Anglesey.'

'It's a holiday place, isn't it?' Callum asked.

31

'No fucking idea, mate,' Red snapped as he came over and gave Michael a hard, 'playful' cuff around the head. 'And now you know, you little prick. We're going right now, so get your shit together, sunshine.'

Michael winced from the blow to his head, but said nothing. One day, Red was going to get what was coming to him.

Chapter 3

A small garage repair shop and warehouse had been quickly turned into a temporary operations centre for the siege that was now taking place at Brannings Warehouse. The area bustled as police officers came and went, relaying snippets of intel and their latest conversations with the GMP top brass or the police media and press unit.

Laura sipped the last of her lukewarm coffee as yet another ARV arrived – she'd counted six so far. That meant close to forty AROs were now on site. Most of the firearms officers were in their vehicles or sitting on boxes and work benches in the main body of the old repair garage. They were checking their weapons and kit as they chatted in low voices or smoked, waiting for the order that would see them leap into action. A stack of ballistic shields rested beside one ARV, making it look vaguely medieval. She heard whispered snippets about their planned MOE – method of entry.

She was overcome with anxiety and walked outside for something to do. Her husband and his colleague Louise were being held hostage somewhere inside the enormous warehouse opposite. Since the gun battle, there had been no contact from anyone inside. They had no idea what the gang wanted, or even if they were prepared to negotiate for the two police officers' release. What if they just shot them? Or what if they were getting their kicks by hurting them? It didn't bear thinking about.

As the wind picked up, she looked skyward, noticing that a black and yellow police helicopter had appeared above them in the milky haze of early morning and was circling the area. Over to the west the sky had darkened, casting an ominous canopy of black, which would soon mask the summer sun.

Please let Sam come out of there alive and unharmed, she pleaded to whatever Higher Power was up there.

The wind swirled again and the large steel gate at the end of the warehouse rattled as if it was desperate to open.

The quiet and stillness were unnerving. At times like this, she wished she still smoked. Sam had forced her to quit after Rosie was born.

DCI Pete Marsons came outside, took a package of ciggies from his pocket and offered her one.

She waved it away. 'No, ta.'

'Sorry, I forgot.' Pete took the packet away. 'I remember when Sam made you quit. You were a grumpy bloody cow for about two months.'

'I tried everything. Gum, patches, acupuncture,' she said. 'I can't even remember how I did it.'

'Will-power and bloody-mindedness,' Pete said, raising an eyebrow. 'Both of which make you a bloody good copper, but sometimes a stubborn pain in the arse.'

Laura didn't reply. She was finding it hard to focus on anything.

Pete looked at her. 'It's gonna be all right, Laura. We're gonna get them both out of there, okay?'

34

Pete might have been her boss, but they were also mates. She, Sam and Pete had trained together in the nineties and stayed friends ever since. Pete and Sam still played five-a-side football every Tuesday with other coppers. They had even been on a couple of family holidays together to Pembrokeshire as Pete had kids a similar age to Rosie and Jake. Laura and Pete's wife, Anusha, got on like a house on fire – she'd even been to Anusha's fabulously tacky hen-night in Blackpool.

'Intel says that there was a lot of activity here this morning, just after dawn,' Pete informed her with a frown. 'Vans moving stuff out. We've also got a report of a lorry carrying away some machinery. I guess that's why Sam and Louise were here.'

'Well, why didn't someone bloody tell us that?' Laura thundered.

'Apparently a new switchboard operator delayed passing that information on to Dispatch,' Pete informed her, shaking his head. 'Something went wrong somewhere down the line.'

Laura growled. 'That's not good enough. People's lives are at stake here.'

'I'm sure the operator will be made fully aware of that,' Pete said dryly.

'I hope they get both barrels.' Laura then frowned as she processed what Pete had told her about the early-morning activity. 'Sounds to me like they were dismantling the factory.'

'Yeah, it does,' Pete agreed as he blew a couple of smoke rings into the air. 'And only a few hours before we're due to do a raid. Fucking fishy, if you ask me.'

'Something's not right,' she agreed and gave him a dark look. 'You think they were tipped off, don't you?'

Pete considered his answer as he took another long drag of his cigarette. 'I don't wanna think there's someone bent in our nick.'

'But?' she prompted.

He shrugged. 'You're a police officer, Laura. We don't believe in coincidences, do we?'

'No, we don't . . . Any ideas?' she asked, but she found it hard to concentrate on anything with Sam still inside the warehouse.

Pete gestured across the road. 'Let's get Sam and Louise out of there safely, eh? Then we can think about whether they knew we were coming or not.'

She gave him a grateful nod. 'Thanks, boss.' She might have called him 'boss', but she often thought of Pete as the brother she'd never had. Luckily they'd never been in a situation at work where their friendship had hindered their ability to work together.

'If only we had an experienced hostage crisis negotiator here, we might just stand a chance,' Pete remarked sardonically.

As well as being a Detective Inspector, Laura was one of the top negotiators on the force. She could remember the very moment she decided to pursue that particular specialism. In 2016, she attended an incident in Rusholme where a drunk, estranged father had taken his three young children hostage with a shotgun. Laura had watched DI Frank Droy, a renowned crisis negotiator in the Manchester Met, work his magic. Droy had spent five hours listening calmly and slowly building a compelling rapport with the father, who finally broke down in tears and handed himself over. Laura would never forget the emotional moment when the three children were reunited with their mother, who had been waiting fretfully with officers close by.

Having spent a year completing the specialist negotiator training all over the UK, Laura had attended over a hundred hostage or crisis situations in the past three years. She had even been to America on secondment to the FBI for a month to see their negotiators in action.

'Yeah, it's very different when you're negotiating for your husband's life though,' she said, pulling a face.

'I know that.' He gave her a compassionate look. 'And I know it's not even ethical. But I've checked and it's going to take hours to get anyone else down here. Are you gonna be okay?'

'If I'm honest,' she said, 'I wouldn't want anyone else talking to the men inside that warehouse while I watched on.'

'Fair enough,' Pete agreed. 'I'll trust you to remain as detached as you can.'

She was desperate for there to be some kind of contact with the gang inside. If there was no communication, she knew that the next step would be to send in armed officers. And that kind of operation became incredibly dangerous for everyone, especially Sam and Louise.

At the far end of the street, she spotted a second response team on standby – a Tactical Support Team in an armoured Land Rover, its huge diesel engine idling. Its menacing presence only added to the tension outside.

Out of the corner of her eye, she saw a young PC approaching them at speed. His face was angular and even though he had a beard, he still bore the ruddiness of youth in his cheeks.

'Sir, ma'am,' he said. 'We've got the landline up and running in the garage. The phone company have run a line test for us and there are three separate land lines inside Brannings Warehouse.'

'And they're all functional?' she asked.

'Yes, ma'am,' he replied. 'They must be still connected from before the warehouse closed down a few months ago.'

Pete thought for a second. 'Except we don't know if there are any actual phones in the building, do we?'

'No, sir. That is a possibility.'

Laura glanced over at Pete and then gestured to the PC to lead her to the operations centre. 'There's only one way of finding out, so come and show me.'

The PC led her inside and across the garage over to an enormous table that was now covered in electronic tracking and sound equipment. She spotted a phone to one side, attached to a laptop and speakers.

'Is this it?' she asked.

'Yes, ma'am,' the PC replied as a Technical Forensic Officer moved so she could get to the table.

Picking up the phone, she held out her hand. 'Anyone got the numbers?'

The PC handed her a piece of paper with the three warehouse landline numbers written down in biro.

She dialled the first and waited as it rang. Pete looked over at her as the tension built.

Nothing.

After two minutes of ringing, she groaned and hung up.

'Try the next one,' she muttered to herself as she dialled the next number and let it ring.

If they weren't able to establish some kind of communication with the gang members inside, how could they negotiate getting Sam and Louise out of there unharmed?

The line clicked as someone answered the phone and there were a few seconds of uneasy silence.

'Hello?' she finally said, in a light, gentle tone.

'Who is this?' asked a gruff voice with a thick Mancunian accent.

'My name's Detective Inspector Laura Hart,' she replied. 'How are you doing over there?'

There were a few more seconds of silence. She wondered if the line had gone dead.

'How the fuck do you think we are, bitch?' the voice snapped.

Nice.

'Is anyone injured?' she asked.

'Are you jokin', love? Your lot just turned this into the Wild fucking West and you wanna know if anyone's injured,' he sneered. 'Unless you're talking about the dibble sitting here tied up?'

Dibble was Mancunian slang for the police.

'How are Sam and Louise?' she asked, using their names to instantly humanise them in the mind of the gang member.

'Sam and Louise? Is that their names?' the man mocked. 'Shagging each other, are they?'

'I just wondered if they were okay?' Laura asked, gritting her teeth.

'Well, me mate here doesn't like dibble, so he's battered the bloke. Blood everywhere.' The man laughed. 'And I'm not gonna tell you what he wanted to do to the other one. He's had a look at her tits but I managed to stop him there.'

She took a breath. The anger and fear were overwhelming, but she knew she couldn't show it. She needed to remain calm and unemotional. 'I'd really like you to release them before they come to any more harm.'

'Oh yeah, bitch?' the man growled. 'And what you gonna give us if we do that?'

'What do you want?' she asked.

'I tell ya what we want. We want a helicopter out of here.'

Jesus. Nothing much then? she thought furiously.

'It's going to take me a while to get that for you,' she replied.

'Well, you've got two hours, love. Or I let my mate loose on these two. And let me tell you, he's a fucking animal.' The man snorted.

A chill ran up her spine at the thought of what that might mean. 'Okay, but please don't hurt them any more.'

'Aww, you're breaking me heart, love. They your mates,

39

are they?' He laughed. 'And by the way. We've strapped high explosives to your friends here. And this place is now covered in petrol. So, if we get so much as a whiff that someone is coming in here, we're gonna light a match and this place and your mates are gonna go up like a fucking volcano.'

Chapter 4

Taking the freshly made pot of coffee from the SMEG machine, Laura poured herself a big mug and added a dash of oat milk. She walked across the wooden floors of her kitchen and the heels of her boots clacked with an echo. Moving over to the window, she took a long swig of the strong Peruvian blend. She could feel the heat of the liquid on her top lip as she breathed on its surface.

That's so good, she thought. She didn't know whether Peruvian coffee was significantly better than Colombian, French or wherever else, and didn't really care. Anyone who claimed they did, in her book, was a wanker.

Gazing out at the view from their first-floor kitchen, she took in the stunning vista. A calm strip of water, the Menai Strait, lay in front of Beaumaris. She imagined it was what those great rivers with iconic names – the Mississippi, the Nile or the Ganges – looked like at their widest points.

Behind the dark blue ribbon of sea lay the Welsh mainland coastline that was only three miles directly across from the town itself. The towering darkness of the Snowdonia mountains, which even in summer were continually shrouded in traversing patches of mist at their dark summit, loomed menacingly over the tableau. At its centre was Snowdon. Laura had read in the papers of a growing movement in North Wales for the mountain to be known only as *Yr Wyddfa*, meaning 'grave' in Welsh, as myth had it that the giant Rhita Gawr was buried at the mountain top after a battle with King Arthur. Locals pointed out that in Australia, what had once been known as Ayers Rock was now known only by its Aboriginal name, *Uluru*.

Above the Snowdonia mountains, the endless, cloudless, azure sky seemed too perfect today. That's what she'd missed when she first moved to Manchester – the Anglesey sky and the feeling of endless space.

Beaumaris' Gallic-sounding name dated back to the thirteenth century and King Edward I, who was French-speaking. *Beau Mareys* meant *beautiful marsh*, which she always thought an amusing oxymoron.

The tide was out, so she could see the sand flats, known as the Traeth Lavan or the Lavan Sands. Little pools and shallow streams glistened and rippled in the early-morning sunlight and Eurasian Oystercatchers, with their pepper-red bills and distinctive *peep-ing* call, patrolled the sands in twos or threes looking for shellfish.

The central sandbank itself stretched across the whole of the Menai Strait, measuring over five miles in width. To the north of Beaumaris was Dutchman's Bank, a dark presence because of its involvement in several major shipwrecks. The most infamous of these had been the *Rothsay Castle*, a 2,000-tonne paddle-steamer that travelled across from Liverpool in August 1831. The boat hit the sandbanks close to Puffin Island and 131 lives were lost. Laura found the disaster particularly poignant after she spotted a grave on a visit to a churchyard in the village of Llansanffraid Glan

Conwy to see the grave of her taid, which was Welsh for 'grandfather', on her mother's side. The gravestone read:

Here lies the body of John Tarrey of Bury, Lancashire. Aged 2 years, he lost his life on the Rothsay Castle on 18th August, 1831

A year after losing Sam she'd decided to leave the police force and move back to Beaumaris on Anglesey. It wasn't a decision she took lightly. Being a detective was all she had ever dreamed of. But working as a serving police officer made it impossible to get over Sam's death. There were just too many reminders. And too many unanswered questions. The whole issue of what Sam and his partner, Louise, had been doing at Brannings Warehouse that morning still plagued her. And no one seemed to be able to provide any adequate answers. Her thought patterns and behaviour became obsessive.

Laura found herself attending crime scenes, spotting a dark-haired, middle-aged officer in uniform, and for a moment believing it was Sam. Such moments were devastating, and they impacted on her ability to do the job properly. Her mental health deteriorated rapidly, and once she was diagnosed as having PTSD, she retired early 'on grounds of ill-health'.

She soon found an old three-storey house just off Altt Goch, meaning 'Red Hill'. The derivation of the name fascinated her. A local farmer, Dewi Hughes, had told her it referred to all the blood that poured down it after a battle, but no one could agree on exactly which battle the name referred to.

Some claimed it dated back to the Roman invasion of Anglesey in 60 BC, when Roman troops crossed the Menai Strait in flat-bottomed boats and landed close to Beaumaris and fought the local Welsh population. Others thought that it referred to the violent resistance to the removal of the people from the village of Llanfaes in the 1280s, during the reign of Edward I, and the building of a new castle at Beaumaris. The last theory was that the name referred to a bloody battle before the siege of Beaumaris Castle in the English Civil War in 1648. Laura just loved the colourful range of historic possibilities and thought the fact that no one could agree on the actual derivation made the name even more interesting.

The house itself was a double-fronted villa with bay windows and a roof with two peaks. When they had first moved in, there were still some of the remnants of the elderly couple who had lived there since the 1960s. Pale green curtains, linoleum in the hallway, and a larder with a generous helping of woodlice. In the living room there was a remarkably decorative cast-iron lamp bracket that seemed completely out of keeping with everything else. Upstairs there was the obligatory avocado-green bathroom suite which Rosie, her eighteen-year-old daughter, thought was 'cool' and 'totally vintage'. Laura assured her it would be going as soon as she had the money to replace it.

She finished her coffee. As the sun peered from behind a solitary cloud, she watched the golden light stream down onto the water's surface and sparkle. She remembered her early-morning swim and encounter with Gareth. It gave her a little thrill to think of it. She wondered what it would be like to kiss him. She liked the fact that he seemed both authoritative and easy-going at the same time.

'You can never get bored with that view, can you?' said a voice.

She turned.

It was Sam.

She felt guilty for a few seconds and then said, 'No. I just wish you could have seen it.'

Sam shrugged. 'I'm looking at it now, silly.' He leaned over her shoulder, kissed and nuzzled her neck, and then pointed out of the window. 'We have Conwy Mountain over there to the east along the Carneddau Hill, and over to the west, the Snowdon Horseshoe.'

'Get you!' She laughed as she rubbed her ear and cheek against Sam's face. He had just shaved and his skin felt smooth and smelt fragrant.

'Talking to yourself again, Mum?' asked her daughter Rosie as she breezed in noisily. She opened the fridge and sneered. 'Why don't we ever have any food? What the hell am I supposed to eat?'

Laura rolled her eyes. This was a daily conversation. 'Cereal, toast, fruit. You know, stuff that the rest of the population eat for breakfast?'

Rosie growled. 'This is why I have to resort to buying protein bars online.'

Elvis jumped up from his bed and trotted over as Rosie crouched down, stroked his face and made a general fuss of him.

'At least someone loves me in this house, eh, Elvis?' Rosie joked.

Laura knew Rosie had an uncomfortable relationship with food. She had become terribly self-conscious recently and wore baggy clothes to disguise her figure. Luckily it had come at a time when pop artists such as Billie Eilish made shapeless clothing fashionable.

Jake wandered in, bleary-eyed, and sat down at the table. He reached for a *pain au chocolat* and stuffed it in his mouth.

'Jake, you don't need to inhale your food.' Laura shook her head. 'And what are you taking for your lunch, young lady?'

'Young lady? Cringe!' Rosie gave her a withering look. 'I think we've established that there isn't anything.'

Laura pointed to the fruit bowl. 'Banana?'

'Yeah, because I just love green bananas.'

'Apple?'

'I hate red apples.'

'Well, make sure you get something from the canteen, please,' Laura suggested, trying to remain calm. 'Jake, your packed lunch is in your bag.'

Rosie went over and ruffled Jake's hair. 'Haven't you got a school trip today, mophead?'

Laura frowned. 'Have you?'

'I don't know.' Jake shrugged, chewing the last of his *pain au chocolat*, much of which appeared to be smudged around his mouth.

'Yeah, it's next week,' Laura said.

Elvis wandered over to Jake, looking expectantly at his food.

'You can't eat this, silly!' Jake said, patting his head.

'And neither can you, by the looks of it.' Rosie handed her brother a tissue. 'You've got chocolate all around your mouth, you loser.'

For all of her faults, Rosie had been an incredible support to Jake in the past three years since Sam's death. They both worried that Jake had become quite withdrawn and suffered from anxiety when things weren't explained clearly to him. A child psychologist had told Laura it demonstrated Jake's need to feel in control. The death of his father had turned his world upside down, and Jake needed to keep control of as much as he could. It was why he had a hang-up about time and getting everywhere early.

Laura glanced up at the clock. 'Come on, you two. The bus will be here in a minute. Go, go, go.'

'Bye, Mum!' Jake yelled as he shot out of the door. He was more worried about getting the bus than giving her a kiss or hug these days.

'Have a nice day, Laura.' Rosie grinned and then waltzed

46

out after her brother. She had started to call her mum 'Laura' a few weeks ago as a joke.

'Love you guys,' Laura called after them as she got to the door that led to the staircase down to the road.

Walking back into the kitchen, she tidied up and grabbed her phone, remembering that she had spotted it was Gareth's birthday on Facebook.

Why didn't he mention it when he saw me on the beach earlier?

Gareth and Laura had first encountered each other when Laura's flat had been burgled only a month after they arrived in Beaumaris. Gareth was a DS at that time, and there had been a clear flirtation between them. They had talked about Laura's time in the Manchester Met, before she decided to leave the force. She thought Gareth was handsome and very funny. Ever since then, they bumped into each other regularly in the local pub or supermarket. In fact, it had got to the point where Laura was a little disappointed when a trip to Tesco's didn't result in a chance encounter with Detective Williams.

When Gareth was promoted to DI they had agreed to meet up for dinner at The Bull so he could pick Laura's brains about her time as a DI back in Manchester. Even though she knew he was married, Laura agreed. It was just one ex-copper helping another, wasn't it?

She wouldn't know as it didn't end up happening. Jake came home with a raging cold that day and, despite various attempts to reschedule, they hadn't found a time that worked for both of them to meet again since. But in recent weeks, she had found herself thinking about Gareth more and more. And however difficult it might prove to be initially, she also found herself thinking how nice it would be to have someone in her life again.

Looking down at her phone, Laura typed out a quick message.

47

Why didn't you tell me it was your birthday this morning, you sod! Happy birthday. I'll have to take you out for a birthday drink! Have a lovely day. Laura

Peering at the message, she wondered if she should add a kiss? She and Gareth didn't sign off their texts with an *x* but maybe they should start to?

Why don't you just do it and see how he responds? Or maybe you should stop acting like a teenager and get on with the day?

'Who are you texting?' a voice asked, startling her. It was Sam again.

'Bloody hell, Sam!' Laura exclaimed. 'I thought you'd gone. You made me jump out of my skin!'

'Guilty conscience?' he asked with a laugh. It was his cocky laugh that she still found so appealing. The quick downward glance, followed by a scratch of his chin and a confident chuckle.

'No. I texted Miss Hughes. Rosie thought Jake was on a school trip today, but I'm pretty sure it's next week.'

'Where are they going?' Sam asked.

'Trip to Puffin Island, I think.'

8.50 a.m.

Sitting at the front of the main CID office, Gareth ran his hand over his head as he contemplated the intel they'd received about the drugs drop over at Beaumaris Beach. He wished they had a more specific time for the gang's arrival.

He let out a sigh, swigged his coffee and felt with his fingers where his hairline was receding at the front. *I used to have long hair twenty-five years ago.* In the early nineties, before he joined the force, Gareth was a wannabe house music DJ in the north-west of England. He remembered his long, butter-blond hair, seventies-style shirts, beads and a predilection for Ecstasy every weekend. If he wasn't DJing, then he was humping great big crates of records around to venues for mates who were. *Christ, those were the bloody days! Forty-eight-hour parties, Dennis The Menace pills and a three-day comedown.*

His phone vibrated in his trouser pocket, breaking his train of thought. It was a text from Laura Hart. His pulse quickened a little. She'd wished him a happy birthday and promised to take him out for a birthday drink. He smiled to himself. He and Laura had been trying for months to meet for a drink and compare notes about working as a DI. Even though he was still living in the marital home, Gareth didn't feel too guilty about having a drink with 'Lovely Laura'. His marriage was over. They hadn't slept together for over three years and had maintained separate beds for over two. They merely co-existed in the house like frosty, indifferent house-mates.

It sometimes made him incredibly sad to think about the collapse of their relationship. It had started to unravel five years ago when he and Nell had finally given up trying to have children after four unsuccessful bouts of IVF treatment. Gareth had been diagnosed with Klinefelter syndrome, which meant that he had been born with an extra X chromosome. The syndrome itself had had no discernible effect on his life as he grew up. It did, however, make fathering a child very difficult. And even though Nell would never admit it, he knew she sometimes resented the fact that they didn't have children. And deep down he feared that now Nell had moved in with Leith, he would get the inevitable message that Mr Super-Sperm had given her the one thing he couldn't.

Unfortunately, Laura knew about his marital woes as Gareth had bumped into her at the end of a boozy night at The Bull in town one night. He vaguely remembered telling Laura how *lovely* she was and going into the fine details of

Nell's affair, and he'd spent that Sunday lying on the sofa, hungover and wincing at the memory of their drunken chat. He hadn't been able to bring himself to reach out to Laura since, and their run-in this morning was the first time he'd seen her in a few weeks.

Holding his phone, he wondered what to text back. Eventually he wrote:

Hiya. Thanks, I will. And I'll hold you to that drink! Gareth

He wondered whether or not to put a kiss. She hadn't, so that would be weird, wouldn't it? He sent the text and hoped he might get some response so they could continue the conversation. He wondered what it would be like to actually kiss her.

Gazing around the room, Gareth could see that the CID team were now fully assembled for what was an unscheduled briefing.

'Right, guys,' he said, getting up from his chair. 'If we can settle for a second, please?' he said, waiting for a moment as the chatter died down.

His team consisted of eight detectives, six of whom were men. Despite what CID officers from the major cities would have others believe, the team at Beaumaris were dedicated, experienced and intuitive coppers and, as far as Gareth was concerned, could hold their own against any in the UK.

'Slightly impromptu meeting,' he began. 'We have intel from Merseyside Police that an OCG from that area is planning to drop a consignment of drugs close to the pier on Beaumaris Beach early this week. It's part of a county lines operation that they are trying to establish on Anglesey.'

There were a few mutterings from the detectives.

'I thought they were going through Holyhead?' DC Andrea

Jones asked. She was early twenties, full of energy and enthusiasm. Gareth rated Jones's sharp, intuitive feel for police work. In fact, she was the one officer in CID that he thought could, and would, climb the ranks to dizzying heights.

'Seems that our efforts to stop drugs coming through Holyhead have just resulted in the gangs looking for quieter places to make their drops,' Declan explained.

Andrea rolled her eyes. 'Great.'

'Now, we don't have any more intel other than the drop will be this week,' Gareth informed them. 'But we have to be on a state of high alert around the clock.'

'You paying for overtime then, boss?' Andrea quipped to a murmur of laughter in the room.

'Not yet, Andrea.' Gareth rolled his eyes. 'Okay, remind me again who the Authorised Firearms Officers are in here?'

The three CID officers who were firearm-trained and allowed to take a firearm to any operation put their hands up.

'Okay, guys. Thanks,' Gareth said. 'I'm taking no chances with this shipment. They could be armed, so we are all wearing vests when we get the go-ahead. I think that's everything at the moment.'

'No, it's not!' Andrea shouted as she stood up holding a cake with one candle in the middle. 'Happy birthday, boss!'

As Andrea approached, and the whole of CID sang 'Happy Birthday' loudly, Declan went over and answered a ringing phone.

'Which tosser let the cat out of the bag?' Gareth chuckled. He saw DC Ben Corden grinning on the other side of the room. 'Thanks, Ben!'

Ben was in his late twenties, blond and boyishly handsome. Ben had a similar background to his own. Born in Beaumaris, they'd gone to the same local schools – although he'd attended in the eighties and Ben in the noughties, which was frightening.

'Thirtieth, is it, boss?' Andrea asked as Gareth bent to blow out the candle.

'I bloody wish,' he moaned with a chortle. 'Fifty-fucking-two.'

'I assume the first round is on you at The Bull later?' Ben asked.

Gareth snorted. 'I'm not buying you a bloody drink now you've stitched me up, you sod.'

Out of the corner of his eye, he spotted Declan putting down the phone and signalling that they needed to talk. He wore a serious expression on his face.

'What's up with you? You're not going to fuck up my birthday, are you?'

'Maybe.' Declan lowered his voice. 'That CHIS in Merseyside has come back with more intel.'

Gareth gave him a quizzical look. 'What's the problem?'

'That drugs drop is going to take place this morning.'

'What? When?'

'Ten a.m. on the dot.'

Gareth glanced down at his watch: nine a.m.

Oh shit. They weren't remotely prepared for any kind of operation!

'Right, everyone!' he yelled loudly. The mood in the CID office changed immediately and all of the officers stopped what they were doing to pay attention as Gareth rarely shouted. 'We have a serious situation and I need all of you to listen *right now*!'

Chapter 5

9.08 a.m.

Michael glanced down at his watch, its silver face glinting in the morning sunshine. Armani. Callum had bought it for him last Christmas. Reckoned it was worth over a grand. It looked dead smart. The spray from the boat splashed over his wrist and he quickly wiped the watch, saw it had just gone nine a.m. and pulled the sleeve of his North Face bomber jacket over it.

Must be nearly there now, he thought as his stomach clenched. He wasn't gonna let on to the other two that he was nervous.

Glancing around the fifteen-foot-long black Zodiac Pro RIB, he saw Red still standing with his legs apart, gripping the steering wheel and giving the odd whoop of excitement.

He thinks he's in some bloody action film, Michael thought. *He's such a dickhead.*

'You all right, kid?' Callum asked as Michael wiped more spray from his eyes.

'Sound,' he replied in a tone that implied, *Why are you asking me that?* 'Except I can't see a bloody thing.'

The sea had been calm all the way from the docks in Liverpool, but at the speed Red was going, the spray still flew up occasionally as they bounced along the water's surface.

Michael pointed over the coastline to their left. 'What's that then?'

'It's Wales, you divvy!' His brother laughed.

Michael shook his head. 'I know that. Which bit?'

Callum shrugged. 'Dunno. I think that bit that sticks out is near Llandudno.'

'Dad took us to Llandudno once, didn't he?' Michael asked.

Callum chuckled. 'Yeah, he took us on that cable car and you shat yourself.'

Michael frowned. 'I don't remember that.'

'You were only about four,' Callum added. 'I think you were scared of heights.'

'I still am . . . So, what's that then?' he asked, gesturing to the flatter coastline to their right. He was keen to change the subject.

'That's Anglesey.'

'Anglesey's an island?' Michael asked.

'Bloody hell, mate. Didn't they teach you nothing at St Joseph's?' Callum asked with a snort as he playfully ruffled Michael's hair.

St Joseph's was the Catholic primary school they were sent to when they were taken into care in November 2014. Their 'arl fella' – Scouse for 'father' – was arrested for manslaughter and banged up in HMP Walton. Some stuff had happened when they went camping with the 12th West Derby Scout Group – it was something Michael didn't want to remember or talk about, and he and Callum never broached the subject – and their dad, Neil Cole, took the law into his own hands and had been sent to prison as a result. Auntie Kerry told Social Services that she already had five kids of her own, and they couldn't afford to bring up Michael and Callum as well, so they spent the next few years at Southlea, a care home in Formby for 'looked after' children. 'Looked after' was the latest label. However, it wasn't long before the kids at local schools reminded them they were just *fucking orphans*.

'Where's your mummy and daddy gone, you slum rats?'

A family called the McCanns had fostered them for a time. They were Christians and meant well, but weren't prepared for two very 'naughty boys'. Callum, in particular, had become an incredibly angry teenager and was permanently excluded from two secondary schools by the time he was fifteen. Instead of taking his GCSEs he dealt drugs for a local gang called the Deli Mob who were based around the Everton, Kirkdale and Walton areas of Liverpool, and used the money to take care of himself and Michael. The Deli Mob were infamous for doing armed robberies on rival gangs, stealing their drugs and selling them on. Their name originated from Delamore Street in Kirkdale, where many of the original members had lived. A year or two later, Callum hooked up with the Croxteth Crew.

'How long?' Michael asked as he stared ahead at the broad strip of water in front of them.

'Twenty minutes, bro,' Callum reassured Michael, giving him a playful slap on the cheek. 'What you worrying about?'

'The dickheads they've sent out here to work county,' he said, referring to the kids that had been sent from Liverpool to start up county lines drug dealing on Anglesey and who were organising picking up the stash at Beaumaris. Michael knew they were idiots. 'I don't want to get there and find a load of bizzies all over the place.'

Callum smiled, unzipped his jacket and showed Michael what was sitting in the waistband of his jeans. A Glock 17 handgun.

'Don't worry. No one's gonna be causing any trouble this morning, lad.'

Michael's eyes widened. 'Bloody hell, Callum!' He had seen plenty of guns in the past but he didn't know Callum possessed one or that he was going to bring it with him. The sight of the gun made him feel more nervous.

Callum gestured over to Red and the Puma bag. 'You think this is impressive? That psycho has put a fucking machine gun in there just in case anything goes wrong.'

'What?'

Callum laughed. 'Yeah, one of them Czech Skorpions. Thirty rounds in a mag. Nine hundred rounds a minute. No one's fucking with us today, sunshine, so relax, eh?'

Chapter 6

9.03 a.m.

It had just gone nine a.m. by the time Beth Hughes took the register for her Year 6 form group. She was a little flustered today. Taking Year 6 on a boat trip from Beaumaris Pier out to Puffin Island was part of their mammals project, and even though the class was relatively small – only twenty pupils – a boat trip took some serious planning. Parental permission slips, risk assessment for the governors, medical conditions . . . the list went on. Basically, it was her responsibility to bring them all back in one piece, and it was only her second ever trip as a teacher.

Beth had just turned twenty-two. Her oval face radiated a warmth and genuine kindness beyond her years. She was an individualist. Her black hair, which was held back by an olive vintage hairband, had a hint of dark red and fell onto her shoulders in ringlets. Her eyebrow was pierced and arms tattooed. When she wasn't teaching, she wore vintage fifties clothes – headscarves, swing skirts or pencil dresses.

Beth had been teaching at St Mary's Primary School for just over a year. It was her dream job. All the women in her family were teachers. Her mum, Sian, had once been the head teacher at the local secondary school until taking early retirement, and her sister, Fiona, worked as a drama teacher over in Welshpool. They had warned her that she looked too edgy to get a job as a primary-school teacher, but she had proved them all wrong.

Having finished the register, Beth checked all the permission slips and risk assessment documents in her folder.

'Okay, Year 6,' she said, getting up from her desk and smiling. 'Hands up who's looking forward to going on our trip to see the puffins today?'

A sea of hands went up, except for a small boy in the corner who stared out of the window.

'Jake?' Beth laughed. 'Are you with us this morning, Jake?'

Jake turned to look at her and blinked. 'Yes, miss. Sorry.'

'Are you looking forward to our trip, Jake?'

He beamed. 'Yeah.'

Wow. Jake smiled. I haven't seen him smile in weeks, she thought.

Jake was a thoughtful but shy boy. His father, Sam, a police officer, had been killed three years ago in Manchester and Beth could see that the event had had a profound effect on Jake. She made sure she kept an eye out for him and she was happy to take him to one side for their 'little chats' if he needed them.

'Okay, class!' She clapped her hands together. 'We've got a bit of time left before we get on the coach. Has everyone got their packed lunches with them?'

There were lots of nods and yeses.

'I've gone for ham salad in my sandwiches today,' she informed them. 'And a banana and bottle of water.'

'I've got cheese and pickle, miss!' boomed out Charlie, a local farmer's son.

A girl in pigtails rummaged in her lunchbox. 'My mum's given me jam because she says I'm fussy.'

'Ooh, I love a jam butty.' Beth laughed. 'Now then, if we can settle down, we've got some time to look at our Second World War project.' She cast her eye down her markbook. 'It's Bella's turn to tell us about what's she found out, so I want us all to be quiet while she's talking.'

Bella was a tall, confident girl who sat at the front of the class and attempted to answer every question that Beth asked. If she was honest, Beth found her a little annoying. She had met Bella's dad, Gary, occasionally at parents' evening and he was an arrogant cockney who clearly spoiled his daughter rotten, which explained Bella's grating assertiveness.

Moving her chair back, Bella took her exercise book, looked out at the class and cleared her throat.

Oh God, here we go, Beth thought.

'The outbreak of the Second World War was on 1st September 1939. Part of the German tactics to win the war was to bomb major ports such as Liverpool. As it was so dangerous, they evacuated many children from Liverpool to North Wales and Anglesey. Many pupils from the Blue Coat School in Wavertree, Liverpool, made the journey by train from Liverpool to Anglesey and were looked after by families in Beaumaris. The town welcomed 270 children and 30 adults from Liverpool. The Red Hill House was used to create a school for all the new children.

'Joan Gordon, a pupil from the Blue Coat school, wrote the following:

"Moving to Anglesey was an incredible experience, although I saw less of my mother than previously. I think I only saw her once during the entire six years of war, as travel was so restricted. While the school was a lifeline for helping my family, it was very intimidating

for someone shy like myself to be away from home at such a young age. But Beaumaris was a lovely place, and the people were very friendly.'

Bella gave a satisfied smile and sat down.

Beth clapped and the whole class joined in. 'Well done, Bella. Really interesting. It's nice to know that the people in Beaumaris were very friendly to the evacuees. And it also touches on something that I talked about before, which is all the connections that we have between Beaumaris and Liverpool. Can anyone remember some of them?'

A blond boy with glasses shot his hand up. 'The Liverpool Arms Pub, Miss!'

'Good,' Beth said. 'Anything else?'

'My Nana and Taid are from Liverpool,' another boy suggested.

A girl at the back of the class shot her hand up. 'I know. My dad supports Liverpool but my mum supports Everton.'

That's not quite what I meant, but okay.

Beth laughed. 'I was thinking more about the historical links. You remember I told you it was builders from Anglesey that went across to Liverpool in the 1800s to help build the city? And think of all the thousands of tourists who come here from Liverpool in the summer.'

Bella put her hand up. 'Can you get to Anglesey from Liverpool in a boat, Miss?'

Beth frowned. 'You know what, Bella, I'm not sure. I'll find out and tell you all tomorrow.'

Something outside the window caught Beth's eye and she watched as the coach pulled up outside. She felt the slight pinch of nerves in the pit of her stomach.

'The coach is outside, miss!' yelled Reece, who was already standing and getting his stuff ready.

'Okay, Year 6,' Beth shouted over the din. 'Get your things together very calmly, and go and form a single line beside the coach and wait for me there, please.'

Right, here we go then, she thought to herself with a deep breath. *First school trip on a boat. What's the worst that could happen?*

By the time Geoff Clegg pulled his battered old Toyota pick-up truck into a parking space on the grass in Beaumaris, he could see that he was running ten minutes late. Geoff, now in his sixties, had grey-green eyes, greying beard and heavy facial features like those of an old boxer. It was his walk that was the key to his true character. It was an easy-going lope. Nice and steady. Not too fast and not too slow. A powerful but relaxed walk, without concern. Someone once remarked that he walked just like Baloo the bear in the film *The Jungle Book*. He had been working for Beaumaris Cruises for nearly ten years now, and he and his best mate, Steve Clarke, took cruises out to Puffin Island on the Menai Strait several times a day. At the height of summer, the cruises would sell out days in advance. Having spent twenty-five years in the Royal Navy, Geoff just enjoyed being out on the water. He also loved spending time with Steve as they got on famously – so it was his perfect job.

Glancing over at the Beaumaris Pier, he saw a few elderly couples walking towards its end or taking in the view. After a failed marriage, and nearly a decade single, he missed having someone in his life to share things with. In recent months, he had begun to worry about what it would be like to grow old alone.

There were a couple of kids laughing, shouting and hanging over the railings with lines dangling down to the glistening beach. Geoff chuckled to himself. They were clearly bunking off school to go crabbing in the sunshine, just as he had done back in the seventies. *Good for them,* he thought. *Far too much bloody pressure on kids at school these days.*

Putting on his cheap sunglasses, Geoff cut across the grass and headed for the pier. His left knee was playing up. He'd injured it during the British attempt to retake South Georgia during the Falklands War in 1981. As part of the Special Boat Service, they landed at Hound Bay and tried to move across Cumberland Bay to a position south of Grytviken. They were stopped by the ice and that's when Geoff fell down a ravine and broke his leg. It took three of his platoon to lift him out and his knee never recovered, so he walked with a slight limp. Yet he chose never to tell the story of how he damaged his leg. He felt it made him sound like a show-off, so he just made a joke of it and put it down to 'old age'.

On the pavement by the pier was a ticket booking kiosk marked *Fishing Trips*. There were two large Welsh flags waving from its top and a chalkboard that promised *A Good Day Out!* Megan, who ran the excursions with her husband, waved him over. She was in her fifties, with a ruddy face, lively chestnut eyes and raven-coloured hair.

'Starting to get busy?' she asked in a loud voice. Megan said everything in a loud voice, to the point where Geoff had wondered if she was actually partially deaf.

Geoff nodded. 'Aye, it's picking up. And the school trips are keeping us going.'

'Pop over for a brew later, eh?' she suggested with a knowing smile as she tapped the side of her nose. 'I've got something to tell you that'll make you piss yourself laughing.'

'You always do.'

She gave him a look of mock indignation. 'I hope you're not implying I'm a gossip, Geoffrey Clegg?'

'A gossip? God no,' he laughed. 'What's that saying? Gossip is the thing we all claim to dislike, but actually enjoy.'

'Well, I like to call it "intelligence gathering", so make sure you pop by later,' she insisted.

'Will do,' Geoff replied with a grin as he strolled away, whistling happily. She was a constant source of hilarious anecdotes. And if anything was going on in Beaumaris, then Megan would know about it. But she had a heart of gold and spent her spare time running the local branches of the Brownies and Girl Guides. It was her passion and she had recently received the prestigious Laurel Award for her outstanding contribution to guiding.

As Geoff wandered away down the pier, he spotted one of the lifeboat crew opening up the double doors to the lifeboat station. The rest of the crew were doing some maintenance work on the boat while listening to the radio. He wished he had time to have a chat and nose around. He loved anything to do with boats.

Getting to the end of the pier, he saw Steve waving at him. Like Geoff, his friend was in his sixties, but with sandy hair and a thick beard.

'Come on, you tosspot, you're late!' Steve chuckled as he clanked open the metal gates to the walkway that led down to the *Anglesey Princess* – a Starlight Ocean Cruiser with fifty-six seats.

'Tosspot? Charming. So, what have we got this morning?' Geoff asked as he stepped off the jetty and onto the boat.

Steve peered down at his clipboard. 'School trip at ten a.m.'

'Which school?' Geoff asked. In his experience, the kids from the local primary schools were almost always impeccably behaved. Those from the larger secondary schools were sometimes problematic.

Steve squinted and ran his finger down the list. 'St Mary's?'

'That's my old primary school.' Geoff laughed and then he looked up at the clear sky and sun.

63

'I finished that book you gave me last night,' Steve said. 'I didn't guess the ending either.'

'I did,' Geoff bragged with a grin. 'When they found all that blood at the farm, I knew it had been planted there.'

'Smart arse,' Steve teased him. 'It's nice to read crime books set in North Wales though because I know all the places.'

'Yeah, that's what I told you,' Geoff agreed. 'I'm on book seven now.'

Their eyes met for a moment – Steve's eyes were chestnut brown – and Geoff felt a warm glow of friendship as he smiled at Steve. They were so close that he sometimes wondered if it could be more than friendship . . .

'Nothing like a good murder, eh?' Steve laughed.

'Too right,' Geoff replied as he gazed out across the Menai Strait that now glimmered in the sunshine. He took a deep breath of the sea air. 'It's gonna be a lovely morning.'

Steve rolled his eyes. 'Famous last words, mate.'

Chapter 7

August 2018

Laura gazed over at Brannings Warehouse. She was waiting for Chief Constable Stephen Bryant, the head of Greater Manchester Police Force, to come back with some decisions about what they could offer to the gang in return for releasing Sam and Louise. She already knew a helicopter was out of the question but she feared that CC Bryant would take a tough stance and decide that they would not negotiate with known members of a drug gang.

And that left them with only one option – direct force.

She suspected that was the way things were going as the influx of tactical firearms officers and specialists meant that the garage and surrounding area now resembled a military camp.

She saw Pete approaching.

'We've received a phone call from Whitehall. The Home Secretary is now monitoring the situation,' he informed her.

She pulled a sarcastic face. 'That's comforting to know.'

'We'll get them back, Laura. Don't worry,' Pete reassured her.

I wish people would stop saying that!

'If those idiots in Whitehall and Scotland Yard won't give me anything to negotiate with, then we only have one other option,' Laura stated grimly as she looked over at the AROs. She knew that sending in armed officers might be the only solution to getting Sam back. However, she also knew that it would put Sam and Louise in a huge amount of danger.

Pete glanced at her. 'Let's take it one step at a time, eh, Laura?'

The phone rang from inside the garage and the answering PC glanced at her anxiously and beckoned her over. 'Ma'am.'

Breaking into a jog, she got to the table and picked up the phone.

'Hello?'

There was a few seconds' silence.

Her mouth was dry and the pit of her stomach tense.

'You need to tell me what the fuck's going on or you're going to be burying your mates next week,' a voice growled. It was the same gang member she'd spoken to earlier.

'The helicopter is on its way.' She spoke calmly, lying through her teeth. 'It just takes time. Is there anything you need in the meantime?'

'What?'

'If you guys need food or drink, I can arrange that for you while you're waiting in there,' she suggested.

The man laughed. 'You think we're gonna wave our hands in the air and come out if you buy us a friggin' pizza and beer? Jesus!'

'That's not why I'm suggesting it,' she assured him. 'I just want everyone in there to be comfortable, okay?'

'I'm not fuckin' thick,' the man sneered. 'You're stalling for time.'

'I'm not, I promise you,' she informed him gently. 'We're

getting the helicopter to fly over from Lancashire. That takes time.'

'I don't give a fuck about that, you bitch!' he thundered down the phone line. 'We're not pissing about here. You've got an hour before I'm gonna cut off one of their heads and chuck it out for you all to have a kickabout with. Do I make myself clear?'

The line went dead.

Chapter 8

9.10 a.m.

Laura scanned the room and surveyed the dozen or so clients of Engage Business Skills who had signed up to take her company's latest course – *Tough Negotiating in Business*. They ranged in age from twenties to sixties. Two of the men had arrived in sharp suits and ties, whereas a couple of the older clients were dressed in far more casual attire. She could tell a lot just from what a client wore and how they sat. The young man in the suit and tie sitting at the front with a laptop open was keen but needy. The man in his early sixties who sat cross-legged at the back with his arms crossed exuded an air of pomposity, as if to say, '*It's down to you to impress me, love.*'

The last year had seen Laura's business management company go from strength to strength. She'd rented new premises in the middle of Beaumaris, on the first floor above a lovely little café, and three months ago she'd hired her first employee, Annabelle Potter.

'Morning, everyone,' Laura said brightly as she perched herself on the table at the front of the room. 'Put your hands up if you've eaten a decent breakfast.'

Seven of the twelve clients put their hands up.

'Okay. I'm going to tell you why I asked. People are more likely to feel positive, happy or focused when their blood sugar levels are high. So, if you're going to have an important conversation with your boss or a client, it's best done early in the day. In fact, data has shown that UK judges are more likely to grant parole to a prisoner straight after breakfast than a few hours later.' Laura unscrewed her bottle of water, took a swig and continued. 'I'm guessing that many of you signed up to this course because of my background in hostage and crisis negotiation when I worked as a police officer. And the reason I like to start by talking about food is because it's also a powerful weapon in a hostage negotiation, especially when used as a reward.'

Getting up from the table, she went over to her MacBook, hit a button and the first slide in her deck was projected onto the wall – *Tough Negotiating in Business*.

'So, let's a have a look at what you're going to be learning on this course and the nine key principles I used to succeed when it mattered most, when people's lives were at stake.'

The summer sky was clear as Gareth pulled the unmarked black police Astra onto a large grassy area at the far eastern end of Beaumaris Beach. At this time of year, the expanse of grass that ran beside the seafront was turned into a car park for tourists. He spotted a couple of twenty-somethings who were checking that everyone who had parked had bought a ticket.

Gareth got out the car and took stock. Now that the sun had burnt away the early-morning clouds, the sky consisted of varying tones of blue. Gazing over at Snowdonia, he longed for those rare moments he had found peace there. Lying on a mountain top and watching the clouds drive across the sky above. Or the sound of the waves breaking onto an empty shoreline. They were the moments when he had let his poor, struggling life mingle effortlessly with Nature, felt the slow beat of her heart and gained perspective on his very being. And for a split second he thought of Laura.

The sudden noise of cars drawing up alongside him broke his train of thought. There were two other CID cars and three uniform patrol cars. He checked his watch: 9.40 a.m. Twenty minutes before the drop. He could feel his heart start to thump against the inside of his chest at the thought of what might come next.

Gareth had spent the last forty minutes putting together an operational plan, as well as informing his Super and the Chief Constable of North Wales Police of the developments. Two Armed Response Vehicles had been scrambled from the Welsh mainland, but by Gareth's calculations, they wouldn't make it in time. It was down to the small number of officers that he had with him right now to make sure the operation was a success.

Getting out of the car, Gareth saw Declan approaching.

'We're ready to go, boss,' Declan greeted him.

'Right, let's get on with it then,' Gareth said.

He had organised for CID and uniform officers to get into position on the west side of the pier, and assigned two armed CID officers and several uniformed officers to spread out around the area of the main road and seafront.

As they marched over to the beach, the colder air currents blew in from the water. It was warm, salty and smelt of seaweed.

Gareth's radio crackled. 'Three-nine to Gold Command. Echo Charlie three and four are in position, over.'

Gareth's call-sign was Gold Command as he was in charge of the entire operation. Nothing happened without his authority.

'Gold Command received,' Gareth replied. The codes told

him that the officers to the west of the pier were now in place.

Now harried, he wondered how this was going to play out.

As they reached the bend of the beach, Beaumaris Pier came into view. The tide was coming in and only the final third of the pier had sand underneath it.

Declan looked over. 'Why ten a.m., do you think? Seems like a weird time, doesn't it?'

Gareth frowned. 'I think it's like the perfect time. It would be highly suspicious for a few men to be seen unloading stuff from a boat onto the beach under the cover of night or at dawn.' He gestured to what they could see in front of them. 'Look at it now. You've got tourists arriving for a day on the beach. Fishing trips and boat tours coming and going from the pier. All shapes and sizes of other boats zipping around, mooring up or leaving. Who's going to notice a couple of blokes arriving on the beach in broad daylight? Unless they're wearing balaclavas and waving around AK47s, how would anyone know they were gangsters?'

Declan nodded. 'Fair point, boss.'

Gareth spotted something over on the main road that concerned him. Taking his binoculars, he focused in on a coach that had parked up with its hazard lights flashing beside the ticket booking kiosks at the pier.

'Don't tell me . . .' he muttered.

Declan frowned at him. 'Problem, boss?'

As Gareth watched, a young woman stepped down off the coach, holding a folder. A few seconds later, a procession of what looked to be ten- and eleven-year-old children followed and lined up on the pavement where she pointed. They began to make their way towards the pier in pairs.

'I've got a horrible feeling that we've got a primary-school party arriving for a boat trip,' Gareth grumbled.

'Can't we just stop them?'

Gareth looked again. It was going to take him over five minutes to reach the pier from where they were. 'If we try to take them back off the pier and explain what's going on, it'll be chaos. And anyone waiting to meet the shipment might well clock our presence. I don't want to take that risk. I just hope they're on the boat and out on the Strait by the time we go to make our arrests.'

All Michael could hear was the intermittent drone of the boat engine mixed with the incessant screeching of gulls until Red finally reduced the throttle on the boat and let the engine die. For a moment, Michael closed his eyes against the sunlight, feeling its warmth on his eyelids. The smells and sounds took him momentarily back to digging in wet sand, damp trousers clinging to his legs, and warm, cheap cola from a two-litre bottle his father had brought with them. The tender simplicity of the memory was a fleeting relief from the morning's incessant anxiety.

Beaumaris Pier and beach were now about a mile or two ahead of them, to the right. The sun blazed down, and even from where Michael sat, he could see the sunlight glinting off glass and buildings in the nearby coastal town. Close to the shore, four long white bungalows gleamed. Behind them, dark pine trees in a small coastal woodland swayed and rattled in the sea breeze.

'Why we stopping?' Michael asked Callum. He knew he sounded scared, but he *was* bloody scared. In fact, he was bloody bricking it – he just didn't want Red to know.

'Waiting for the signal to go in,' Callum replied, and then reached over and ruffled his hair again. 'Keep calm.'

'I am bloody calm,' Michael protested in a virtual whisper. He really wasn't.

Callum gestured to Red, who was still standing with his

legs apart over by the steering wheel and throttle. 'Yeah, well, I'm just saying, all right? Cos he's a fucking bully.'

Michael agreed, but his brother's words had done little to settle his nerves. His stomach began to churn and his breathing felt shallow again.

Come on, lad, you can do this! he said to himself.

The air was still and hot. Michael dangled his hand in the cold water and then rubbed it over his face. It felt dead nice. A droplet ran down his cheek, all the way to his lips, and, for a second, he got the salty taste of the sea in his mouth.

About 500 yards away, a twenty-foot yacht glided along the surface of the water and turned. Its gleaming blue hull tipped towards them and threw a plume of white water into the air. Then a sharp noise of the sail billowing and flapping, like the brisk sound of laundry being shaken to remove its creases.

'Here, you need to put these on,' Red growled as he pulled off his black ski hat. His orange hair seemed more fiery in the sun.

Reaching into the black Puma bag, he pulled out three brightly coloured baseball caps.

Looking down at the bright orange baseball cap, Michael saw a blue and white sailing boat in the centre of the cap and the word '*Sailing*' scrawled underneath.

'Fucking 'ell,' Michael snapped. 'I'm not wearing this thing. I'll look like a right dickhead.'

Callum rolled his eyes. 'That's the point, you divvy!'

Michael frowned. 'What?'

Red approached Callum aggressively. 'Haven't you taught him nothing?'

Callum tried to ignore Red and glanced at Michael. 'We're meant to look like dickheads. Dickheads who are messing about on a boat. Hence the stupid baseball caps. We don't want to look like a bunch of scallies, do we? Think about it, eh? We can't rock up in balaclavas, can we?'

Michael put the cap on. It made sense now Callum explained it.

'Hey, Callum, look at these,' Red chortled as he fished out a pair of Oakley wraparound sunglasses. 'I got a pair of these bloody things, like they all wear.'

Callum laughed, but Michael could tell he was just humouring Red. That's what everyone did. Humouring him was a form of self-protection.

Red glared at Michael and pointed to his jacket. 'And you wanna get rid of that bloody jacket, kid, if you're staying up here for a bit. You wear North Face and you've got a Scouse accent, you might as well wear a sign for the bizzies that says "*I'm working county lines*".'

If he was honest, Michael was looking forward to a few weeks in a town like Beaumaris, doing a bit of dealing and having time out of the continual glare of Red. He was a scary prick.

Looking down at his mobile, Red turned. 'Right, ladies. We're fucking on!'

He started the engine, which gave a deep rumble, and floored the throttle.

Before he could get a grip, Michael had been thrown back. Grabbing the side, he got his balance and stared out ahead as they sped towards Beaumaris Beach.

Chapter 9

Looking up the pier, Geoff could see a young female teacher followed by twenty or so pupils heading his way. Glancing down at his watch, he saw it was nearly 9.50 a.m., so they were cutting it a bit fine to leave bang on ten a.m. His forearm was a little red from where he'd caught the sun the day before and his naval tattoo appeared more faded. The tattoo was over thirty years old and featured a long dagger pointing up, a parachute and a scroll that read '*By Strength and by Guile*'. At the bottom, another scroll that read '*Special Boat Service*'.

The SBS was the elite special forces unit of the Royal Navy and was formed during the Second World War. Even though he was proud of his time in the Royal Navy, he often regretted having the tattoo so prominently on his arm as it allowed know-it-alls to start a conversation about his time in the SBS.

'Sorry we're late,' panted the young teacher as she arrived, clutching the tickets. She appeared flustered.

Geoff smiled reassuringly. 'No problem. There's no rush.' He admired teachers – he knew he didn't have the patience to do their job. He then gestured to the pupils. 'In fact, St Mary's is my old school.'

The teacher laughed. 'Wow. Small world. I'm Miss Hughes. Beth.'

'Hi, Beth,' he said. 'I'm Geoff. If I can just take those tickets off you and check them.'

Beth handed over the tickets and seemed to have relaxed a little. 'Oh, yes. Of course.'

Underneath her top and short sleeves, he could see that she had tattoos. *Good for her,* he thought. *When I was young, the only place you would have found a woman with tattoos was in the circus.*

Geoff grinned at the pupils in the line. 'So, my name is Geoff. And the nice man who drives the boat and is going to tell you all about Puffin Island, and the other things we're going to see, is called Steve.'

A young girl peered up at him, squinting in the sunlight. 'If he does all that, what do you do?'

Beth looked at him and gave an apologetic roll of her eyes.

'No, no. That's a fair question.' He chuckled. 'And what's your name, young lady?'

'Isabella. But I'm known as Bella,' she announced.

Now there's confidence, and there's precociousness! he thought.

'Well, Bella,' Geoff explained. 'While Steve is doing all that, I'm just fighting off all the sharks and stuff like that.'

Beth laughed but Bella pulled a face.

'There aren't any sharks out there, are there?' she asked.

'Not many,' Geoff joked. 'But don't worry, if there are any, I'm trained to deal with them. In fact, I'm trained to deal with anything that comes our way.'

Beth gave him a smile. 'Well, guys, it sound like we're in good hands, doesn't it?'

*　　*　　*

Laura walked across the room, hit a button on her laptop and projected a slide up onto the wall which read '*Mirroring*'.

'Okay, this is a very powerful negotiating technique,' she explained. 'It's essentially imitation. Neurologically, when humans or animals copy each other in a non-confrontational way, it comforts us and puts us off our guard. The person who is being mirrored is rarely aware that it's happening. In a crisis situation, or in a business situation, it can establish an unconscious rapport or bond that then leads to trust. It says to the other person, "*You and me, we're alike. You can confide in me.*"

'Just over ten years ago I went on secondment to the FBI in America to spend a month working with FBI negotiators. It was fascinating, and I noticed that one simple trick they continually use is to repeat the last three words that a person has said in the form of a question. So, I'm going to use the exact conversation that an FBI negotiator used during a bank robbery in Washington DC, where I worked as an observer.'

Sipping from her coffee, she clicked through to the next slide on her MacBook. She couldn't help but get a little thrill when playing the FBI card. She loved to see the reactions on clients' faces as though this made her what Americans would term 'a big shot'. Sam used to tease her about it unremittingly, doing his best Anthony Hopkins as Hannibal Lecter, saying '*You know what you look like, with your good bag and cheap shoes? You're not more than one generation away from poor white trash. You could only dream of getting out, getting anywhere, getting all the way to the F . . . B . . . I.*' She would roll her eyes, telling him he was just jealous.

Up on the wall the following was projected:

FBI Agent: We haven't managed to find your car out here on the street yet.

77

Bank Robber: Yeah, because you guys chased our driver away.

FBI Agent: We chased your driver away?

Bank Robber: Yeah. As soon as he saw cops, he cut.

FBI Agent: What a jerk. He saw cops and he cut?

Bank Robber: I know, can you believe it? Should have never used an out of town guy.

FBI Agent: He was an out of town guy?

Bank Robber: Boston. You know, Southie.

FBI Agent: Southie? Yeah, well, you can never trust the Irish.

Bank Robber: Too right. Crooked as the day is long.

Laura turned back to her clients. 'So, by using the mirroring technique, the FBI agent found out that they were looking for an Irish getaway driver from South Boston. I don't think the bank robber would have been so open if the agent hadn't used that technique. So, for the next few minutes, I want you guys to practise this technique in the pairs you worked in earlier. Take it in turns to mirror each other and then write down how it feels being on each side of the mirroring strategy. Okay, so off you go and we'll feedback in a group in ten minutes.'

A young man in a suit and tie, whom Laura had pegged as an estate agent, put up his hand. 'Can I ask a question before we do that?'

'Of course,' she replied.

'Do you believe you can negotiate with anyone?' the man asked. 'You've shown us you can negotiate with a bank robber. But what about someone who is a bully in the board-room? Someone who is unreasonable, or even uses threats?'

'That's an excellent question,' she said, not wanting to sound too surprised. She had had the young man down as another wannabe property tycoon with half a brain. 'My belief is that you can negotiate with anyone. For instance, the bully in the boardroom doesn't actually want to fight. And don't be misguided into thinking that what they want is power. They want *status*. They want to appear more important than anyone else. They want to win. To them, the negotiation is a game. So, my advice in that situation is to also treat it like a game. Acknowledge the bully's status, *but* stand firm on what you want. Does that answer your question?'

The man gave a quizzical look. 'Sort of.'

'Don't worry,' she reassured him. 'We're going to be doing a session on this type of thing this afternoon. I'll make sure that we come back to your question and go into it in more detail then.'

The young man nodded and as the clients got into pairs, she went over to her desk and sat at her MacBook. She wanted to check her emails and do some other admin stuff while the clients were working together. Opening her inbox, a name struck her she hadn't seen in several months. DCI Pete Marsons.

That's weird. Pete never sends me emails. He usually texts me.

Hiya lovely
Hope all is good with you guys? Is Rosie learning to drive yet? Has Jake stopped supporting that ridiculous team and come to the sky blue side of Manchester?
I still cannot track down Martin Barratt. The trail on him has gone completely cold. The last intel I have on him shows that he is working in Dublin. Also no progress with Mandy Cooper, I'm afraid. She and her family have moved out of Manchester to Portsmouth.

There is, however, something else that I have discovered. You know we've always wondered about how the Fallowfield Hill Gang knew there was going to be a raid that morning? And we've always suspected that there might have been a leak somewhere in the GMP? I've continued to dig and I think I've found something. The attached clip of CCTV shows Danny Wright, a leading member of the Fallowfield Hill Gang, in a car park in the Bredbury Park Industrial Estate. He gets out of the BMW X5, goes over to an Audi A5 and hands a large envelope to the driver. I've checked the plates against the PNC and the Audi is registered to a company called Clayton Vale Holdings. A director and part-owner of Clayton Vale Holdings is Jack Taylor . . . and Jack Taylor's daughter Leanne is married to Superintendent Ian Butterfield. Laura, we now have a direct link between Ian Butterfield and the Fallowfield Hill Gang.

Laura sat back for a moment in shock. Was Butterfield really bent? He had been the Gold Commander on the operation at Brannings Warehouse.

She and Pete had made their concerns, that someone had tipped the gang off about a raid earlier in the day, known to the IOPC – the Independent Office for Police Conduct – and there had been a full investigation but it had concluded there was no evidence of any police corruption. Even though she knew the IOPC was a reliable and independent body, she also knew that their conclusion wasn't definitive. They had made mistakes before.

'Butterfield?' asked a familiar voice.

She spun around and glared at Sam. 'What are you doing here? I've told you not to come to work. And I've also told you not to read things over my shoulder.'

'I'm just feeling very uncomfortable today. I can't seem to settle,' Sam said. 'Does Pete think Butterfield is bent?'

She shrugged. 'He thinks there could be a direct link between Butterfield and the OCG.'

'I always thought Ian Butterfield was a prick,' Sam grumbled. 'But that's Leeds fans for you.'

'This isn't funny, Sam,' she whispered.

'Sorry,' Sam said. 'You know what I'm like. I use humour when I feel uncomfortable.'

'Weren't there loads of rumours when Butterfield got married?' she asked, thinking out loud.

'I think it was common knowledge that Leanne Taylor's family were dodgy,' Sam agreed. 'I think her brother did time for armed robbery, didn't he?'

'Something like that,' she said. 'It's the first time we've found a link between someone in the GMP and the Fallowfield Hill Gang.'

Sam looked at her. 'Why is this so important to you?'

'Why is it so important to find out if a bent copper in the GMP was feeding information to an OCG and was therefore responsible for your death?' she growled.

'I understand all that,' he said thoughtfully. 'And I know that if you could find out who was responsible for my death, that might bring you some closure.'

'Of course it would. I might be able to move on with my life.'

Sam gazed at her momentarily as though he had something important to say. 'The funny thing is, if you can find some kind of answer that would allow you to move on, I guess I won't be around as much.'

There were a few seconds of uncomfortable silence. He was probably right.

She looked at him as a lump came into her throat. 'Yeah, I know that, Sam. But it just feels like the right thing to do.'

Talking with Sam, as she had done since the day of the funeral, had been incredibly comforting. However, Laura was becoming aware that it was neither healthy nor sustainable if she wanted to get her life back.

* * *

Beth watched as the last pupil from St Mary's walked across the steel gangplank and stepped down onto the *Anglesey Princess*. She then followed and stood looking around the boat. Apart from her Year 6 class, there were twenty or so other passengers on board, mainly pensioners.

Holding up her hand to get her pupils' attention, Beth hollered, 'Okay, listen up, Year 6. I want us to have a lovely trip, but there are a few things for you to remember. You are out in public today, so you are representing St Mary's and I want you all to be on your best behaviour, please. I want you to stay in your seats during our trip. You are not to go wandering around the boat. There is no use of phones or eating food. It's going to be hot, so if you want to put on suncream or your caps and drink water from your bottles, then that is absolutely fine. Our trip today is going to be part of our wildlife and nature project, so I also want you all to take out your project books. When our guide begins to tell us about all the interesting things you can see today, I want you to take notes as next week you are each going to have to do a presentation for the whole class. So, let's have a lovely trip, and if you need me, I'm going to be sitting just here.'

Beth smiled at them and sat down.

Phew.

The tannoy on the boat crackled and there was the sound of a voice saying, 'Good morning, everyone, and welcome to Beaumaris Cruises' trip to Puffin Island. My name is Steve, and my glamorous assistant for today is Geoff. He's the hairy old bloke you might have seen when you were getting on.'

Beth and some of the other passengers laughed.

'We've got to give you a little safety briefing before we get away, guys. It's nothing to worry about though as the conditions this morning are perfect for going out and looking at wildlife and we're not expecting any dramas today. So, firstly, our life-jackets are located in the wheelhouse. If there is an emergency, myself and Geoff will distribute the life-jackets to everyone and make sure that they are fitted correctly. On the roof of the boat there are four Solas life-rafts, which can be both manually and automatically inflated in an emergency situation, and we carry all the necessary fire-fighting, first-aid and rescue equipment required for a vessel of this kind. We would also ask you to remain on the boat throughout the trip. It's going to be a hot, sunny day and the water might look inviting, but there are two big propellers underneath the boat and we don't want you tangling with them, do we? So, we're going to be setting off now and I'll be back with you when I can start to point out things of interest.'

The tannoy crackled again as it switched off.

Grabbing her sunglasses, Beth gave a satisfied sigh.

An hour and a half of sitting in the sun on a boat with beautiful views. There are definitely some benefits to being a teacher.

Chapter 10

August 2018

Laura stood looking over at Brannings Warehouse. She felt utterly helpless. Superintendent Ian Butterfield had just clarified that the GMP would not negotiate with criminals who have taken police officers hostage as it would – apparently – set a dangerous precedent. She knew what Butterfield had said was true, and that they just couldn't give in to an OCG like the Fallowfield Hill Gang, but Sam was her husband and she would do anything to get him out of there unharmed.

She saw Pete approaching.

'Don't worry. We're going to get them out of there, one way or another,' he said.

'That's what everyone keeps saying,' she snapped loudly. The stress was really getting to her. 'It doesn't mean their lives aren't in great danger or that I'm not terrified.'

'Sorry. No more platitudes from me today,' Pete apologised.

Laura took a breath to calm herself and shook her head. 'Sorry, boss.'

'Forget it,' he said. 'I've told the Super that there is growing suspicion that those scumbags were tipped off about the raid.'

'What did he say?'

'The usual bullshit,' Pete moaned. '"The IOPC will carry out a full enquiry, blah, blah, blah."'

Suddenly, a thunderous noise came from the sky and Laura glanced up to see a dark, ominous shape blocking out the sun.

A helicopter.

As it hovered and then landed on a disused car park about 200 yards away, she could see that it wasn't a police helicopter. It was a black Eurocopter Dauphin. It touched down, throwing dust and grit into the air, and the rear doors opened slowly. Within seconds, about eight men dressed head to toe in black protective equipment jumped out and ran to an area where they assembled.

The Special Air Service – the elite special forces unit of the British Army.

The time for negotiating was well and truly over.

All the SAS officers were wearing breathing equipment. It made her shudder for a second. The SAS had been using CS gas as a prelude to their operations as far back as their infamous assault on the Iranian Embassy in 1980.

She hated feeling this helpless. The operation was completely out of her hands and she wasn't used to that. She shuddered to think of Sam and Louise being held against their will, while the warehouse filled with CS gas and SAS officers fought a gun battle with armed gang members.

There must be a way of getting them out before this all kicks off, she thought.

Pete glanced at the SAS officers and quipped dryly, 'Here we go. *Who Dares Wins.*' It was the well-known motto of the Special Air Service.

Laura was terrified. 'I do not want Sam and Louise caught up in the middle of some hideous firefight.'

'Neither do I,' Pete admitted. 'But I think we're out of options.'

As they watched, the SAS officers adjusted their body armour and balaclavas before checking the magazines in their Heckler & Koch assault rifles. Then they crouched, fanned out and disappeared around the back of the warehouse.

Laura did a double-take. They had landed, disembarked and entered the warehouse in less than two minutes. She guessed that was their MO – in and out with terrifying speed and force.

Pete's Tetra radio crackled. 'All units from Gold Command. Proceed with caution to target location.'

She and Pete crouched and then moved forward, finding cover behind a nearby wall.

Suddenly, there were sporadic cracks of gunfire. The SAS officers had clearly encountered the gang members.

Then everything went silent.

A sweet wrapper skittered along the ground beside them.

The wind picked up and blew a strand of hair across her face.

This is way too quiet.

She turned and looked at Pete, who was crouched by her side. 'What's going on?'

'Maybe they've given themselves up?' He shrugged. 'Faced with CS gas and masked special forces I'd surrender myself pretty sharpish.'

Then she saw him looking up at the sky and frowning.

'That's definitely not CS gas,' he stated, gesturing upwards.

She glanced up to where he was looking and saw a growing plume of thick black smoke swirling up into the blue summer sky above the warehouse.

'Shit! There's a fire coming from somewhere in there,' she cried. 'And that place is covered in petrol and explosives.'

'Come on,' he yelled as he clicked his Tetra radio. 'Gold Command from nine-five, over.'

'This is Gold Command, received, over.'

'We have smoke coming from target location. We are proceeding to the entry point at target location immediately, over.'

Laura and Pete scuttled across the yard and took cover over by the double doors, which were covered in corrugated iron and daubed with graffiti.

She could see the full extent of the smoke, which now dominated and darkened the sky above them.

This is not good! Sam is in there somewhere!

There was more gunfire, but this time it was close by. Too close.

Without warning, a man in a balaclava and holding a handgun smashed through the double doors.

In a flash, he had grabbed Laura, spun her around and put her in a choke hold. He then jammed the handgun hard into the side of her head.

'Get back or I'll shoot her!' the man shouted at Pete.

As she tried to get her breath, she recognised his voice. He was the man who she had talked to on the phone.

Pete put up his hand. 'Hey, take it easy, mate.'

The man dragged Laura back, his forearm hard against her throat. 'Right, me and her are walking out of here, got it? If anyone comes anywhere near us, I'm going to kill her!'

Pete nodded. 'Fine. I just need you to calm down.'

A figure appeared at the double doors – an SAS officer holding his Heckler & Koch assault rifle against his shoulder, ready to fire. He immediately spun and pointed the gun at the man who was holding Laura.

'Take the gun away from her head!' the SAS officer snapped.

'Don't get any funny ideas, pal,' the man hissed through gritted teeth. 'Otherwise I'm gonna blow her brains out!'

'Drop your weapon now!' the SAS officer barked again.

The man snorted. 'No chance!'

They staggered backwards, away from the warehouse. Laura's head was starting to swim from lack of oxygen. The gun barrel was jammed so hard against her skull, she thought it was going to crack. She tried to pull his forearm away from her throat.

'You're suffocating me!' she gasped.

'Shut up, bitch!' he growled, continuing to pull her backwards and away from the burning warehouse.

For a second, she thought she was going to lose her balance and fall.

Then something caught her eye. The red laser sight glimmering from the SAS officer's gun. It was still trained in their direction.

Then she remembered something from her Tactical and Combat Training.

Making eye contact with the SAS officer, she tried to indicate she was about to make a move that would allow him to have a safe, clean shot.

'Just so you know,' he whispered. 'I had a good time kicking the shit out of your copper mates in there.'

GO FUCK YOURSELF!

Raising up her foot, she stamped with all of her strength down onto the gang member's instep. In that split second, he loosened his grip on her throat and she bit as hard as she could into the flesh of his forearm.

'ARRGGHHH', he yelled in pain and released her from the choke hold.

In that moment, she dropped to the ground as fast as she could and covered her head.

CRACK! CRACK!

Two bullets hammered into the man's chest and he crumpled into a heap. He was dead before he dropped.

'Jesus!' she gasped, getting up.

Pete went to her. 'You okay?'

But she had other things on her mind.

'Where are the police officers?' she asked frantically as she stumbled towards the SAS officer.

He shook his head. 'We can't find them.'

Thick black smoke now billowed like an onrushing tidal wave out of the double doors. All Laura could see beyond was the inferno of the warehouse burning inside.

Please God, let Sam be alive!

The SAS officer looked at her and coughed heavily in an effort to expel the soot and smoke from his lungs. 'Don't worry,' he gasped. 'I'm going back in. I'll get them out.'

Suddenly, the air ripped apart with noise and flames as the windows along the front of the warehouse exploded in an eruption of fire and glass.

It felt as though time was trapped in slow motion. Laura reached out, as if she was pushing her hands through sand. Her mouth opened, but any sound was stuck inside her chest. She was frozen.

Then she was picked up and flung backwards by the force of the blast.

She landed heavily on her back and lay there winded.

For a moment, everything became silent. An eerie darkness, as if all the light had been drained from the sky.

She sucked in oxygen, but the air felt hot and thick. She didn't know if she was drowning or suffocating, and the silence had now been replaced by a high-pitched ringing in her ears.

At last, she got her breath back. Drawing in as much air as she could, all she could smell was dust and petrol fumes.

And then she felt a strange sense of rain as bits of stone from the warehouse fell noisily all around.

She coughed for a moment and looked at Pete. His face was blackened by soot and debris. He said something, but the ringing in her ears drowned out his words.

Then she stared at the warehouse in a daze. All that was left was a shell that was now engulfed in a blazing, flaring cauldron of fire.

Sam!

Then everything went black.

Chapter 11

CRASH! The RIB smashed into a wave and white spray flew into the air. The beach and pier at Beaumaris were getting closer and closer and Michael felt the knot in his stomach tighten as the spray covered his face again. This was it. He gripped the webbing for dear life as they continued to bounce and hurtle along the rippled surface of the sea. The wind whipped at his face so that it was difficult to breathe.

BANG! The RIB hit the wake of a nearby fishing boat and leapt off the water for a few seconds before clattering back down again. The force threw him forward, and he grabbed the webbing with both hands to steady himself. More spray hit his face. It stung his eyes. The air smelt of seaweed and diesel fuel.

Come on, lad, you've got this! he told himself as he steeled himself for what was to come. He wasn't going to let his brother down. Especially not in front of Red.

The sound of gulls was now drowned out by the Yamaha 4-stroke, 250hp engine as Red pulled down the throttle with a roar. They hammered across the water at 40 knots. It felt a lot faster. A small blue yacht flew past in a blur. Michael thought if he stretched out, he might have touched it.

Jesus! That was close.

Pulling left, Red took the Zodiac Pro RIB away from the coast slightly in a wide arc. They zipped through a gap between two red buoys, heading to the beach on the far side of the pier as arranged.

The tone of the engine dropped as Red lowered the revs and slowed the RIB down. If Michael was to guess, he'd say they were about 500 yards from the shore when the RIB came to a standstill.

Michael looked over at Callum, who wore the bright green baseball cap that Red had given him. 'You look like a dickhead, mate.'

Callum beamed and gave him the finger.

'Oi!' Red yelled at them. He pointed to a mobile phone. 'Just waiting for the word, ladies.'

There was a loud thundering sound above them. Looking up into the clear blue sky, Michael saw the enormous shape of a yellow helicopter flying low above them and then heading inland towards Anglesey.

'Jesus!' Michael frowned. 'What the fuck do they want?'

'Don't worry, lad.' Callum laughed. 'That's not a bizzy helicopter.'

'How do you know that?'

'Bloody hell.' Callum groaned. 'Don't you know nothing? That's an RAF helicopter heading to the base over there. Remember that Prince William was stationed there for a while?'

Michael shrugged. He hadn't got a clue what his brother was talking about.

Which one's William? The ginger one?

'Don't you watch the news?' Callum asked.

'No,' Michael replied.

'Bizzy helicopters are black with a bit of yellow round the propellers,' Callum explained. 'You're getting paranoid.'

Red waved the mobile phone at them. 'Right, girls, we are fucking on. Time to grab your buckets and spades cos we're going in.'

And with that, Red yanked down the throttle. The engine roared as they sped towards Beaumaris – and whatever awaited them.

Gareth took his binoculars and scanned the Menai Strait from where he, and several other CID officers, lay hidden in the sand dunes close to Beaumaris Pier.

Nothing.

He had stationed two other CID officers on the pier itself to make sure members of the public didn't get caught up in anything if the arrest got nasty.

As the wind picked up, he peered at his watch. It was 10.10 a.m.

'Looks like they're running late,' he remarked.

Declan, who was crouched next to him, chuckled, trying to break the tension in the atmosphere. 'They're Scousers, boss. They're late for everything.'

'Nice regional stereotyping,' Gareth joked dryly.

For a few seconds, he stared over the glistening water of the Strait and then the looming presence of the Snowdonia mountains that towered over the horizon. It was a view he had seen thousands of times before, and one that he took for granted. To the left, the misty peak of Carnedd Llewelyn, the second-highest mountain in Wales, shimmered in the sunlight.

Where are they? I hope this intel isn't one big wild goose chase, he thought.

He looked again. The sunlight flared in the lens of the binoculars for a moment before he was able to focus them.

In the distance, a black RIB was zipping towards the beach at high speed. It skimmed like a flat pebble across the water, throwing clouds of spray into the air. At this range, he couldn't be sure how many people were on board but it looked like two, maybe three, white males.

'I think we're on,' Gareth said, handing Declan the binoculars. 'Have a look.'

Declan squinted and agreed. 'Yeah, boss. That's definitely them.'

'How long before they're on the beach?'

Declan narrowed his eyes. 'Two minutes.'

With his pulse racing, Gareth took his Tetra radio and pressed the long grey speak button on its side. 'Gold Command to all units. We have a visual on Target One. A black RIB with unidentified IC1 males heading for our target location, over.'

'Gold Command, this is Echo Charlie three and four,' a voice crackled on his radio. 'Received. We have visual on Target One and we are moving into position, over.'

Gareth took a breath. This was it. His heart was hammering against his chest.

'Okay, all units, stand by. ETA of Target One is two minutes.'

Chapter 12

09.59 a.m.

Looking out from the wheelhouse, Geoff could see that the conditions were just perfect for being on the water. He stepped outside onto the deck and the cool breeze blew against his weathered face. It reminded him of when he had been aboard HMS *Vanguard* in the early nineties when it had accompanied the aircraft carrier HMS *Invincible* on a five-day visit to the United States. They had sailed along the Hampton Roads, a wide strip of water, much like the Menai Strait, that served as a channel for the James, Nansemond and Elizabeth rivers in south-eastern Virginia and North Carolina. It was a beautiful part of the world, with miles of waterfront properties and beaches. Geoff had promised Steve that if he ever won the lottery, he would move there and take him with him.

'Sir, is there a toilet on the boat?' asked a voice. It was the little girl from St Mary's who had doubted his story about the sharks in the Menai Strait. She was now wearing Ray-Ban glasses with green plastic frames.

'It's Bella, isn't it?' Geoff asked with a smile. He had a granddaughter, Libby, almost the same age, living down in

Kent. However, he and his daughter, Steph, didn't get on after the divorce, so he only saw Libby and his grandson, Oscar, who was eight, once or twice a year. It broke his heart when he allowed himself to think about it. The last time he was down there, he had taken Oscar to see the Hugin, which was a reconstructed Viking longship at nearby Pegwell Bay.

'Yes, sir.' Bella nodded.

'It's just there.' Geoff pointed to the blue door on the left.

'Thank you,' Bella chirped as she skipped away.

What a cheerful soul, he thought as he resolved to make a more concerted effort to have contact with his grandchildren. Maybe he would drive down to Ramsgate when the summer tourist season had died down a bit.

His marriage to Julie had ended over ten years ago. He wasn't really sure what had happened, except they had just fallen out of love. Drifted apart. And when it came to him moving out, they had packed up his stuff like old friends and hugged . . .

A loud thundering noise broke his train of thought.

Turning to look, he saw a long black RIB hammering past on the water, heading towards Beaumaris Beach.

Jesus Christ! What the hell are they doing going that fast?

There were three young men on board and there was something about them he didn't like the look of. Driving an expensive RIB that fast was incredibly dangerous and irresponsible. With their bright baseball caps and sunglasses, he assumed they were flash bastards with too much money.

Looking out over the water, Geoff could see the enormous wake the RIB had created – it was heading their way. A few seconds later, the *Anglesey Princess* rocked harshly.

Bloody yobbos!

'Who the hell were they?' Steve asked, stepping out of the wheelhouse with a frown.

Geoff shook his head. 'Oh, you know the type. In my day,

they were called "Flash Harrys". If they don't slow down, they're going to hurt someone or themselves.'

He watched as the RIB zipped across the water towards the beach area.

Morons! I bet they're bloody footballers or something, he thought.

With the binoculars pushed tight against his damp eyebrows, Gareth watched the black RIB approaching at high speed. He could now see there were three young men inside the craft. With their brightly coloured baseball caps and designer sunglasses, they didn't look like members of the Croxteth Crew. Maybe that was the point? Or maybe the intel they'd been given was wrong?

The RIB slowed down to a crawl and turned. They were only 200 to 300 yards from the beach.

Gareth studied them again. The men in the RIB looked nervous as they surveyed the area of the beach.

No, it's definitely them. So, what are they waiting for?

Gareth chewed on his lip and then clicked his radio. 'Gold Command to all units, stand by.'

He could feel the anxiety growing as his breathing became shallow. The next few minutes were going to be critical in getting them arrested and the drugs seized. It was going to be a major triumph for Beaumaris CID, especially given recent rumours the station might be closed due to budget cuts. He didn't know why they weren't closing down the station at Benllech. They couldn't even run a bath, let alone a decent criminal investigation.

Gareth watched the RIB warily. He knew at the first sign of anything suspicious the gang members would turn and disappear back down the Menai Strait from where they had come. And with no police boats or helicopters on hand, they could easily escape back to Merseyside.

Scouring the beach quickly, Gareth searched for the other members of the gang who would be on hand to help pull the RIB up onto the beach, bring the drugs ashore and act as protection. There was no one who even remotely fitted the bill.

'Come on, you tosser, just land the boat,' Declan snarled under his breath.

The RIB had now virtually stopped. Gareth could see the men scanning the beach for the best place to land.

Come on. Two more minutes and you fuckers are mine! he thought to himself.

Suddenly, he saw something out of the corner of his eye.

A small boy at the end of the pier, who had been leaning precariously over the rails while crabbing, had fallen into the sea. His friends immediately ran to the railings and shouted and screamed for help, pointing to their friend in the water.

They didn't look very old – maybe seven or eight.

'Shit!' Gareth exclaimed.

'Something wrong, boss?' Declan asked.

'A boy just fell off the pier into the sea.' Gareth grabbed the radio and got to his feet. His overwhelming instinct was to go and help. 'Gold Command to all units. I've just spotted a boy falling from the right-hand side of the pier into the sea, over.'

Without thinking, Gareth ran out of the dunes where he had been hiding and sprinted towards the pier.

His Tetra radio crackled. 'Gold Command, this is Charlie Echo five. We have visual on the boy. We're on our way, over.'

As he reached the flat, wet surface of the beach, he no longer needed his binoculars. There were members of the public looking over the railings, shouting and screaming for help.

As he paused for breath, he could see that the two CID

officers he had stationed under the pier were already out and running towards the water. Ben threw his radio to one side, kicked off his shoes and dived into the sea.

'Jesus!' Declan exclaimed as he caught up to Gareth.

As Gareth jogged towards the pier, his attention went back to the stationary RIB, which was now only a hundred yards from the chaotic scene.

The three men inside were watching the events unfold.

This is not good.

His priority was to get the boy out of the sea alive, but he couldn't help worrying that the police presence on the beach was now blatantly obvious.

The man at the wheel of the RIB then turned and looked directly at him.

A second later, Ben came out of the water with the boy in his arms, put him down on the sand and checked on him. The boy was coughing, but he could sit up, so that was a good sign.

'Thank God,' Gareth muttered and then glanced anxiously back at the RIB.

A man with ginger hair locked eyes with him again. He then reached down, revved the RIB's powerful throttle and turned the boat away from the beach.

Shit! They've seen us.

The undercover operation had been detected, and the suspects were escaping.

Chapter 13

The RIB lurched as Red slammed down the throttle and the engine roared. Michael lost his balance and tumbled backwards against the side of the boat.

What the fuck is going on? he wondered as he grabbed a rope and scrambled into a seat.

Red glanced back at them, his face full of thunder. 'Fucking police everywhere!'

Having just spotted the young boy being pulled from the sea, Michael had been relieved to see that he was alive. He had been too focused on watching the events unfold to see anything else.

He looked back at the beach. Two middle-aged men were watching them. One of them had a walkie-talkie. The other was watching them through binoculars.

Shit! Bizzies.

As the RIB hit full speed, it zipped past the end of the pier. Callum pointed to three more men on the pier who were hurrying over. They all had walkie-talkies.

'What do we do now?' Michael yelled.

Callum was scared. 'We get the fuck out of here!'

The RIB hit a wave and left the water for a moment before slamming back down with a violent judder. Michael pushed his foot against the side of the boat to steady himself. His pulse was racing as the adrenaline surged through his body.

They were now fifty yards past the end of the pier. Red turned hard left as they headed back the way they had come.

What was going to happen to them? Scanning the Menai Strait, Michael anxiously searched for signs of a police boat he assumed would now chase them. He couldn't see anything – yet!

Turning with an icy stare, Red looked at them both. 'How the fuck did they know we were coming?'

Callum shrugged. 'They must have had a tip-off.'

'Well done, Sherlock!' Red shouted. 'I meant, *who* the fuck tipped them off?'

Michael avoided Red's glare. He knew he was now under suspicion, and that was dangerous. His stomach was in knots.

Callum moved over. 'Don't worry, kid. We'll be back in Croxteth in a couple of hours, having a bevvy and laughing about all this, eh?'

Michael glanced at him for a moment and said quietly, 'It wasn't me, Callum, you do know that, right?'

Callum pulled a face. 'Don't be a twat. No one thinks that you've been grassing to the bizzies. Jesus, I'm your brother for starters.'

Michael gestured to Red, who was standing with his legs apart and gripping the steering wheel with both hands. 'He does. He thinks I'm a grass.'

'No, he doesn't. He's just not right in the head. He's paranoid,' Callum assured him as he put his hand on Michael's shoulder and winked. 'Just let me deal with him, eh?'

Michael could feel the sense of relief that only his older brother could bring. He loved the very bones of him. It was the Cole brothers against the world. That's what Callum had always told him.

As his shoulders dropped a little, Michael stared ahead. Just over to the right was a large cruise boat. It had *Anglesey Princess* written across the side. On the deck of the boat were lots of schoolchildren and a few pensioners taking photos and looking out at the view. He guessed it was one of those cruise boats that took tourists around to look at the local area. He didn't think he'd ever been on a school trip. It was usually a chance to go on the wag with Callum and get into trouble.

Suddenly, the RIB lost power, as if someone had cut the engine.

They slowed. Now that the engine had stopped, the only sound was the hull swooshing through the water.

What the hell is going on?

Red pulled the throttle up and down – nothing. He hit the starter button, but it was completely dead. He kicked the dashboard in utter frustration. 'FUCK!'

Michael looked at Callum. *Shit! This is not good.*

Callum got up and went over to where Red was frantically trying every lever and button to no avail.

'What is it?' Callum asked.

Red shook his head. 'I don't fucking know, do I! We've got fuel, so it's not that. The engine is just dead.'

Callum glanced around. 'And we're stuck here like idiots.'

Red kicked the controls again in sheer fury. 'Fucking hell!'

'Any way of fixing it?'

Red pulled a face. 'I don't know nothing about bloody boat engines, do you?'

The blood had drained from Callum's face as he shook his head.

Red's eyes roamed around nervously. 'It's not gonna take long before the bizzies find us here and we get nicked.'

'And if we chuck the guns and drugs, we're gonna owe Jay and Danny over a hundred grand,' Callum stated, thinking out loud.

Red gritted his teeth angrily. 'And that means we won't live to see fucking Christmas.'

'What the fuck do we do?' Michael asked nervously.

For a few seconds, no one said anything. A gull cawed noisily overhead.

Red pointed over to the *Anglesey Princess*. 'We'll hitch a ride home on that.'

Callum frowned. 'That's a cruise ship. It's not going to Liverpool.'

'It'll go where we tell it to go,' Red growled.

Michael looked over at the *Anglesey Princess*. The cruise boat had slowed to a virtual stop as the tourists stared towards the Welsh coastline. They were taking photos.

'Red, the boat's full of schoolkids,' Michael muttered.

'Fine, then I'll just leave you two faggots here.' Red shrugged in anger. 'You'll get fifteen years for intent to supply crack cocaine and possession of firearms. Or you can dump the lot and go back to Croxteth, take your chances, and end up dead in the Mersey. Up to you.'

Callum and Michael looked at each other – they really didn't have a choice.

Taking one of the mooring ropes, Red turned the steering wheel so that the current moved the stationary RIB towards the *Anglesey Princess*.

Reaching down, Callum grabbed a paddle and used it to propel them towards the cruise boat.

'Hello?' Red bellowed as they got closer. 'Hello?'

A couple of the schoolchildren waved at them as the RIB got to about twenty yards away.

Callum gestured to them with a cheery wave and shouted, 'Can you get the captain of the boat for us? We've broken down.'

They nodded and disappeared.

Red, Callum and Michael all shared a look as they waited. Michael couldn't quite believe this was happening. Were they really going to board a boat and then take the passengers hostage until they got to Liverpool?

A few seconds later, a man in his sixties appeared by the railings and peered over. 'You guys okay?'

'Engine's dead and I've no idea why,' Red yelled.

'I've got some diesel if you need some,' the man suggested.

By now, there was a growing crowd of schoolchildren looking over at them to see what was going on.

'We've got over half a tank left. It's not that, mate,' Red explained and then he gestured to the *Anglesey Princess*. 'Any way we can catch a lift back to Beaumaris with you?'

The man scratched his chin for a second. 'We're not insured to tow other boats.'

Red shrugged. 'It's okay. It's my uncle's boat. We'll moor it here and he can come and fix it later.'

'It's going to be another hour before we get back to Beaumaris,' the man commented.

Callum shrugged. 'It's going to be a lot better than just sitting here.'

The man smiled and pointed to the mooring rope that Red was holding. 'Throw that to me and we'll pull you over then.'

'Thanks, mate.' Red grinned as he tossed the rope across the water. 'Here you go.'

The man pulled the RIB slowly over to the cruise boat under the watchful gaze of everyone on board.

As the side of the RIB pulled parallel, the man reached over, grabbed Red by the arm and helped him step across the gap to the *Anglesey Princess*. Callum took the Puma bag containing the drugs and the machine gun and followed.

'I'm Steve,' the man informed them warmly. 'Welcome aboard.'

Michael reached over, jumped across and gave him a friendly smile. 'Thanks.'

'We're heading down there to Puffin Island,' Steve explained. 'So, if you want to make yourselves comfortable.'

Red tossed the mooring rope back into the water, and the RIB floated away. He looked at Steve. 'Yeah, sorry, mate. Slight change of plan. We're going on a bit of a detour first.'

Chapter 14

10.11 a.m.

Having sprinted to the end of the pier, Gareth couldn't believe what he had just seen through his binoculars. The gang had boarded a cruise boat that looked like it was heading over to Puffin Island. He had no idea why. Surely it would have been quicker and easier to stay on the RIB? The only thing he could assume was there had been something wrong with the RIB, which meant they couldn't use it.

'Jesus Christ!' Gareth turned to Declan with a grim expression. Just when he thought their only issue today was going to be the aborted arrests of some Scouse drug dealers . . . 'We now have a *very* serious problem.'

Most of the Beaumaris CID team were now assembled around the area at the end of the pier. A few had binoculars and had been watching the events unfold with the RIB and the *Anglesey Princess*. There was a palpable sense of shock at what they had just witnessed. Things like this just didn't happen in the sleepy seaside town of Beaumaris.

Holding his hand up to get everyone's attention, Gareth gave a loud whistle. If he was being honest with himself, he felt completely out of this depth. 'Right, listen up, everyone! As most of you have seen, our operation this morning has had a serious development. Our Target One, the suspects who we believed were part of an OCG operation to land drugs on that beach, have now boarded one of the tourist cruises that travel from Beaumaris to Puffin Island and back – the *Anglesey Princess*. I can only assume they had some kind of mechanical failure on the RIB.'

There were some mutterings from the CID officers. It was frightening to think about three gang members boarding a boat with fifty or more tourists on board.

'Do you think they've got firearms, boss?' Declan asked.

'I'm not sure. I'm praying that they don't,' Gareth said as he took a breath. 'Because it gets worse. I believe that there is a primary-school trip on board, so I estimate there are twenty to twenty-five children on the boat.'

'Jesus Christ! My nephew Alfie goes to the local primary school,' Andrea exclaimed in alarm.

'This time of year, it could be any primary school on Anglesey,' Declan pointed out, trying to allay her fears.

'Right, we need to do everything we can to get those children, and the other people on that boat, back safely.' Gareth's tone was deadly serious. The adrenaline was pumping through his veins, which was making him jittery but also highly focused. 'I want this pier cleared of anyone not involved in this operation. Andrea?'

'Boss?' she answered.

'Get to the Anglesey Cruises kiosk down there,' he said, pointing to the other end of the pier where the main road was situated. 'We need a passenger list. If there is a primary-school party, then I need to know which school and which class. They will have a teacher with them. What's their name? Are they going to go to pieces? Do they have a teaching assistant with them? I want the names of the whoever is running the tour. Who are they? Any background information could be helpful. There must be a way of contacting the boat, so I need to know if it has some kind of radio. My guess is that it will have a VHF or two-way radio. What channel does the boat use in an emergency? Take Sian with you.'

'Yes, boss.' Andrea and DC Sian Taylor jogged away down the pier.

Gareth's head was spinning with everything they needed to think of. A rapid fire of questions, problems and then solutions flashed through his mind. 'Declan?'

'Boss?' he replied, taking two steps forward. He looked like a sprinter warming up before walking over to the blocks. It was all the nervous energy.

'I need any more information that we can get from Merseyside Police. Do we have any names for the men that were on that RIB? Any details that can tell us who they are or how they're going to react. Can we have access to the CHIS that they're running? It's probably a no, but any connection we can make with these men could be vital.'

Declan nodded, took his mobile phone out and moved away as he made the call. Gareth didn't know what he'd do without Declan as his DS and right-hand man.

'Ben and Dan,' Gareth said to the two CID detectives who had rescued the boy from the sea. 'Are you okay?'

Ben looked at him. His shirt was still wet from going into the sea.

'Yes, boss. The boy's parents arrived about five minutes ago. They're going to take him to the Gwynedd Hospital over in Bangor just to be on the safe side,' he informed him.

'Well, good work, lads. You saved that boy's life.'

Ben looked a little embarrassed by the statement. 'Thanks, boss.'

'Dan, can you and Ben chase Holyhead Police? We need their launches over here asap. And then talk to the NPAS at

Hawarden and get them to send over the helicopter. Ring RAF Valley and see if they're willing to help us out with a chopper.' Gareth took a breath as he surveyed the rest of the team. 'Have I missed anything?'

'HMS *Queen Elizabeth* is up the coast,' Ben informed Gareth. 'It's an aircraft carrier so it might have helicopters on board?'

Gareth nodded. 'Worth a try. Let me know what they say, Ben.'

Ben looked at him. 'Boss, if this is going to be a hostage situation, shouldn't we have a trained police negotiator here?'

Gareth agreed. 'Good point. Ring North Wales Police and see who they've got and how long they're going to take to get here.'

'Yes, boss.'

Gareth knew it could take hours to get a negotiator over from the mainland. He didn't relish the idea of talking to the gang members himself. It was going to require delicate and skilled negotiation techniques that were way beyond his skillset.

However, he did have a Plan B up his sleeve.

As Laura pushed open the door to the small kitchen area in her office, she saw that her PA and office manager, Annabelle, was sitting on the tiny sofa with the television on. On the floor beside her, Elvis was sprawled out in his usual daytime position. He moved his head, rested it on the floor and looked up at her with his enormous brown eyes.

Heading over to the kettle, she didn't say anything, but she was annoyed that Annabelle wasn't manning the phones or doing any of the tasks they had discussed earlier that morning. It wasn't like her. Annabelle was uber professional and always conscientious about her work.

'I'm just grabbing a quick coffee while the clients watch

a video,' she explained, but she knew Annabelle wasn't listening.

She's acting very strangely.

Annabelle was in her early twenties, polite, cheery and super organised. She was just what Laura needed. She ran the diary, answered emails and generally made sure the business ran smoothly. Laura knew she'd be lost without her.

'Sorry?' Annabelle mumbled.

'Everything all right?' she asked as she approached. What she wanted to say was, *What are you doing?*

'There's something going on in Beaumaris. It's on the news,' Annabelle told her, pointing to the television. 'It was on about a minute ago, but now this bloody Bo Jo story is on. He's such a dick.'

Annabelle loved to use the cheesy nickname for Prime Minister Boris Johnson, although her political awareness was no more sophisticated than Jake's.

'Beaumaris was on the news?' Laura asked, not really paying any attention. 'We're never on the news.'

She assumed it was some terribly parochial local interest piece. Yesterday, there had been a five-minute news item on BBC Wales about some protestors who had stopped work taking place on a 140-year-old disused school that was being converted into luxury holiday rentals. On Anglesey, it was always a slow news day.

'I know,' Annabelle replied and pointed again. 'It'll be back on in a minute. Something was going on down at the beach, by the pier. There's police everywhere. My mum rang me and told me to put it on.'

Annabelle's words made Laura uneasy. If a tiny seaside town like Beaumaris was on the national BBC News, then something dramatic or serious must have happened. She switched her focus from making a coffee to the television.

The news anchor looked at the camera and said, 'We are

getting reports of a major police operation in the town of Beaumaris, which is on the south coast of the Island of Anglesey, off the coast of North Wales.'

A map appeared on the screen to the side of the news anchor to show where Beaumaris was in the UK.

'Early reports suggested that there was an issue with one of the tourist boats that regularly sail from Beaumaris to visit wildlife on the local Puffin Island or sail around the Menai Strait. It was believed that police were mounting a rescue operation for the fifty or so tourists on board the boat, which is called the *Anglesey Princess*. However, we have just had another report suggesting that the tourists on board the boat have in fact been taken hostage. At the moment, North Wales Police are refusing to make any comment about the nature of their operation. We will, of course, keep you up to date with any developments as and when we get them.'

Annabelle looked aghast at Laura. 'Oh my God! That's terrible.'

'I wonder what the hell is going on down there,' Laura said. The word *hostage* had made her concerned. She got up, walked back over to the kettle and clicked it again to re-boil the water so that she could make herself a coffee.

Her thoughts then turned to Gareth, who she knew would be at the centre of what was going on. She was aware that whenever she thought of him, she got a little frisson. She remembered running into him that evening in The Bull in town when Gareth had confessed that his wife Nell was having an affair. She also remembered wondering how the wife of someone as good-looking and amiable as Gareth could do that. It just confirmed what she had always suspected. You could never understand the nuances of someone else's marriage unless you were in it.

'Laura?' Annabelle said urgently.

The BBC News anchor was on television again. 'And once again, if you are worried about anyone who you believe might be on the *Anglesey Princess*, Beaumaris Police have set up a helpline with a dedicated number. That number is 01248 810319. I'll repeat that number once again, 01248 810319.'

Chapter 15

10.17 a.m.

Having shown Steve the Glock 17 handgun in Callum's waistband, the gang members hauled him into the wheel-house. The pupils and other tourists gave them curious stares as they disappeared from the deck area.

Michael's breathing was shallow. *What the hell are we doing here? There's loads of little kids on the boat. This is not what I signed up for.*

As Steve turned to them inside the damp, musty wheel-house, Michael could see that he was shaking. On the wall, there were maps of the island and a photo of Steve and another man giving a thumbs-up while sitting outside a pub.

'I really don't want any trouble,' Steve yammered nervously.

Red fixed him with one of his psychotic stares. 'You do as you're told, mate, and there isn't gonna be any trouble. All right?'

'Yeah.' Steve looked frightened. 'What do you want me to do?'

'I need you to take us to Liverpool,' Red replied.

113

Callum frowned. 'Liverpool?'

Red snapped. 'Where did you think we were going, you dickhead?'

Michael furrowed his brow. 'The bizzies aren't gonna let us go all the way to Liverpool on this boat.'

'Why the fuck not?' Red growled. 'We've got a boat full of kids and we've got guns. We can do what we like.'

Michael swallowed. They were completely out of their depth. They were going to end up on the bloody telly and in the papers. And then they were going to go to prison for the rest of their lives.

Callum looked increasingly agitated. 'What if they bring in snipers or something?'

Red laughed. 'Where from? We're too far from the coast now.'

'Helicopters?' Callum asked with a shrug.

'Jesus Christ, Callum!' Red chortled and shook his head. 'They're not gonna try to take a pot shot at us from a helicopter with a boat full of kids. Behave.'

Michael's stomach was churning with fear.

Red stared at him. 'I still wanna know how the bizzies knew we was arriving on that beach at that time.'

'What you looking at him for?' Callum asked aggressively.

'Who should I be looking at?' Red then spun and moved a step towards Callum so that their faces were only a few inches apart. 'Should I be looking at you, la? Maybe the two of you are fucking grasses?'

Before Callum could reply, Steve pulled a face and stammered, 'I c-can't take you to Liverpool.'

Red scowled, turned and went over to him. 'What the fuck are you talking about?'

'We haven't got enough diesel to get to Liverpool,' Steve explained, backing away slowly.

Red nodded slowly and then, without warning, shot out

his hand and seized the handgun from where it was resting in Callum's waistband. He took a step towards Steve and jammed the Glock 17 against his temple.

'Tell me again.'

Steve was shaking uncontrollably. 'We h-haven't got enough fuel to get us all the way t-to Liverpool.'

Red leaned in and snarled in a virtual whisper, 'Steve. Today is not the day to play bloody hero.'

'I swear,' Steve stuttered. 'I swear on my kids' lives. I could try to get you to the Wirral. West Kirby. I promise you though, we d-don't have enough to get to Liverpool.'

Michael could see that Steve was clearly telling the truth. He was too scared to have the balls to lie to Red like that.

Red laughed as he took the gun away from Steve's head. 'The Wirral it is then, Steve.' He then turned to Callum and Michael with a smile. 'The Wirral sounds good to us, eh, lads?'

He really is fucking mental, Michael thought to himself.

'How long is that going to take?' Red asked.

'Two hours,' Steve replied. 'Maybe longer, depending on the currents.'

Red nodded. 'Right, in that case I'd better tell the passengers that there's been a change of plan.'

Taking the Puma bag with him, Red left the wheelhouse and made his way out onto the deck where the pupils and other tourists were basking in the sun. Michael and Callum followed him.

The gulls hovered and swooped, making loud cawing sounds.

Michael thought of the times when they were younger when he and Callum had made up stories about sailing away to find a new life together somewhere far away. One night at the care home in Southlea, they'd pushed their beds together to build themselves a pretend sailboat. Callum grabbed an old atlas from downstairs and they gazed at maps, finding places they could sail away to. Michael identified the island of Comoros, off the eastern coast of Africa. Neither of them had ever heard of it. But it looked tiny, and they were convinced that they would be the only people there. Callum remembered a film where some boys survived on a desert island by building their own huts, killing wild pigs and drinking coconut milk. It sounded perfect.

'Right, everyone, can I have your attention!' Red yelled, breaking Michael's train of thought.

Most of the passengers went quiet and frowned. A couple of them murmured to each other.

'I'm afraid there has been a slight change of plan this morning,' Red continued as he unzipped the Puma bag. He pulled out the Skorpion machine gun and held it in the air and stood up on a seat. There were a few gasps and a scream. Some of the children cowered. Their teacher gestured to them, trying to tell them not to worry. 'Me and my colleagues here have . . . commandeered – is that the right word? – anyway, we've taken over this boat for a bit. And Steve has kindly agreed to drop us over on the Wirral.'

A small boy with spiky hair got out of his seat and ran across the deck, and the teacher put her arms around him protectively.

'Now, no one needs to worry. We just need to get to where we're going without any fuss,' Red said with a slight smirk. 'Does anyone have a problem with that?'

The passengers were silent except for an old woman who was crying and hugging her husband.

'Okay. Well, if you all sit tight, then I'm sure we're gonna have a lovely trip.'

Chapter 16

August 2018

Moving slowly, Laura felt a stabbing pain in her ribs as she took in a breath. She tried hard to blink open her eyes, but she couldn't. She was aware of noises – a car revving its engine, the distant sound of an airplane, the wail of schoolchildren in a far-off playground.

Where the hell am I? I can't seem to get myself awake.

She let out a long, slow breath.

She saw a little girl in a school hallway standing as still as a statue. A puddle of urine slopped against her black school shoes. She was six and the terrifying headmistress, Miss Peabody, had scolded her for running down the corridor. Miss Peabody smelt of coal tar soap and cigarettes. When she was reprimanding pupils, spittle got trapped between her front teeth and top lip.

Then the colour faded from the scene until all that was left was the white of a winter snow scene.

'Laura? Laura?' said a voice she recognised.

With a glaring flash, she was back at the warehouse. Bits of rubble falling around her in a silent shower. Something dark and dreadful pervaded her whole body. A blackened face looking down at her quizzically. It was Sam.

Oh my God, he's alive!

Then the voice again. 'Laura? Laura?' It wasn't Sam's voice calling her.

And then she saw a man's body lying on a grass verge. She ran over and saw that it was her father.

Running left, running right, Laura found herself back in the cold school corridors. She was late for something. She couldn't remember what. An exam? Time was running out. If she didn't get there, it was going to be disastrous. The anxiety was overwhelming. *Where the hell is the exam hall? I'm sure it's down the corridor,* she thought. It wasn't. Spinning on her heels, she sprinted back the way she had come, zig-zagging past pupils who all knew where they were going.

And now the image of a blackened, burnt body. *No!*

She couldn't get the image out of her head. It kept repeating like the endless photos from an old-fashioned slide show.

'Laura? Laura?'

Where the fuck am I? Who the hell is that?

Moving her fingers, she felt a sheet beneath her. And then a blanket against her other hand. The top of her right hand was tender and sore.

God, I am so tired, just let me drift here for a while.

Laura opened her eyes.

At first, all she could see were shapes. A long overhead light, a blue curtain of some sort. Then the sound of the continual bleep from a nearby machine kicked in.

'Laura?'

Who is that?

As her eyes focused, she could see her sister, Emma, looking down at her.

What the hell is Emma doing here? She lives in Kent!

118

'You're in the Manchester Royal Infirmary, Laura,' Emma whispered.

Am I?

Laura tried to move herself in the bed, but she ached all over.

Christ, I feel like I've been hit by a bloody bus!

Emma put her hand gently on her arm. 'Try not to move, eh?'

Then it started to come back to her.

The siege at Brannings Warehouse. The non-negotiations with the gang member. And then the SAS and the fire and explosions.

Oh God, no.

Where was Sam?

Her breathing became shallow as she panicked. She was suffocating.

'Try to take a deep breath,' Emma advised her in a whisper.

Laura didn't care if she could breathe or not.

'Is he dead?' she asked on a gasp.

Emma looked at her but didn't say anything as her eyes filled with tears.

She gritted her teeth. 'Emma? Is he dead?'

At first, Emma was motionless. Then she nodded almost imperceptibly. 'I'm so, so sorry.'

Laura shook her head slowly. 'No. He can't be.'

She searched her sister's face urgently, looking for the smallest hint that she misunderstood her.

Emma wiped the tears from her face and bit her lip. It was true.

No. This isn't happening. This isn't real.

'Please . . .' Laura implored her, as she looked into her sister's eyes. Sam couldn't be gone. It wasn't possible. 'No, no.'

Emma reached out and held her hand.

I don't understand. Maybe it's a mistake.

As her eyes roamed the room in terror, she knew there was no mistake.

'What am I going to do?' she whispered.

A deep, terrible pain, like nothing she had experienced before, came like a black wave and overtook her.

It was unbearable.

How could she go on if she was never going to see Sam again?

Chapter 17

10.26 a.m.

It had been twenty minutes since Geoff had gone down into the hold of the *Anglesey Princess* to check the oil pressure and levels. The gauge in the wheelhouse had showed they were both lower than normal and the boat's engine had also stalled twice, which could be a sign that there was a bigger problem. He had suspected that the engine bearings were worn, which wasn't surprising given the boat's age and mileage. The excessive wear reduced the original flow restriction and so the pressure would consequently drop.

It had been just as Geoff was checking the oil level on the dipstick between 'add' and 'full' that he had heard the men coming aboard. Although the wooden deck was thick, if you listened hard enough, you could hear what was going on. When he heard the Scouse accents, he had immediately become suspicious.

What the hell are they doing on the boat? he wondered.

At first, he had assumed that another boat had had a mechanical failure and Steve had picked them up so they could hitch a ride back to Beaumaris.

Having heard several people moving towards the wheel-house, Geoff had positioned himself underneath the wheelhouse floor – and with a growing sense of dread, heard everything. It sounded like the men had at least one gun, if not more. He had listened to them threaten Steve and demand that they be taken over to Liverpool. He thought he also heard Steve tell them they could only get as far as the Wirral.

Fuck that! Geoff thought to himself. *They're not taking this boat to Wirral. In fact, they're not taking this boat anywhere.*

Looking around, he reached out and grabbed a grubby spanner. He started to unscrew the pipe that led from the steel oil tank to the engine itself. It was incredibly stiff and, even with all of his strength, it was only moving millimetre by millimetre.

It was baking hot and stuffy in the hold, and he soon had sweat pouring down his forehead and dripping into his eyes, which stung. Looking down, he saw the drips of sweat forming a speckled pattern on the wooden floor.

Some bloody birthday, he thought to himself.

He was born on Monday 24 June 1957. His father, Huw, had told him that Elvis Presley's 'All Shook Up' was number one in the charts. His father and mother Maggie had been at the pictures in the Llandudno Palladium while they were there visiting her family. They were ten minutes before the end of *Around The World In 80 Days* when Maggie's contractions became unbearable, and Geoffrey Ernest Clegg had been born in the Llandudno General Hospital at two minutes to midnight, weighing a mighty eight pounds.

Hearing a scream from the deck overhead, Geoff stopped what he was doing. Straining to hear what was going on above, he could make out a man's voice. It sounded like he was addressing the passengers.

Shit! This is not good, he thought as his body tensed with anxiety.

Various questions raced around his mind. Why had the men boarded the boat? Why did they want to be taken to Liverpool? Did the police, or anyone else, know what was happening? The nearest radio was in the wheelhouse so that was a non-starter. Maybe they were prisoners on the run?

The main thing was that he was hidden in the boat's hold and they didn't know he was there. That gave him the element of surprise – and that was key in any combat situation. The importance of stealth and concealment had been drummed into him during his SBS training at the British naval base at Hamworthy, which was close to Poole in Dorset. New recruits were made aware of the pride and history of the unit from its origins in the Second World War, where folding canoes were used for covert attacks on enemy railways, port facilities and airfields, to their raids in the Aegean Sea, where the SBS adapted local fishing boats to operate unnoticed among the area's enemy shipping fleets.

Looking down, Geoff could feel that the fitting around the oil pipe was beginning to loosen. Encouraged, he twisted it until it was loose enough for him to use his thick, powerful fingers. He yanked the pipe and, with a loud metallic clunk, the two parts of the pipe came apart.

Geoff stood back to admire his handiwork, as litres of thick, black engine oil spewed out of the pipe into the hold. After about thirty seconds, the flow decreased and then spluttered and stopped. Standing still, he held his breath, hoping that his act of sabotage had worked.

CRUNCH!

With no oil, the metallic parts of the engine ground together with a dreadful screech. The engines juddered and banged.

After a minute of deafening noise, the hold went quiet.

The temperature inside the hold was now fierce from the

metallic friction inside the engines and the air was thick with the fumes of hot metal and the burning of oil residue. It sounded like the piston rings had come loose.

Fearing that he might cough and give himself away, Geoff crouched and crept down the hold away from the smoking engines.

He smirked to himself.

The Anglesey Princess *isn't going anywhere, you scumbags!*

Beth glanced at Jake, who was sitting beside her. He blinked nervously as his eyes roamed around the boat. His brown hair was spiky on top and shaved close to the scalp at the sides and back.

'Don't worry,' Beth whispered. She put a comforting arm on his shoulder. 'It's going to be all right.'

Jake gave the faintest of nods, but she wasn't sure that he had actually heard her. He had freckles along the length of his nose and a few scattered across his cheekbones. His face was just starting to narrow from the chubby, rounded face of a young boy to that of a pre-teen.

Gazing back to where they had come, Beth could see that they were still only half a mile or less from Beaumaris Pier and beach. She wasn't sure if it was her imagination, but the boat was slowing down. Looking around to the left, she could see the town of Bangor across the Menai Strait in the distance. If she remembered correctly, it was the oldest city in Wales and its name meant *wattled enclosure*, or something like that. It had been two years since she had graduated from Bangor University with a first-class honours degree in QTS Primary Education. Graduation day had been the proudest day of her life, even though her mother had spoiled the evening by drinking too much and making barbed comments.

As the wind picked up, she tucked tousled strands of hair behind her ear. Two of the men who had boarded their boat sat together talking in low voices on a seat at the back of the deck. Now that they had discarded their baseball caps, she could see that they had distinctive haircuts. A small patch of hair on top was combed forward, and the sides and back were shaved to the scalp. Both of them wore Adidas sports gear and silver chains around their necks. They looked just like any other stereotypical scallies from Liverpool, she thought.

They're a bloody cliché!

The deck was strangely silent. For the past ten minutes, she had deliberately made eye contact with all the pupils in Year 6 to check that they were okay. Nearly all of them had nodded with serious expressions. She was so proud of how they were dealing with what had to be a terrifying experience at their age. A couple of the older tourists had also given the pupils comforting words to make sure they were okay.

As she scanned the deck, she made eye contact with the youngest member of the gang. He could have only been seventeen or eighteen. While the man next to him was relatively relaxed as they talked, the boy couldn't hide his anxiety in his face and his body language. For a few seconds, she actually felt sorry for him. He had that kind of face. The innocence of someone who was completely out of their depth. They held each other's gaze for a second or two before he looked away. She wondered why the men were on the boat. She assumed they were on the run from the police but she didn't know why.

The leader of the gang, who had distinctive ginger hair and beard, appeared from the wheelhouse with the boat's captain, Steve. He walked with a swagger and was chewing gum. There was something unnerving about him compared to the other two. As he came out onto the deck, he took the sunglasses from on top of his head and put them on. She studied the angular shape of his jaw and saw a thick scar that led over to just under his earlobe.

He stared at the passengers, puffing out his chest. The small machine gun was in his right hand, dangling by his side.

'Okay, listen up, everyone,' the man shouted. The volume of his voice made Jake flinch next to her.

'It's all right,' she whispered as she put her hand on his forearm and gave it a reassuring squeeze. In some ways, it was easier to focus on making sure Jake and the other pupils were okay, rather than fixating on the feelings of dread and unease that were making her nauseous.

The man grabbed a black bin bag Steve was holding nervously. He then looked over at the teenage boy and gestured for him to come over. 'We're gonna go around and collect all your mobile phones. We don't want anyone being clever and trying to contact anyone. And we don't want no photos or videos, okay?'

'Ta,' the teenage boy mumbled as the man handed him the bag.

'And don't you be getting any funny ideas about trying to keep your phone,' the man growled. 'If you keep your phone and I find it, I'm gonna have to shoot you and dump you in there.' He gestured to the dark water that stretched over to the Welsh coast.

An elderly woman let out a howl of fear as she buried her face in her husband's chest. Beth's stomach churned.

Please, God, let us all get out of this alive.

The teenage boy circulated and the passengers and pupils dropped their phones into the bag. He came to an elderly couple and the old man muttered something.

'What's the problem?' the gang leader barked.

The teenage boy looked over. 'He reckons they don't have a phone.'

'Jesus Christ!' the red-headed man snapped as he stormed over and put the machine gun to the elderly man's head. 'Stand up!'

126

The elderly man was visibly shaking, and his wife cried. 'I'm sorry. My wife has a phone, but we didn't bring it with us.'

The teenage boy shot the man a look as if to say, *What the hell are you doing?* 'Red?' he said under his breath.

His real name, or a nickname because of his ginger hair? Beth wondered. The man spun and glared at the teenage boy.

Beth knew he was furious that he had used the name. She had seen enough crime dramas on the telly to know that using a name was a cardinal sin amongst criminals.

'Search him!' Red barked.

The teenage boy frisked the elderly man and confirmed with a nod that there was no phone.

'Do I need to search her?' Red sneered at the elderly man.

The blood had drained from the elderly man's face as he shook. 'No, no . . . I promise. We just don't use one.'

The teenage boy collected the rest of the phones and approached where Beth was sitting with Jake.

Jake looked at him and shook his head.

Beth touched Jake's arm. 'It's all right, Jake. You can give him your phone.'

Jake shook his head again – he wasn't going to hand it over.

The teenage boy crouched down, pointed to the red Manchester United shirt Jake was wearing under his hoodie and smiled. 'You've got the wrong shirt on, mate. United?'

Jake frowned. 'I support Manchester United.'

The teenage boy raised an eyebrow and asked gently, 'Why do you support United then?'

'My dad supported United,' Jake replied.

'You watch the games with him, do you?'

Jake hesitated. 'No. He's dead.'

The teenage boy looked at Jake and then up at Beth.

'Sorry to hear that, mate,' he said.

Beth touched his arm again. 'Come on, Jake. Just give him your phone.'

Jake dug into his hoodie pocket, pulled out the phone and handed it to him.

The teenage boy gave him a wink and put it in his pocket. 'Don't worry, mate. I'm gonna put it in here for safekeeping, okay?'

Jake nodded.

The teenage boy looked at Beth again as she placed her phone in the bag. He was clearly trying to show to her he wasn't a psychotic monster like his friend Red. She didn't care. He was part of a gang that had captured a boat and were terrifying children. That made him an utter scumbag in her eyes.

As the teenage boy walked away, he handed the bin bag over to Red.

'Sorry, guys!' Red shouted as he shrugged and then tossed the bag straight over the side and into the water. Then he stopped for a second as he peered down at the sea. 'Why have we stopped?'

There were a few seconds of tense silence.

Steve blinked nervously – the question was clearly aimed at him.

Red turned, marched over to Steve and pushed the gun's muzzle hard into his head. 'I said, why have we stopped?'

'I-I don't . . . don't know,' Steve stammered. 'I promise. I've no idea.'

Red gestured to the wheelhouse. 'Well, get in there and sort it out. Or I'm going to start shooting passengers!'

Chapter 18

10.37 a.m.

Beaumaris Pier was now teeming with police officers and CID had set up a temporary operation centre in the lifeboat station on the pier itself, where they had access to electricity, a phone line and wi-fi.

Having left members of the CID team back at the lifeboat station to continue setting up what they needed, Gareth had jogged down to the end of the pier again with Declan. The *Anglesey Princess* was aiming east down the Menai Strait. However, he had no idea where exactly they were heading or why.

Looking through his binoculars again, Gareth saw something peculiar. He handed the binoculars to Declan. 'Have a look and tell me if you notice anything strange?'

Declan peered for a few seconds and then turned to him. 'The boat's stopped moving.'

Gareth agreed. 'Yeah. That's what I thought.'

Declan shrugged. 'What are they up to?'

'I assumed that when they headed east, they might be

129

trying to get back as close to Merseyside as they could get,' Gareth explained. 'But now they've stopped, I've no idea.'

He noticed a presence behind him and turned to look.

Superintendent Richard Warlow, dressed in his uniform, stared back at him with a dour expression. He was tall and wiry, with a mop of grey hair, and wore glasses. Gareth had little time for Warlow. He was petty, controlling and lacked any sense of humour. In CID they called him Partridge, after the comedic television character Alan Partridge. Not only was Warlow inept, but he also had an inflated sense of his own importance and spent more time self-promoting than doing his actual job.

Warlow also had a strange sniff, like a nervous tic, which meant you could identify him coming down the corridor before he arrived. Declan used to joke that he sniffed like an old bloodhound. Gareth had joked that all Warlow could sniff was his next promotion.

'Sir,' Gareth said, forcing a smile.

'Have you contacted the gang yet?' Warlow asked. Even at five yards, Warlow's breath stank of extra-strong mints. Gareth had him down as a secret drinker.

'Not yet, sir,' Gareth said and then gestured out to the water. 'The boat seems to have stopped but until we speak to them, I don't know what they want or what they're planning.'

'Any news on if we have any bloody boats yet?' Warlow asked.

'Two police launches are coming round from Holyhead, sir,' Gareth reported. 'But they're going to be another hour or more. I've tried to contact the NPAS helicopter that's over near Hawarden but they're attending a nasty RTA on the A55.'

'Great!' Warlow raised a sardonic eyebrow as a gull screeched overhead. 'What about a hostage negotiator?'

130

Declan glanced over. 'North Wales Police have two hostage negotiators. One is on long-term sick leave and the other is on maternity leave, sir.'

'Jesus!' Warlow sighed and shook his head.

'I've spoken to Merseyside and Greater Manchester Police, but they're a bit stretched. They're going to try to come back to me,' Gareth explained.

'We don't really have time for that, do we?' Warlow asked rhetorically.

'No, sir,' Gareth agreed.

'You up to talking to them if we get a secure line, Gareth?' Warlow asked.

Gareth shrugged. 'I'll give it my best shot, sir.'

A young PC approached with a sense of urgency. 'Sir, we've got the VHF radio up and running. We've also confirmed which channel and frequency the *Anglesey Princess* is using.'

'Thank you, Constable.' Gareth looked at Warlow. 'I'd better see if I can contact them, sir.'

Marching down the pier towards the lifeboat station, he glanced over at Beaumaris Beach, which had now been cleared of tourists. He spotted more uniform officers taping off the main road by the beach and redirecting traffic.

The council and the tourist board are going to love this.

The double doors to the lifeboat station were wide open and the constable showed him to a temporary desk that was now fitted with a VHF radio and recording equipment.

'Here you go, sir,' the constable said as he gestured Gareth ahead of him.

Taking the VHF marine radio, which was attached to a small monitor with a digital read-out, Gareth took a breath.

Here we go.

'*Anglesey Princess, Anglesey Princess*, do you read, over?' he asked.

Gareth and the constable listened intently, but all they could hear was the low hiss of static and white noise.

'*Anglesey Princess, Anglesey Princess*, do you read, over?' he repeated.

Nothing.

Gareth could feel a growing frustration – if they couldn't speak to the gang, how could they resolve the situation?

'Who is this?' growled a voice with a thick Scouse accent.

Bingo! We're on.

'Hi there. This is Detective Inspector Gareth Williams from the Beaumaris Police,' he began, his heart pounding against his chest. His negotiating skills were basic, and only what he had picked up along the way as a police officer, but he knew that the most important thing was to gauge the mood of the criminal, and then listen for any clues or tells in what he was saying.

'So, what do you want?' the man snapped.

What do I want?

'I just wanted to check if everyone is okay out there,' Gareth said gently.

'Is everyone okay?' the man snorted. 'You having a fuckin' laugh, mate?'

Gareth didn't know what he meant or what he was getting at. He panicked.

Now what do I say?

Taking a deep breath, Gareth started to speak again. 'I know there are a lot of children on the boat. And I wanted to check that they're all okay.'

'Oh yeah, mate. They're all having a belter of a trip out here,' he replied sarcastically.

The man didn't sound nervous. He sounded confident and aggressive.

'Can I talk to their teacher?' Gareth asked. 'To check everyone's okay?'

'You takin' the piss, copper?' the man sneered. 'No, no, you can't.'

'Sorry, I—'

'I just told you everyone is fine! Are you calling me a liar?' the man thundered furiously down the phone.

Jesus. He sounds unhinged.

'I'm really sorry. That's not . . . not what I meant . . .' Gareth stammered.

'What did you mean then?' the man barked.

With his head spinning and his pulse racing, Gareth was fast running out of ideas. 'I meant that we've got a tricky situation here and before I ask you what you want, I just wanted to check that everyone on board is okay.'

'Are you fucking thick, mate?' the man boomed.

'No, I . . .' Gareth's mind was going blank as he began to panic.

'You're calling me a liar!'

'I'm not, I promise.'

'Because you're acting like such a prick, I've got a good mind to go and shoot one of those kids and toss them in the fucking sea.'

'Please don't do that . . .' Gareth pleaded.

'Okay, officer prick. This is what is going to happen. You're going to arrange for a speedboat to come out here to pick us up. You're also going to deliver us a bag with two hundred grand in cash. Then we're taking a couple of these kids and we're going on a little journey. When we get there, we'll let the kids go. Any funny business, any sign of coppers, we kill the kids. Do you understand?'

'Yes,' Gareth replied in a virtual whisper. 'But it's going to take some time to get the boat and the money.'

133

'Yeah, well, you've got an hour before I start throwing bodies into the sea.'

The line went dead.

Gareth felt sick as he let out a breath. The Liverpudlian gang member had just run rings round him on the radio. He needed an experienced negotiator to talk to them instead.

I've got a phone call to make.

Chapter 19

August 2018

St Stephen's Church, in central Manchester, was packed with Sam's friends and colleagues. GMP officers were in full dress uniform, including their white gloves. The hearse carrying Sam's body was decorated with ornate flowers that read *No 1 Daddy*. Six of his closest colleagues, including Pete, carried his coffin, which was draped with a traditional police blue flag with the red Greater Manchester Police emblem at its centre. A solo piper played 'Amazing Grace' as the pallbearers slowly carried the coffin inside and down the aisle to the sanctuary.

Outside the church, several hundred members of the public, who had come to pay their respects, congregated in respectful silence. Some had thrown flowers at the hearse from the pavement as it arrived. In the weeks after his and Louise's untimely deaths, a sea of floral tributes and candles had arrived outside the wreckage at Brannings Warehouse. Laura had been so touched by the messages that she had read there.

When the service was over, Rosie and Laura came out of

the church and into the fresh air. The wind flicked a wisp of Laura's hair and the sun was warm on her face. All she could hear were snippets of polite conversations about *a nice service* and *the sunny weather*. She was in a surreal daze.

Laura didn't care about any of it. A terrible grief ripped at her very insides. Rosie's hand felt warm in hers as they led the congregation out to the graveside. She had decided that Jake was too young to attend. He had completely shut down since his father's death and it was painful to watch him struggle with what had happened. He and Sam had been so incredibly close. They played football in the park together, they watched United together, they played on the Xbox together – and sometimes they fell asleep in the spare bed together while watching *Match of the Day*. Laura knew only too well the torment her son was going through.

Nothing about the day so far felt real. Her attempt at some kind of eulogy had been interspersed with tears and deep breaths. She couldn't even remember what she had said now. It was as if she was watching everything through the lens of a film camera. Removed and remote.

Stopping close to the mounds of black earth that had been dug from Sam's waiting grave, Rosie squeezed her mother's hand.

'It's okay, Mummy,' Rosie whispered, her eyes glassy with tears.

How is she being so strong today? Laura wondered. Sam would have been so proud of her.

Her daughter's words stayed with her. She was wrong.

Nothing is okay. Nothing is all right. How is it possible that Sam has been ripped from our lives? How is that fair? How are we going to go on without him?

Laura looked at the coffin and pictured Sam inside. She had picked up Sam's black police dress uniform from work and then dropped it off at the funeral directors.

What a strange, cruel thing death is.

'I'm never going to see him again, am I?' Laura mumbled with trembling lips.

The pain of that thought was just too much to bear. For a moment she felt dizzy, nearly lost her footing, and Rosie and others had to support her.

'Sorry . . . I'm all right. It's okay, darling,' she whispered, looking at Rosie's sad face.

She watched as the police officers lowered the coffin slowly into the ground. Then she and Rosie stepped forward, took some earth, and sprinkled it on top.

I don't want to say goodbye to you. And I wish so much that I could believe I'm going to see you again in a better place.

Turning back from the grave, Laura felt Rosie place her arm around her shoulder.

'Where's Nana?' Rosie asked. 'I thought she was coming?'

Laura shrugged. 'She's not well so she changed her mind.'

'She's very strange, isn't she?' Rosie said.

'I'm afraid she is, and she always will be,' Laura sighed.

Nana, or Geraldine Hart, was Sam's rather cold, unemotional seventy-year-old mother. Although she had never actually left Sam's father, Nigel, Geraldine had run a small B&B in Northern France for nearly twenty years. Over the years, Geraldine had managed to come to their wedding and a couple of the kids' birthdays, but that was all. She had rung three days earlier to say she was recovering from chemotherapy and was too ill to travel over for the funeral. Laura had no idea if it was true, but she had long since given up trying to understand the motivations of her mother-in-law.

'You know what Dad would want us to do now?' Rosie asked quietly.

'Get drunk and listen to Wham!' Laura said. The tiniest glimmer of a smile appeared on her face at the thought of Sam singing 'I'm Your Man' word perfect.

'Exactly,' Rosie said.

A figure moved towards her. It was Pete. He stepped forward from where he was standing with his wife, Anusha, and took Laura in his arms.

'I'm so sorry. I just don't know what else to say.' His voice quivered.

'You don't have to say anything,' Laura whispered as she held him tight. 'He loved you, you know that?'

After a few seconds, she moved back and looked up into his face.

'Thank you,' she said.

'There's something I need to talk to you about,' Pete whispered.

'Can it wait until we get back to the house?' Laura asked.

'Of course. No problem. In fact, it can wait for another day altogether.'

The wake back at Laura's home in the leafy suburb of Sale was drawing to a close. She had spent twenty minutes in the bathroom upstairs, trying to get her head together. She had drunk too much. The whole thing felt like some terrible nightmare that she was going to awake from any minute.

Someone knocked on the door. 'Laura? Are you in there?' asked a gentle voice.

It was her sister, Emma. She had been a rock since Sam's death.

Most people could tell they were sisters. They shared the same jawline, high cheekbones, the same arch to their eyebrows that people took for being unapproachable. Emma had the same blonde, wavy hair, the light blue eyes that twinkled when she found something amusing or ridiculous.

Taking a deep breath, Laura stood up from where she was sitting on top of the closed toilet, went over to the door and unlocked it.

'Sorry, I just needed to get away,' she mumbled as she opened the door.

Emma reached over and touched her arm. 'Hey, that's fine. You need to do whatever you need to do.'

'I couldn't bear any more conversations about Sam,' she admitted. 'I'm never going to forget him. Never. But I just needed a few minutes to focus on something else.'

'I couldn't find Rosie when I checked around,' Emma said. 'I'm sure she's okay though.'

'I'd better come downstairs and check on her.'

As they turned to walk down the landing, Laura saw Emma was limping more than usual. She had been diagnosed with MS last year and her symptoms seemed to come and go. It was a devastating diagnosis for Emma in particular because all she had ever wanted to be was a PE teacher, and now she was head of PE at a prestigious girls' grammar school near Canterbury. The doctors had told her that the MS would eventually prevent her from doing that job – they just couldn't predict when that would happen.

Spotting a photo on the wall at the top of the stairs, Laura stopped. It featured Laura, Emma and their parents, Gwen and Owen, who had both died from cancer, six and seven years ago respectively.

'Jesus.' Laura snorted. 'I forgot Dad went through a whole moustache phase in the mid-eighties.'

'Look at your hair!' Emma giggled. 'Back-combed to death with a whole can of Studio Line hairspray.'

'Yeah, well, your haircut resembles a Franciscan monk.'

'Hey!' Emma protested. 'That's because Mum cut it to save money. It's hideous.'

'That was Mum for you.'

'*If you look after the pennies, the pounds will look after themselves,*' they said in unison and then laughed. It was their mother's favourite saying.

Laura smiled ruefully at her sister. 'We weren't really close when we were younger, were we?'

'God, you really are drunk,' Emma said, raising an eyebrow.

'You know what I mean.' Laura knew that her words were sticky around the edges and she was beginning to slur. 'Not like now. We tell each other everything now.'

'Five years was a big gap when we were that age,' Emma said. 'I was only twelve when you went off to university.'

She reached out and took her sister's hand. 'Thank you. I wouldn't have got through this without you, you know that?'

'You're stronger than you think.' Emma moved a lock of hair from her face and then frowned. 'I'll tell you what though, I think you've got some grey hairs.'

Laura wrinkled her nose. 'Piss off.'

'Oh come on.' Emma laughed. 'Mum was virtually grey by the time she was forty.'

Their mother had often been the object of ridicule and suspicion in the local village. She didn't dye her hair, but instead let it grey and then go a beautiful silver.

Laura raised an eyebrow. 'You know what she always said.'

'Yeah, she said it was because she was too brainy and that had taken all the melanin from her hair.'

'And don't forget the fact that hair is actually originally white and that melanocytes pump pigment into hair follicles,' Laura said, reminding her of their mother's well-worn statement.

Emma snorted, 'She was one in a million.'

'Thank God!'

'And I can't believe that Sam's mother didn't come over,' Emma said with a frown.

'I can.' Laura gave her a knowing look. 'And I know I'm drunk, but she's a selfish, self-absorbed bitch so I'm glad she's not here. We never got on.'

'Hey, get off that fence and say what you really think about her,' Emma joked.

Laura shrugged. 'I don't care. His stepdad is a right oddball too. He came over, mumbled something without making eye contact, patted my arm and then shuffled away. I don't know how much we'll see of them now Sam's gone.'

'Doesn't sound like a great loss. Come on. We'd better go and check on Rosie. And I think you should drink some water, rather than any more wine.'

Laura followed her sister down the stairs. Looking left, she saw there were around six members of her extended family standing talking and eating in the kitchen.

Thank you for coming, but please sod off so I can have the house back to myself, she thought.

Hearing a noise to her right, she saw that the door to the room they used as an office and study was open by about six inches. She was pretty sure that she had locked it.

Pushing the door open gently, she saw Rosie sitting at the desk in the large, black, padded office chair. She was facing the small sofa at the back of the room and talking in a whisper.

'Hello, darling,' Laura said gently. 'You okay?'

Rosie spun around in the chair and looked at her. 'Hi . . . I just wanted to be on my own.'

Laura smiled knowingly. 'Yeah. I've just been hiding upstairs in the bathroom until Auntie Emma found me.'

Rosie gave a half-smile and then said, 'I've been talking to Dad.'

'Have you?' Laura asked, trying not to cry. 'Well, that's a

good thing. I'm sure he's everywhere in this house and I'm sure he can hear you.'

'Yeah, I know he can,' Rosie said confidently.

'Do you need anything, darling?'

Rosie got up from the chair. 'I'm a bit hungry now. I might get something from the kitchen.'

'Be careful. Your great-uncle Len is in there. If he explains the roads he took to get here, and the ones he intends to take on the way back, make a run for it.' Laura chuckled.

'I will.' Rosie gave a half-smile as she slipped out through the door.

Walking slowly over to the desk, she sat down in the padded office chair and pushed so that the back reclined a little. She looked up at the ceiling. The tiny threads of a spider's web hung from the cornice. What was it they said about spider silk? It was lighter than cotton, a thousand times thinner than human hair, but stronger by weight than steel.

As her eyes returned to the desk, she caught sight of a photograph of her father. She wondered what he would have made of the events of recent weeks. He was the ultimate stoic. A man of few words or emotions, he was the son of a farmer and spent his whole life working the land on Anglesey. Her favourite memories of him were walks over the clifftops at Trearddur Bay. They would stand, hand in hand, looking down at the churning water below. Then they'd make their way to Laura's favourite spot. An enormous slab of rock that was seemingly balanced precariously on top of a cliff. She would sit or stand on it, shouting 'Help' or making frightened noises, as if the slab was going to fall from where it had stood for thousands of years and plummet into the sea below. Her father just watched her and laughed. Years later, she would return on her own to that place as a teenager. Wrapped in a woollen hat and scarf, listening to her Oleta

Adams *Circle of One* cassette on her Walkman, she'd gaze out at the horizon and watch the breakers crash, the gulls or oystercatchers fly out to sea. *I don't care how you get here, just get here if you can.* She'd wanted to escape the mundaneness of her island for the glowing metropolises of England.

Next to the photo of her father was a wedding photo. Sam grinning, his hair and collars flecked with confetti.

'Sam, what the hell were you doing there that day?' she asked out loud as she let her weight bring the chair upright with a jolt. It had been gnawing away at her in recent days. Why were her husband and his partner at an OCG drug factory only an hour before it was raided?

As she glanced at the photograph again, it dawned on her that Sam was never going to get old. His face was going to remain the same as it was in photos. Blinking away the tears that now filled her eyes, she gritted her teeth in anger. She wanted to grow old with him. To snuggle on the sofa, under blankets, in front of a log fire.

'You fucking twat, Sam!' she sobbed. 'You utter fucking twat.'

The computer monitor in front of her was switched off. In its reflection, she thought she saw something move behind her.

'That's a bit harsh,' said a familiar voice. 'And by the way, I thought I was doing my job that day.'

She spun and realised that Sam was sitting on the sofa, his legs crossed, just as he had done a hundred times before. He was dressed in a black V-neck, white T-shirt and jeans.

She shook uncontrollably. *Oh my God! What . . .*

She looked at him again. *Am I going mad?*

Getting up from the sofa, Sam crossed over to her and took her in his arms.

She didn't care that it didn't make any sense. It felt real.

He felt real. She wrapped her arms around him and pulled him tight to her.

I don't understand. I can smell him. I can feel him.

'Sam?' she wept.

'I'm sorry. I'm so, so sorry,' he whispered.

'Why?' she gasped.

'For leaving you. For leaving all of you.'

Chapter 20

10.38 a.m.

Laura strolled across the meeting room, went to her laptop and clicked it. A slide was projected onto the wall, headed: *Create the Illusion of Control*. Even though she was trying to focus on the course she was teaching, her mind kept going back to what she had seen on the news about Beaumaris.

Come on, Laura. Concentrate, she told herself.

'This is key,' she stated as she strode over to the wall and pointed to the phrase. 'Successful negotiation involves getting your opponent, your boss or your client to do the work for you and suggest *your* solution himself, or herself. Give them the illusion of control, while you are the one defining and running the conversation. The key to this is open-ended questioning, or what we in the trade call "calibrated questioning". And it also involves removing all hostility or aggression from the conversation that you're having. Think of the difference between these two questions . . .'

Another slide was projected, headed: *You CAN'T leave OR What do you think you'll achieve by leaving?*

'So, for example, in a hostage situation I was once in, we needed to know that the hostage was alive. If we were going to use calibrated questioning, then we needed to avoid verbs like *can, is, are, do* or *does*. They are close-ended questions that allow a one-word answer, like *yes* or *no*. So, the question isn't "*Can I speak to the hostage?*" The question is "*How can I be sure that the hostage is okay?*"'

There were several nods from the clients as they acknowledged the point she was making.

The door opened and Annabelle popped her head in.

I wonder what she wants? I'm in the middle of a workshop.

'Hi, Annabelle,' Laura said with a forced smile.

'There's a phone call for you, Laura,' Annabelle announced, looking awkward.

She gestured to the room and clients. 'I'm kind of in the middle of something here. Can you take a message?'

'Sorry. The man said it was an emergency.'

Laura's stomach lurched. Her immediate thought was that it was one of the kids.

'Did he give you his name?' she asked.

'Detective Inspector Williams.'

Laura looked at her clients. 'I'm really sorry about this. I won't be more than five minutes.'

Following Annabelle out of the room, she got to the phone on the desk and picked it up. Her heart raced as she feared the worst.

'Hi, Gareth, is it one of the kids?' she asked breathlessly.

'No, no. It's nothing to do with them, honestly,' he assured her. 'Have you seen what's going on down at the beach and pier?'

'I caught something on the news,' she replied. 'What's happening?'

'Members of an OCG went to do a drugs drop on the

beach. We were there to nick them, but they spotted us and headed back out onto the Strait. There must have been some kind of mechanical failure because they've now boarded one of those cruise ships going out to Puffin Island,' Gareth explained.

'Jesus, Gareth,' she breathed. 'Do you know who's on the boat?'

'We're still waiting for the passenger list. But we've got a school party on there. Primary school by the looks of it.'

'Oh God. That's horrible.' She was glad that Jake's class wasn't due to go until the following week. 'How many gang members are there?'

'Three.'

'Are they armed?' she asked, finding herself going back instantly into DI mode.

'I'm not sure. They threatened to shoot the kids, so I'm guessing they are.'

'Jesus. What do they want?'

'A speedboat and two hundred thousand in cash. They're taking hostages with them on the speedboat until they know they're safely away.'

She thought for a few seconds. 'Don't take this the wrong way, Gareth, but why did you call me?'

'I've talked to the leader of the gang. He's a nasty piece of work. He says if they don't get the boat in an hour, he's going to start killing children and throwing them into the sea.' He sounded rattled.

'It sounds like you need a trained police hostage negotiator down there,' she said.

'Laura, you *are* a trained police hostage negotiator.'

'Not any more, Gareth.' She could already feel the impending warning signs of a panic attack.

Gareth sighed. 'Laura, we can't get anyone down here at the moment. I'm desperate.'

Laura's breathing was becoming more rapid and shallow. She blew out her cheeks for a second, trying to regulate her breath. 'I can't.'

There were a couple of seconds of silence as an overwhelming feeling of guilt for not being able to help the police operation took control. But she was terrified that if she was put in a high-pressure hostage negotiation, she would just go to pieces, potentially making things worse and putting people's lives at risk.

'That's fine. I'm sorry. I shouldn't have asked,' he apologised, but he sounded disappointed.

'No, I'm really sorry, Gareth. But there's a reason why I left the police and why I can't do that kind of work anymore.' Her voice broke a little. There was a lump in her throat.

'I completely understand. Please don't worry.'

'Thank you, Gareth,' she murmured. 'Bye now.'

She ended the call and began to shake. The conversation had taken her right back to August 2018. She couldn't catch her breath.

'Hey, remember deep breaths,' said a voice. 'In for the count of ten, hold for the count of ten, and then gently out for the count of ten.'

It was Sam. He looked at her as she sucked in a breath and then tried to hold it. It was an effective technique for dealing with panic attacks.

'I just wish I could go down there and help,' she said.

'I know you do. I hate to see you like this.'

'I'll be fine in a minute.' She gasped and then let out a long, slow breath.

'Better?' he asked after about thirty seconds.

'A bit.' She sighed. 'It's what I'm trained for. I feel so bloody stupid for saying no.'

'Come on, Laura,' Sam said. 'You need to give yourself a break once in a while.'

He took a step forward, put his arms around her, and they hugged.

Geoff wiped the sweat from his forehead with his sleeve. He was concerned that by sabotaging the boat, he had now put Steve in danger. He had already heard the arguments in the wheelhouse as Steve tried to explain that the oil pressure and gauge were both at zero. The man who Geoff assumed was the gang leader was frustrated, angry and therefore dangerous.

Hearing movement from above, Geoff listened intently to where Steve and the gang members were moving up on deck.

Without warning, the hatch to the hold door clicked.

Shit! They're coming down here! he thought as he moved quietly back down the hold and hid behind the huge Leeward Ballast Tank.

Peering back towards the hatch and the small set of steps down, Geoff saw Steve appear. A rough-looking man in his twenties with short ginger hair and a beard followed him.

'Show me where it is?' the man growled and shoved Steve forward.

The man had some kind of machine gun. It looked a bit like the Israeli Uzi, in that it was short and compact. That changed everything. Had they been armed with knives, he might have been able to pick them off in a fight. But guns made the whole thing more dangerous, especially with all the schoolchildren on board.

'This is the oil tank here,' Steve said.

The man stared at all the oil that had spilled onto the floor. 'What the fuck is this stuff all over the place?'

'It's oil,' Steve said nervously as he went over to inspect the tank. 'The pipe from the oil tank to the engine has come loose and the oil has leaked. That's why there's no oil pressure.'

'So, now what?' the man snapped.

'The engine has overheated without the oil. It needs repairing,' Steve told him.

'Can you do that?' the man asked.

Steve shook his head. 'I'm not a boat mechanic. And even if we could fix the engine, we don't have any spare oil on board.'

'Fuck!' the man yelled. 'So, we're not going anywhere?'

Steve shook his head as his eyes roamed anxiously around the hold.

He's probably wondering where the hell I am, Geoff thought to himself.

As they turned to go, the man spotted the spanner that Geoff had used to unscrew the oil pipe. He picked it up and frowned.

'Is there anyone else on this boat?' the man asked, looking around suspiciously.

'How do you mean?' Steve asked.

'Crew,' the man snapped. 'It's just you, is it? You drive the boat, do all the chat and that?'

Steve nodded. 'Yeah, of course.'

The man got into his face and looked at him. 'And you're sure about that, are you? You haven't got someone else hiding on the boat somewhere?'

Steve shook his head. He looked utterly terrified.

Geoff could feel his pulse racing.

The man turned back and walked down to the hold towards where Geoff was hiding.

Shit!

Geoff froze. Would he be able to overpower the man before he shot him? Possibly. But there could also be deadly consequences if the machine gun fired randomly and bullets flew up through to the deck where the passengers were sitting.

The man continued to move slowly down the hold. He was now only ten yards away.

Geoff tensed as he prepared to pounce and attack. He held his breath.

The man stopped and peered at the tank that Geoff was hiding behind. 'What's this?'

'Ballast tank,' Steve murmured.

'What's in it?'

'Water,' Steve replied.

The man took another step forward.

This is it!

Suddenly, there was a thunderous noise from somewhere above them. A rhythmic mechanical juddering. It was deafening.

The man frowned and looked up. 'What the bloody hell is that?'

The hatch opened, and another man appeared who Geoff assumed was part of the gang.

'You need to come here,' he yelled over the deafening noise. 'We've got company.'

The ginger man spun on his heels, headed back down the hold and out through the hatch.

Geoff let out a breath. *Jesus! That was bloody close.*

Then he realised what the noise above them was.

A helicopter.

Chapter 21

Gareth watched as the black Eurocopter EC145s hovered low over the *Anglesey Princess*. Having liaised with the National Police Air Service, he had asked for reconnaissance photos to be taken of the boat and deck. He needed to see where the passengers and gang members were positioned on the boat.

His Tetra radio crackled. 'Alpha Zero to Gold Command, are you receiving, over?'

It was an officer from the helicopter.

'Alpha Zero received, go ahead, over,' Gareth replied.

'We have visual contact with our target vessel. We also have visual contact with at least two suspects, over.'

'Okay, thank you Alpha Zero, I—'

There was a noise, and the radio crackled for a few seconds.

'Alpha Zero? Do you copy?' Gareth asked.

'Alpha Zero to Gold Command, Code Zero. I repeat Code Zero. We are under fire from target vessel, we are leaving the target area, over,' the officer replied, sounding a little shaken.

'Alpha Zero, received,' Gareth said, now aware that someone was approaching. It was Warlow.

Oh good. Just what I need. A supercilious prick on my case.

'Problems?' Warlow asked.

Gareth gave him a grim expression. 'One of our kidnappers just opened fire on the helicopter.'

'Jesus! So they've definitely got guns?' Warlow exclaimed.

That's right, Sherlock.

'Sounds like it,' Gareth said.

'I've spoken to the Chief Constable,' Warlow continued. 'He wants us to stall them for as long as we can.'

Gareth peered down at his watch. 'Well, sir, we've got forty minutes before they claim that they're going to shoot hostages. What about the speedboat and cash?'

Warlow pulled a face. 'I think we can sort out the speedboat. But I'm pretty sure they're not going to sanction handing over a bag with two hundred thousand pounds in it. It would set a precedent for any OCG to start taking hostages in return for cash.'

Gareth groaned. 'What am I supposed to tell him?'

'I'm sure you can think of a way of broaching the subject, Gareth,' Warlow said.

'What if he shoots someone?' Gareth thundered. 'Do we give them the cash then?'

Warlow rubbed his chin ruefully. 'I understand that this is a very stressful situation.'

'Which is why I need a trained negotiator here now!' Gareth snapped. 'I'm not up to it.'

'Ah, well, we have found someone in Cheshire,' Warlow said, 'but it might be an hour or two before they arrive.'

'We haven't got an hour or two, sir!' Gareth complained, shaking his head.

A harried-looking WPC approached. 'Sir, we have someone

on the *Anglesey Princess* wanting to talk to whoever is in charge.'

Gareth turned and broke into a run as he made his way back down the pier towards the lifeboat station. His head was spinning.

Running over to where the VHF radio was, he picked up the handset. 'Hello?'

'Send another fucking chopper and I'll empty a whole magazine into its propellers and put it in the sea!' the man bellowed.

'We were just checking that the children were safe,' Gareth explained.

'Yeah, well, you've got forty minutes to get that boat and money out here before I start shooting the kids,' the man barked.

Just as Gareth was thinking of how to reply, the line crackled.

'Hello?' Hello?' he asked.

Nothing.

The anxiety was growing in the pit of his stomach as Gareth closed his eyes for a second. The situation was getting out of control. Was the gang leader really going to shoot a child?

Andrea approached, holding a computer print-out. 'Boss?'

'What have you got?' he asked, hoping that it was good news.

'Finally got the passenger list for the *Anglesey Princess*. The primary-school trip is from St Mary's from just up the road. Year 6 class. Not that it really helps, but it's not my nephew's school.'

No, but I'm pretty sure that Laura Hart's son Jake is a pupil in Year 6 at St Mary's, he thought. It wasn't a phone call he was looking forward to making, but he didn't want anyone else breaking the news to Laura.

'Okay, we need to liaise with the school to notify all

154

parents of what has happened,' Gareth said. 'Although there might be some who are already aware from watching the news.'

'Some are already here.' Andrea raised her eyebrow as she gestured to a huddle of people over by the police tape. 'They started to arrive about half an hour ago, boss.'

'And you've told them they're better off staying at home?' Gareth asked.

'Of course,' Andrea replied. 'They want to be here though so there's not a lot we can do.'

'I can understand that. So as long as they stay out of our way . . .'

Andrea gestured to the passenger list and notes she was carrying. 'Teacher is a Beth Hughes. She's twenty-two and has been teaching at St Mary's for just over a year. There's no teaching assistant with them.'

Taking out his mobile, he scrolled through his contacts.

He rang the number for Engage Business Skills, but it was busy. He would try again in a few minutes.

11.03 a.m.

The tension inside the wheelhouse was growing. Michael could see that Red was becoming increasingly erratic – and even more dangerous than usual. He could also see that his brother had lost the cool, calm exterior that was his usual manner. They were all going to prison for a very long time unless they could find a way of escaping. Boarding the boat and taking the passengers hostage at gunpoint had made the potential severity of their sentences much, much greater – and they all knew it.

'What are we going to do?' Callum asked in a hushed voice.

Red, who could not stand still for more than a second, frowned. 'What d'you mean, what are we gonna do?'

'You've told the bizzies that you're gonna start shooting passengers in half an hour,' Callum said.

Red shrugged. 'So what?'

Taking a deep breath, Michael looked at them. 'Yeah, well, we're not doing that, are we?'

Red glared at him. 'We'll do what I fucking say, right, lad?'

Michael shook his head. From somewhere, he had found a bit of inner strength. Dealing drugs was one thing. He wasn't going to stand by and let that psycho start shooting people.

Red moved towards him aggressively. 'What you shaking your head at me for?'

Despite feeling sick with nerves, Michael glared at him. 'We're not shooting anyone.'

Red moved to about six inches from his face. 'And what are you gonna do about it?'

Michael frowned but didn't flinch. 'We're not shooting anyone!'

Callum gave Michael a concerned look. 'Michael?'

Red sneered. 'You'll do what I fucking say you, you little prick. Or I'll be fucking shooting you.'

In a moment of fear and anger, Michael snapped and grabbed Red by the throat, pushing back across the wheelhouse. He wasn't going to let him bully him anymore. And he certainly wasn't going to let him shoot any of the innocent passengers on this boat.

They struggled for a moment as he pinned Red against the wall. Then Red head-butted him in the nose.

Michael winced, reeling from the blow. For a second, he couldn't see anything and was unsteady on his feet. Before he knew it, Red had pounced on him and thrown him to the floor.

Now practically foaming at the mouth with his teeth

clenched, Red pinned him to the ground. He reached up, pulled the Skorpion machine gun from where he had left it resting on the boat's dashboard and rammed it hard between Michael's eyes.

'Red?' Callum asked uncertainly.

Red fixed Callum with a glare. 'Shut the fuck up!'

Red was pushing the gun's muzzle so hard into Michael's head that it felt like he was going to crack his skull.

Michael flinched. *Shit! I think he's going to shoot me!*

'You fucking little rat,' Red seethed, his chest heaving.

'Red,' Callum pleaded. 'Come on, get off him.'

Michael's breathing was fast and shallow. Was this it?

Looking at Red's hand, he could see it was shaking as his finger trembled on the trigger.

Oh God. Please don't let me die.

Callum came over and put his hand on Red's arm. 'Come on, Red. We're all fucking stressed, mate. Take the gun out of his face.'

Red didn't move. He was still clenching his teeth. 'You ever fucking do something like that again and I'll blow your tiny little brains out!'

As Red got off him, Callum pulled Michael to his feet and scowled at him. 'You'd better get outside and calm down, before you get yourself killed.'

Avoiding Red's glare, Michael stepped out of the wheelhouse and walked out to the deck where the passengers were sitting. He looked over the side of the boat, trying to clear his head and waiting for his heart to stop thumping.

For a moment, he let the cool breeze blow across his face. It reminded him of sitting by the Mersey and drinking cans of beer they had stolen from Asda. He knew how close he had just come to death. He didn't care. He wasn't going to let anyone innocent die today.

Spotting the teacher, he saw she was trying to calm the

young boy who was wearing the Manchester United shirt. The boy was struggling to breathe.

'Is he all right?' Michael asked as he approached.

The teacher gave him a withering look. 'No. Of course he's not all right.'

Michael crouched down and looked at the boy. 'What's his name?'

'Jake,' the teacher replied. 'He doesn't have asthma but he can't seem to get his breath.'

Michael glanced at her. 'He's having a panic attack.'

'How do you know that?' she asked.

'I used to get them when I was his age.' Michael put his hands on Jake's arms and looked directly at him. 'Listen, Jake, I want you to take a deep breath and then I want you to hold it. When I give you a nod, I want you to let it out really slowly. Can you do that for me, mate?'

Jake's eyes were full of tears. He was frightened.

'Okay, take a deep breath in,' Michael said as Jake sucked in air and his chest rose. 'Now hold it. See if we can get to ten, eh? One, two, three, four, that's it, keep it going, mate. Five, six, seven, eight, nine, ten. Brilliant, mate. Now let it out nice and slowly.'

Jake let out an audible sigh as he let out the breath.

Michael was aware that the teacher was watching him intently. She was pretty, and he hoped she didn't despise him too much.

'Try it again for me, Jake,' Michael suggested gently.

Jake took a deep breath, held it and then let it out slowly. He blinked as he looked at Michael.

'How's that? Any better?' Michael asked.

Jake nodded.

'Great. You're doing great, mate,' Michael said. 'Try it one more time.'

The teacher peered at him. 'How do you know how to do that?'

Michael gestured back towards the wheelhouse. 'My brother used to do that with me when I had my panic attacks.'

The teacher glanced over to the wheelhouse. 'He's your brother?'

'Yeah,' Michael replied.

The teacher seemed surprised. 'Oh, okay.'

'Why do you say it like that?' he asked.

The teacher shrugged. 'The other two seem really rough and scary.'

Part of Michael was relieved that he didn't fit the profile of a 'rough and scary' drug-dealing gangster.

'So, I'm not scary then?' he asked, studying the teacher's face in more detail now. She had dark, wavy hair that was tinted red and big brown eyes.

She shook her head. 'Not really, no. Sorry . . .'

Michael shrugged. 'It wasn't my idea.'

'Yeah, well, that's no excuse, is it?'

Michael frowned as he thought about what she had said for a moment. 'No, not really.' Then he looked at her. 'What's your name?'

She snorted. 'I'm not telling you my name.'

'Fair enough.' Michael shrugged and then looked over at Jake, who looked a hundred times better. 'How you doing, Jake?'

Jake nodded. 'Good.'

'Nice one.' Michael allowed himself a half-smile as he got up. 'I'm glad you're feeling better, mate.'

As he turned to go, the teacher looked at him. 'Beth,' she said quietly. 'My name's Beth.'

Chapter 22

11.10 a.m.

'We've got a boat!' Ben exclaimed as he approached Gareth at the end of the pier.

'Where is it?' Gareth asked, looking at his watch. They had twenty-seven minutes before the deadline the gang had given them.

Ben pulled a face. 'Holyhead. Police over there say they've got a RIB.'

Gareth's heart sank. 'Jesus Christ!'

'It's on a trailer, boss,' Ben continued. 'They reckon they can get it to us here in forty minutes. An hour, tops.'

Gareth scratched his chin and thought for a few seconds. There was nothing he could do but to contact the *Anglesey Princess* and try to stall them. Their last exchange didn't fill him with much hope. The man they were dealing with was very aggressive about what he wanted.

'Okay, thanks, Ben,' he said. 'Let me know when it gets here.'

In the back of his mind, he also knew that he needed to call Laura again. He would head back to the lifeboat station and ring her now. Part of him wondered if the fact that her son was on the boat would make any difference to her decision. From what she had told him in the past, Gareth knew Laura had been negotiating with the OCG gang who had had her late husband as a hostage. Something had gone wrong, and he had died. It might well be too difficult and emotional for her to negotiate with the men that now had her son.

'Boss,' Declan called over. 'I need a word.'

'What is it?' Gareth asked as he walked back down the pier towards the lifeboat station.

'You see the fella down there?' Declan asked surreptitiously.

Gareth glanced over to see a man in his forties standing by the police tape. He was well built, shaved head, designer clothes. Even from this distance, Gareth could see that he had the air of a man who could handle himself.

'Expensive clothes? Looks like a bouncer?' Gareth asked.

'That's him,' Declan replied. 'Gary White.'

'Why do I know that name?' Gareth asked.

'He's a local businessman, originally from London. He owns a couple of clubs up in Holyhead. Very rich and very flash,' Declan told him. 'Lots of rumours about how he's made his money.'

Gareth gave him a quizzical look. 'You mean he's involved in criminal activity?'

'I think he has a lot of very dodgy friends,' Declan replied.

'Has he got a record?' Gareth asked.

'As far as I remember, he's got some stuff from when he was younger. Assault, petty theft. Nothing heavy since then.'

'What does he want?'

'He said he thinks he can help with what's going on,' Declan replied. 'But he's only talking to the person in charge.'

Gareth gave an exasperated sigh. Even though he didn't really have the time, he was curious about how White was going to help them. 'Right, I'll go and see what he wants.'

Marching towards the crowd at the start of the pier, Gareth took out his sunglasses. The sun was beating down and reflecting off the white-painted beach walls. To his right, the lido was empty. Normally it would be full of children playing in the water. The centre of Beaumaris was now in lockdown and, except for a huddle of parents, the promenade was deserted on both sides.

'You the bloke in charge?' White asked as he approached. He had a thick cockney accent.

'Mr White?' Gareth asked. 'My sergeant said that you think you can help us?'

'My daughter, Bella, is out on that boat,' White growled. 'And there's no fucking way I'm leavin' her out there.'

Gareth frowned. He didn't like the tone of White's statement. 'What are you suggesting?'

White pointed out towards where the *Anglesey Princess* was sitting. 'What do they want?'

Gareth frowned. 'What do you mean?'

'The blokes that are holding everyone hostage on the boat? What do they want?'

Gareth shook his head. 'I'm afraid I can't discuss that with you, Mr White.'

'I heard a rumour that the RIB they were in broke down out there.' White gestured to the Menai Strait. 'That's why they boarded the boat. Is that right?'

Oh shit! How does he know that?

'As I said, I'm not prepared to discuss that with you.'

White's face twisted with utter contempt. 'I'll tell you what you should understand. If any of them lay a fucking finger on my daughter, I will fucking hunt them down, kill them and then kill their families.'

There was something very intimidating about White that Gareth had only seen in a few criminals in his career.

'I'm not sure that's the wisest thing to say to a police officer, Mr White.' Gareth pointed back to the lifeboat station. 'Now, I've got a lot of things that I need to do so—'

'They want a boat for starters, don't they?' White interrupted him.

'What do you mean?' Gareth asked.

'Stands to reason,' White retorted. 'They were clearly trying to get away from your lot in a RIB. It broke down. Now they're stuck. So, they need a fast boat to get out of here.'

'That's an interesting theory,' Gareth said. There was no way he was giving White the faintest hint that he was on the right track.

'And I'm guessing that if they're chancing their luck, they'll ask for some money as well,' White suggested.

'Listen, Mr White, I really am very busy so—'

'I'll tell you what I'm gonna do, shall I?' White asked rhetorically. 'I've got a bloke who knows how to handle himself, if you know what I mean. I've also got two very fast Scarab speed boats about five minutes down the road. And I've got a lot of cash. So, I'm gonna do you lot a favour. I'm gonna give my bloke a big bag of cash and then me and him are gonna drive out to that boat. We give the cash and one of my boats to these blokes who've hijacked it. Then I'm going to pick up my daughter and bring her back here safely. Then, once those blokes sod off with my cash in my boat, it's down to you to get everyone else. How does that sound?'

Gareth couldn't believe what he was suggesting. 'I'm sorry, Mr White, but I can't let you do that. It's incredibly dangerous.'

'Listen, I'll do anything to get my daughter back,' White snapped. 'And you can't stop me!'

163

White turned away to leave.

'Mr White!' Gareth yelled after him.

'You can thank me later, when you get all those kids back safely, eh?' White said over his shoulder as he walked away.

Chapter 23

Laura looked at the clients in the room as she perched casually on the table in front of them. She wasn't relaxed at all. Her conversation with Gareth had completely rattled her. All she could think was that she had let down the Beaumaris Police, and the poor people out on the boat.

'I get the feeling that some of you are already aware that we have an ongoing situation in Beaumaris at the moment,' she said calmly.

The young man pointed to the phone he was holding. 'I just read it on Twitter. Something about some hostages on a boat.'

There were a few concerned murmurs from the clients who weren't aware of what was developing only three miles down the road.

'I think that the roads in and around Beaumaris are going to get clogged in the next few hours with emergency vehicles, media and general onlookers who want to see what's going on,' Laura explained. 'I know that some of you have come a long way to get here and have a long journey home. But

I don't want you to get stranded here overnight. So, my suggestion is that we finish for the day and I will find some other suitable dates that I can run the rest of this workshop for you all. If you want a full refund though, that's not a problem. I can only apologise for having to cancel the rest of today's session, but I hope you understand that what's going on is out of my hands.'

The pompous man at the back gave her a withering look. 'Are you willing to reimburse our travel costs for today?'

She forced a rueful half-smile. 'If you can provide me with receipts, then naturally I'm happy to reimburse you. How far did you come?'

'Llangefni,' he replied.

Are you kidding? That's about ten miles away!

By her calculations, she would owe him less than £2. What a petty moron.

Once she had seen the clients out to the car park, her focus returned to the events on the *Anglesey Princess*. Marching back into the office, she spotted Annabelle was back watching the television news.

'What's going on?' she asked as she plonked herself down on the sofa.

'Nothing really,' Annabelle told her. 'Some police bloke came on and said that they were negotiating with the kidnappers and listening to their demands.'

'Right.'

Annabelle turned and looked at her. 'I don't know why they don't ask you to go and talk to them. That's what you used to do as a job, isn't it?'

Laura nodded, feeling uncomfortable. She wasn't about to tell her that they had asked for her help and she had turned them down.

'Yeah, I did,' she mumbled as she peered at the television

166

screen. 'A long time ago though.' She was keen that the conversation didn't continue.

'What was it like working with the FBI?' Annabelle asked. 'That must have been so exciting. I watched that *Silence of the Lambs* the other night. She was an FBI agent, wasn't she? The main character?'

'I think so,' Laura replied.

The BBC anchorwoman came back onto the screen looking concerned. 'And now back to our main story today. A boat off the Island of Anglesey has been captured and its passengers taken hostage. We had reports that a police helicopter had been fired at, so we're going over to our correspondent, Hannah Chilwell, who is at the scene for us. Hannah, is there anything you can tell us about the reports of gunfire?'

Hannah was standing in front of the seawall with Beaumaris Beach and the pier behind her. 'It was about ten minutes ago when a police helicopter hovered directly over the *Anglesey Princess* for a few minutes. It was then that I heard what sounded like gunshots, and an eyewitness reported seeing a man firing a gun at the helicopter from the boat's deck.'

For a few seconds, Laura drifted away. She remembered the last time she had been glued to the BBC News like this was in August 1997, when Princess Diana had died in Paris. Her American friend, Hayley, used to tease her and claimed that was the day the British finally lost their stiff upper lip. Instead of cold stoicism, the British public had become a weeping mess. Hayley alleged that from that day on, the British people were at last allowed to grieve in public.

The office phone rang, breaking Laura's train of thought.

'I'll get it!' Annabelle chirped as she got up from the sofa.

Picking up the phone, Annabelle looked over and pointed to the receiver. 'It's that policeman again.'

What does he want from me! I've told him that I can't help.

Laura took the phone from Annabelle.

'Gareth?' she asked.

'Laura,' Gareth said. 'I've got some bad news.'

'What is it?'

'I've just got the passenger list.' Gareth stopped for a few seconds. 'The school trip that's on the *Anglesey Princess* is the Year 6s from St Mary's.'

'What?' She gasped in horror. 'Are you sure?'

'Yes. I've spoken to the head, Mr Peters. I'm really sorry. That's Jake's class, isn't it?'

'Yes,' she whispered, thinking back to the conversation they'd had at breakfast. 'We'd all forgotten he had a trip today. Oh God!'

'Don't worry. We're going to get them all back safely. I promise.'

She had heard those fateful words before – just before Sam was killed.

'Okay,' she muttered in a daze. 'Thanks for ringing me, Gareth.'

Putting down the phone, she stared into space.

Please, God, don't let anything happen to my son.

Her stomach clenched as she took in a breath.

'What is it? Annabelle asked as her eyes widened.

'Erm . . . I need to go outside,' she muttered as she left the office and headed out to the large first-floor balcony that looked north over the Anglesey countryside.

Blowing out her cheeks, she could feel her heart hammering in her chest.

'You know you need to go down there, don't you?' said a voice.

She turned to see Sam looking at her. His expression right now was the one she most disliked. Very calm, slightly parental and a little pompous.

She shook her head as the anxiety flooded her body. 'I can't. Seriously, I can't do it.'

Sam looked upset. 'He's our son, Laura.'

She held out her hand. It was shaking. 'Look at me! I can't go anywhere near this.'

He went to her and put his hands gently around her arms. 'Please. You know what Jake's like. He's going to be terrified on that boat.'

'I know, I know,' she said through gritted teeth. 'And I hate myself for that!'

'You can't sit here and do nothing.'

'The last time I did anything like that, you ended up dead,' she snapped. 'I can't lose him as well.'

'It wasn't your fault. They gave you nothing to work with. You did everything you could.'

'Yes, but it wasn't enough, was it?'

'Please, Laura. Go down there, talk to them, do what you do best. And get our son back safely.'

She looked at him, her eyes wide with fear. 'I can't. I just can't. I'm sorry.'

Chapter 24

Laura took a few moments to take a breath and look up at the low ceiling of the living room. They had spent the day moving into the new family home in Beaumaris and Rosie and Jake were now upstairs unpacking their stuff and arranging their new bedrooms. Her sister Emma had helped with the move and was now heading home to Kent. Laura didn't know what she'd do without her.

There were dozens of unpacked boxes scattered throughout the house, which created a frustrating labyrinth. On the floor was a broken lamp that one of the removal men had dropped by accident. He had been mortified, promising to pay for it, but Laura had brushed it aside, saying that it was just an old lamp. But it wasn't. It had been a wedding present from her parents. She had been touched they had gone all the way to Habitat to buy it as they knew she and Sam liked 'nice things from Habitat'.

She thought of her mother, Gwen, in that moment. Even though she tried her best, she had never really fitted in with the other mothers in the small village of Rhosmeirch.

170

Everyone in the village had an opinion about her and it was seldom a positive one. She was intelligent, politically aware and opinionated. She made her thoughts on organised religion very clear. And that made her an outsider in their rural home. She started running and eventually ran a couple of marathons. Laura could remember her doing her keep-fit routine to a Jane Fonda workout VHS in the mornings. The only problem with having a mother like hers was the feeling of being an outsider. While other parents at school met in the pub or for barbecues, hers were ostracised for being different.

Laura looked around the room again. Many of her friends and colleagues had thought her decision to leave the police force and move back home to Anglesey was impulsive. And of course they were right. But she knew that if she and her children were going to survive Sam's death, they needed a fresh start. Even though both her parents had passed away in recent years, she still knew many people on the island. It was where she had grown up. It was home.

She gazed up at the photographs that lined the mantelpiece over the fireplace. For some reason, they had been the first things she had unpacked. At the far end was a picture of the four of them at Knowsley Safari Park. It had been about five years ago. She remembered that halfway through their drive around the park, Jake had told them he was desperate for a wee. Sam had groaned and told him he would have to wait. As they entered the tiger enclosure, they all spotted two huge tigers ambling past the car and over to a fallen tree trunk. Suddenly, there was the noise of the door opening and Laura had spun around to see Jake's door open by about a foot. For a moment, everyone froze. Then Rosie dived across the car and slammed it shut. When they had asked Jake what he was doing, he had just shrugged and said that he was getting out for a wee. And when it was pointed out that they were in the tiger enclosure, he shook his head and pointed. *They're over there, silly. They're miles away from where I was going to wee.* They ended up giving him an empty Ribena bottle, which did the trick.

Stretching out her legs, she yawned before arching her back and standing up. She wandered over to the window and looked out. The setting sun had coloured a strip of cloud a rich, dark orange, as if the sky itself was on fire. The black ridges of Snowdonia cut a ragged line through the flaming band. The sky would soon soothe itself to a scarlet and purple hue, before a wash of sapphire blue signified the onset of night.

'You don't get views like that in Sale,' said a voice. It was Sam.

'We never did get up Snowdon, did we?' she whispered.

He laughed. 'You wanted to take the train.'

She pulled a face of mock indignation. 'So? I've got little legs. It would have taken all day to walk up to the top.'

'Wimp,' Sam snorted, and then looked at her. 'I really hope you and the kids are happy here. I don't want you sitting inside being all mopey and moody.'

Laura raised an eyebrow. 'Hey, I've got to get on with my life, mate. And so have Rosie and Jake.'

'Oh . . . I'd hoped that you'd miss me a bit sometimes. Just not all the time.'

'God, you're so needy,' she joked as he went back to the sofa. In the light of dusk, the room was awash with a hue of apricot.

Her phone rang. It was a number she hadn't seen for a few weeks. Pete Marsons. Sam looked over and saw who was ringing.

'If he wants to speak to me, I'm not in,' he joked.

'Very funny,' she said, rolling her eyes as she answered the call. 'Hi, Pete.'

'Hey. How's moving day?' Pete asked.

'Exhausting,' she replied.

'I told you I'd come and give you a hand,' he said.

'It's fine. Emma helped out and we're nearly there now. When are you coming to visit?' she asked.

'Definitely before Christmas,' he promised. 'I've got Jake a signed United football shirt, even though it killed me buying it!'

'Oh, thanks. He'll love that,' she said. 'How's Anusha?'

'She's fine. She said to say hello.'

'Tell her I used her recipe for roasted tandoori cauliflower and tahini yoghurt the other night,' she said. 'It's incredible.'

'I know. She's started putting her recipes online.'

'Brilliant idea,' Laura said. 'How are the kids?'

'You know. Argumentative, entitled and messy.' He laughed.

'I know that one,' she groaned.

There were a few seconds of silence.

'Is everything all right?' Pete asked. 'You said that you wanted to speak to me about something.'

'Yeah,' she admitted quietly. 'I've done some digging around.'

Once Laura had started to recover from the trauma of Sam's death, she found herself wondering about what he had been doing at the warehouse that day. Something about it didn't sit right with her. Coupled with the fact that OCG seemed to have been tipped off that they were going to be raided that morning, she had a nagging feeling there were more to the events of 12 August 2018 than the IOPC and Manchester Met had concluded.

'You remember we tried to track down the number that called the station to tell us that there was suspicious activity at Brannings Warehouse?' she continued.

173

'Yeah, it was a burner phone and we couldn't trace it,' Pete replied.

'Well, I spoke to that mate of mine in Digital Forensics about it again a few weeks ago. She told me they had managed to triangulate the phone signal using the masts in the area,' she explained. 'It's just that no one ever asked to see the trace.'

'Why not?'

'I don't think anyone took our concerns about that initial phone call seriously. And now I know why.'

'That sounds ominous. The trace would still only give us a rough area of where the phone call was made from. It could have been someone walking down the street or sitting in the car,' he said, thinking out loud. 'What did you find out?'

'Digital Forensics tracked the phone call to Trafford Police Station.'

There were a few seconds of silence. Her discovery had clearly surprised him as much as it had her.

'Pete?' she said.

'What? Are you sure?'

'Yes.'

'That doesn't make any sense.' He sounded utterly baffled. 'Why would anyone inside Trafford Police Station ring the switchboard to give an anonymous tip-off of suspicious activity?'

'That's what I thought. Central Park Trading Estate was Sam and Louise's patch. All those roads around Trafford Park, that's where they patrolled. If you knew that, then you would know that they would be contacted by CAD and be first on the scene at anything going on at Brannings Warehouse.'

'You think they were deliberately targeted?' he asked, unable to hide the disbelief in his voice.

'I don't know yet,' she said. 'Looking at the log I photo-copied before I left, Sam made five PNC checks and one check on HOLMES in the week leading up to his death. Looks like he was trying to play detective about something.'

'Yeah, that doesn't sound right does it?' Pete agreed. 'Since when does a uniform officer start running checks on PNC and HOLMES?'

'Have you got any way of checking what he was looking at?' she asked hopefully.

'I could ask the Digital Technology Unit to see if they can trace them,' Pete suggested. 'I also need to see if we can get a recording of that phone call.'

'That would be great. I'm sorry to trouble you with all this, but I thought you'd want to know.'

'Of course I want to know, Laura. I wish I could say that I knew what he was up to, but I just don't. Leave it with me,' he reassured her. 'I'll get back to you as soon as I get anything else back.'

'Thank you, Pete. There was something off about that whole day.'

'Yeah, I know. Listen, I'll let you get back to unpacking and sorting yourselves out.'

'Okay. I'll speak to you soon,' she said as she finished the call.

As she tried to process what she had discussed with Pete, there was a noisy clattering on the stairs, followed by foot-steps coming down the hallway.

Rosie and Jake came pelting in. They were laughing.

'Can we get a takeaway?' Rosie yelled as she dived onto the sofa next to Laura.

'Nando's?' Jake suggested.

'Domino's?' Rosie hollered.

She beamed and looked at them. 'Sorry, guys. I don't think there's a Nando's or a Domino's in Beaumaris.'

'What?' they cried in unison.

'Actually, I'm pretty sure we can't get food delivered here,' she told them.

Rosie looked gobsmacked. 'Are you actually joking?'

'No. We're not in Manchester anymore,' she said.

Chapter 25

Sitting on a wrought-iron chair on the first-floor balcony, Laura took a long deep breath of fresh air. She had managed to regain some composure even though her mind still whirred with the thought of Jake, what he might be going through and her maddening inability to go and help him.

Sam reached over and took her hand. 'I think you're right,' he said after a few minutes' silence.

'About what?' she asked. Her heart had started to slow to a relatively reasonable level.

'If you go down there and just lose it, you could make things worse,' he replied.

She furrowed her brow as she looked at him. 'You've changed your tune, haven't you?'

'I can see how much the thought of it terrified you, that's all.'

'But that's my job,' she sighed in frustration. 'I'm trained to negotiate for the safe release of hostages.'

'To do that properly, you have to be detached,' he said. 'You need to be clear, calm and unemotional, don't you?'

'I suppose so.'

'There's your answer then. He's your son, so that's impossible.'

'They don't have anyone down there that can do it, Sam,' she said in a fraught voice. 'And Jake is sitting out there, on that boat, scared to death.'

For a moment, he looked directly at her with a tender expression. 'Do you remember when he was born?'

'Yes, of course. Birth isn't something you forget when you're a mother,' she snorted dryly. 'And you spent most of your time watching *American Pie* on that telly on the wall and laughing.'

'It's a funny film,' he shrugged. 'And you'd had more drugs than Keith Richards.'

'I think my exact words were *Give me more fucking drugs!*' she admitted with a wry smirk.

He looked directly into her eyes with a loving smile. 'And there was a moment when I was holding your hand, and you looked at me and said *I can't do this anymore, Sam. I'm too tired. I can't do it.* And I said *Come on, Laura. Just one more big push. You can do this.* And about a minute later, our baby son was born. And he was perfect.'

She smiled at the memory of it. 'He was so tiny and so perfect wasn't he? He still is.'

And then it struck her.

What the hell am I doing just sitting here?

Getting up from the chair, Laura took a band from her pocket, pulled back her hair and fastened it into a ponytail. She took a deep, audible breath and looked at him.

And in that moment, she knew exactly what she needed to do.

'Going somewhere?' Sam asked.

'Yes. I'm going down there,' she replied.

'Okay.' Sam frowned. 'What's changed your mind?'

178

'Jake is our beautiful little boy. And I'm his mum. And it's my job to make sure that he's safe. So, I'm not going to let someone else take the responsibility for that. I have to go down there now.'

With his clothes now soaked with sweat, Geoff sat at the far end of the hold with his back resting against the hull. His hair was wet and sticking to his scalp. He hadn't experienced anything like this since his basic training in 1981.

After two days of briefings at the SBS base in Hamworthy, he had been subjected to four weeks of endurance testing, mainly in the Brecon Beacons in South Wales. It was very similar to SAS training, and he remembered the torture of timed marches wearing heavy Bergens – the military rucksack weighing 25 kilos. The climax of this training was known as 'the long drag': a 40 km march that had to be completed in less than twenty hours. It was the test that in 2013 had seen three recruits die on the Brecons from exhaustion and prompted an official inquest.

After that came the SBS jungle training in the rainforests of Belize, which had tested Geoff and the other recruits to the limits of their endurance. Finally, there were four weeks of combat survival, where recruits were hunted down and captured by members of the Royal Marines or the Parachute Regiment. They were then subjected to interrogation and psychological torture to see if they would break.

Geoff realised that his training had taken place forty years ago, but he still knew how to take his body and his mind to the limits of their endurance. Standing up, he listened. It had been a while since anything significant had happened up on deck. Nothing really since someone in the gang had fired shots, presumably at the helicopter overhead.

He grabbed the top of the large water ballast tank again and unscrewed the plastic cap. It was just about wide enough for him to get his fingers inside and into the water. Pulling his fingers out, he could drip water into his mouth and then repeat the process. It was laborious, but he knew how important it was to get some water into his body, given the heat inside the hull.

'Geoff? Geoff?' whispered a voice. It was Steve.

Peering cautiously around the ballast tank, Geoff saw that the hold door was open and Steve had crept in.

Jesus! What the hell is he doing? He'll get himself shot.

'Geoff? Geoff?' Steve whispered.

Geoff appeared and put his finger to his lips to signal for Steve to be quiet. He approached slowly.

'What are you doing down here?' Geoff whispered, putting a comforting hand on his arm.

'I told them I'd see if the oil pipe could be repaired,' Steve explained as he glanced nervously at the open hold door.

'What for?' Geoff asked.

Reaching inside his trousers, Steve brought out a mobile phone. It was Geoff's.

'I found this in your rucksack. They didn't look in there. I thought you might be able to use it. I heard one of the gang call the leader Red.'

Geoff frowned. 'Red?'

Steve nodded. 'Yeah, Red. He's got ginger hair, so it might be that. The young one called the other one Cal.'

'Cal?' Geoff asked to clarify.

'Callum, maybe? I don't know if I'm onto anything, but I think they might be brothers. They look similar.'

'Okay.' Geoff gave Steve another reassuring pat on the arm. 'We're going to get out of this, old son. I promise you.'

Steve looked terrified. 'I'd better get back and tell them it's definitely fucked.'

Geoff smiled. 'Take it easy up there, okay? Don't do anything stupid.'

He watched as Steve turned, headed back to the hold door and left. Even though he had never articulated it, in this moment he realised Steve was the most important person in his life.

11.36 a.m.

As Laura marched past Beaumaris Beach towards the pier, she pulled out her sunglasses and popped them on. Looking left, she could see the *Anglesey Princess* stationary on the Menai Strait. Jake was out there on his own. She couldn't bear to think how scared he must be. It was down to her to help bring him back home safely.

The main road and pier had been cordoned off with blue police tape, which was being manned by several uniformed officers.

As Laura got closer, it took her back to the days when she would take out her warrant card and breeze past the police barrier, moving towards the crime scene. Now she was just a civilian. There was definitely part of her that missed being a copper.

A young female police officer gave her a kind smile as she drew near.

'Is DI Williams around?' she asked.

'Erm, I'm not sure,' the PC replied with a frown. 'I think he's pretty tied up at the moment.'

She gave a wry smile. 'Yeah, I can imagine. He's asked me to come down and help him.'

The PC raised an eyebrow. 'Really?'

Oh God, she must wonder what the hell I'm talking about.

'My name is Laura Hart. I used to be the Chief Hostage Negotiator for Greater Manchester Police. He's asked me to help him.' She hoped she hadn't come across as pompous.

'Sorry, ma'am,' the PC mumbled awkwardly as she lifted the tape for her to proceed. She didn't have the energy to explain that she wasn't a copper anymore.

Striding up the pier, as she had done thousands of times before, she knew that she needed to remain focused. If she let herself get too emotional, then all of her training as a negotiator would go out of the window. And that would put Jake, and everyone else on the boat, in more danger.

Gareth did a double-take when he saw her. 'Oh, my God. Aren't you a sight for sore eyes?'

Despite the stress of the situation, she still couldn't help but be pleased to see his handsome face beaming at her.

'Where do you need me?' she asked, the adrenaline pumping in her veins.

'Follow me,' he said, gesturing to the lifeboat station. 'What made you change your mind?'

'Someone who knows me very well told me that my son was on that boat and to go and help save him.'

'Well, whoever that was, I owe them a very big drink.'

She didn't think now was the time to tell Gareth about her conversations with her late husband . . .

They marched into the lifeboat station and over to where the audio equipment and VHF radio were sitting on a table. On the other side of the room, they had set another table up where two CID officers were sitting at laptops and another was on the phone.

Andrea came hurrying across to them. 'Boss, we've got someone on the line claiming that they're calling from the *Anglesey Princess* on a mobile phone.'

'What?' Gareth asked with a frown. 'Who is it?'

Andrea pointed over the sound equipment. 'He says his name is Geoff Clegg. He's one of the guys from Beaumaris Cruises.'

'Have we checked that out?' Gareth asked.

'Yes, boss. He's on the passenger list Beaumaris Cruises gave us as one of their employees,' Andrea said. She pointed at the laptop. 'The tech boys have patched the call through to here.'

Laura exchanged a look with Gareth, who gestured to the laptop. 'Time to work your magic.'

She moved swiftly over to the table, sat down and moved the computer so that it was in front of her.

Here we go.

'Hello, Geoff?' she said.

'Hello?' whispered a voice through the laptop speakers.

'This is Laura. I work for the North Wales Police,' she said calmly. 'I understand that you're on the *Anglesey Princess*?'

'Yeah, I'm hiding down in the hold.'

She exchanged a look with Gareth. 'Have you been down there since the men boarded the boat?'

'Aye. I heard them come aboard.'

Christ, that's an interesting development, she thought.

'Do you know if everyone is okay on board the boat?' she asked, even though her mind was fixed firmly on how Jake was doing.

'As far as I know.'

'Do you know how many men boarded the boat?'

'Three.'

'Is there anything you can tell us about them you think might help us? Any accents, names or descriptions?'

'Aye. They're from Liverpool. The leader is called Red. One of the others is called Cal, which may be short for Callum. I think his brother is the third one,' Geoff said quietly.

'That's fantastic, Geoff. That's incredibly helpful,' she said encouragingly.

'They wanted Steve to take them over to Liverpool, but I dismantled the oil pipe. The boat's going nowhere.'

183

He's sabotaged the boat? Brilliant! I knew I liked the sound of Geoff.

Geoff continued. 'If I was to guess, I'd say they've got a handgun and some kind of machine gun by the sounds of it. Possibly small calibre.'

Laura pulled a face at Gareth. 'You sound like you know your stuff, Geoff.'

'Ex-military. Royal Navy,' he said shortly.

'Royal Marines?' she asked.

'The SBS actually.' He sounded almost apologetic. 'Long time ago.'

Laura's eyes widened – they had an ex-member of the SBS hiding in the boat's hold. A very interesting development indeed.

'Do you think there's anything else you can tell us that might help?' she asked.

There were a few seconds of silence.

'I can't think of anything,' he replied.

'That's brilliant, Geoff. Keep yourself hidden and safe for now, okay? We'll call you back as soon as we can.'

'Aye.'

Laura finished the call, looked at Gareth and, without thinking, immediately went into her default police negotiator mode.

'I'm going to need PNC, NOMS and HOLMES checks on anything we know about anyone in the Croxteth Crew with a nickname Red. Also, check the name Callum and see if he has a brother.'

'We're in contact with a DCI in Merseyside who has a CHIS that is involved with the Croxteth Crew. That's how we got the tip-off about the drop-off at the beach this morning,' Gareth explained.

For that moment, Laura had been so caught up in the police work it was as if she were back to being a DI. Then

184

she remembered Jake and prayed to God that he was going to come out of this unharmed. The thought of anything happening to him terrified her.

Keep it together, Laura. Jake needs you to stay focused, she thought, giving herself a sharp reminder to say calm.

She frowned, deliberately moving her thoughts back to what was required. 'At the moment, they're facing sentences for possession of firearms, kidnapping and intent to supply. So, they're probably looking at sentences of ten to twelve years?'

Gareth nodded. 'Sounds about right.'

'They shoot someone in cold blood, they get life. I need to speak to them and make that very clear. If you get twelve years, you can be out in six. You commit cold-blooded murder, you're going to serve twenty-five at best.'

'And that's got to be incredibly persuasive,' he agreed. He then gave her a grim look.

'What's the matter?'

'According to my watch, we've just run out of time. This "Red" gave us an hour to get the speedboat and money to him.'

'I need to buy us some more time,' she said calmly as she turned and grabbed the VHF radio. 'Hello, *Anglesey Princess,* can you read me? Is anyone there, over?'

Silence.

She looked at Gareth. The fact that they hadn't contacted them at the point of the deadline running out was worrying.

'Hello? *Anglesey Princess?* Is anyone there, over?'

The radio crackled and a gruff voice came on.

'You're late!' Red growled.

'Hi there. My name is Laura. I—'

'I don't give a fuck what your name is.'

Not a great start.

'Okay,' Laura said gently. 'Before we begin, could you tell me how everyone is doing over there?' She wanted Red to be

185

reminded that he had a boat full of scared adults and children.

'No, no, I can't. Now what do you want?'

'I have a big favour to ask you. My guess is that you don't want to hurt anyone on that boat, do you?'

After a few moments of tense silence, Laura looked at Gareth and narrowed her eyes. She was finding it hard to get Red to engage with her.

'I said, what do you want?' Red eventually growled.

'I'd like you to give us a little more time,' she said in a composed tone. 'We're very close to being able to get you what you've asked for, but I just need a bit more time.'

'I don't remember agreeing to give you more time, bitch,' Red sneered. 'You must think I'm some kind of mug.'

'No. I promise you I don't think you're some kind of mug at all,' she said, mirroring his words. 'I think you're a young man who has got himself in over his head and you're looking for a way out. I completely get that. And I want to work with you so that everyone can get out of this situation unharmed. To do that, though, I need you to do me a massive favour and give us a bit more time. Can you do that for me?'

'Yeah . . . I think I can give you some more time.'

That was easy.

She sighed with relief. 'That's great. I know that me and you are going to be able to work this out together.'

Gareth gave her a look as if to say, *Well done. We're now on the right track here.*

'You said your name was Laura, is that right?' Red asked.

'Yes. My name's Laura.'

'You see, Laura, there is a slight problem,' Red continued. 'I gave you an hour, and I said that if I didn't get what I wanted, then I would start shooting children.'

Laura frowned and looked at Gareth.

What's he talking about? We've just been through all this.

'I understand that. And I've asked that you give me a little more time to get together what you've asked for.' She was now uneasy. She couldn't quite tell what Red was up to and it had thrown her a little.

'Yeah, but Laura, I'm a man of me word,' Red replied. 'I can't be seen to back down on what I've said. I've got my reputation to think of, d'you know what I mean?'

She could feel her pulse quickening. 'I've got a feeling that deep down, you're a reasonable, intelligent young man. If you could just give us a bit more time we'll get you exactly what you've requested.'

'Nah, I don't think so, Laura.'

Laura's mouth had gone dry.

What does he mean by that?

She looked up at Gareth, who was also clearly concerned.

Before she could reply, Red said, 'I've got a young boy here. He won't tell me his name. I think he's scared, to the tell the truth. In fact, he's wet his pants. But that's because I've got a gun pressed against his head.'

Oh my God!

She felt sick. She couldn't believe what he was saying.

What if it's Jake? Please God, don't let anything happen to him.

'Please, whatever you're thinking of doing, I'm begging you not to . . .'

There was a terrible silence.

She couldn't get her breath. She looked up at Gareth – the colour had drained from his face.

CRACK! CRACK!

From down the radio, there came the unmistakable sound of gunfire.

Chapter 26

11.37 a.m.

Beth and Jake flinched on the deck. There had just been two gunshots in the wheelhouse. She had no idea what was going on, but it was terrifying to hear. All the passengers were sitting safely, but they were now clearly frightened.

Two girls from her class were crying so Beth got up and went over to comfort them.

'You need to stay in your seat,' warned the teenage boy.

Beth glared at him as she put a comforting arm around the girls.

The teenage boy looked at her. She could see that he wasn't like the other two. In fact, he had spent most of his time onboard looking nervous, apologetic or both.

'What are they shooting for anyway?' she growled at him.

He shrugged and gestured to the two girls. 'I don't know. I'm sorry if it's scared them.'

'You've scared everyone on this boat!' Beth snapped, and then gestured to the girls. 'Do you actually think this is okay?'

The teenage boy didn't reply and looked down at his feet.

'Look at them!' she yelled. 'Oh, that's right, you can't, can you?'

The teenage boy looked up.

Beth looked at the girls. 'We're going to go back soon and you can see your parents. I promise.'

The girls nodded and seemed reassured.

Going back to her seat beside Jake, Beth sat down and saw the teenage boy looking at her.

She fixed him with a stare.

He looked lost and briefly put his head in his hands. Then he looked up at her. 'I'm sorry, I really am.'

'Then do something about it,' she advised him, having regained her composure.

He shrugged. 'I can't.'

'Can't or won't?' she asked, and then in a quieter tone added, 'What are you doing here? You don't seem to be anything like either of those two.'

He thought for a moment. 'It's a long story.'

She gestured to the wheelhouse. 'So, what's the plan? This boat hasn't moved in nearly an hour.'

'It's not working,' the teenage boy replied.

'What? So, we're just going to sit here for ever?' she grumbled, giving him a withering look.

'We're waiting for a speedboat and then we'll be going.'

'Thank God for that,' she said, looking out over the water in frustration. 'How long does it take to bring a speedboat out here?'

'I dunno.' The teenager shrugged.

There were a few seconds of silence before he looked over at her. 'I like your tattoos.'

'What?' she asked with a frown.

'I really like your tattoos.'

Beth looked down at the array of colourful tattoos on her

189

arms. His attempt to pacify her was both pitiful and endearing at the same time.

'I don't normally like girls with lots of tattoos, you know?' he admitted. 'But they really suit you.'

There were a few awkward seconds. Beth wasn't sure what to say to that. It amused her that he was trying to make a connection with her in such a tense situation.

'I'll take that as a compliment, I think,' she said, playing along. 'My taid was a tattoo artist, so I guess it runs in the family.'

'Taid?' he asked with a frown. 'Is that his name or something?'

She frowned. 'No. Taid's Welsh for grandad.'

He pulled a face. 'Sorry. I didn't know that.'

'Why would you?' she snapped. 'You're not Welsh.'

'Yeah, but me arl fella is. He's from Rhyl.'

'Is he still in Rhyl?' she asked.

The boy bristled and then shook his head. 'No. Not anymore. We've lost touch with him.'

'You mean, you and your brother?'

'Yeah.'

'Oh, right. So you don't even know where he is?'

Something about the questions had unsettled him. 'No.'

'What about your mum?'

For a few seconds, the teenager stared into space. Then, without looking at her, he muttered, 'She died.'

'I'm sorry to hear that,' Beth said. 'My mother died last year. It was horrible.'

The boy looked at her. 'Sorry. Yeah, me mum died when I was only three, so I don't really remember her. Just photos and that.'

'That must have been really difficult for you and your brother?'

'Yeah. When me arl fella went away, it was me brother who brought me up, you know? He did everything for me.'

190

'You must be very close then?'

The boy agreed. 'Yeah, we are. We're dead close, me and Cal.'

'His name's Callum?' she asked.

The teenage boy looked awkward. 'Yeah, but I didn't tell you that, okay?'

She shrugged. 'Okay.'

For a moment, he smiled at her. It was the first time that she had seen any expression on his face other than a scowl or a frown of concern. His eyes twinkled. She wondered how his life would have turned out if he had been brought up in different circumstances. He'd probably be still sitting in school or college.

There was a sudden movement from the wheelhouse as the ginger-haired man and the other man, whom she now knew as Callum, came out onto the deck.

The ginger-haired man rushed to the side of the boat. He frowned as he peered back towards Beaumaris.

'What's going on?' the boy asked.

'Come and have a look, lad,' Callum said, beckoning him over.

Getting up, the teenager joined the other two and looked shocked as he saw what they were staring at.

Laura had controlled another panic attack and sat taking deep breaths. The anxiety of not knowing what had happened and if Red had actually just shot the boy was overwhelming.

Getting up from her seat, she felt like she was in a surreal nightmare.

'This is why I can't do this kind of stuff anymore,' she said to Gareth as she headed towards the open double doors of the lifeboat station. She just needed to get out and get away. Despite knowing that Jake was on the boat, she couldn't bring herself to go back.

191

'You're going?' Gareth asked.

'I'm sorry, I just can't do this.' Her heart was still thumping and her breathing shallow.

'Anything I can do to persuade you to stay?' Gareth asked.

'No!' She pointed over to the laptop and sound equipment. 'Not after that.'

'For what it's worth, my instinct is that he didn't shoot anyone.'

'You don't know that!' she snapped.

'I don't. I might be wrong. But I pray that I'm right . . .'

Laura shrugged. 'I've got to go. I'm sorry.'

She spun on her heels and started to march away.

'Hello?' shouted a voice on the radio. It was Red.

Laura stopped in her tracks.

'I think you lot have suffered enough,' Red sneered. 'And you're fucking lucky I didn't actually kill anyone.'

What?

She looked at Gareth, who closed his eyes and let out a sigh.

Thank God!

Turning back, she looked at the microphone.

Do I leave and let Gareth deal with this? Or do I go back?

Taking a deep breath, she jogged over towards the laptop and grabbed the microphone. 'Hello?'

'And I'm glad you've seen sense,' Red said. 'By the looks of it, those boats will be here in about five minutes. And then we'll be on our way.'

She frowned at Gareth.

What the hell is he talking about?

'What boats?' Gareth asked no one in particular. 'We've got a boat arriving by road from Holyhead in about a quarter of an hour.'

Laura clicked the button on the microphone. 'Hi there. We're a bit confused. You said something about boats?'

Red gave a sarcastic laugh. 'You taking the piss, love?'

'No. I don't know what you're talking about.'

'Well, there are two speedboats heading this way,' Red explained. 'So, who the fuck's on them?'

Gareth signalled to Laura that something had occurred to him and he needed to talk to her.

'Let me just check that for you,' she said. 'Just give me a few seconds.'

Gareth looked at her. 'Is that mic off?'

Laura nodded. 'Yeah.'

'About twenty minutes before you arrived, some bloke called Gary White, whose daughter Bella is in Jake's Year 6 class, had a chat with me,' Gareth told her.

She knew exactly who he was talking about. Gary White was a flash cockney who picked up Bella from the school gates in his Bentley with a personalised plate. 'Yeah, I know who he is.'

'He claimed he had a bloke who "could handle himself". He reckoned he had two speedboats, and he wanted to drive them out to the *Anglesey Princess*, exchange one of the boats for Bella's release and bring her back.'

'Jesus! What did you say?' she asked, her eyes widening.

'I told him that there was no way he could do that,' he replied.

She gestured out to the water. 'You think it's him?'

Gareth shrugged. 'It's the only explanation.'

She pulled a face. 'Shit!' She went back to the microphone. 'Hello? *Anglesey Princess*? Hello?'

Nothing.

'Hello?'

Still nothing but static noise.

'For God's sake!' she growled.

Laura huffed. She couldn't believe that the father of one of the children was just going to take the law into his own hands, despite police warnings not to.

'Hello? *Anglesey Princess*?' she asked as she looked at Gareth.

Gareth grabbed his binoculars from the table and gestured to the open doors. They broke into a run as they came out onto the pier.

Declan sprinted towards them. 'Boss, we've got two unidentified speedboats heading directly for the *Anglesey Princess*.'

Gareth rubbed his hand over his head. 'Yeah, I know.'

'What the hell does he think he's playing at?' Laura thundered. She had no idea how Red or the rest of the gang were going to react to someone turning up and trying to trade a speedboat for their daughter. It could all go horribly wrong.

Gareth passed her the binoculars and growled. 'They're going to be there in less than a minute.'

Taking the binoculars, she soon spotted the two boats bouncing through the water.

Jesus! This is not good.

Chapter 27

The two speedboats were now only 200 yards away. From what Michael could see, there was one man driving each speedboat and they looked a lot more powerful than the RIB they had travelled from Liverpool in. Their hulls were black and red and shaped so that they cut through the water with ease.

'Bizzies don't know who they are,' Red shouted as the noise of the speedboat engines grew louder.

Callum frowned. 'What d'you mean? I thought we asked for a speedboat to get us out of here.'

Red shrugged. 'I dunno, mate. But we'll soon find out what the fuck is going on.'

Michael was looking over and listening to their conversation. Red caught his eye and glared at him. He got the feeling that Red was still angry after their tussle in the wheelhouse. Part of him was scared that Red was going to attack him at some point to get his revenge.

The two boats slowed as they reached the *Anglesey Princess*. Michael could now see the two men driving them.

One was short and well built, with a tanned bald head. He was wearing sunglasses and a thick gold chain around his neck. The man driving the other boat was younger, taller and wore a black baseball cap.

As the two boats approached, both men steered, so that they were side on to the *Anglesey Princess* and then went to fetch the mooring ropes.

The bald man looked over at them and pushed his sunglasses up onto his head. 'I hear you might be looking for a speedboat?'

Michael could hear that he had a cockney accent.

Red puffed out his chest and frowned. 'And who the fuck are you?'

'Gary,' the man said calmly. 'I'm guessing you're the man in charge here, are you?'

Red sneered at him. 'Yeah. What the fuck d'you want?'

'Well, for starters, can you put that fucking thing away? I don't like guns,' Gary said, pointing to the machine gun Red was holding. 'And then, if you tie us up to your boat, I've got a proposition for you.'

Red looked over at Callum and scratched his beard. 'What d'you think?'

Callum shrugged. 'Let's see what he says.'

Red gestured, and Gary and the other man threw their mooring ropes over. Callum and Michael took the ropes and tied them to the side. Gary grabbed a large rucksack, then stepped off the speedboat and onto the deck.

'Daddy!' came a cry. It was one of the little girls from the school.

Gary looked at her. 'Hello, sweetheart. You okay?'

She nodded from where she was sitting and blinked nervously. 'Yeah.'

'You just stay there for a second while Daddy talks to these men, eh?' Gary said with a smile.

Michael couldn't believe how calm and controlled Gary was being, given the situation they were in. It was impressive.

'She's your daughter?' Callum asked, looking confused.

'Yeah.' Gary nodded. 'And the deal is that she comes back with me and my friend in one of the speedboats. And you get to have the other one.' He patted the rucksack and put it down. 'There's a hundred grand in there. It's all I had in my safe.'

Red raised an eyebrow. 'What's stopping me shooting you both, taking the money and having two boats?'

Gary gave a huge laugh. 'Fucking hell. You've got some balls, I'll give you that, son.'

The baseball cap man pulled out a handgun and pointed it at Red.

'Oh, I didn't introduce you. This is my friend Charlie,' Gary explained. 'He used to be in the special forces. And if you piss me about, he's gonna shoot you all.'

Red scoffed. 'Is he?'

'Yeah, he is . . . Listen, mate, this isn't a dick-swinging competition,' Gary sneered. 'You give me my daughter. You get my boat and my cash. What's the problem?'

'You're the problem, *mate*,' Red growled.

Michael could see that Red was wound up, and that made him unpredictable.

'Oh yeah,' Gary smirked. 'Why's that then?'

'I hate fucking cockneys,' Red snarled, looking directly at him.

'You believe this bloke, Charlie?' Gary laughed and looked over at Charlie. 'Yeah, well, I ain't all that keen on Scousers. But I didn't come out here to make friends, so shall we get on with it, you twat?'

For a few seconds, Red just stared at Gary. Michael prayed Red didn't start shooting.

Red then looked at Michael and gestured. 'Get the girl, will you?'

'That's the spirit, eh?' Gary grinned.

Michael led Bella over to where the men were standing at the side of the boat. She wrapped her arms around Gary.

'Daddy,' she cried.

He crouched down and looked at her. 'Don't worry, sweetheart. Daddy's taking you home now.'

Red put out his hands. 'Give us the keys then, eh?'

Gary shook his head as he took Bella's hand. 'All in good time, son.'

Red pointed the gun at Bella. 'Give me the keys, dickhead, or I'll blow her head off.'

Gary dropped Bella's hand, turned and glared at Red. 'It's your lucky day today, you know that? Cos normally if anyone threatened my daughter like that, two seconds later they'd be fucking dead.'

'Oh yeah?' Red held his gaze as they locked eyes. 'Give us the keys, old man.'

Gary reached into his pocket, dangled the speedboat keys in mid-air and then dropped them on the deck. 'There you go, you prick.'

As Charlie continued to point the handgun at Red, Gary and Bella stepped off the *Anglesey Princess* and onto one of the speedboats.

Callum went over, picked up the speedboat keys and inspected them. He indicated to Red that they looked legitimate. He then went over to the rucksack and pulled out a wad of cash.

Charlie backed off the boat, still holding the handgun, and got into the speedboat. He started the engine and they pulled away.

Gary turned, took several steps down the boat and glared at Red as the speedboat turned and picked up speed.

He grinned and gave Red the finger.

CRACK!

Michael flinched at the sound of a gunshot.

He saw Gary grab his stomach, crumple into a heap and fall to the floor of the boat. The little girl screamed as she saw her father drop.

Red had shot him.

Callum spun and glared at him. 'What the fuck did you shoot him for?'

Red shrugged. 'He was a dickhead, and he was pissing me off. What do you care?'

'What if he dies? Red?' Callum snapped. 'We get done for accessory to murder!'

Red sneered. 'Well, you'd better hope he doesn't die then.'

Chapter 28

11.58 a.m.

Gareth and Laura had been watching events unfold on the *Anglesey Princess* through binoculars at the end of the pier.

'Did someone just shoot Gary White?' Laura asked. She had heard a gunshot and seen him clasp his stomach and fall.

'Yeah, I think so,' Gareth replied. 'Looks like the daughter, Bella, is okay though.'

'We need to get some paramedics on standby,' Laura said, thinking out loud.

'Yeah, I'll get someone to ring Bangor Hospital Trauma Unit and tell them they've got a victim with a gunshot wound.'

'I'll see if I can find Bella's mother so she can met her off the boat,' she said. 'She's going to be very distressed.'

'Good thinking,' Gareth said. 'And we'll need a witness statement from the guy driving the boat.'

Laura gestured out to the *Anglesey Princess* with a tentative sense of hope. 'At least now they've got a boat.'

'Don't worry. I expect them to be on the move very soon.'

'Please, God,' she said.

'Jake will be back here before you know it,' he said with the kind of confidence and certainty that made him very attractive.

Their eyes met for a second longer than was customary. Despite the tension, there was something exciting about the way their minds worked in tandem. Even though they'd never worked together before, they were incredibly in sync.

The moment was broken by a thundering noise as the black police Eurocopter hovered over Beaumaris' empty beach, throwing clouds of sand up into the air, before it slowly touched down and landed.

If you ever wanted to clear the beach of sunbathers, that would be how, Laura thought dryly to herself.

'Gold Command to all units,' Gareth said into his Tetra radio. 'We need paramedics at Beaumaris Pier as soon as possible. We have a victim with a possible gunshot wound coming ashore. Can someone alert the Bangor Hospital Trauma Unit that the victim will arrive within the hour, over?'

'Gold Command, this is Charlie Alpha. Received, over and out.'

As Laura took the binoculars again, she scanned the *Anglesey Princess* for signs of movement. Naturally, her thoughts turned to Jake. She couldn't bear to think about him being so scared out there on that boat.

'It's okay,' said a voice. 'Jake's going to be all right.'

As she put down the binoculars, she saw it was Sam. Glancing over at Gareth, she saw that he was now talking to the police helicopter pilot and briefing him on what needed to happen next.

'What are you doing down here?' she hissed.

'You do know that no one can see me, don't you?' Sam asked with a grin.

'That's not the point,' she whispered as they walked over

201

to the other side of the pier. 'I don't want people to think that I'm totally bonkers, do I? I'm talking to someone who died three years ago.'

'Okay, no need to rub it in,' Sam said. Then he gestured to Gareth. 'He fancies you, you know that, don't you?'

She rolled her eyes. 'No, he doesn't.'

'Of course he does. You saw his face when he saw that you'd come down here to help him.'

'He just thinks I'm good at what I used to do,' she argued. 'He's married anyway.'

'She's having an affair, and he's about to get divorced.'

'Legally he's still married.'

'Oh, so you would be interested, if he wasn't?' he teased her.

'No, that's not what I meant.' She sighed. 'And I don't think you're in a position to be jealous, are you?'

'What, because I'm dead?' Sam asked.

'It is a pretty major factor standing in the way of us having a proper relationship,' she commented sardonically.

'Well, why don't you ask him out then?' Sam suggested acerbically.

She didn't answer but instead looked out over the Menai Strait again and at the stationary *Anglesey Princess*. She wondered if Sam would disappear if she ignored him.

'I have an idea,' Sam piped up.

'Oh good,' she quipped.

'Why don't you try his mobile phone?' he suggested.

Laura frowned. 'What?'

'Why don't you try Jake's mobile phone?'

Shit! Why didn't I think of that?

'I'm guessing that the gang will have taken them,' she said.

'What if they didn't?' he asked. 'Or what if Jake just didn't hand it over? If you FaceTime him, he wouldn't have to speak. You could just see him, and check that he was okay?'

202

She agreed. It had to be worth a shot, she thought.

'I'll do it in a minute,' she snapped impatiently.

'If you do speak to him, tell him that I love him,' Sam said with a growing sadness in his eyes.

'He knows you love him,' she stated with a benign smile.

'Laura?' said a voice.

This time it was Gareth.

He pointed over to the beach where several police officers were manoeuvring a large RIB, with NORTH WALES POLICE written on the side, into the sea.

'Bloody hell! It's too late now.' Laura sounded exasperated. 'They've already got a boat. Now what do we do?'

Gareth gestured out to the *Anglesey Princess*. 'We have to see what their next move is going to be.'

Red, Callum and Michael had agreed it was time to leave the *Anglesey Princess* and make their escape. Having checked the Strait, they had concluded that there were no police launches or boats in the vicinity.

Swaggering out to the middle of the deck, Red looked at all the passengers with a twisted smile. He was clearly enjoying the feeling of power.

He's such a prick, Michael thought to himself.

'Okay, everyone. Listen up!' Red barked loudly, making the passengers flinch. 'I've got some good news and some bad news.' Red looked over at Callum and Michael. 'Good news is that me and my associates here are going to leave the boat now. And I'm guessing it won't be long before you're all rescued and taken to shore.' Red then pulled a face. 'The bad news is that we're gonna need to take a couple of you with us, just for insurance purposes. We don't want the police blowing us out of the water, so I need to pick the lucky two who get to come with us.'

A man in his sixties, who was sitting beside his wife, stood up and looked over. 'I'll come with you. I don't want you taking women and children.'

Red glared at him. 'Yeah, sit the fuck down, *Iron Man*.'

Out of nowhere, Michael heard a mobile phone ringing. Then it vibrated in his pocket. It was the phone he had taken from Jake, the nervous, spiky-haired boy in the United shirt sitting with his teacher Beth.

With his teeth gritted, Red sneered as he looked around. 'Who the fuck's got a mobile phone?'

Looking terrified, the passengers urgently checked bags and pockets, or shook their heads to signal that it didn't belong to them.

'It's me,' Michael said to Red. 'I took it off one of the kids. I just forgot to put it in the bin bag, that's all.'

Red held out his hand as Michael took it from his pocket. 'Yeah, well, give it here, will ya?'

Looking at the screen, Michael could see a woman was FaceTiming Jake, and it read '*Mummy*'. However, in the background, behind the woman, it looked like there were police officers.

Red snatched the phone from him and looked down. Pointing it down to the floor, so that the caller couldn't see anything, he pressed the answer button.

'Hello?' whispered a female voice. 'Jake?'

Silence.

'Jake? If you're okay, just give me a signal, like a thumbs-up, to tell me you're okay,' the female voice said. 'Listen, you're going to be okay. I promise you'll be back here with me very soon.'

'Hello?' Red said.

'Hello, who is that?' said the female voice. 'Who am I talking to?'

Red frowned. 'Laura?'

'Yeah, who is this, please?' the voice asked.

Red took the phone, covered the camera with his finger so she couldn't see him, and smirked. 'I thought I recognised your voice. This is perfect. So, your son Jake is on this boat, Laura? Small bloody world, eh?'

Silence.

'I wondered what you looked like. You're older than I thought you were.'

'Please, don't hurt him,' she pleaded.

'Don't worry. Jake is just going to come on a little trip with us. And as long as we get away safely, little Jakey boy is going to be fine. So, I'll say bye-bye for now.' Red ended the call, turned and threw the mobile phone into the water.

Michael went over to Jake, who looked frightened and confused. Crouching down, he looked at him. 'Listen, Jake, you see that speedboat over there?'

Jake stood up so he could see over the side of the boat. He nodded.

'Well, you're going to come with us in the speedboat,' Michael whispered. He didn't want him to be frightened. 'But you're gonna be fine. Honest, mate.'

Jake shook his head. 'I don't want to.'

Beth looked at Michael. 'I'm coming with him then.'

'There you go, mate. Your teacher's coming with you.' Michael gave Jake a wink. 'Does that make it better, mate?'

Jake nodded.

Red approached and snapped, 'Come on. We need to get going.'

Michael indicated Beth, 'She's coming, too. She's the kid's teacher.'

'Make no difference to me.' Red shrugged and then gave Beth a lecherous grin. 'In fact, it might be fun having you on board.'

Michael promised himself that if Red laid a hand on Beth, he would kill him.

Moving over to the side of the boat, Michael gestured for Jake and Beth to follow him across the deck and climb down into the speedboat.

Suddenly, a voice boomed, 'You're not going anywhere with those two!'

A man in his sixties, with a greying beard and hair, appeared from over by a hatch beside the wheelhouse. He was covered in sweat and holding a pistol.

Where the hell did he come from? Michael thought. *And what the hell is he doing?*

'Who the fuck are you?' Red thundered.

'Never mind that,' the man growled. 'I want you off this boat. But you're not taking anyone with you.'

Red laughed. 'Is that a flare gun, old man?'

'Yeah,' the man nodded, 'and if I fire it into your face, it'll burn you to death. So, get into the boat, go and leave us all in peace.'

Red sighed and shook his head. 'You know what, old man? You're very brave. But you're also very stupid.'

There were several tense seconds and they looked at each other.

Michael was frightened. He didn't want all hell to break loose on the boat. And he wasn't keen on taking Jake and Beth with them.

'I'm not going to tell you again,' the man growled. 'Get in that boat and go crawl back under whatever rock you came from.'

'That's not very nice.' Red twisted a sneer. 'You should be careful how to talk to people.'

In a flash, Red pulled up the gun and, before the man could react, shot him in the top of his arm.

CRACK!

The man reeled backwards, dropped the flare gun and crashed to the deck, holding his shoulder.

'Jesus Christ!' Steve exclaimed as he rushed over to him.

'Come on, let's get onto the boat and get the fuck out of here!' Red bellowed as waved his gun towards Beth and Jake, ushering them onto the speedboat.

Michael jumped down into the boat and turned to give Beth and Jake a helping hand down.

Walking over to the steering wheel, Red took the speedboat keys, turned on the ignition and revved the engine.

He pulled down the throttle, the boat lurched, and they sped away.

Chapter 29

12.11 p.m.

Standing by the end of the pier, Laura had been overwhelmed by the FaceTime call she had just had with Red. If only she hadn't given into Sam's suggestion to FaceTime Jake, he might well have been left on the boat with the rest of his class. Once the gang had left the *Anglesey Princess*, Jake would have been safely returned to her. Now he was a hostage with a dangerous gang heading to Liverpool on a speedboat.

Gareth approached, looking uncomfortable. He gestured to the mobile phone that was still in her hand. 'After that call, I'd understand if you want to go.'

Fuck that! She wasn't going to sit around and wait for others to get her son back.

'Go?' she snapped. 'I'm not going anywhere until I get Jake back. And I'll do anything to make that happen.'

'Of course. Whatever you need to do.' Gareth seemed relieved that she wasn't leaving. He pointed to the beach. 'The helicopter is ready to scramble as soon as we see them make a move from the boat. We can follow them all the way.' He put a reassuring hand on her shoulder. 'We're not going to let Jake out of our sights, okay?'

She got a little tingle from the touch of his hand on her. Maybe Sam was right? Maybe he was attracted to her? And maybe she liked the idea?

'Boss?' Andrea said, approaching them. She pointed out to the Strait over to the right of the pier. 'The launches have arrived from Holyhead.'

Two police launches, with blue and yellow paintwork and the word POLICE on the side, honed into view. They were still quite some way from shore and even further than the *Anglesey Princess*.

'Too late,' Gareth grumbled.

'Why are they *too late*?' Laura asked with a frown. She thought that having two police launches nearby would be a good thing.

'Now they've got a speedboat, there's no point trying to pursue them on one of those,' he explained. 'They've got a top speed of about 15 knots, which in layman's terms is about the same in miles per hour. That Scarab speedboat can do 80 knots. It would leave them for dead.'

'You know a lot about boats?' Laura remarked.

'I'm from Beaumaris. I grew up around boats.' He looked at Andrea. 'Once the gang have made their move and are away safely, we're going to have a rescue operation on our hands. There's nearly sixty passengers and crew that we need to get from the *Anglesey Princess* back to shore safely. Can you liaise with the launches so that they're on stand by to pick up passengers when we tell them to?'

Andrea nodded, 'Will do, boss.'

Grabbing his binoculars, Gareth moved forward and peered towards the boat. Then he turned to Laura. 'They're off.'

'What?'

'They're in the speedboat and moving away from the boat,' he said, handing her the binoculars.

'Is Jake with them?' Laura asked as she looked anxiously across the water.

Gareth looked at her. 'I couldn't see.' He grabbed his radio. 'Gold Command to all units, suspects are leaving the vessel. I repeat, suspects are leaving the vessel. Proceed, over.'

'Alpha Zero to Gold Command, received,' said the helicopter pilot. 'Stand by.'

The thunderous engines and the central propeller of the helicopter started.

Gareth looked at Laura with a curious expression. 'I've got an idea. Come with me.'

'Where are we going?' she asked.

'We need to go quickly,' he said, not answering her question.

Gareth broke into a run, and she had no choice but to follow him.

What the hell are we doing?

At the end of the pier, he ducked under tape and headed left across the beach. It was hot, and she was getting out of breath.

'Where are we going?' she repeated, but the whining sound of the helicopter was now deafening and drowned out her shout. It threw clouds of sand up into the air as it waited for its central propeller to get up to full speed.

As she reached Gareth, who was standing by the water's edge, she could see that he was looking at something else.

The black police RIB that was bobbing around in the shallow water.

'We're taking that!' Gareth shouted over the growing noise.

'What?' she asked.

'Come on,' he yelled as he waded into the water towards the RIB.

210

Jesus Christ!

Striding into the sea, she could feel the icy water on her feet and then her legs. What a surreal thought it was that she had been swimming in this very stretch of water nearly six hours earlier.

Jumping into the boat, Gareth turned and put out his hand. A moment later, she reached him and he pulled her into the boat.

'You know how to drive one of these?' she shouted about an inch from his ear.

The helicopter was now twenty feet above the beach.

Gareth yelled back, 'Of course.'

Marching forward, he looked at the steering wheel and throttle. He turned the key, the engine burst into life and he pulled down the throttle. The RIB lurched forward at speed, knocking her off balance.

As they hurtled past the pier, he clicked his radio. 'Gold Command to all units. I am currently in pursuit of suspects in target vessel, over.'

'Sierra three-six to Gold Command. Received, over. Will advise.'

Moving up the boat, and clinging to the side for dear life, Laura looked at Gareth.

'Let's not lose these bastards,' Gareth shouted over the noise of the engines. 'And make sure we get your son.'

'Yes,' she said. 'Yes.'

There was something incredibly attractive about the way Gareth had taken charge of the situation. And about the way he stood holding the speedboat steering wheel as he skilfully manoeuvred through the waves.

He's incredibly sexy, she thought.

Beth could taste the salt water in her mouth as the spray washed over her. She had her arms around Jake, who hadn't

211

said a word since they had got onto the boat. She was trying to work out how this was going to play out. She assumed the gang were going to take the speedboat to somewhere in Liverpool Docks. They would be met by other members of the gang who would help them escape, leaving Beth and Jake dockside. She prayed that there was no reason for them to come to any harm, although the police helicopter which had hovered over them five minutes earlier had certainly rattled the gang members.

Jake stretched out a finger and pointed to a tattoo on her forearm. It was a green shamrock with the word *Athair* written underneath. She had had the tattoo done four years ago when her father, Liam, had died. She and her brother Shaun had gone to Anglesey Ink in Holyhead to get them done together. Shaun was only sixteen at the time, but he had fake ID. To be honest, Beth was sure that the tattoo place wasn't particularly fussed.

'It's a shamrock,' Beth told him as they bumped along in the speedboat. Jake frowned but didn't say anything. 'It's a plant, just like clover. You know, like a four-leafed clover?'

Jake moved as he looked at her. 'Oh, yeah.'

'But it's also a symbol of Ireland,' she said.

Looking at Jake, she realised how much he reminded her of Shaun when he was younger. She thought of Shaun, aged eleven. The way he would work at the kitchen table with his head bowed, tongue between his lips, as he did his homework. He always hummed when he did maths, and he would sing out loud while writing stories or drawing, especially when he suspected that no one was listening. 'I Got A Feeling' by The Black-Eyed Peas was his favourite. He used to sing it on a loop for hours.

'What's it for?' he asked, looking at her tattoo.

'I had it done for my dad. You see this word here, *Athair*? It's Celtic for "father".'

212

'What's Celtic?' he asked.

'It's the language they speak in Ireland.'

'Is it like Welsh, then?'

For a second, she was caught off-guard. Jake had spoken hardly at all while she had taught him in Year 6. And he had probably only asked three or four questions the whole year.

What a time to come out of himself, she thought.

She smiled at him. 'Yes, it's very similar to Welsh.'

'So it's like "tad" for "dad" then?'

Beth was glad it was compulsory for Welsh Primary Schools to teach Welsh to children as she believed it was an important part of their culture and heritage.

She nodded. 'Yes, just like tad.'

'Does he like it, then?' he asked.

Beth frowned. 'Sorry?'

'Does your dad like the tattoo you had done for him?'

She took a second before answering. 'I'm afraid he died when I was younger. I had the tattoo done in memory of him, so he never got to see it. But I'm sure he would like it.'

'That's like my dad,' Jake said.

She gave him a benign smile. 'Yes, I know . . . You must miss him?'

'Yeah. My mum still talks to him. She thinks me and my sister can't hear her. Rosie says that my mum is bonkers.'

'I suppose she just misses him. And if she talks to him, he can probably hear what she's saying.'

Callum frowned and walked down the speedboat towards the back, where Beth and Jake were sitting. For a moment, she was scared.

What the hell does he want?

Then she saw he wasn't looking at them at all. He had his eyes fixed on something on the water behind them.

Beth turned. Although it was quite a long way away, she

could see that there was a RIB following them along the Strait.

Callum pointed to it and shouted back to Red and Michael. 'Looks like we've got company.'

Chapter 30

Now they were out in the middle of the Menai Strait, Gareth rapidly built up speed and Laura could feel the power of the RIB's enormous engine as they hit 80 knots. She gripped a thick rubber handle, which was attached to the gunwale on the starboard side, with one hand and the seat in front of her with the other as the RIB smashed through the water.

She sat forward a little, peering through the spray. 'Where are you, you bastards?'

The Scarab speedboat was still a long way ahead – more than half a mile.

But they were closing.

The RIB hit a wave and left the water for a second before slamming back down with a violent jolt.

Gareth took a quick look at her. 'You've gone white.'

'Not a big fan of speedboats, if I'm honest,' she admitted as her stomach lurched.

They went hammering past a large, moored yacht, which flashed by.

The Scarab speedboat was getting closer – they were gaining.

Gareth pulled left as they sped between two enormous orange buoys.

She was trying to work out what they were going to do if they caught them up. The main thing was to keep them in sight. She didn't want the gang members disappearing with Jake.

Gareth grabbed his Tetra radio. 'Gold Command to all units. We are heading east along the Menai Straights. We have Penmon Point due north from here and Puffin Island north-north-east. We have visual on target vessel, range just over 500 yards, over.'

'Gold Command, this is Alpha Zero. Received, over.'

'We're not letting them get away,' he said with a steely determination, dropping the throttle to increase the revs.

She knew that Red and the gang wouldn't stop and would be driven on by fear and adrenaline.

Two minutes later, they screamed past the coastline of Puffin Island. They were going so fast, a huge spray of water momentarily blinded Laura.

The RIB was now only 500 yards away.

As she looked up, she could see there was a small gap between Trwyn Du Lighthouse and the rocky cliffs at the southern tip of Puffin Island.

The Scarab speedboat zipped through the gap and disappeared around the eastern edge of the tiny island.

Shit! We've lost them.

Gareth wasn't for slowing down as they came hurtling towards the gap.

Then it occurred to her. The police RIB they were travelling in was significantly wider than the Scarab speedboat!

Oh my God! We're going to crash into the rocks!

Her eyes widened with alarm – there just wasn't enough space to get through.

Gareth dropped down the throttle and the engine roared uncomfortably.

She closed her eyes and held her breath.

Please God, I don't want to die!

They made it past the rocks with centimetres to spare.

'Shit! That was seriously close!' he yelled as he stared fiercely ahead, searching for where the Scarab speedboat had gone.

Laura spotted it off to the left, close to the Puffin Island coastline. 'There!' she bellowed. 'Just don't lose them!'

If they lost the speedboat, they might get to Liverpool and go into hiding somewhere.

Suddenly, a fishing boat came from behind a stack of rocks and moved directly into their path.

Gareth swung the RIB hard left.

Laura held on for dear life as everything in the RIB slid violently to the left of the boat.

For a moment, she wondered if they were going to flip over and capsize.

'Bloody hell!' Gareth shouted, as he straightened the wheel and the RIB righted itself with a crash.

There was a thunderous noise from above.

Laura looked up to the sky to see the dark shadow of the police Eurocopter flying overhead. The wind from its propeller whipped her hair into her face.

The Eurocopter shot past them and was soon above the Scarab speedboat, which had put more distance between them again. The Eurocopter hovered over them for a few seconds before ascending and looping away.

'Alpha Zero to Gold Command, are you receiving, over?' came a voice on Gareth's radio. It was the helicopter pilot.

'Gold Command to Alpha Zero, go ahead, over,' Gareth said.

'Visual contact with target vessel and suspects. Confirm

217

there are three male suspects on target vessel, along with two hostages, one female and one male child, over.'

Laura looked at Gareth.

Who is the female hostage?

Could it be Beth Hughes, Jake's Year 6 teacher? Jake had a soft spot for her and being with her might allay his fears a little.

'Gold Command to Alpha Zero, received. Stand by,' Gareth said.

Out of the corner of her eye, she spotted something moving. It was way out to the right, almost on the horizon.

She squinted. It looked like several boats heading in their direction.

Reaching over to the seats in front of her, she grabbed Gareth's binoculars.

Focusing, she couldn't believe her eyes.

Three enormous Royal Navy attack RIBs were crashing through the water towards them. Inside each craft, she could see six men in combat uniform, helmets and body armour, carrying firearms.

On the side of each RIB was a white flag with a red cross and Union Jack in its corner, and the words ROYAL MARINES.

Oh, my God. Now that's what I call back-up!

'Gareth! Gareth!' she yelled, handing him the binoculars and pointing at what she had seen.

Grabbing them, Gareth slowed the RIB for a second, peered towards the horizon, and then looked back at her.

'Bingo!' he exclaimed, as his face brightened a little. 'Here comes the bloody cavalry. Thank you, HMS *Queen Elizabeth*!'

Callum was now sitting at the back of the speedboat. He was keeping a close eye on whoever was following them. It was still too far away to see anything except that it was a black RIB.

Beth then saw Callum race across to the right-hand side of the speedboat. Using his hand to shield his eyes from the sun, he peered across the water towards the Welsh mainland.

'What is it?' Red shouted.

'Look!' Callum yelled as he pointed.

Shifting in her seat, Beth turned right and squinted.

There were three small boats speeding through the water and heading their way.

Michael turned to look as well and pulled a face. 'Shit!'

Beth looked at Michael and gestured to the boats that were coming their way. 'Who is it?'

Michael looked blank. 'Not the police.'

Red had slowed the boat so that he could leave the steering wheel and get a proper look.

'Who the fuck is that?' Callum thundered.

'They've got Royal Navy flags,' Red growled.

'What does that mean?' Michael asked.

Red gave him a withering look. 'It means that they're not the bizzies for starters.'

Callum frowned. 'So, they're soldiers?'

Red shook his head. 'No. It's the Royal Navy, you dickhead. And that means they're Royal fucking Marines.'

Taking in what they were saying, Beth could feel herself tense. If three boats of Royal Marines were heading their way, did that mean they were going to get rescued? But Red and Callum had guns. The thought of a terrible gun battle made her shiver with fear.

'Fuck that!' Callum pointed to Beth and Jake. 'We've got them on board. They're not going to do anything.'

Red had a face like thunder. 'Don't be a dickhead. They could have a couple of marksmen with them with laser sights.

219

And within thirty seconds of them getting within a hundred yards, we've got bullet holes between our eyes.'

It was the first time since Red had got onto the boat that she had seen him remotely rattled.

'What do we do then?' Michael asked.

Red cranked up the throttle and pointed left towards the shore of Anglesey. 'We find a different way of getting back to Liverpool.'

Chapter 31

1.02 p.m.

Fifteen minutes later, Red guided the Scarab speedboat towards the flat sandy beach on the north-eastern coast of the island. Although the water was shallow, it had a green hue due to the prevalence of seaweed. They were close to Traeth Coch, which translated meant 'red beach', although the English named the area Red Wharf Bay.

As the wind picked up, Michael steadied himself on the side of the boat, took hold of the rope mooring line that was attached to a steel cleat, and jumped into the sea. The water was freezing and came up to his knees. There wasn't time to think about how uncomfortable it was or that his new hundred-pound Nike trainers were now full of sea-water. They were being chased.

Callum leapt into the shallow water on the other side of the boat. Taking the thick rope of the mooring line, Michael walked backwards as he and Callum pulled the boat until its hull scraped onto the sand and then rested on a seaweed-strewn dune. The air was salty and thick with the pungent smell of the shiny caramel-coloured seaweed that lay like thick noodles in the shallow water.

Reaching up, Michael helped Beth and Jake off the boat and onto the wet sandy ground.

They were in a cove and this made it impossible to see how close the Royal Marine boats or the police RIB were. Either way, Michael knew they had to get moving – and fast.

'Come on, come on,' Red growled impatiently at Beth and Jake.

Looking around, Michael spotted a steep pathway that led from the beach upwards towards the clifftops.

'Over here,' he said, leading the way.

The group trekked up the beginnings of a footpath that dropped by uneven steps. A tangle of flowering shrubs and trees clung to the steep bank on either side, interspersed with large weeds with swollen stalks and dark, thick-veined leaves. A cluster of huge gulls soared on the wind currents above, cawing loudly as if they were discussing the strangers that had just arrived on the beach.

The pathway was steep but dry. As they got towards the top, dotted around the rocks were the small white flowers of the mouse ear plant. Further along, buckler fern, sea-lavender and juniper bushes bordered the path.

Michael turned to check that Beth and Jake were okay and able to climb the pathway. He saw Red was at the back, holding the Skorpion machine gun at his side. Callum was next, carrying the Puma sports bag over his shoulder and the rucksack with Gary White's money. Beth stopped for a moment, uncertain where to put her foot next.

'Get a fucking move on!' Red snarled.

Michael leaned down, gave her his hand and pulled her up. 'Here you go.' He gave Red a withering look as they locked eyes for a second.

'Thanks,' she said as she got her balance.

Michael reached down and pulled Jake up onto the same section of the pathway. 'Here you go, Jake.'

Turning, he continued up the last hundred yards until the bracken cleared and the path reached its end. They were now on top of the cliffs, looking out across the sea on both sides. To the north, the sea swept endlessly into the distance, the next land being the Isle of Man nearly 200 miles away. The wind was powerful and noisy as it whipped around him with a deep groan.

Covering his eyes from the sun, Michael glanced back at the Menai Strait where they had come from. The police RIB was speeding along the coast to the beach where they had landed. About 200 yards behind them were the three Royal Marine attack boats. His stomach tightened – how were they going to get away?

'Shit!' Red growled as he looked in the same direction. He then pointed inland and barked, 'Get a move on!'

There was a narrow pathway across the clifftop that led towards an old wooden stile and gate beside a single-track road.

Marching at a fast pace, Michael led the way. He knew that if they were going to make their escape, they needed some form of transport. He had seen enough programmes on the telly to know they weren't going to outrun Royal Marines across country. And even if they had a car, how were they going to get off Anglesey undetected? Surely every police officer in North Wales would be looking for them?

They arrived at the stile. Grabbing the wooden rail, Michael swung his leg over the gate and jumped down the other side. Beth and Jake followed.

Suddenly, the air was filled with a deep, thunderous noise.

Shit! Police helicopter!

Red and Callum reacted, pushing them all against the hedgerow.

'Get down!' Callum shouted as he looked skyward.

The helicopter flew past and then hovered behind them over the clifftop and the beach they had arrived on.

'Now they know where we landed.' Red pointed with a grimace. 'Up here!'

They continued down the narrow country lane, which was flanked by high hedges and undergrowth on either side. Hawthorn was entwined with dogwood and honeysuckle, which had attracted Welsh Black honeybees and orange-tip butterflies.

Michael was thinking that he was pretty sure he'd never been in such a remote area in his whole life when a ramshackle white farmhouse became visible about a hundred yards up on the right-hand side.

Red and Callum exchanged a look.

As they approached, Michael could see the farmhouse was wide, with storage sheds and dark wooden outbuildings. Half a dozen chickens pecked at the dirt. The air smelt of straw and freshly cut grass. There were clothes hanging up on the line and a radio was playing classical music from somewhere inside.

Someone was definitely home.

Parked to one side was an old, navy blue Land Rover Discovery that was streaked with mud. Beyond that were two old red tractors and some other farming equipment.

Red turned to everyone, narrowed his eyes and put his finger to his lips. He then looked at Callum and gestured over to the Land Rover.

Callum walked gingerly across the yard, cupped his hands and looked inside the car. Michael assumed he was looking to see if the keys were still in the ignition. He looked over at Red and shook his head. They weren't.

'Can I help you?' asked a voice. A woman in her sixties, carrying a basket of washing, appeared from a side door. She frowned at them with a baffled expression. She had short, neat grey hair and thin disapproving lips.

'It's all right, love,' Callum said calmly. 'We're not gonna hurt you.'

She spotted Red was carrying the Skorpion machine gun at his side. She dropped the washing basket to the floor as her eyes widened in fear. 'Oh my God!'

As she moved backwards, Red looked at her with contempt. 'We're just going to take your car, that's all.'

'Frank!' she screamed. 'Frank!'

'Jesus!' Red thundered.

Moving swiftly towards her, Callum put his hand over her mouth and put her in a neck lock.

'Leave her alone!' Beth snapped loudly.

Red stepped forward and put the gun to Beth's head. 'Make another noise and I'll shoot you, you bitch!'

Michael bristled. He hated to see Beth looking so scared.

'Take the gun from her head,' Michael growled, looking Red directly in the eyes.

Red frowned. 'What did you say?'

'Take the gun from her head,' Michael snapped.

Before Red had time to respond, there was a noise from over by one of the sheds.

'Right, dickhead, make sure these two don't go anywhere,' Red barked at Michael as he set off for the sheds with his gun now in both hands.

Michael looked at Beth. 'It's gonna be okay.'

'Is it?' she hissed angrily and gestured to the yard. 'How is any of this okay?'

She brought Jake closer to her and put her hands protectively on his shoulders.

'Mary?' shouted a man's voice from somewhere over by sheds. 'Mary, are you all right?'

A man in his late sixties appeared from behind the tractors. It was Frank, and he was carrying a shotgun. His wrinkled face dropped when he saw Callum had Mary in a headlock and his hand over her mouth.

'Let her go!' he thundered, as he marched forwards.

From out of nowhere, Red crept up behind Frank and pushed the muzzle of the gun into the back of his head. 'Drop the shotgun, Grandad.'

Frank didn't react for a few seconds.

'Don't do anything stupid. Otherwise, he's gonna break her neck,' Red said. 'And then I'm going to blow your brains out.'

Frank put the shotgun slowly down onto the ground. 'What do you want?'

'Anyone else here?' Red asked.

Frank shook his head and replied calmly, 'No. It's just the two of us.'

Red moved from behind Frank and kept the gun trained on him. 'My mate and your wife are going to go inside. I want the keys to that car, a mobile phone and any cash in the house. Okay?'

Frank looked over to Mary and gave her a reassuring look. 'Do as he says, Mary. It's all right.'

'Callum?' Red said.

Callum looked over.

'If there's a landline, cut the wire. Don't want these two calling the bizzies two seconds after we've left.'

There was a tense silence as Callum and Mary went inside.

Frank frowned as he looked over at Michael, Beth and Jake. 'You're from that boat that was hijacked, aren't you? It was on the radio.'

Red smirked. 'No comment.'

Callum appeared holding the car keys, a mobile phone, cash and a bottle of whisky. 'We're good to go, mate.' Tossing the car keys to Red, he looked over at Michael, Beth and Jake. 'Come on. We're going.'

Chapter 32

3 April 2019

Laura was in the middle of composing a text message to Pete. She had managed to track down the switchboard operator at Trafford Police Station who had answered the call on 12 August 2018 – the day Sam had been killed at Brannings Warehouse. Her name was Mandy Cooper. A little more digging revealed that she was thirty-five years old, married with two children and lived in Longsight, about three miles south of Manchester city centre. However, she had also left the Manchester Metropolitan Police Force at the end of September 2018 – only six weeks after events at Brannings Warehouse. Laura couldn't find out why, but she thought it was strange in terms of timing.

Pete had agreed that it would be useful to speak to Mandy as she was the person that answered the call reporting suspicious activity at Brannings Warehouse at 9.12 a.m. Laura and Pete had discovered that call was made from a burner phone inside Trafford Police Station. What they didn't know was whether Mandy was aware of that. Did she remember the call or anything about the person who had made it?

Laura had made the decision to go and speak to Mandy and she wanted to know if Pete would meet her there. Pressing the send button, she watched as the text disappeared.

Something knocked against her foot, distracting her. She spotted the small bundle of caramel fur scampering around on the rug and smiled. Elvis was an eight-week-old puppy who looked more like a beautiful teddy bear than a dog. He stopped in front of her and cocked his head with an adorable, curious expression. She thought he was the most delightful creature she had ever seen.

Jake had been asking about getting a puppy for the last few months and she knew how excited he would be when he got home and found Elvis waiting for him. The idea of a Mountain Mastiff dog called Elvis had originally been Sam and Jake's idea, but she had vetoed it. Too big, too slobbery and too much hair. But she hoped that getting Elvis now might allow Jake to still feel connected to his father. She knew that her son was still struggling to come to terms with Sam's death.

'I can't believe it!' said a voice. It was Sam, and he was shaking his head.

'What?' She shrugged innocently. She knew exactly what he was going to say.

Sam gestured pointedly. 'So, Elvis is in the building?'

'I know,' she cooed. 'He's sooo cute, isn't he?'

'Yes, he is. But aren't you forgetting something?' he asked with a raised eyebrow.

'Sorry?' she asked with a rueful smile. She was teasing Sam. 'What have I forgotten?'

'That's my dog,' he exclaimed. 'I mean, that's the dog I wanted.'

'You sound like a spoilt child, Sam!'

'I'm just trying to point out the irony, that's all,' he snorted with an apologetic smile.

'If I remember correctly, you only decided you wanted a dog like this when you saw some terrible film with Mark Wahlberg where he lived up in the mountains and shared a bottle of beer with his mountain dog, which I believe was actually called Sam?'

Sam shrugged. '*Shooter* is not a terrible film, actually.'

'Really?' she huffed, raising an eyebrow. 'And you need to remember that Jake wanted this dog too.'

'I know that . . . It just seems a bit tight that I had to die for you to allow a dog like that into the family home,' he grumbled. 'You can see why I might be miffed.'

'Sorry.' She pulled an apologetic face. 'But I can't wait to see Jake's face when he gets home from school.'

Sam smiled. 'I know. He's going to be so excited.'

'It's like your shoes,' she said.

Sam frowned. 'What's like my shoes?'

'I used to complain all the time about the fact that you left your big size-eleven shoes all over the house. You'd take them off wherever you sat down and then leave them there. It drove me mad.'

'I know it did. But you've kind of lost me there, kid.'

'And now I sit here and I would give anything to see your bloody huge size-eleven shoes lying on the floor beside the sofa.' A lump came to her throat, and she blinked. 'Or anywhere, come to think of it. And I hate myself for having been so uptight about it.'

'So you got a dog?' Sam asked sarcastically.

'You know what I mean. You're being facetious, Sam,' she moaned. 'I should have let you and Jake have that dog in the first place.'

'Hah, so you admit it?' he said triumphantly.

'Yes, you win. Well done.' She sighed. 'God, I forgot you were so bloody competitive.'

'You even went for naming him Elvis?'

'That's what you and Jake agreed on, wasn't it?' she asked with a frown. 'I didn't even know you like Elvis.'

'Yes, you did,' Sam protested. 'I sang "Suspicious Minds" to you in that karaoke bar in Leeds once.'

'Oh, yeah. And it wasn't even that bad,' she remembered. 'Except for the excessive thrusting.'

Sam laughed. 'My dad loved Elvis. He had all the old records. Me and my brother once counted them. He had forty-seven Elvis albums. He loved the whole fifties rock'n'roll era.'

'I think I favour Elvis in a leather suit, for obvious reasons,' she responded with a cheeky grin.

'I loved the seventies. Cool sunglasses, bling jewellery, shooting TVs, popping pills and dying on the toilet,' Sam said. 'As an allegory, it was a perfect story of the failure of the American Dream.'

'Thanks. I didn't need a lecture on the cultural significance of Elvis Presley,' Laura scoffed. 'Just why we've called our dog after him.'

There was a noise from the front door and the familiar sound of Rosie and Jake coming in, kicking off their shoes, hanging up their coats and then running down the hallway.

Laura smiled as Jake skidded into the living room in his socks on the polished wooden floor and looked at her. He looked suitably dishevelled.

'How was school?' she asked him.

He shrugged. 'Good. Have we got any crisps?'

'We've got a visitor, Jake,' she said, pointing to the puppy, who headed over to see him. 'Meet Elvis.'

'Oh, wow!' Jake's eyes widened in utter excitement. Dropping to his knees, he put his hand out gingerly to stroke Elvis' tiny, fluffy head.

'What do you think?' she asked.

'He's perfect,' Jake said as he ran his fingers through his fur.

She looked over to where Sam had been sitting – but he had gone.

She wondered when she would be ready to let Sam finally go. If she was honest, it felt too frightening to be without the version of Sam she still had in her life. She'd be lost without him. The simple answer was, *One day, but not yet.*

Her phone buzzed with a text. It was from Pete.

Hi Laura. Yes, let me know when you're going to see Mandy Cooper and I'll meet you there. Hope you and the kids are okay? How's Elvis? Pete x

Chapter 33

Laura was sitting opposite Frank and Mary at their kitchen table. They both looked very shaken as they recounted what had happened. It had been fifteen minutes since Laura and Gareth had spotted the speedboat, landed on the beach of Red Wharf Bay and followed the group's most likely route inland. The Royal Marines had been in contact. Given that they had no vehicles on Anglesey, there was very little they could do to help the search, so they had returned to HMS *Queen Elizabeth*. Having come across the farmhouse, Laura and Gareth had knocked to see if anyone had seen anything or anyone coming past.

Laura cast her eye around the hundred-year-old farmhouse, a sprawling, higgledy-piggledy building that had been added to at regular intervals. It was clear they had applied nothing more than the obligatory slap of cream paint in decades. Tired net curtains hung at the streaked windows. There was a slight sag in the ceiling between the two wooden beams which bisected the room. There was a strong smell of clean washing and fabric softener. A Welsh dresser stood in the corner with a collection of commemorative china. A plate with a photo of Princess Diana at its centre and the dates '1961–1997' caught her eye for a second.

'There was a woman in her twenties. She had a young boy with her,' Frank said.

Laura's ears pricked up immediately. 'How did they seem?' she asked.

'Very frightened.'

Mary blinked and then gave a slight nod. 'They were scared. Not surprising.'

Laura couldn't imagine what it must be like to be only eleven years old and going through all that Jake had witnessed today. Just thinking about it overwhelmed her. She wanted him to be in her arms and safe. She would give anything for that.

Gareth came into the kitchen and took out his notepad. 'Can we have the registration and make of the car that was stolen, Mr Greaves?'

'Of course.' Frank nodded with an expression that showed he was eager to help. 'It's a 2005 navy Land Rover Discovery. DT05 BRV.'

'Thank you,' Gareth said. 'That's very helpful.'

'Can you show us where it was parked?' Laura asked, getting up and re-focusing herself. Any scrap of evidence could be vital. She remembered once finding a screwed-up till receipt that had fallen out of the trousers of a burglar in a car he had stolen and then abandoned.

Frank got up and showed them the way.

Gareth clicked his Tetra radio as they came out into bright sunshine in the dusty yard. 'Gold Command to all units. Suspects are now travelling in a navy-coloured Land Rover Discovery. Licence Delta Tango zero five, Bravo, Romeo, Victor. I repeat, suspects are now travelling in a navy-coloured Land Rover Discovery. Licence Delta Tango zero five, Bravo,

Romeo, Victor. Last known position is Red Wharf Bay. They are possibly travelling south on the A5205, over.'

'Gold Command, this is Charlie Alpha, received, over,' came the reply from the helicopter pilot. Gareth wandered away from them and continued to talk into the radio.

Frank gestured to where the Land Rover had been parked and Laura crouched down to take a look. There were scuffs and tyre marks in the dry dirt. Then she saw the pattern of a small trainer print, about a size four. It had to be Jake's footprint. For a second, she was engulfed with emotion. Taking a deep breath, she stood up and steadied herself.

Gareth marched across, looked at her and said very quietly, 'Are you okay?'

She nodded and gestured. 'I saw Jake's trainer print and it just got to me for a moment.'

'Of course it did.' He put a reassuring hand on her arm and looked at her. 'I know I keep saying it, but we're getting him back safely. I promise you that.'

'Thank you,' she said, snapping herself out it. 'Right, what do we need to do?'

'We may need to close the bridges off the island. I've contacted North Wales Police in Bangor. They're sending patrol cars to check the traffic coming off Anglesey. They've got the make and registration.'

Laura frowned. 'Can't we close both the bridges now?'

'We've got 14,000 people coming back and forth to Anglesey over them every day,' he said with a shrug. 'Can you imagine what would happen if we closed the bridges for the next couple of hours?'

Frank looked at them. 'They won't get as far as the bridges, anyway.'

Laura frowned. 'What do you mean?'

'There can't be more than ten miles of diesel in that car,'

Frank explained. 'I kept meaning to fill her up. I got jerrycans full of diesel over there for the tractors.'

Gareth raised an eyebrow. 'Looks like they're going to need fuel from somewhere then.'

Laura could feel the wind pick up and swirl around her.

'We need to get back to Beaumaris and run this operation from there,' Gareth decided.

'How long is that going to take?' Laura asked. 'We haven't even got a car.'

'It's fifteen minutes in a car,' said Frank. 'If I had one I'd give you a lift.'

A loud, juddering sound came from above them.

Glancing up into the air, she saw that the police Eurocopter was descending slowly into an adjacent field.

Gareth gestured. 'They're going to drop us at Beaumaris Beach before they go searching for the car, so we'll be there in two minutes. How are you with helicopters?'

Laura wrinkled her nose. 'I like helicopters almost as much as I like speedboats!'

Blinking his blurry eyes open, Geoff tried to work out exactly where he was and what was going on. As his vision cleared, he could make out that he was lying in the shadowy wheel-house of the *Anglesey Princess*. He got a familiar waft of ageing timber and stale coffee.

He tried to sit up, but a white-hot pain shot down his right arm from his shoulder. Then he remembered what had happened. He had been shot. As he looked down, he saw that someone had dressed his shoulder wound and put his right arm in a sling.

'You need to stay still, mate,' said a familiar voice. It was Steve.

Geoff winced with the pain. 'Jesus!'

'You're lucky, old son!' Steve grinned.

'I don't feel very bloody lucky,' Geoff complained.

'Firstly, the bullet went clean through the flesh at the top of your shoulder and missed the bone. Otherwise your collar bone would be in pieces,' Steve explained. 'Secondly, you've lucked out by having an ex-army medic captaining this boat today.' Steve put his hand gently on Geoff's and looked at him. 'Just lay back, matey. I don't want you going into shock.'

Geoff knew about shock. He had seen it in the Falklands War.

Reaching into a cupboard underneath the ship's wheel, Steve brought out a blanket and came over.

'I know it's hot, mate,' he said. 'But I'm going to put this over you. Trust me, gunshot wounds can do all sorts of strange things to the body.'

'What happened?' Geoff asked. 'Did those blokes leave with that boy?'

'Yeah.' Steve nodded grimly. 'They took the teacher, too.'

'I should have shot him in the face and not threatened him,' Geoff stated angrily.

Steve shook his head. 'And then the others would have killed you!'

Geoff leaned back and looked up at the ceiling of the wheelhouse. 'What's happening now?'

Steve gestured out towards the deck. 'A couple of the passengers spotted two police launches heading our way. I'm guessing we're getting rescued. And you, you daft bugger, are going to hospital.'

'Oh great,' Geoff grumbled.

Steve crouched down next to him and put a water bottle to his lips. 'You need to keep hydrated too.'

'I'd prefer rum,' Geoff joked, trying to smile through the pain.

'I'm sure you would.' Steve laughed as he felt Geoff's

forehead. 'Yeah. Good news is that you're not clammy. First sign of trauma shock.'

For a moment, Geoff looked up at Steve, and their eyes met. It was hard for him to admit what he felt for him. And he was convinced that Steve felt the same way. But he was far too afraid to say or do anything about it. What if he was wrong? Their friendship might be over for ever, and that was unthinkable.

Steve gave him a benign smile and pointed to the skin on his left arm, which was exposed since he had cut Geoff's shirt off while he was unconscious. There were at least ten circular scars the size of a fivepence piece.

'I saw these on your arm,' Steve whispered. 'I wondered how you got them?'

Geoff let out a breath, and he blinked. The memory of it was painful.

'It's all right if you don't want to talk about it,' Steve whispered. 'None of my business, is it?'

'No, I want to . . . My dad used my arm as an ashtray,' Geoff said with a lump in his throat. In nearly fifty years, he had never really spoken about it.

'Why?' Steve asked with a horrified expression.

'He said I was a faggot,' Geoff murmured. 'In fact, everyone said I was a faggot. The kids at school. My brother. And my dad. He told me if he ever found out I was gay – *poofter*, I think, was the actual word he used – he'd kill me.'

'Jesus.' Steve frowned and shook his head. 'I'm so sorry.'

'So I joined the Marines, then the SBS, ran around shooting and blowing stuff up to prove them all wrong.'

'I suppose you did,' Steve said with a wry smile.

A tall man in his late fifties appeared at the wheelhouse door and looked in. 'Thought you should know, the first police launch is about to dock alongside us. Do you need a hand getting him up and over to it?'

Steve smiled. 'Yeah, he's a bit of a lump so I'm definitely going to need help.'

'Piss off, I've been bloody shot,' Geoff joked as he gave a groan. 'No respect for the elderly these days, is there?'

'Geoff?' Steve said.

'Yes?'

'Shut up and try to concentrate on getting up on your feet, old man.'

Chapter 34

1.49 p.m.

Having landed on Beaumaris Beach ten minutes earlier, Laura and Gareth were now back at the temporary operation centre inside the balmy interior of the lifeboat station. The main boat-house was a hive of activity. Both CID and uniformed officers came and went, speaking on phones or working on laptops. Laura was trying to remain calm while she collated intel that might be useful when negotiating with the gang members.

A uniformed sergeant walked up to her and stopped. It was now so hot that sweat trickled from the roots of his short black hair, making his face shiny.

'Ma'am, we've had information from the *Anglesey Princess* concerning a Geoff Clegg,' he informed them.

'Is he okay?' she asked the sergeant. She wondered why they hadn't heard from him since the gang had left the boat.

'He threatened the gang with a flare gun. Then one of them shot him,' the sergeant reported. 'But it's just a flesh wound in the shoulder, so he should be okay.'

'Thanks for letting us know, sergeant,' she said, thinking that Geoff was probably lucky not to be dead.

Gareth, who was holding his Tetra radio, approached. 'Helicopter has done two passes over that area. No sign of the Land Rover yet. We've got three cars in the area now. Without diesel, they're not going far. We'll find them, don't worry.'

Laura gave an audible sigh. It wasn't the finding or even stopping of the car that worried her. It was getting Beth and Jake safely away from the armed gang members. She looked up as Declan came in and blew out his cheeks. It was baking hot outside as well.

'Boss, passengers are disembarking from the *Anglesey Princess* and getting on the first launch,' Declan said.

Gareth nodded. 'Good. How many can we get on the launch at a time?'

'They reckoned only twenty to be safe.'

'Okay,' Gareth said. 'We're going to need some kind of initial statements from everyone off that boat. Grab a couple of uniformed bods. I want names and addresses. I don't want anyone disappearing only for them to pop up in court for the defence in a year's time.'

'Boss. We've also got the paramedics standing by for Geoff Clegg.'

'I'm not sure if he's very brave or very stupid,' Laura said with a raised eyebrow. 'What I do know is that he's bloody lucky to be alive.'

Declan agreed. 'Yes, ma'am.'

Gareth ran his hands over his scalp and asked, 'Have we managed to get units over to the bridges?'

'Two patrol cars at both,' Declan told him.

'Thanks, Declan,' Gareth said. As Declan left, Gareth turned to Laura and gave her a sympathetic look. 'How are you doing?'

'Fine,' she lied as she blinked. She found herself swinging between overwhelming fear and how she was feeling at the moment – a steely focus and aggression in her quest to get

Jake back. 'We've got three things we need to achieve. Find them, stop them and persuade them to hand over Jake and Beth without anyone getting hurt.'

'Sounds about right. And the first two should be the straightforward part.' Gareth sighed. 'Anything come back on the gang members?'

Laura pointed to her laptop. 'Merseyside Police think they can identify all three.'

Gareth came closer and leaned over her shoulder to look. She could feel his presence and got a waft of something fragrant and citrusy.

'I can smell grapefruit,' she said with a frown.

'Yeah, that's my shower gel,' he said. 'Apparently it's "a zesty way to start the day".'

'Is it indeed?' she chortled, forgetting herself for a moment and imagining being in the shower with him.

Gareth pointed to the screen. 'Well, that's a decent start.'

Focusing her mind again, she nodded. 'We've got Paul Griffin, known as Red because of his ginger hair. Aged twenty-nine. Criminal record stretches back to when he was ten.' She pointed to a photograph that had appeared on the screen. 'Grew up in Norris Green. Father, John, mother Sheila. When he was sixteen, he was convicted with five others of manslaughter after a seventeen-year-old rival gang member was kicked to death in Croxteth.'

'Jesus! What about the other two?' Gareth asked.

Laura tapped the computer and two photographs came up. 'Callum and Michael Cole. Mother died in 2007 of cancer. Michael was three and Callum was six. They were brought up by their father, Neil, who was then imprisoned for manslaughter in 2014.'

'Dysfunctional families,' Gareth sighed. She felt the heat of his breath on the side of her neck. 'It's just an ongoing cycle, isn't it?'

'I'm not sure it is with these two,' she said with a frown. 'Neither of them had any form of criminal record until they went into care in 2014.'

He shrugged. 'Late bloomers then?'

'There might be something here that helps us.' She pointed to the laptop. 'Neil Cole was accused of the manslaughter of Kevin Hopper. He alleged in court that Hopper had tried to abuse both Callum and Michael while they were in the local Scout group. The defence couldn't provide any evidence of this.'

'You think you can use that?' he asked.

'Possibly,' she said. 'Neil Cole was released on parole three weeks ago from Walton Prison. He's in a bail hostel in Mold.'

'Do we think that Callum and Michael know that?'

'Hard to say, but given their involvement with organised crime, they may have lost touch.'

'How does his release help us?' Gareth asked.

'I want to bring him here. Now,' she said.

Gareth frowned. 'Really?'

'These were average kids. I'm not condoning what Neil Cole did but I know what I'd want to do if someone tried to abuse one of my kids. Callum and Michael ended up in care and got themselves into a lot of trouble. I'm not trying to say they're not responsible for their actions. But if Neil Cole knew what his two sons were mixed up in, maybe he would come here and try to talk to them. And that might give us an edge when it comes to getting Jake and Beth back safely.'

He nodded enthusiastically – clearly he thought it was a good idea. 'Yeah, that might work. Brilliant. I'll see if local plod will go and pick him up. They could probably have him here in just over an hour if they find him right away.'

'Okay, then let's do that,' Laura said decisively. She was pleased that she had obviously impressed him. 'Anything that gives us any kind of leverage is worth a try in my book.'

Gareth looked directly at her, with a twinkle in his eye. 'And from what I hear, you virtually wrote the book.'

However inappropriate the timing, he really is very handsome, she thought.

Michael buzzed down a back window to get some fresh air. They had been driving for less than ten minutes and it was already baking inside the Land Rover. The atmosphere was tense.

In the distance, a small village sat at the foot of a series of overlapping hills. A church steeple was visible at the far end. In the fields that bordered the road, sheep grazed idly in the sunshine.

Red and Callum were sitting in the front, with Michael, Beth and Jake in the back. Michael tried to give Beth and Jake a reassuring look, but both of them were gazing into space. There was no way he was going to let Red hurt either of them.

With a sudden turn of the steering wheel, Red pulled into the entrance of a field that was covered in grass. The Land Rover smashed through the wooden gate and pieces of wood flew into the air.

'Jesus!' Michael exclaimed.

'What are you doing?' Callum asked.

'We're going cross-country,' Red snorted with a chuckle.

'Thanks for the warning,' Beth snapped.

Callum looked at Red and frowned. 'Why?'

'Why d'you think, you divvy?' Red thundered. 'There are probably only a couple of roads we can take from here to the bridges. And the bizzies will have them blocked off or they'll be patrolling them. They can't do that if we go cross-country.'

Callum nodded. 'And we're in a Land Rover, which is supposed to go cross-country.'

'Exactly, mate.' Red laughed as he grinned over at Callum.

If he was honest, Michael hated the close relationship that had formed between Red and Callum in recent months. He thought Callum sucked up to Red and hero-worshipped him. Sometimes it was bloody embarrassing. And as for Red, well, he was just scum.

The car bounced and jolted along the uneven surface. Beth reached up to hold on to the plastic grab handle to stop herself from being thrown around the car. The dust from the dry field had settled on the windscreen, forcing Red to use the windscreen wash and wipers.

Callum was looking at his mobile phone. 'There's no bloody service out here.'

'We're in the middle of nowhere, dickhead,' Red snapped.

Up ahead, Michael saw an old man walking across the field with his black Labrador. When the man heard the noise of the Land Rover, he stopped, looked back and gave them a cheery but slightly bemused wave as they passed by.

Christ, if only he knew what was going on, Michael thought to himself.

'We really need some fucking petrol,' Red growled for the third time to no one in particular.

Michael leaned forward in his seat and tapped his brother on the shoulder. 'There might be a spare can in the boot?'

'Can you have a look?' Callum asked.

Moving the seatbelt, Michael turned, only to see that the parcel shelf was covering the boot. 'I can't see. You'll have to stop.'

Red swung the car over beside a large wooden gate to another field and slammed the brakes on hard, throwing everyone forward. 'Let's have a look then, eh?'

What is his problem?

Flinging open the driver's door, Red got out of the car and

245

headed for the boot. Michael was dying for a pee, so he opened the door and headed over to a nearby bush.

'Where the fuck are you going?' Red snapped.

Michael ignored him as he peed in a blackberry bush. He must have been dehydrated, because his urine smelt strong.

As he zipped up, he saw Red kicking the car angrily and slamming down the boot.

'For fuck's sake!' Red yelled.

'No petrol?' Michael asked. If they ran out of the petrol, then they really were fucked.

Red frowned as if Michael had said something inflammatory. 'What did you say?'

Michael could see that Red was like a wound coil. Usually, that would have terrified him, but his contempt for Red was now overwhelming.

Michael gestured to the boot and said with a slight air of sarcasm, 'You kicked the car, so I'm guessing there wasn't a petrol can. And that means in about five miles we're going to run out of petrol.'

'You think this is funny?' Red barked, taking an aggressive step towards him.

'Not really,' Michael said dryly. 'Going to prison isn't funny, is it?'

Red took another pace forward and narrowed his eyes. 'Who the fuck said anything about us going to prison?'

Michael shook his head and sighed. 'Don't be an idiot, Red. We're not going to get out of this. Even if we had petrol, where would we go? Any bridges off this island are going to be swarming with police.'

Red gritted his teeth for a moment. 'What did you call me?'

'What?'

Red's nostrils flared in utter fury. 'You think I'm an idiot? You called me an idiot?'

'I think you're an idiot if you think we're going to drive off this island and get back to Liverpool.' Michael knew Red was about to explode – but for some reason, he was beyond caring. In fact, he wanted to provoke him.

In a flash, Red lurched forward and grabbed Michael by the throat. 'You think I'm a fucking idiot? I tell you what, I'm a fucking idiot for believing that you're not a grass. The bizzies were waiting on that beach for us. And you told them we were coming.'

Michael used all of his strength as he shoved Red in his chest and face. 'Fuck off, Red. I'm not going to grass on my own brother.'

Red moved forward again.

Michael scoffed at him, 'Not so hard now you haven't got that gun, are you, Red?'

In a flash, Red threw a punch which landed square on Michael's jaw. He saw stars as his legs wobbled and he collapsed to the ground.

Jesus! That really hurt!

Callum got out of the car. 'Will you two fucking pack it in?'

Red crouched over Michael and came close to his face. 'Fuck with me again and I'll bury you.' As he turned back towards the car, Red spat on Michael.

'Why don't you keep your bloody mouth shut, eh?' Callum gave him a withering look as he got to his feet. He then gestured to his mobile. 'Hey, I've got a signal. And there's a petrol station about three miles over that way.'

Michael's head was still ringing as he opened the door and got back in the car.

A moment later, the car pulled away with a jolt and they sped across the field.

Chapter 35

2.07 p.m.

Laura and Gareth had utilised a large map of Anglesey that was pinned to the wall of the lighthouse station. As they studied it, it was clear there were only three roads that the gang could have taken in the stolen Land Rover – if they were heading for the two bridges that linked Anglesey to the Welsh mainland.

Laura was exasperated. 'I don't understand why they haven't been spotted.'

Gareth's Tetra radio crackled. 'Gold Command from Alpha Zero, over.' It was the Eurocopter, which was scouring the area between Red Wharf Bay and the two bridges that led off Anglesey.

'Alpha Zero received, go ahead,' Gareth replied.

The radio crackled, and the pilot stated, 'We have no visual on target vehicle or suspects, over.'

Gareth looked despondent. 'Received Alpha Zero, received. Stand by.'

Looking again at the map, Laura had checked online that there were no petrol stations within the radius that Frank had suggested when he told them they only had around ten miles of diesel left in the Land Rover.

'Maybe they've just run out of petrol and they're now on foot,' she suggested, thinking out loud.

'They won't get very far.' Gareth came to get a closer look at the map. 'Unless they've stolen another car?'

She gave him a grim look. It was a distinct possibility and then they would have no idea where Jake's captors were or what vehicle they were travelling in.

Declan came in and went over to the map. 'Boss, we've established that there are no petrol stations within range,' he reported as he pointed. 'But just here is Talwrn. There's a shop there cunningly called the Talwrn Convenience Store. And it's got two petrol pumps outside. It's just not registered as a petrol station on our database.'

'Okay. It's definitely en route.' Laura put her finger on the map and found the tiny village of Talwrn. 'Have we got a number for the shop?'

'Yes, ma'am.' Declan handed her a scrap of paper.

'Actually Declan, I'm a civilian, so it's Laura,' she said with a kind smile.

Declan furrowed his brow. 'Sorry.'

'Don't worry,' Laura said as she turned and marched across the lifeboat station to the table where the phone and sound equipment were situated. She grabbed the phone and dialled the number.

'Hello?' said a voice. It sounded like an elderly man.

'Hello, this is the Anglesey Police. Can I ask who I'm speaking to, please?' she asked.

'Dai Lewis,' he replied, sounding concerned. 'Is everything all right?'

'My name's Laura. I understand you own the Talwrn Convenience Store, is that right?'

'Yes.' Dai sounded even more perplexed.

'Can you tell me if anyone has stopped for petrol or diesel today?'

'No, not yet. We don't get many people stopping here for that. Most of them go down to Asda to get their fuel now. It's much cheaper, you see?'

'And you haven't seen anything suspicious today?'

'No, no. Nothing out of the ordinary here, I'm glad to say.'

'We're particularly interested in a navy blue Land Rover Discovery,' she informed him. 'The licence plate is DT05 BRV.'

'Okay, well, I'll look out for it, shall I?' he asked.

'Listen, the men inside that car are probably armed and very dangerous,' she told him, hoping she wasn't going to scare him to death. 'Do not challenge them or signal that you know who they are if you do see them.'

'Well, what if they stop here for diesel?' he asked nervously. 'What should I do?'

'Let them have the fuel. And then contact us when they've gone. Okay?'

'But I haven't got any diesel. I'm not expecting a delivery until tomorrow,' he said.

Oh shit!

'Then I want you to explain that to them nice and calmly.'

'Okay,' he said, but his voice now sounded jittery.

Laura looked over at Gareth. 'Dai, we are going to send a patrol car over to you right now.'

Gareth gave her a thumbs-up to confirm that while she had been on the phone, he had radioed a patrol car to drive over to Talwrn.

'O-okay, then,' Dai stammered. She could hear the nerves in his voice.

'They'll be with you very soon,' she said, trying to reassure him.

* * *

250

Beth watched as Red slowed the Land Rover as they entered the tiny village of Talwrn, which lay between Llangefni and Pentraeth. It was the place that Callum had identified as having some kind of petrol station. Reaching over, she gave Jake's hand a squeeze, and he looked up at her. She couldn't imagine what was going through his mind. After all he had suffered after the sudden death of his father, to be put through an ordeal like this was cruel and traumatic.

They had been generous with space when they built the houses in the village, in that they were unremarkable except for their sense of isolation from each other. Front gardens and driveways were unusually large. As she looked up, the sunlight strobed through the tall trees, dappling everything with shapes. Looking left out of the car window, there were fields with a scant smattering of well-fed sheep. Behind that, rolling hills dominated the azure sky. On any other day, it would have been the perfect weather for a drive and a pub lunch, she thought darkly.

She glanced at the clock on the dashboard. It was 2.12 p.m. So much had happened in the past four hours, it was hard to feel that it was real. It felt that at some point a director was going to jump up and shout 'cut' and tell them that they could all go home.

She looked down at her hands. Even the bones inside her fingers were trembling. Her head was pounding from the stress and she was finding it hard to sustain any rhythm to her breathing. Maybe it was the effect of having too much adrenaline pumping through her veins. She wondered how this was going to end. In many ways, she wanted the gang to get away. For them to leave them somewhere on the roadside, escape back to Liverpool and disappear. There was a simplicity and safety to that. What she feared most was the appearance of armed police officers and a terrible gun battle where anything could happen.

'Just up there.' Callum pointed to a shop on the left-hand side of the road.

Outside were two old rusty petrol pumps that looked like they had been there for decades.

'Nice one,' Red said as he pulled the Land Rover over.

'I need to go to the toilet,' Jake blurted.

Red turned to look at him. 'You're going nowhere, sunshine. We're filling this car up and then we're going.'

Beth glared at Red and pointed to the sign that read CUSTOMER TOILET with an arrow that showed it was to the side of the building. 'Come on. I'll take him. I need to go too. You don't want us going in the back here, do you?'

Red narrowed his eyes and then glanced at Michael. 'You take them. And stand outside. I don't want them trying to run away.' He looked at Callum and gestured. 'Give your brother your gun.'

Callum pulled the Glock from his waistband, turned and handed it to Michael.

'And if they try to do a runner, shoot them,' Red said coldly as he got out of the car.

Opening the rear door, Michael gestured for Beth and Jake to get out and follow him.

It was a welcome relief to get out of the stuffiness of the car. Beth reached out and took Jake's hand. His fingers were icy.

'Are you okay?' she asked as she crouched down to look at him.

Jake nodded blankly. There was too much for him to process and too much going on inside his head. The skin under his eyes had a purple hue. He looked exhausted.

'It's going to be okay. You do know that?' she asked, looking at his face for a sign that he understood.

Jake shrugged and stared at the ground. He looked broken.

'Trust me. Come on,' Beth said as she took his hand again

and they walked past the shop and headed for the toilets around the side.

In the distance, she could hear the helicopter flying low, searching for them. Was it strange that there was now a growing part of her that didn't want them to be found? She had once read about Stockholm Syndrome and wondered if that was what she was suffering from.

They took it in turns to use the toilet, then Michael led Beth and Jake back to the shop. He noticed Red had put the nozzle of the petrol pump into the Land Rover – but he was looking confused.

'It's not bloody working,' he grumbled as he pulled the lever on the pump again.

Beth pointed to a sign over the pumps that read PLEASE ASK INSIDE FOR THE PUMPS TO BE TURNED ON and tried not to look smug.

Maybe he can't read?

Red didn't say anything as he stormed inside the shop.

Michael looked at her, rolled his eyes and then sat down on a low concrete wall and gazed into space. She wondered what was going on in his mind.

Beth and Jake followed Red into the shop. She had her bank and credit cards in a thin wallet in her trouser pocket. 'I'm getting you something to drink. What would like?'

'Sprite, please,' Jake whispered as they went over to the fridge.

Callum was in the other aisle picking up crisps and biscuits.

'Crisps?' she asked.

Jake blinked nervously. 'Walkers cheese and onion, please.'

'Excuse me, mate,' Red called in a very loud, annoyed voice, 'Can you put the pumps on for us? We're in a bit of a hurry.'

An elderly gentleman looked over at him, a little startled.

Even from where Beth was standing, she could see that he looked frightened. 'Did you want petrol or diesel?'

'Diesel,' Red answered.

The elderly man shook his head. 'I'm really sorry. We're out of diesel, I'm afraid. I'm getting a delivery tomorrow, if that helps?'

'No, it doesn't,' Red snorted as he looked over to Callum and pointed to the door. 'I need a word.'

Beth watched as Red and Callum had an animated conversation outside the door. With a sideways glance, she then spotted the elderly man pick up the phone. He kept glancing over at the door nervously. As he went to dial, she could see his hand was shaking.

Oh shit, he's calling the police.

In a flash, Red was back in the shop and glaring at the elderly man. He was holding the Glock handgun, which he had retrieved from Michael.

Red marched towards the shop counter with the handgun now pointing in front of him.

'Put the phone down!' he thundered.

Beth gasped as the elderly man's eyes widened in terror.

He dropped the phone so that it swung from its plastic cord like a pendulum.

'Who were you calling?' Red growled.

'No one,' the elderly man yammered. 'I . . . I mean my wife. I don't want any trouble.'

Red had now reached him and put the gun against his head. 'I asked who you were calling.'

Jake tucked his head against Beth's side and closed his eyes.

'The p-police,' the elderly man stammered. 'But I didn't speak to anyone. I'm sorry.'

Red held out his hand. 'I need the keys to your car.'

The elderly man shrugged. 'I don't have a car. Not here.'

Red narrowed his eyes. 'Then how the fuck did you get to work this morning?'

'My wife dropped me off. She needs the car to visit her sister.'

Red moved the gun from his head. 'I need somewhere to hide that car outside.'

The elderly man pointed to the rear of the building. 'There's a garage at the back here. I've got the keys. You could put it in there?'

Red held out his hand, clicked his fingers and snapped, 'Keys!'

The elderly man was now shaking all over as he dug into his pockets, pulled out a plastic fob with a small key on it and placed it in Red's palm.

God, he looks like he's going to have a heart attack, Beth thought. It was horrible to see an innocent old man so frightened.

Red turned to Callum and tossed it to him. 'Right, go and hide that car quickly while I tie grandad here up.'

9 April 2019

It was mid-afternoon by the time Laura and Pete drew up outside a small, semi-detached house on Clitheroe Road in Longsight, to the south of Manchester. Even though it wasn't as deprived or violent as the neighbouring boroughs of Moss Side and Fallowfield, it was still rundown and neglected.

The houses were neat, red-brick with a small flat roof over the front door. Laura spotted a bin with a large white '73' painted on it. It was the address they had for Mandy Cooper. There were some teenagers on bikes whizzing up and down the road and shouting.

Laura raised an eyebrow as they walked up the path to the white laminate front door. 'Haven't done this in a while.'

'You miss it?' Pete asked as he gave the door a knock.

'Yeah, of course,' Laura said with a nod. 'It was my life for twenty years.'

The front door opened and a woman in her mid-thirties, with brunette hair to her shoulders, glasses and too much make-up, peered at them curiously. 'Hello?'

Pete held out his warrant card. 'DCI Pete Marsons, Manchester CID. We're looking for a Mandy Cooper?'

'Yes. What do you want?' Mandy asked in a tone that immediately told them she wasn't happy to see them.

'Can we come in?' Laura asked.

'No,' Mandy snapped. 'What do you want?'

Pete put his warrant card away. 'We'd like to ask you some questions about events of 12 August 2018. Does that date mean anything to you?'

Mandy snorted. 'Joking, aren't you? Of course it does.'

For a few seconds, Mandy looked up and down the street. She clearly didn't want them on her doorstep for the neighbours to see, so she ushered them inside.

'You've got five minutes,' she growled as she led them into a living room that was untidy and cluttered with toys and folded washing, and pointed to the sofa. 'You can sit there.'

She's a little charmer.

Pete sat forward and looked at her. 'We know that you took a call on the switchboard at Trafford Police Station from someone at 9.12 on the morning of 12 August. Do you remember that?'

Mandy raised an eyebrow sarcastically as though that was a stupid question. 'Yes.'

'Do you remember who made the phone call?' Laura asked.

'It was anonymous,' Mandy said.

Laura nodded. 'Was it a man's voice?'

Mandy scratched her face nervously. 'I can't discuss that with you.'

What's she talking about?

'Could you tell us why?' Pete asked.

Mandy shook her head as her eyes roamed anxiously around the room. Her initial hostility had clearly changed to fear. 'No.'

Pete gave Laura a baffled look. Something was definitely wrong.

Laura frowned. 'You don't work for the Manchester Metropolitan Police any more, do you, Mandy?'

'No. No, I don't,' she said in a bitter tone.

'Can I ask why you left?' Laura enquired.

'No, you can't. It's none of your business.'

Pete furrowed his brow. 'I'm a bit confused here, Mandy. I'm a Detective Chief Inspector with CID. I'm looking into the events of that day but you say you can't talk to me about it. Can you tell me why?'

Mandy's breathing was becoming shallow. 'I was told not to. And that's all I'm going to say.'

'You were told not to discuss an anonymous 999 phone call?' Pete asked, sounding bewildered.

There is something very suspicious about all this, Laura thought.

'I don't want any trouble,' Mandy said. 'But I can't talk to you.'

Laura gave her a concerned look. 'Mandy, did someone warn you not to talk to anyone about the phone call that morning?'

'Please,' Mandy implored them. 'I have three children. I left that place to get away from all this. If you need to talk to someone, you should talk to Martin Barratt.'

Pete shrugged. 'Martin Barratt?'

'He was the CAD operator I passed that call on to,' Mandy

explained. 'I'm really sorry, but unless you're going to arrest me, I can't tell you anything else.'

Laura looked at Mandy's hands lying in her lap. They were shaking. Something about their visit had seriously spooked her.

Chapter 36

Geoff was in the far corner of the Astor Ward on the third floor of Bangor Hospital. The doctors had confirmed that he wasn't in any danger but they needed to keep a close eye on the gunshot wound as it would be prone to infection. He was also dehydrated, so he was on a saline drip.

The sun streaked in through the lopsided blinds close to his bed. His mind immediately went to the little boy and his teacher who Red and his gang had taken with them when they had left the *Anglesey Princess*. He prayed they were going to be okay.

A figure approached. It was Steve. He was holding a blue plastic bag, which he waved at him as he sat down on a chair beside the bed. The air was thick with the smells of disinfectant and hospital food.

'You can go home, you know,' Geoff said.

'And miss seeing you in pain? I don't think so,' Steve joked. 'Anyway, I've been shopping.' He gestured to the plastic bag. 'Hobnobs, Hula Hoops, full-fat Coke.'

Geoff snorted. 'Christ, am I that predictable?'

'Yes.' Steve looked at him. 'You're also a bloody idiot!'

'What?'

'I haven't said anything until I knew you were all right for certain,' Steve admitted. 'But what the hell were you doing with that flare? They had a machine gun.'

'I was trying to persuade them to leave without taking any hostages,' Geoff explained, although it did sound ridiculous now. Maybe the heat and dehydration had affected his thinking.

'Well, you're bloody lucky you're not dead, aren't you?' Steve scolded him.

'Oi, you're not my wife,' Geoff replied. To be fair, they'd been told on many occasions that they acted like an old married couple.

'If I was your wife, I'd have slapped you,' Steve chuckled. 'Silly bugger.'

'I can't stop thinking about that boy and the teacher,' Geoff said. 'Have you heard anything?'

Steve shook his head. 'BBC News was on the television in the cafeteria, but they said the search for the gang and their two hostages was still ongoing.'

'I wish I'd shot that Red bastard in the face,' Geoff growled.

'And then you'd be dead,' Steve snapped. 'And the other two would have still taken the boy and his teacher.'

Geoff started to shrug, but a sharp pain shot through the length of his arm. He winced.

Steve looked at him. 'Do you want me to get a nurse?'

'No, don't be bloody daft. I've been shot. It's going to hurt a bit, isn't it? It's not a big surprise.' Geoff groaned.

'All right, tough man,' Steve teased him. 'The BBC showed some shots of the rest of the children from that school getting off on Beaumaris Pier and being reunited with their parents.'

'Thank God,' Geoff said. 'They're going to need counselling or something.'

'It's certainly a day they'll never forget,' Steve sighed.

'I think the most dramatic thing that ever happened at our school was when Wally Simkins spread shit all over the walls of the changing rooms and got expelled.'

'Nice story.' Geoff pulled a face. 'I didn't really like school, did you?'

'No. Definitely not. I always felt like a square peg in a round hole,' Steve confessed.

Geoff nodded in total recognition. 'Yeah. That's exactly how I felt. The other kids breezed through school without a care in the world. I spent my whole time worrying about something. I was always dead nervous.'

Steve grinned. 'God, I was a nightmare. Mr Hitchens asked me to read out a poem about a red, red rose. I just panicked and ran out. I got my mum to write a note asking for me not to be asked to read out in class again.'

'It's Robert Burns,' Geoff informed him.

'What is?'

'That poem. It's "A Red, Red Rose" by Robert Burns.'

'How the hell do you know that?'

'O my Luve is like a red, red rose / That's newly sprung in June; / O my Luve is like the melody / That's sweetly played in tune,' Geoff said, surprising even himself that he could remember the words.

'Get you!' Steve laughed and then looked at him. Their eyes met for a few seconds. 'You really are full of surprises, aren't you, Geoff Clegg?'

The gang was now holed up in the Talwrn Convenience Store. Red told Michael and Callum that they needed to wait for a car to stop outside so that they could then steal it at gunpoint and make their escape. Until then, they must keep out of sight. The police helicopter had passed overhead twice in the last ten minutes. There were probably police cars patrolling the area, too.

261

Red locked the door to the shop and turned the sign to read CLOSED. He then pulled all the blinds down at the windows.

Callum frowned. 'Why have you put the CLOSED sign on the door? How are we going to steal a car?'

'Well, genius,' Red explained, giving him a withering look. 'They'll have to stop, get out of the car and come to the door to actually see the CLOSED sign, it's that small. Then we can make our move.'

'Okay.' Callum nodded.

'And if the bizzies stop to have a look,' he said, 'it just looks like the shop is closed for some reason.'

They had found out that the shop owner was called Dai Lewis. He was now sitting on a chair in the back, tied up. Michael thought it was faintly ridiculous to tie him to a chair. He was old, frail and didn't look like he could harm a fly.

Taking a bottle of whisky from the shelf, Red unscrewed the top and glugged it. He then pulled a cigarette from a packet, lit it and blew out a long, bluish stream of smoke.

The shop was eerily quiet aside from the low hum of the fridges that ran down the right-hand side.

Callum was sitting on the far side of the shop, his back to the shelves of sweets and crisps. He was inspecting his nails and jigging his foot nervously.

Michael went over to where Beth and Jake were sitting with their backs to the storeroom door. It was out of the sight of the windows and shop entrance. Jake was resting his head on Beth's shoulder and staring into space.

'You guys want a drink?' he asked them in a whisper.

Jake nodded.

'He wants a Sprite,' Beth informed Michael wearily.

'What about you?' Michael asked. He was worried that she hated him. Why wouldn't she, after all they had been

262

through? He couldn't help thinking she had lovely, kind eyes and long eyelashes.

'Water, please,' she said, sounding tired.

Walking over to the fridge, Michael grabbed their drinks, got himself a beer and returned.

'I need to go to the toilet again,' Jake whispered.

Michael gestured silently for them to follow him.

Red stared over as Beth and Jake got to their feet. 'Where the hell are they going?' he snapped at Michael.

'Toilet,' Michael explained.

'Again?' Red growled.

'He's nervous,' Beth snapped at him. 'What do you expect?'

Red looked at Michael. 'She can stay over there. You take him.'

Michael glanced at Beth as she returned to where she had been sitting. He then looked down at Jake and tried to give him a half-smile. 'Come on, mate.'

They walked across the back of the shop, out through the door and to the toilet. Even though it was a hot summer's day, the back rooms of the shop were cold and smelt damp.

Jake went in and turned to close the door.

'Leave the door open, eh, mate?' Michael suggested. 'Don't want you locking yourself in there and having to get you out.'

Jake pulled an embarrassed face. 'I need to close the door.'

Michael frowned. 'Why?'

Jake looked down at the floor in embarrassment. 'I . . . I need to sit down on the toilet.'

Michael nodded. 'Oh, okay, mate. No worries. Close the door, eh? Sorry.'

As he waited, Michael walked into an adjacent dark stockroom. It smelt of spices but also sweet. He scanned the rows of goods that were stored there. Once he might have scoffed at someone who ran a small shop like this. He would have seen it as boring. However, after the events of the past eight hours, Michael thought how nice it must be to have the simplicity of running the village store. Friendly faces of locals popping in to get their groceries and to have a chat. Nothing to worry about except for the fact that the shop was running low on baked beans. He bet Dai didn't have to continually worry about going to prison or being stabbed or shot by a rival gang.

Spotting a packet of fig rolls on the shelf, he thought of his father. Fig rolls and a cup of tea were his daily routine when he got in from work. He had worked as a local plumber. It was hard to think about the terrible events that led to him going to prison. He and Callum had been watching the telly when the police arrived to arrest him. A woman from Social Services had arrived at the same time and told them they would have to go into care while their father was on remand and awaiting trial.

For a second, Michael got a flash of what had happened with Kev, the bloke that ran the 12th West Derby Scout Group. In August 2014, there had been an overnight Scout camping trip to The Sanctuary, a 40-acre community wood over in Knowsley. Michael had only just moved up from the Cubs to the Scouts and was sharing a tent with Callum when Scout Master Kev decided to pay them a midnight visit. Michael had tried to block out what had happened that night. Callum had eventually wrestled Kev out of the tent, but the damage had been done.

The door to the toilet opened, breaking Michael's train of thought. He realised that he now had a tear in his eye and a lump in his throat.

'Can I wash my hands?' Jake asked.

Michael wiped the tears from his eyes, trying to hide his emotion. He cleared his throat. 'Of course, mate.'

Jake went over and very precisely washed his hands.

Michael realised that Jake was the same age as he had been when his life had been turned upside down. He wondered how Jake would be when all this was over. He had said his father was dead.

Michael sat down on some big boxes of tins. 'Who's your favourite United player then, Jake?'

Rubbing his hands dry on his jeans, Jake shrugged.

'Bruno Fernandes? He's quality.'

Jake shook his head. 'Rashford's my favourite player.'

Michael agreed with a nod. 'Yeah, he's rapid.'

'I also like Giggs,' Jake admitted. 'But that's cos he was my dad's favourite.'

'Was he?' Michael asked with an approving look. 'Giggsy is a legend. And he's Welsh.'

There were a few seconds of silence.

Michael leaned forward and looked at Jake. 'It's gonna be all right, mate. You're gonna be back home very soon, okay. I promise you that.'

Jake's eyes roamed nervously around the passageway.

'Come on then.' Michael gestured for them to go back into the shop.

As they took one step inside, a voice hissed at them, 'Get down! Bizzies!'

Michael instantly crouched, pulling Jake down with him. He glanced over at the door and saw a police officer cupping his hands to look inside. He was saying something into his radio and then banged hard on the door to try to attract someone's attention.

His heart pounded. What was Red going to do if they managed to get in? He didn't even want to think about it.

Looking to his left, Michael's eyes met Beth's. He knew she wasn't stupid enough to shout or make a noise.

There was more banging on the window and a voice called, 'Mr Lewis? Are you in there? Mr Lewis, it's Anglesey Police.'

Then everything went quiet.

Michael's mouth was dry and he could feel himself hardly daring to breathe.

Then he heard the sound of a car engine starting and the crunch of gravel as the patrol car pulled away.

Going over to the window, Red moved the blind and looked out.

'Panic over, ladies and gentlemen,' Red said. 'They've gone.'

Chapter 37

3.32 p.m.

'Gold Command from Alpha nine-zero, are you receiving, over?'

Gareth clicked his radio and gave Laura a meaningful look. It was the patrol car they had sent over to the Talwrn Convenience Store. She prayed they had got there in time and no harm had come to Dai Lewis.

'Alpha nine-zero from Gold Command, receiving, go ahead,' Gareth said.

'We're at Talwrn Convenience Store. It's shut up and locked. There's no sign of the proprietor, suspects or anyone else, over.'

That doesn't make sense.

Gareth frowned as he exchanged a look with Laura. 'Received, Alpha nine-zero. Continue with search of local vicinity for target vehicle and suspects, out.'

Laura looked at him. 'Maybe he decided to close for the day and go?'

'But he didn't say he was going to do that.'

'He seemed very scared,' she pointed out, as she ran

267

through various scenarios in her head. 'You wouldn't blame him. Do we have a home address for him?'

Gareth went to the laptop and tapped some buttons. '29 Cresswick Close. Looks like it's about a mile from the shop, which I'm guessing at Dai Lewis's pace is a fifteen-minute walk.'

Laura looked at her watch. 'So, if he locked up after our call, he would be arriving back home right now.'

Gareth gestured to the laptop. 'I've got a landline number. I'll give it a call.'

She watched him walk away. On a professional level, they were totally in sync with each other. But what about on a personal level?

He's strong, intelligent, funny and very attractive, she thought. *But does he like me in that way? I can't tell. I think he does.*

'A car has just arrived with Neil Cole in it. I think you and the boss wanted to talk to him?' said a voice, breaking her train of thought. It was a male PC who had arrived by her desk without her even noticing.

God, I really was miles away, wasn't I?

'Definitely,' Laura said as she processed his question and nodded emphatically. 'Can you bring him in here for us?'

The PC gestured to the door. 'He's just outside, ma'am.'

'Brilliant,' Laura said as she got up and followed the PC over to the front of the lifeboat station.

Outside the open door was standing a man in his forties. He had short, cropped blond hair and a rounded chin and face. He had his hands thrust into his jeans pocket and looked nervous.

'Mr Cole?' Laura asked as she approached and shook his hand.

He snorted but smiled kindly. 'Long time since anyone called me Mr Cole. It's Neil.'

'If you want to follow me?' She gestured back into the lifeboat station. 'I don't know how much you know about what's going on?'

'The copper who picked me up explained that Callum and Michael were caught up in something in Anglesey and you needed my help. I've been reading the news on my phone, so I put two and two together.'

'Have a seat,' she said, pointing to a spare chair. 'We believe that Callum and Michael are part of an OCG operation – sorry, that means an Organised Crime Group . . .'

Neil gave her a wry smile. 'It's all right. I watch *Line of Duty*, so I know what an OCG is.'

'The OCG planned to make a delivery of drugs by boat to their associates, who were going to be waiting for them on Beaumaris Beach,' Laura told him. 'We had a tip-off but when they realised they were walking into a trap, they turned the boat around and left. However, their boat broke down and they boarded a local cruise ship full of tourists and schoolchildren heading for Puffin Island. And they were armed.'

'Jesus Christ!' He closed his eyes for a moment and shook his head. 'I can't believe they've got mixed up in something like this . . . Are they still on the boat? Do you want me to talk to them?'

She shook her head. 'They got hold of a speedboat and took an eleven-year-old boy and his teacher hostage. They were forced to land on Anglesey where they stole a car at gunpoint. We don't know where they are at the moment, but we don't think they could have got very far from where they landed.'

'Bloody hell,' he said on a gasp. 'What a mess.'

'Did you have regular contact with them when you were in prison?' she asked.

'At first, yes,' he said, leaning forward. 'I had an agreement

269

with my sister, Kerry, if anything ever happened to me, she would look after Callum and Michael. When it came to it, she let me down and said she couldn't cope with it. But the care home was very good about bringing them to see me regularly. In recent years, since they've been mixed up in all this type of thing, I've hardly seen them. Michael came to see me last Christmas and brought me a present. It's probably two years since I've seen Callum.'

She looked at him. 'I've read the case notes about what happened in 2014.'

Neil pursed his lips together. 'I'm not making any excuses for what I did.'

'Callum and Michael had made an allegation against Kevin Hopper, is that right?' she asked.

He nodded. 'Yeah. He . . . sexually assaulted them both on a camping trip they went on with the Scouts.'

'But he wasn't arrested?'

He shook his head. 'It was his word against theirs. The police were investigating it when I killed him.'

'What did Callum and Michael think about what you'd done?'

'Callum said that Hopper deserved it,' Neil admitted. 'I'm not sure about Michael. He's quite sensitive and shy. He didn't really say anything.'

'I think it's probably sensible for me to tell you that the little boy they've got with them is my son, Jake. He was on a school trip on the boat.'

'Oh my God.' His face fell. 'I'm so sorry to hear that. Of course I'll talk to them. I'll do anything I can do to help get your son back. And the teacher.'

Laura gave him a benign look. He seemed genuinely upset by what she had told him. 'Thank you, Neil. If you can wait here for a bit, I'll tell the officer in charge what we talked about.'

Spotting Gareth ending a call on his mobile phone, Laura approached him and gestured over to Neil. 'That's Neil Cole, Callum and Michael's father. He said he'd do anything to help and is more than happy to talk to them.'

'Great.' Gareth pointed to his mobile phone. 'I've tried Dai Lewis's home three times now. No reply.'

'He claimed his wife was going out to see her sister,' Laura suggested.

'I suppose he might just not be back yet?'

She thought of something and gave him a dark look. 'And what if Red and the others turned up, and he's now being held captive in his own shop?'

'Okay,' he said, pausing for thought.

'We need someone to check the road from his shop to his home, and then check that he's not sitting at home drinking tea and watching the telly.'

'I'm loath to take another patrol car away from the search in case we're barking up the wrong tree,' Gareth admitted and then glanced at his watch. 'If I put the blues and twos on, we could be there in fifteen minutes.'

'Then what are we waiting for?' she asked with a wry smile. She guessed there were worse ways to spend time than hurtling through the countryside with DI Gareth Williams.

Michael grabbed two cold beers from the fridge, scurried across the shop to where Callum was sitting and handed him one.

'Ta,' Callum said as he pulled the ring. 'How many of those have you had, kid?'

'A couple,' Michael protested. 'It's just Fosters, mate.'

'Yeah, well, you're gonna need to keep your wits about you when we have to steal the next car that comes.'

There were a few seconds of silence.

Michael sat and drank his beer. 'What the fuck happened to us, Cal?'

'What d'you mean?'

Michael gestured to the shop. 'Here. All this. We're out of our depth and that nutter is going to get us life sentences, if we're not careful.'

'You know what your problem is?' Callum reached over and gave Michael a friendly tap on the face. 'You worry too much.'

'Yeah, well, I won't have to worry for much longer.'

Callum took this in and then frowned. 'What does that mean?'

'After this is all over,' Michael said, 'I'm gone. It's all over for me.'

'What are you saying?'

'You know what I'm saying, Cal,' Michael said. 'This isn't me. It isn't you, either. I'm getting the fuck out of Liverpool and I'm never coming back.'

'Yeah, well, there are few people who might not let you do that,' Callum whispered as he looked over at Red.

'What does that mean?'

'You know what it means,' Callum said. 'You can't just say, "*Sorry, lads. Thanks for everything but I'm off now.*"'

'What?' Michael narrowed his eyes and looked at his brother. 'I've got to do this for the rest of my life? No way. No fucking way.'

'Then they'll find you floating in the Mersey. I'm not joking.'

Michael took a long swig of his beer. His head was a little fuzzy from the alcohol. 'Yeah, well, I'll take my chances.'

'As long as I'm around, you're safe, Michael,' Callum said. 'Once you're out there on your own, I can't help you.'

'Safe?' Michael snorted. 'Jesus, that's a joke.'

Callum frowned. 'Sorry, you've lost me there, kid.'

'It's too late to protect me, Cal.' Michael pushed his lips together. 'I needed protecting seven years ago. Now I'm just damaged fucking goods.'

272

Callum turned his head slowly towards Michael. 'Don't even fucking go there.'

There was a long, uncomfortable silence.

Whether it was the beer, the events of the day or seeing Jake looking so fragile and helpless, Michael wanted to talk about what had happened that night at the Scout Camp. He *needed* to get it off his chest. It had been crucifying him for the last seven years. The question that he had never dared ask.

'Why didn't you do something, Cal?' he whispered. 'You lay there and let him do that.'

Callum didn't react. It was as if he hadn't heard what Michael had said.

Getting to his feet, Callum mumbled. 'I'm going for a piss.'

Michael finished his beer as he watched Callum walk away and wiped the tears that were oozing through his eyelashes.

Chapter 38

Laura and Gareth were hammering across country towards Talwrn. The search for the gang, the missing Land Rover and, more importantly, Jake and Beth was becoming frustrating. It seemed to Laura that they had simply vanished. They had a helicopter and several patrol cars scouring the area from where the Land Rover had been taken close to Red Wharf Bay, across to the Menai and Britannia Bridges that led to the Welsh mainland and then England. However, there hadn't been the slightest hint of a sighting.

'I think they've switched cars,' Laura said, thinking out loud.

'I'd agree, but we haven't had any calls reporting an armed car-jacking anywhere,' Gareth pointed out. She knew he was right. That kind of serious crime would have been reported within minutes.

Gareth gestured to the Talwrn Convenience Store as he pulled up outside. 'Let's have a look and then track Dai Lewis's movements if he did head home.'

Getting out of the car, Laura squinted up at the blazing

sun and put her sunglasses back on. The thin, wispy clouds had slowly morphed into a cloud that looked like a fish skeleton.

She looked down at the various sets of tyre tracks that had been left in the dirt and gravel beside the petrol pumps.

Where are you, Jake?

While Gareth went over to the windows of the shop, she approached the door, which had a CLOSED sign. Behind that was a tired-looking roller blind which had been pulled down so that it was virtually impossible to see inside. The blind had been bleached by the sun, except for its edges, which retained the original tan colour.

Cupping her hands to block out the sunlight, she saw an inch gap in the blind. Inside the shop was dark and empty. Her eyes scanned the floor, looking for anything that would indicate that the gang had been there. There was nothing.

She tried the door, but it was locked.

'Anything?' she asked, looking over at Gareth. She already knew their visit was proving to be futile.

He shook his head. 'I don't think they're in there, if I'm honest. But let's go to Dai Lewis's home, check he's there and then head back to Beaumaris if all else fails.'

It wasn't what she wanted to hear. They weren't making any progress.

Laura gave an audible sigh. 'Where have they bloody gone, Gareth? I don't understand it.'

'All I can tell you is if we're being logical about it, they didn't vanish into thin air,' Gareth replied as they made their way back to the car. 'And if a helicopter and patrol cars can't see them on the road, my instinct is that they are hiding somewhere out of sight. Maybe they think it's safer to make their move by night?'

As she got into the car, she gritted her teeth in frustration. It wasn't going to get dark until nearly ten o'clock that night.

275

She couldn't bear to wait that long. She wanted this night-marish day to be over and to have Jake back in her arms.

'I thought we were taking the next car that stopped here?' Callum asked, sounding frustrated.

A minute earlier, a car had pulled up and two people had looked in through the door and the windows. Because of the sunlight and the blinds, all Beth could see were their shadows peering inside. She had held her breath, waiting for Red to charge outside with his gun and commandeer the car.

But nothing had happened and whoever had stopped had now gone – and she didn't know why. The whole thing had just added to her feeling on edge.

'Why did you let them go?' Callum asked after getting no reply from Red.

'They were coppers, you divvy,' Red snapped as he puffed on the cigarette that he had just lit. The smoke rose and caught the slices of sunlight that came from the thin gaps in the blinds.

Callum furrowed his brow. 'How d'you know that?'

'I saw them when they got out of the car.' Red was getting angry at being questioned. 'I know a fucking bizzy when I see one. They look different, they walk different, so shut your mouth, will ya?'

There were a few uneasy seconds of silence.

'Yeah, well, I'm fed up just sitting here,' Callum groaned.

'Oh yeah, Callum, I'm having a bloody party here, lad,' Red snapped. 'I suppose we should have just gone out there, waving our guns around, only to find a load of armed coppers sitting around the corner. Then we'd be dead or nicked. That's really smart thinking, you dickhead.' And with that, Red flicked the remainder of his cigarette over at Callum. It hit his chest and red embers showered over his clothes. He brushed them quickly off before they burned the material.

'For fuck's sake, Red!' Callum yelled.

Red took a long swig of whisky, exhaled noisily and then glared at him. 'You wanna say something, la? You wanna go?'

Beth could feel the tension in the shop was about to boil over. At this rate, they were going to end up shooting each other.

Without warning, Callum jumped to his feet, pulled the handgun from his waistband, pointed it at Red and walked towards him. A sneer creased his face.

'Yeah, I wanna go, lad. Fucking flick a ciggie at me! Who the fuck are you?'

Red jumped down from the counter where he had been sitting. He grabbed the Skorpion machine gun and walked towards Callum. 'Think you're a big man, eh? It takes guts to shoot someone, but you wouldn't know about that, would you? So, go 'head.'

Red took the barrel of Callum's handgun and pulled it so that it was pressed against his own forehead. 'Come on then! Shoot me. Splatter me fucking brains all over this shop, lad. Do it! Go on, do it!'

Jake whimpered and buried his head in Beth's side. She could feel him shaking. It felt like something was about to explode.

Even though her heart was hammering, she couldn't take it any longer. 'Oh my God! Will you shut up? I teach ten-year-olds that are more mature than you!'

They ignored her.

'You really want me to shoot you?' Callum growled through gritted teeth.

'Come on, pussy boy,' Red sneered again, pushing his forehead hard against the barrel. 'Do it.'

Callum looked at him, took the gun away from his forehead and turned. 'I'm not serving life for you, prick.'

Red gestured with his hand. 'That's it, pussy. Go and sit down and stay out of my fucking way.'

Red took another swig of whisky, grabbed a cigarette and hopped up to sit on the counter. He looked over at Beth, who was looking at him.

'What?' he snapped.

'Nothing,' she replied, but she could see that the more drunk he was getting, the angrier and more irrational he was.

She glanced out towards where the petrol pumps were located and wondered when the next car would stop and park. Although she had no desire to watch someone have their car stolen at gunpoint, she knew it was safer for them to be on the move than cooped up in an increasingly hot shop where tempers flared.

Gareth and Laura walked up the garden pathway to the front door of 29 Cresswick Close, where Dai Lewis lived with his wife. The front garden was immaculate, with beautifully tended flower beds. Several hanging baskets, with a mixture of white and purple petunias, swung in the warm, gentle breeze. A couple of bees buzzed and flitted around the flowers before flying away.

Gareth gave an assertive knock on the door, took a step back, and pulled out his warrant card. A few seconds later, there was the metallic sound of the door being unlocked. A woman in her sixties, who they assumed was Mrs Lewis, answered.

'Hello?' she asked with a perplexed look. Her face was weather-worn and lined. Her outdated glasses sat flat against her face and she was wearing a hearing aid. Despite the heat, she was wearing a pale cardigan and a thick woollen skirt.

'Mrs Lewis?' Gareth asked, showing his warrant card. 'I'm DI Gareth Williams from Anglesey Police. This is my colleague, Laura Hart.'

'Yes?' She peered at them. 'Is something wrong?' She spoke in a thick North Wales accent. Laura immediately had her pegged as someone whose first language was Welsh. It was the way she had pronounced the *g* in *wrong* as hard.

Laura smiled at her. 'We're looking for your husband and we wondered if he was at home?'

Mrs Lewis opened the door wider and shook her head. 'No, no. He'll still be at the shop in the village.'

'We've been to the shop, and it's all closed up,' Gareth explained. 'The closed sign is hanging in the window, the blinds are drawn and the lights are off.'

'What?' Mrs Lewis said with a perplexed frown. 'No, no. That can't be right. We don't close until six.'

'Could your husband have popped out for something and closed up the shop?' Laura suggested gently. Something was starting to make her feel uneasy.

'No, no. Dai would never do that.' Mrs Lewis shook her head emphatically. 'We've been running that shop for over thirty years and I've never known us shut except for the day of my mother's funeral.'

Gareth pointed to the road they had travelled down from Talwrn. 'And if your husband was walking home from the shop, he would have come down this road, would he?'

'Yes. That's right. But it's too hot for him to do that today.' Mrs Lewis was looking increasingly worried. 'Besides, like I said, he would have no reason to close up early and walk home. I don't understand.'

'I spoke to your husband earlier about some men that are on the island in a stolen car,' Gareth explained. 'I wanted to see if he had seen them. I got the feeling that I might have scared him a bit. If he had decided to close the shop and leave, is there anywhere else he might go?'

'No.' Mrs Lewis blinked nervously. 'Where would he go?'

'A friend's house? Or a relative?' Laura suggested.

279

'No.' She shook her head again. 'We're the only ones that live in Talwrn these days. Oh dear, I don't understand what's happened to him.'

Gareth tried to give her a reassuring look. 'I'm sure he's going to be fine. If you stay here, we'll give you a call as soon as we hear anything, okay?'

Mrs Lewis nodded. 'Erm . . . all right. Yes.'

Laura looked at her. 'Have you got anyone who could come and sit with you until we find your husband?'

'My sister might be able to come over, I suppose,' Mrs Lewis said, now lost in thought. 'I could give her a ring.'

Laura smiled. 'Why don't you do that.'

'Yes, okay.'

Laura and Gareth walked down the garden path as she closed the door behind them. It had been horrible to witness how frightened Mrs Lewis had become during their questioning. She would be sitting there panicking until they found out what had happened to her husband.

Gareth looked at Laura as they reached the car and asked, 'What do you think?'

'Something's definitely not right,' Laura replied. 'I'm worried that something horrible has happened to Dai Lewis.'

Chapter 39

4.57 p.m.

Laura and Gareth were making their way back to the Talwrn Convenience Store. Something about the empty shop didn't sit right with her – but she didn't know what it was. And if she had learned anything as a detective, it was to trust her instinct.

Looking down at the floor, she moved an empty can of Diet Coke with her foot. The inside of the car was untidy and strewn with empty cans, crisp packets and sandwich wrappers.

God, Sam would have had a mild coronary seeing a car like this, she thought to herself.

Gareth's mobile phone rang, and he answered it. After a few seconds, he said. 'Okay, thank you.'

Laura raised an eyebrow as if to ask the nature of the phone call.

'Gary White just died in Bangor Hospital.'

'Shit!' she exclaimed.

'That is not good news,' he mumbled.

'I just pray that they don't see it. They'll panic and make even worse choices than they already have.' She sighed.

They both knew that Red would now face a murder charge, which made him much more dangerous, as he had far more to lose if he was captured. The other two members of the gang, Callum and Michael, might also face conspiracy to murder charges, as they were part of the kidnapping in which the murder had taken place. Either way, the stakes just went up to a whole new level and it only made Laura feel more uneasy.

As she looked up, she spotted a marked patrol car coming the other way. Gareth flashed his lights, and they both stopped in the road.

Opening the door, Gareth got out and leaned down to speak to the uniform officers inside.

'Has someone emptied a skip in here?' said a voice. It was Sam, who was sitting in the back seat.

'Jesus, Sam! You scared me!' Laura hissed.

Gareth looked into the open driver's door window. 'Everything all right?'

She smiled. 'Yeah. Just talking to myself.'

Gareth looked a little confused but went back to talking to the uniform officer.

She turned and glared at Sam. 'You know what's going on, Sam. So, I need you to piss off so I can concentrate on getting Jake back.'

'He's my son, too,' Sam protested.

'Yeah, but you're not helping by popping up like this,' she complained. 'Are you actually with me all day?'

'What?'

'Are you actually looking over my shoulder all day, Sam?' she asked, but the uneasy feeling she'd had driving away from the shop was still nagging away at her.

'No, of course not,' he said. 'You seem distracted.'

'I am.'

'Why?'

Then she realised what her instinct was telling her. 'They're in the shop, aren't they?'

Sam frowned. 'What do you mean?'

She gestured to the road and direction of the Talwrn Convenience Store. 'Jake, Miss Hughes, those scumbags. I think they're still in the shop.'

'You've just been there. You would have seen something,' he said, 'so why do you say that?'

'I was a copper for twenty years. No one can find the Land Rover. Dai Lewis is missing. The shop is closed up. My instinct is that they're in there working out their next move.'

'And you think they've parked the Land Rover out of sight?' he asked, joining up the dots.

'Exactly.'

'Good thinking, Batman.' He smiled at her. 'I forgot what a good copper you are.'

'I just want Jake back safely,' she said with a serious expression.

Sam nodded. 'Yeah, it's killing me too, not being able to do anything to rescue him.'

She looked at him. 'You understand the irony, don't you?'

'It's killing me?' he joked dryly. 'Yeah, but only after I'd said it.'

The driver's door opened, and Gareth got back in.

'Anything?' she asked him, feeling slightly thrown after her conversation with Sam.

Gareth shook his head. 'Nope. Not a peep. What if they switched cars, and the driver is now being held hostage too?' he asked, thinking out loud. 'We wouldn't have a report of a car-jacking if the driver was with them.'

'Maybe.' She shrugged. 'I can't see them wanting to have more hostages with them though.'

'But it would allow them to switch vehicles without us

283

knowing,' he suggested. 'Or they could have tied the driver up somewhere so they couldn't report the car as stolen.'

She processed what he was saying. 'My instincts are telling me there's something strange about Dai Lewis being missing and the shop being closed. I think they're in there and we just missed something.'

Gareth's mobile phone rang. 'DI Williams.' For a brief moment, he listened to whoever was on the other end of the call and then said, 'Thank you.'

'That was a CAD operator,' he explained in a serious tone. 'They had a 999 call forty minutes ago. The caller didn't say anything and after a few seconds, they put down the phone. They've just traced back the number . . . It's Talwrn Convenience Store.'

Chapter 40

19 May 2019

It was five weeks since Laura and Pete had visited Mandy Cooper. Despite Pete's best efforts, he had been unable to track down a recording of the emergency call made to the switchboard at Trafford Police Station. It had made them both suspicious. They now had an address for Martin Barratt, the CAD operator who had taken the details of the 999 call from Mandy, and had then dispatched Sam and Louise to Brannings Warehouse. Barratt had been relocated to a different CAD all the way over at Pendleton Police Station in Salford four weeks later. Just as with Mandy Cooper, it was suspicious in terms of timing.

Barratt lived in a ground-floor flat in a terraced house in Salford Quays. Walking up to the front door, Pete knocked and took a step back. There was a plastic bag full of beercans to the side of the door and pizza boxes in a pile.

After thirty seconds, Pete banged again but there was still no reply.

Laura walked over to a ground-floor window but the

285

curtains were pulled. She listened. Nothing from inside – no voices, no movement.

'Anything?' Pete asked.

She shook her head. 'Not a peep.'

Pete leaned down and opened the letterbox to see if he could see or hear anything inside. He pulled a face. 'Someone's been on the wacky-backy.'

Laura raised an eyebrow and grinned. 'Did you actually say *wacky-backy*? That's what my dad used to call it.'

Before Pete could respond, there was a metallic noise of keys turning and the front door opened.

A man in his thirties with scruffy blond hair, dressed just in grey trackie bottoms, peered out at them. 'Hello?' He looked half asleep.

Pete flashed his warrant card. 'We're looking for a Martin Barratt?'

Michael nodded. He looked concerned, but then again, a warrant card normally had that effect. 'Yeah. That's me.'

'Can we come in?' Pete asked.

He nodded and pointed inside. 'Can you give me two secs to get dressed, eh?'

Pete shrugged as he looked at Laura. 'No problem.'

Michael closed the door and went inside.

Laura looked at Pete. 'Have you ever known the recording of a 999 call to go missing before?'

'No, never,' Pete said, shaking his head. 'Technically it's not even missing. It just doesn't exist. Effectively, that emergency call was never received by Mandy Cooper and the details weren't passed onto our friend in there.'

Suddenly, they heard the clattering noise of a gate. It came from the back of the house. Laura took a few quick steps to the left and glanced down the scruffy side passage and driveway.

Thirty yards down, a figure in a black hoodie, grey trackies

286

and a black baseball cap was already climbing onto a wheelie bin.

She recognised the trackies.

Shit! He was doing a runner. *You little sod!*

Barrett then jumped and pulled himself up onto the flat roof of a single-storey garage in one move.

'Stop! Police!' Pete bellowed as they broke into a run.

They sprinted down the dank, overgrown alleyway. Barrett stopped on the roof and then looked back at him.

'Martin! Stop right there!' Pete yelled but Barratt turned, headed to the other side of the garage roof and vanished out of sight.

Suddenly, Pete pulled up in agony and clasped his knee. 'Jesus!'

'What's wrong?' Laura asked.

'It's my knee,' he groaned. 'The cartilage is fucked.'

Barratt was nowhere to be seen so she had no choice but to follow.

'Stay there,' she said. 'I'm going to have to go after him.'

'Be careful, then,' Pete warned her.

She smiled. 'It's okay. I've done this sort of thing before.'

Leaping onto the wheelie bin, she jumped and pulled herself up. At first, she thought she was never going to get there. It had been a long time since she pulled up her own bodyweight with just her arms. And she'd put on a few pounds since she left the force.

She began to shake with the sheer effort.

I don't think I can do this.

Eventually, she clambered onto the garage roof, grazing the skin from her forearm on the mastic asphalt roof. It stung but she had no time to think about it.

Laura went to the other side of the roof. Below was a car park on some kind of industrial estate, with half a dozen courier vans parked up beside two vast warehouses. An

287

enormous red articulated lorry was reversing up to some steel shutters, its reversing siren bleeping.

In the distance, she spotted Barratt sprinting out of the car park through a wire mesh gate. He disappeared out of view.

I'm never going to catch him at this rate.

Laura looked down and hesitated. It was high enough for her to break her ankle.

'Sod it!' she thought. She needed to know what happened that morning and why Sam and Louise had been called to Brannings Warehouse. Barratt knew something, otherwise he wouldn't have run.

Fuck it! Here we go!

She jumped, hit the ground with flat feet and felt a white-hot pain shoot up the outside of her right ankle.

'Jesus, that hurts,' she growled as she tried to put her weight on it. It was agony but something was urging her on.

Beginning to run flat out, Laura gritted her teeth against the pain in her ankle as she continued to chase Barratt. As she got to the mesh gate, there was a close of newly built houses in front of her.

Where the hell has he gone?

Then she heard the sound of feet pounding on the ground. Turning left, she spotted Barratt well over a hundred yards away, running down the road.

Laura broke into a full sprint, pumping her fists as she went. She'd managed to run off the pain. To her right, a burger van was dishing out food and Styrofoam cups of coffee and tea. Some of the customers turned to look at her as she sped past. A mother, holding the hands of two toddlers eating orange lollies in the sun, gave her a curious look as she thundered past.

Barratt veered left into a side road and out of sight again.

By the time Laura got to the turning, her feet were numb and the sweat was running down her back. She glanced down the side road.

Barratt had vanished.

Beginning to jog in the direction she assumed Barratt had headed, Laura was feeling dizzy and shook her head to try and stabilise herself.

Between the houses were discarded garages, alleyways, flat pieces of concrete peppered with weeds. It was quiet except for the distant noise of children playing. There were several cul-de-sacs leading from the road. It was basically a maze from here on and Barratt could have gone anywhere.

For God's sake.

A noise came from the side of an old boarded-up house. Slowing down cautiously, Laura jogged across the weeds to take a look.

Then a clatter. Metallic maybe.

Laura moved slowly and put her back against the wall. The brickwork felt rough against her back.

Another click. What the bloody hell was Barratt doing? Did he have a weapon?

Laura took a slow, quiet breath as her pulse thudded in her eardrum. She didn't want to peer down the side of the house only to get a blade shoved into her throat.

The noise stopped.

She moved her shoulder round, face touching the brickwork and inched across to see.

Suddenly, out of nowhere, a cat sprang off an old, stained mattress, yowled and bounded past her towards the fence.

'Shit!' Laura blurted out, jumping out of her skin. 'You little—'

Looking around her, Laura realised that Barratt could be anywhere.

Taking her phone from her pocket, she tried to get her breath as she dialled Pete's number.

'Laura? Are you okay?' Pete asked immediately.

'I'm really sorry, but I've lost him,' she panted.

Chapter 41

5.16 p.m.

Sitting with his back to the fridge, Michael looked over at Beth and Jake. The shop had been in a tense silence for over ten minutes, aside from the burble of a small portable television. There hadn't even been so much as a passing car or tractor in that time. He wondered how long they were going to wait. Red and Callum had found the television out the back. They were now watching BBC News, relishing the fact that they were the lead story. Michael thought their excitement and laughter at being featured on the news were pathetic.

He glanced over at Callum. His brother was not only not talking to him, he was also avoiding eye contact. Maybe he shouldn't have tried to talk to him about what had happened seven years ago? Maybe it was best left locked away? It didn't feel like it though. Michael still had nightmares in which he was being chased by Kevin Hopper. And the nightmares always ended the same – with him being trapped in a small room or some kind of confined space, and Kevin Hopper bearing down on him with his fat, sweaty face and greasy hair.

Michael took a long swig of beer and looked over at Beth. For a couple of seconds, she remained looking at the floor, but then she met his gaze. He gestured for her to come and sit next to him. She shook her head. He made a face at her and beckoned her over again. He wanted to tell her something. He needed to tell her something.

Beth rolled her eyes and slid across the floor while looking over at Red, who was ensconced watching the news.

'What?' she whispered as she sat against the wall next to him.

'I wanted to speak to you,' he whispered.

She frowned. 'About what?'

'I'm going to let you go,' he said.

'What?' She furrowed her brow and then looked over at Red to make sure he wasn't watching them. 'What are you talking about?'

'If I get a chance,' Michael explained in a hushed tone. 'I'm going to let you and Jake go.'

'How?' Beth asked. 'You'll get shot.'

'No, I won't.' Michael shook his head. 'I'll find a time. Just be ready to go when I tell you.'

After a few seconds, Beth gave him a friendly look. 'What are you doing here, Michael?'

'I don't know,' he admitted. He felt lost. 'You know what?'

'What?'

'If I ever get out of this,' he confessed, 'I'm going away. I'm leaving Liverpool and I'm never coming back.'

'Where are you going to go?' she asked.

'Anywhere.' He shrugged. 'Spain, Italy, I don't know. Somewhere where it's hot. I'll go swimming in the sea. Work in a beach bar.'

Beth smiled and, for a moment, put her hand on his arm. 'I really hope you do that, because all this is ruining people's lives.'

'Hey, we're back on the news again!' Callum said with a grin.

Red turned it up. 'Shut up, so we can listen, you divvy!'

He turned up the volume as the BBC anchor looked straight into the camera.

'And now the latest on the Anglesey boat hijacking . . . A fifty-three-year-old man, Gary White, who eyewitnesses say was shot while trying to negotiate the release of his daughter from the hijackers, has died from his injuries. A hospital spokesperson said, "Mr White arrived at Bangor Hospital this afternoon with a serious gunshot wound. Although staff in our trauma unit did everything they could, his injuries were too severe for him to be saved. His family have been informed."'

Red's face was full of thunder as he swigged again from the bottle of whisky. Michael knew Red would now face a murder charge and that he and Callum could also potentially be charged with conspiracy to murder because they were with him when it happened. Everything had just got about a hundred times more serious.

There was a sudden noise from outside. It was a car engine.

Red immediately jumped up from the counter, scurried over to the blind and looked outside.

'Bingo!' he whispered under his breath.

Callum came over. 'What is it?'

'Bloke in a BMW just stopped. He's just got out to look at the pumps.'

Red and Callum hurried towards the door and looked out.

As Laura and Gareth turned into Talwrn, they saw that a white BMW SUV was parked outside the convenience store. A man in his thirties in sunglasses was inspecting the pumps and then he went over to the windows to look inside.

'What's he up to?' Laura asked.

'Tourist low on petrol,' Gareth guessed. 'He's hoping they're open.'

'Yeah, well, I think he needs to go somewhere else – and right now.'

Gareth parked on the left-hand side of the garage and they jumped out.

'Excuse me!' Gareth yelled over, showing his warrant card. 'Anglesey Police. I'm going to need you move your vehicle, sir.'

The man frowned. 'Sorry. It's just that I'm driving on fumes and I don't want to run out. I saw the petrol pumps, so I stopped.' He had a Manchester accent.

Laura's eyes scanned the windows for movement. Nothing.

Gareth pointed. 'If you keep going down that road for about three miles, you'll find a big Asda. There's petrol there.'

The man smiled. 'Nice one. Thanks.'

Out of the corner of her eye, Laura spotted something by the door to the convenience store. Someone was looking out from behind the blind. Shit!

'Gareth!' she said in a controlled, quiet tone. 'Two people looking out of the shop by the door.'

Gareth looked over at the man. 'Sir, I'm going to need you to get in your car right now and drive away.'

The man smiled. 'Yeah, no problem, mate.'

Suddenly, the door to the store flew open.

Two men, both holding guns and carrying bags, moved out quickly. Laura quickly deduced that they were Paul Griffin, aka Red, and Callum Cole.

'Jesus!' The man gasped, his eyes widening. He put up his hands.

With her heart pounding against her chest, Laura moved

slowly back towards their car. She needed to try to get to the radio and ask for back-up.

Red pointed the Skorpion machine gun at the man and yelled, 'Give me the fucking keys!'

'It's . . . it's an automatic ignition,' the man stammered. 'The keys are already in there.'

'In that case, fuck off over there!' Red growled before turning to glare at Gareth, who was also walking slowly backwards towards their car. 'Who the fuck are you?'

Gareth shrugged. 'I'm no one. Just keep calm, okay?'

Laura looked over at the doorway.

Suddenly, Jake appeared with his teacher, Beth Hughes. Behind them was a teenage boy, who Laura knew must be Michael Cole.

Time seemed to stop for a moment as she took in Jake's little face and unruly hair. She just wanted to run and protect him.

'Jake!' she shouted out instinctively.

Jake spun and looked over, his eyes wide with shock. 'Mummy!'

Callum, who had the rucksack over his shoulder, grabbed Jake by the arm and ushered him into the BMW, followed by Beth Hughes.

By now, Gareth had reached the car.

Having opened the driver's door, Red glared at them. 'You're those two coppers who were here before, aren't you?'

Gareth and Laura didn't respond.

Red took the machine gun and aimed it at them.

Laura held her breath. Was he just going to shoot them in cold blood?

She looked him straight in the eye. 'Come on, Red. What are you doing? This is over. It's time to stop now,' she said in an almost maternal tone. Then she remembered the names of his parents. 'What would John and Sheila say if they were here right now, Red?'

Red gritted his teeth with hatred. 'Don't pretend you know me, you bitch!'

CRACK!

He fired a bullet in their direction.

Jesus Christ!

It hammered into the headlight of Gareth's car, and glass exploded everywhere.

Laura flinched and then dived to the floor for cover. She had dirt and dust on her face and in her mouth. All she could think about was Jake and what he was going through.

With her pulse thudding, she held her breath.

If he opens up with that thing, we're sitting ducks here, she then thought grimly.

The BMW's engine started.

'Laura? Are you okay?' Gareth shouted from the other side of the car.

'Fine. You?' she yelled as she scanned the BMW for Jake. She saw the top of his head in the back.

Please keep him safe!

There was the sound of tyres spinning and squealing as the BMW pulled out and sped away.

'I think so.'

Laura got herself up off the ground, rubbing her dirty hands together.

Dai Lewis!

She sprinted across the forecourt and into the shop. Heading towards the back, she saw a door to the right. She flung it open.

Dai Lewis was sitting on a chair, gagged with his hands bound behind his back.

Glancing around the stock room, she grabbed a pair of scissors. She removed the gag and went to work on the string that was wound around his wrists.

'Are you okay?' she asked.

296

He looked very shaky as he rubbed his wrists. 'Yeah, I think so.'

'I'm going to call an ambulance for you.'

'I don't need an ambulance,' he said.

'I'm going to call one anyway, to be on the safe side,' she explained. 'You're safe now. I'll get word to your wife that you're okay.'

He pointed to the shop. 'It's fine. I can ring her from here right now.'

'Okay,' she nodded. 'I've got to go now, but as long you're all right.'

'Go after them,' Dai said urgently. 'They've got that little boy.'

Laura got up, turned on her heels, dashed out of the shop and over to the car.

'Come on!' she yelled as she jumped in.

Gareth revved the engine. 'How is he?'

'Surprisingly fine.'

Gareth clicked his radio. 'Gold Command to all units, are you receiving, over?'

The man who had been driving the BMW stood looking shocked by what had happened as he spoke into his mobile phone. He jumped out the way as Gareth hit the accelerator, spinning the wheels as they roared away in pursuit.

'Gold Command from Alpha Zero. Go ahead, over,' came the reply.

'We're in pursuit of hijacking suspects. White BMW X5, registration Yankee, Bravo, two, zero, Tango, Charlie, Charlie. Heading south-west out of Talwrn on the B5110. Suspects are armed and very dangerous. They have two hostages on board. Proceed with maximum caution, over.'

'Alpha Zero received. Stand by, over.'

'Let's get that bastard,' Gareth snapped.

Once out on the road, Gareth rapidly built up speed and they quickly reached 70 mph. Laura gripped the door handle with one hand and the dashboard in front with the other as the car screamed round a bend. She didn't care as long as they caught up with the BMW.

Gareth sat forwards a little, peering through the windscreen. 'Where are you, you bastard?'

The white BMW came into view, speeding up a hill about a mile ahead.

There they are.

Laura felt the Astra's back tyres losing grip and slipping as they cornered another bend.

Gareth took a quick look at her. 'You okay?'

'Not a big fan of high-speed pursuits, if I'm honest,' Laura admitted as her stomach lurched.

'Not a fan of boats, helicopters and high-speed chases,' Gareth said with a wry smile. 'I can see why you opted to train as a negotiator.'

She noticed that his dark brown eyes twinkled whenever he made a joke.

Gareth went hammering up the hill and over the crest. The BMW was now only about half a mile ahead, and they were gaining. He pulled out to overtake a tractor and silage tanker and shot past them at speed.

Laura was trying to work out what they were going to do if they caught up with the BMW. If armed units arrived, she didn't want the BMW to be stopped and for there to be some kind of stand-off. In those situations, suspects can lose their heads and start shooting indiscriminately.

'Gold Command from Dispatch. We have ARV unit tango two-one heading south on the B5111 towards your location, over.'

Laura knew the stakes were escalating now that an Armed Response Unit was heading their way.

She pressed the button on the Tetra radio. 'Gold Command received, over.'

'Thanks. Now let's take these bastards down and get Jake and Beth,' Gareth said with a steely determination, dropping the car into third as they reached a long hill.

'What's the plan when we stop them?' Laura asked as she was thrown against the door and then back again as they swerved around another bend.

'If they're surrounded, they'll have to give themselves up,' Gareth said confidently.

She looked at him and took a breath. 'And what if they don't?'

'What's the alternative?' he asked. 'Do you want three armed gang members disappearing with Jake in their car?'

'No, of course not.' Even the thought of that made her catch her breath. 'But if we surround them with armed officers, they might lose their heads and start shooting.'

'We have to take the option that gives us the most control over the situation,' he explained. 'If we lose them, we have no control.'

Laura tried to regulate her breathing. This wasn't the time for a panic attack.

She knew Red wouldn't stop now and would be driven on by fear and adrenaline.

Gareth took the Tetra radio. 'Suspects now heading south-east on B520. Two miles south of Talwrn. Speed nine-zero. Over.'

Laura looked over at the dashboard.

Christ! We really are doing 90 mph!

A moment later, they screamed through the tiny village of Penmynydd and screeched round a bend beyond. They were going so fast that Laura felt the houses and stone walls were only inches from the passenger door.

Just up ahead, a tractor pulled out of a field in front of

them. Gareth steered the car onto the opposite side of the road, missing it by a few feet.

'For God's sake!' he bellowed.

Laura thought about the fact that she didn't want to die today and closed her eyes for a second as they careered around another bend. She opened her eyes again as the car flashed past a red sign that read: ARAFWCH NAWR – REDUCE SPEED NOW!

If only, she thought.

'What if we just let them escape?' Laura asked.

'What are you talking about, Laura?' Gareth asked in a slightly condescending tone.

She wondered if her anxiety was preventing her from thinking clearly.

'If we let them escape, they'll drive to Liverpool, drop Jake and Beth on the roadside and then disappear,' she suggested.

Gareth gave her a dark look. 'You don't know that's what they're going to do.'

She shrugged. 'I think that's what they're probably going to do.'

'Red is now facing a murder charge,' he explained. 'The other two a conspiracy to murder charge. Beth and Jake are key witnesses to everything that's happened today. They've seen and heard everything.'

'What are you trying to say, Gareth?' she asked, although she knew exactly what he was getting at and thought of it made her stomach tighten and she felt nauseous at the back of her throat.

'Sorry to be blunt,' he said as he gripped the steering wheel. 'But I don't want to be pulling anyone out of the Mersey.'

She knew he was right. Allowing Jake and Beth to disappear with the gang was basically a matter of Russian roulette. Stopping them put the ball back in their court.

'Sorry,' she said. 'You're right.'

300

'Hey, if it was my kid, I'd be thinking of every scenario to get him back safely too.'

The white BMW was now only 500 yards away. It pulled out to overtake, and whizzed past two cars. However, as Gareth pulled out to do the same, there was a huge articulated lorry coming the other way.

Laura's eyes widened with alarm – there just wasn't enough time or space to get past the second car.

Gareth dropped down into third gear and the Astra roared uncomfortably, but the boost in speed bought them a couple of extra seconds and they made it past with inches to spare.

'Shit!' Gareth yelled as he stared fiercely ahead at the BMW, which was now only 200 yards ahead.

'Just don't lose them!'

Suddenly, another tractor pulled slowly out of a field in front of them. The BMW's back lights glared bright red as Red slammed on the brakes.

'Jesus Christ!' Gareth shouted, as he hit his own brakes hard.

The Astra skidded, and as Laura glanced ahead, she saw the BMW had swerved to try to avoid the tractor.

Please don't crash with Jake inside!

Laura felt like everything in her body was contracting as the Astra continued to skid at speed towards the tractor. She instinctively pulled her knees up and screwed her eyes closed. A metallic thud threw her forwards. The scraping of metal against metal, the sound of cracking glass. A glancing blow against the tractor sent the Astra spinning.

Another bang of metal and crunch of glass, with the sensation of spinning. Now they were travelling backwards. After a few more seconds, they came to a stop.

Laura blinked open her eyes, realised that she wasn't actually dead, and immediately looked over at Gareth. He looked back, blood running from a cut on this forehead.

'You all right?' he gasped.

'I think so. You?' she asked, dazed.

'Yeah. Apart from needing a new neck.'

Through their shattered windscreen, she looked in horror as the BMW sped away and out of sight.

'No!' she shouted.

Chapter 42

5.26 p.m.

Glancing behind, Michael could see that the police Astra had spun and come to a halt. A few seconds later, they had sped around a bend and the police car was out of sight.

Bloody hell, that was close, he thought.

'Woo hoo!' Red yelled. 'Fuck you, coppers!'

Callum reached over and high-fived him. Michael could see that they were clearly getting along again, which annoyed him.

For a while, there was peaceful silence as they drove. The BMW was still new enough to have that showroom smell. There were even small screens in the back of the headrests so that those in the back could watch movies.

Michael buzzed down the window a few inches and took a long, deep breath. The summer air was sweet and fresh. But it was changing.

Gazing at the sky above, Michael saw it had darkened as black clouds rolled in from the south. The sun was now hidden behind a vast canopy of grey, which had sucked the vivid colours from the countryside outside. The first few specks of rain travelled through his window and splashed gently against his face.

Michael's train of thought was broken when Red reached over to the stereo and played around with the tuning to find a station playing hip-hop.

'I want to see my mummy,' Jake murmured.

Michael could just about hear what he had said over the thudding bass of the music.

'Of course you do,' Beth said. 'And you'll see her again very soon. I promise.'

'I don't even know where we're going,' Jake mumbled.

Michael looked over at Jake. 'We're just going on a bit of journey, mate. That's all. Nothing to worry about.'

'But where are we going?' Jake asked.

'I think we're trying to get to Liverpool,' Michael explained gently. He didn't want Red or Callum to hear what they were talking about.

'Liverpool?' Jake pulled a face and then looked down at his Manchester United shirt. 'My dad always said that I should hate Liverpool.'

Michael gave him a wry smile. 'Yeah, not a lot of love lost between United and Liverpool, is there?'

Jake looked blankly at Beth. He didn't know what that meant.

'You want to play for United when you're older?' Michael asked him.

Jake shook his head.

'No?' Michael asked. 'You don't want to be a footballer then?'

Jake shook his head.

Beth put her hand reassuringly on Jake's. 'So, what do you want to be when you grow up?'

Jake looked at them both. 'I'm going to be a policeman, like my dad.'

Michael looked at Beth for a second but was distracted by a noise outside the car.

He frowned as it grew louder, to the point that it was thunderous.

What's going on? It's like we're in a tornado.

Looking up into the sky, his jaw dropped. He saw exactly what was going on.

A black and yellow police helicopter was hovering about 300 feet above them.

Shit! They've spotted us.

Callum glanced up and shouted, 'Red!'

'Fuck!' exclaimed Red, and for a second he lost control of the car and it swerved across the road.

'This is the North Wales Police. Pull your vehicle over to the side of the road,' boomed an amplified voice from the helicopter.

'What's going on?' Jake asked, his eyes wide with fear.

'It's just a helicopter,' Beth said, trying to pretend it was nothing.

The voice boomed again. 'This is the North Wales Police. Pull your vehicle over to the side of the road and stop.'

'Just piss off!' Callum shouted, looking up into the sky.

'Shoot at them!' Red yelled.

Taking the handgun, Callum buzzed down the window and pointed the gun up at the helicopter above them.

In a flash, Michael leaned across the back seat and covered Jake's ears with his hands.

CRACK! CRACK! CRACK!

The sound of the handgun was deafening inside the car.

Beth winced and stuck her fingers in her ears. 'Jesus!'

As he took his hands away from Jake's head, Michael realised there was a high-pitched ringing sound in his own ears from the noise of the gunshots, and the pain that accompanied it was intense. He touched his ears to see if there was blood. There wasn't.

I'm gonna end up bloody deaf at this rate.

Looking up, he saw the helicopter had disappeared – for now.

'We've got to get off this bloody island,' Red growled.

Callum looked at him. 'There will be police on both bridges.'

Red shrugged. 'They can't keep both bridges closed permanently.'

'Yeah, but they know we're in this car,' Callum pointed out.

'What are they going to do with those two in here?' Red asked. 'Shoot at us? We'll drive over the bridge and there's nothing they can do about it.'

Michael glanced out of the window and saw the helicopter fly overhead and then circle back again, like an animal toying with its prey. He took a deep breath and looked at Beth. 'Yeah, that's if we even get to the bridges.'

Callum looked up again. 'Shit! How the hell do we lose them?'

Red turned onto the main road south. He stamped on the accelerator, and the 3.0-litre engine roared as they hit 80 mph.

Michael had a nervous knot in his stomach. How were they going to get out of this?

'I wish they'd just fuck off!' Red growled as he peered up cautiously.

Without braking, Red spun the steering wheel.

The back tyres screeched loudly, and he completely lost the back end of the BMW.

This is it, Michael thought. *We're going to flip over and we're all going to die!*

The car was now full of the acrid stench of burnt rubber.

Jake let out a whimper and Beth checked he was okay.

Spinning the steering wheel back, Red regained control.

'I thought we were going to crash,' Jake gasped.

Michael blew out his cheeks. 'Me too, mate. Me too.'

As they raced downhill away from the A55, Callum peered up into the sky. 'Where are you, you bastards?'

Red was looking in the other direction. 'I can't see them. You think we lost them?'

Callum shrugged. 'I doubt it.'

Suddenly, a black shadow came low across the sky in front of them.

'For fuck's sake!' Red shouted.

Michael knew the helicopter would have radioed their location. It wouldn't be long before there were police cars on their tail or even roadblocks. This wasn't good.

The helicopter hovered above them before flying ahead and circling back again.

As Red looked up, he lost control of the car again and they swerved across the road.

Jesus! Please God, let this day be over and let me live, Michael thought to himself.

Callum leaned out of the window and pointed the gun.

Jake and Beth both covered their ears with their hands.

CRACK! CRACK!

'Callum!' Michael shouted out in frustration.

Callum turned and glared at him. 'Have you got a better idea then, dickhead?'

'A better idea than bringing down a police helicopter?' he asked sarcastically.

Beth put her hand to her face nervously.

'Don't worry. I'll get us out of this,' Red said.

Out of the corner of his eye, Michael spotted a sign reading NEWBOROUGH NATIONAL NATURE RESERVE AND FOREST.

Red saw it too and gestured to the sign. 'Nice one!'

He turned the car sharply, following the signs for the forest. 'Hey, Callum, what do you find in forests?'

Callum shrugged and then peered out of the window nervously. 'What are you talking about, Red? Trees. You find lots of trees in a forest.'

'Exactly.'

Up ahead, Michael could see exactly what Red was talking about and why driving into the forest was a great idea.

There were endless rows of towering pine trees. He was no expert, but they looked like they were close to being 150ft high.

Red shouted, 'Try following us through this, you bastards!'

Callum laughed. 'Woo hoo!'

As they reached the forest, the sky disappeared behind the enormous canopy of trees above.

Red slowed a little. There was a right-hand turn marked YELLOW TRAIL. He slowed right down, and gazed up at the sky, which was virtually invisible through the branches.

Turning left, Red pulled into a small car park and stopped. The rain had started to fall heavily and pattered rhythmically on the roof and windscreen.

For a moment, everyone just sat getting their breath back and composing themselves.

Red and Callum opened the car doors and stepped out.

Michael got out too and stood frozen, listening intently.

Nothing except the soft patter of rain on the ground.

Callum laughed as he peered up at the sky. 'Oh, my God. They've gone.'

Chapter 43

Laura was now at a temporary incident base on the north side of the Menai Bridge. They had been forced to open the bridge as there were ten thousand islanders who commuted daily to mainland Wales, with at least five thousand coming the other way.

As the sky was darkening with cloud cover and the air filled with light drizzle, uniformed officers were slowing cars down on the north side to check the drivers' identities before allowing them to cross the bridge.

The Chief Constable had been in touch with Gareth, clarifying that he wanted a resolution to the situation. The media now had the story and the hunt for the gang was the lead story on every news channel. It was turning into a PR disaster for North Wales Police. How had the gang members managed to escape with two hostages, one of whom was only a child?

Taking a deep breath, Laura gazed north towards Anglesey. *Where the hell are you, Jake?*

Her phone rang. It was Rosie. They had exchanged a few

309

texts and voicemail messages over the day but they hadn't actually spoken yet.

'Mum, is he all right?' Rosie asked. She sounded terrified.

'Yes. And he's with his teacher Beth Hughes, so there's someone looking after him,' she said, trying to reassure her daughter.

'I don't understand. What do those men want?'

'We're not sure yet, darling,' Laura said. 'I'll let you know as soon as I know anything.'

'Where are you?'

'Menai Bridge.'

'Okay,' Rosie said. 'I feel so helpless.'

'I know. Just sit tight and I promise I'll call you as soon as I hear anything.'

'I love you, Mum,' Rosie said, sounding upset.

'I love you too. I'll talk to you in a bit.'

As Laura ended the call, Declan came jogging over. He was holding a map book, which he showed to her.

'Ma'am, the chopper spotted the suspects off the A55 here. Just by a place called Trefdraeth. They followed them up the A55 but then lost them just here in the Newborough Forest.'

Laura looked at the map. 'If they're on the A55, then they're coming this way.'

Declan frowned. 'You really think they're going to come over one of the bridges?'

'I don't see that they have any other choice. Where else can they go? They can't keep driving around Anglesey for ever.'

Spotting a young CID officer taking a cigarette from a packet, Laura went over. 'Mind if I steal one of those?'

'Of course,' the CID officer said as he offered the packet to her. She took the cigarette and he lit it.

'Thanks,' Laura said. 'I owe you one.' She turned and headed back to the side of the bridge and leant over the railings.

Looking east over the Menai Strait from the bridge, she took a deep drag and blew a long plume of smoke up into the air. The day had been a sharp reminder of just how exhilarating, challenging and demanding being a police officer could be. Obviously she was personally involved, but there had been moments when she had been in full DI mode when it felt like the job she had been born to do.

God, I really do miss being a copper.

The black water churned and swirled below her. From where she stood, she could see the power and overwhelming force of the undercurrents and tides that made the Strait so deadly. For a moment, she had a twinge of vertigo and took a breath to keep it in check.

'I didn't know you smoked,' Gareth said with a raised eyebrow as he approached.

She shrugged as she turned. 'I don't. Not anymore.'

She'd had two cigarettes in the past ten years. Both of them were smoked at the funerals of fallen colleagues who were being laid to rest – the latter being her husband's.

'I don't blame you,' he said. 'I used to smoke forty a day. Marlborough Red.'

'Yeah, well, I was never that bad.'

'Oh, thanks,' he said with a wry smile that developed into a more earnest look. 'I don't know how you're keeping it together.'

She gave a droll laugh. 'Neither do I.'

'Seriously,' Gareth said, looking at her. 'I know what you've been through. And I can't imagine what you're feeling right now. You're remarkably strong.'

'Stop, otherwise I might actually lose it,' she said with a lump in her throat.

'Hey, don't worry,' Gareth said in a low voice. He put his hand reassuringly on her shoulder. 'We're getting Jake back today. You have to believe that.'

311

The sincere look in his eyes and the hand on her shoulder overwhelmed her for a moment. There was something so powerful and protective about his presence.

'I do believe that.' She sniffed as she wiped a tear from her face. 'God, I'm sorry. That's really embarrassing.'

'Don't be silly,' Gareth said. 'I can't think of anything more stressful than what you're going through.'

'What if they don't come here?' she asked.

'They *are* coming here.'

'I must look a state.'

'Far from it.'

Their eyes met for a moment. There was something very intense building between them. She could feel it.

Like her emotions, the intensity of the rain was growing too, and the sky was now black with storm clouds. Laura pulled up the collar on her coat.

Gareth's radio crackled. 'Gold Command this is Bravo nine-three, are you receiving over?'

'Bravo nine-three from Gold Command, receiving, go ahead, over,' he said.

'We have a visual on target vehicle travelling south on the A55. They have just passed Gwalchmai, over.'

'Gold Command received, standby, Bravo nine-three,' Gareth said.

He put down his radio and looked at Laura. 'They're travelling south, they're ten miles away and they're heading our way.'

'In that case, where's Neil Cole?' she asked.

Gareth pointed. She saw him standing about a hundred yards away drinking coffee.

'Good,' she said. 'I think we're going to need him.'

Beth gazed out of the window. The surface of the A5 was smooth but wet, which made the tyres turn with a slight hiss.

312

The flat terrain on both sides of the road seemed gloomy and apparently endless. It looked more like they were in the middle of some remote American prairie than North Wales. By now the sky above them was dark with storm clouds and the rain was falling hard onto the windscreen.

Red stepped on the accelerator and sped past a car towing an enormous white caravan. The driver, a middle-aged man in a baseball cap, gave them a thankful wave.

Christ, if only he knew what was going on in this car, she thought.

Callum was busy texting on the phone in the passenger seat.

'Nice one,' Callum said triumphantly, looking over at Red and pointing at his phone. 'Someone's meeting us on the other side of the bridge with a car.'

'Where?'

'Some place called Bethseda?' Callum said uncertainly.

'Bethesda,' Beth corrected him.

'Yeah, that's it. Bethesda,' Callum said. 'We can switch cars there and ditch this one.'

'How far is it?' Red asked.

Callum shrugged and looked back at Beth.

'It's about ten miles on the other side of the bridge,' she explained.

She had an uncle and aunt just down the road in Capel Curig and had spent various family holidays taking walks into Snowdonia, building forts out of logs and sometimes horse riding.

Callum looked at Red and raised his eyebrows. 'Think we can do that, mate?'

Red narrowed his eyes. 'Let them try to fucking stop us, lad.'

Glancing up, Michael saw a sign to Bangor and another to Menai Bridge. It was only ten miles away.

313

They came to the top of a steep hill. As they went over its crest, the valley of the River Cefni stretched out before them. Even in the pouring rain, it was stunning.

'God, it's so beautiful here,' Beth said quietly with a sigh.

'I've never seen anywhere like this before,' Michael admitted.

Beth opened her window and sat back as the wind and rain battered her face. It smelt so fresh and cold.

God, please let me and Jake get through this day alive.

Michael had his mobile phone in his hand and was texting. After a few seconds, he nudged her casually with his elbow and showed her the screen.

When we get to the bridge, there will be police. When I give you a sign, I'm going to distract Red and Callum. I want you and Jake to make a run for it.

Beth read it and looked at him. There was part of her that didn't want to escape from the car on the bridge. What if Red or Callum shot them in the back as they ran? Wasn't it safer to just stay in the car? It had, however, dawned on her that she and Jake were witnesses to everything that Red, Callum and Michael had done and said all day. Did that put them in greater danger? Were the gang really going to just let them go once they reached the safety of Liverpool? Or did they actually plan to get rid of them?

Suddenly, she saw flashing blue lights in their rear-view mirror.

Oh God!

Red pushed down the accelerator, the engine roared and she felt herself pushed back in the seat.

Callum spun around to look at the police in pursuit of them. He looked alarmed. 'For fuck's sake!'

Red pressed the accelerator so that it touched the floor,

and the engine rumbled. 'Don't worry. We can outrun that thing.'

Beth glanced through at the digital speedometer – 85 mph.

'How far are we from the bridge?' Callum asked.

'Less than ten miles,' Michael replied. 'I saw a sign.'

Looking up ahead, they saw that two police cars with flashing lights had blocked off the road.

Red groaned and said, 'Shit! Road block!'

Michael's eyes widened. 'What are we going to do?' he asked. He suddenly sounded very young.

'That's the beauty of being in a car like this,' Red said to no one in particular. Nothing seemed to faze him.

'What is?' Callum asked.

'This is!' Red spun the steering wheel. The car skidded off the road and smashed through a fence as they sped into a field.

The ground was uneven. A series of bumps threw them around the car.

Beth reached up and grabbed the handle above her. 'Jesus!' She looked at Jake. 'You okay?'

He nodded as he gripped the edge of the seat with both hands.

Tearing across the field, Beth could see that Red was already putting distance between them and the police car.

Then, without warning, a large police Ford Ranger appeared from the right. It was heading their way.

'Bollocks!' Red snapped as he saw it.

Turning sharp left, the BMW skidded back and forth, throwing mud and earth into the air.

Beth gripped the seat for all she was worth and glanced at the dashboard – 65 mph.

'Red!' Callum yelled.

Red had been so preoccupied avoiding the police Ford Ranger, he hadn't seen a huge wooden shed right in their path. There wasn't time to stop.

Beth held her breath and threw an arm across Jake to protect him.

CRASH! They hit the wooden wall hard.

For a second, they couldn't see anything except for splintering wood and hay.

Then everything cleared and Beth let out a sigh.

Phew!

Glancing back, she could see the Ford Ranger was now only twenty yards behind them.

'I can definitely outrun that thing on the road,' Red bragged as he looked in the rear-view mirror.

Smashing through a low wire fence, the BMW hurtled back onto a road heading south.

A sign read MENAI BRIDGE – 3 MILES.

Red stamped on the accelerator, and Beth felt the engine kick in again.

Then she heard a mechanical sound. At first, she thought there was something wrong with the car, but as it got louder and deeper she recognised it.

She had heard that thundering sound before.

Helicopter!

Glancing skyward, she saw the black and yellow police helicopter that had followed them earlier come into view.

'Red!' Callum said as he looked up into the darkness.

'I know.'

Callum glanced in the wing mirror and then over at Red. 'Shit!'

Looking in the rear-view mirror, Beth counted four police cars that were now in pursuit. It was like a scene from a film.

We're not going to escape all those, are we? she thought as her stomach tightened. She gave Jake a reassuring pat on the arm.

As she looked outside, she noticed a line of blue metal railings on either side of the road.

316

Where the hell are we?

As they turned the corner, an enormous steel structure came into view.

Menai Bridge.

Red slammed on the brakes. The car skidded as it slowed down and eventually stopped.

Everyone gazed at the looming structure of the nineteenth-century suspension bridge, which towered over 100 feet into the dark sky.

The helicopter was now circling above them with its spotlight cutting through the rain and gloom.

Glancing in the rear-view mirror, Beth could see the police cars had stopped about fifty yards behind them. Some of the officers were getting out.

The bridge was completely blocked and sealed off with police cars. Their blue lights flashed, throwing strobed patterns onto the steel structure.

There was no way they were driving across.

At the sight of their car, police officers scuttled across the bridge and into position. She could see that some of them were armed.

'End of the road, I think,' Beth muttered.

Callum looked at Red. 'What are we going to do?'

Red revved the engine and then turned it off.

There were a few seconds of silence as Red tapped the steering wheel nervously with his fingers.

Then he turned his head and looked at Beth and then Jake. 'Get out of the car! We're walking over the bridge and you're coming with us.'

Chapter 44

Laura sprinted into the freezing water and dived through the icy wave. It was the only way to get in. She had tried the gradual immersion technique, but it was torturous. She had been cold-water swimming off Beaumaris at dawn on Saturday mornings for nearly a year now with the Bluetits, a group of mainly middle-aged or elderly lunatics who met up to face the challenge of sea swimming in all weather. It had been Gareth Williams who had suggested that she join when she mentioned her love of swimming in the sea all year round.

They must have made such a peculiar sight. Twenty adults stripping down to their trunks or swimsuits at dawn and charging into the sea with whoops and hollers. Laura loved the way she could experience the changing seasons and landscape through her swims. The way the water felt was always different. Sometimes dark, thick and velvety. Other times, clear, flat and glassy. They swam when it was barely light and freezing rain or hail peppered the sea's surface. And they swam when the warm early-morning sunshine gently dappled the surface, illuminating the bubbles under the water. They swam on Christmas morning, New Year's Day and Easter Sunday.

She loved it when it was gaspingly cold. The first time she went into the icy winter sea, it felt like her skin was burning. But she learned quickly that the body acclimatises and soon Laura was addicted to the shock and rush of wild cold-water swimming. She used it to numb her pain. To blast away the grief. It became utterly addictive. She even found herself craving the powerful rush of a cold-water high during the day sometimes.

This morning the sea seemed to be almost aquamarine in colour, and as the sun rose, the sky was reflected on the surface of the water. *I'm swimming in clouds,* Laura told herself, watching as a gull descended and landed close to her. Just before they headed in, a seal popped up to watch the group from about a hundred yards away. Laura knew she was probably imagining it, but she was convinced the seal had a bemused look on its face as if to say, *What are they doing?*

The post-swim ritual was just as important as the swim itself. The Bluetits sat huddled on the sand, wrapped in jumpers and blankets. There were hot flasks of tea and bowls of porridge passed around. Laughter. Sometimes bad news or worries were shared. And then it was back home. Hot shower on freezing bright red skin. And several hours of an energetic high, where Laura felt no one could touch her. She hadn't felt like that since she took Ecstasy a few times in the mid-nineties. And the best thing about cold-water highs? No dirty three-day comedown.

By midday, Laura was sitting at her kitchen table looking at the photographs that she and Jake had taken on their morning cycle along the beach from Beaumaris. They had headed south, with the Menai Strait to their left. On their way, they had stopped to allow Jake to take photos of whatever he wanted: the sky, birds, flowers or an interesting road sign. It's how they spent most Saturday mornings while Rosie dozed in bed. Jake had taken photos ever since they moved to Anglesey. It seemed to be a useful creative outlet for him and he would sometimes take them into school to show his teacher and class.

'What have we got?' Jake asked as he came over to sit with her at the table. He was nursing a gargantuan hot chocolate with squirty cream and a flake.

'This one,' Laura pointed to the screen. 'This is called a purple sandpiper.'

There was a photo of a small brown bird sitting on the wet sand.

Jake pulled a face. 'It's a bit boring.'

She clicked onto the next photograph, which was a close-up of a yellow flower. 'What about this one? That's a brilliant photo, Jake.'

He grinned. 'Yeah. I like that one.'

'You know what that's called?'

He shrugged.

'It's called Papaver Cambricum. And it's a Welsh poppy,' she informed him.

Jake frowned. 'I thought poppies were red?'

'Not Welsh ones,' she said. 'Welsh poppies are special. Shall I email it over to Auntie Emma or Nana to show her what we saw today?'

'Why don't we ever see Nana?' Jake asked with the kind of oblivious bluntness only a child could express.

Laura smiled. 'She lives in France, darling. It's a long way away. But I know that she thinks about you and Rosie, and she loves you both.'

'Can we go to France to see her one day?' he asked.

'I'm sure we can,' she replied uncertainly. She was fairly sure that was never going to happen.

Since her failure to show at Sam's funeral, there had been little effort on Geraldine's part to keep in touch with her grandchildren or Laura. Laura didn't know why. Maybe she found it too painful to see them and be reminded of her late son. If she was honest, Laura thought that Geraldine was too self-absorbed to really put the effort in. She remembered Sam telling her that Geraldine's first words to him when he rang her in France to tell her of Rosie's birth were '*Remember, Sam, I don't really do babies.*'

Jake wandered away without singing quietly to himself.

'Don't you want to look at the rest?' she asked.

'Maybe later.'

'What are you doing?'

'*Football Focus* is on,' he explained.

Even when Jake was very little, he and Sam would settle down to watch the BBC's *Football Focus* every Saturday lunchtime.

'No worries,' she said. 'I'll make lunch in a bit.'

She continued to look at the photos on the laptop. Today they had ended up in the Plas Cadant Secret Gardens, which were about five miles away. Laura told people it was Anglesey's best-kept secret. Two hundred acres of historic gardens that she and Jake loved to roam around. It consisted of three separate and very distinct areas. A formal garden with a pool and elegant curved walls. A secret valley garden with a river and three waterfalls. And then an upper woodland garden with a nineteenth-century folly and a series of stone outcrops.

There was a noise from the hallway and Rosie and Jake came in. They were carrying something.

'You guys okay?' Laura asked, wondering what they were doing.

Rosie was carrying an A3 piece of paper. She laid it down to show her. On the front were some photos and crayon drawing, and the top read: *HAPPY BIRTHDAY, DADDY – WE MISS YOU!*

Laura immediately felt a lump in her throat. Tomorrow would have been Sam's forty-seventh birthday and she had promised them they would travel to Leeds to Sam's grave. It wasn't something she would have normally suggested – she had hoped they would do something at home to remember him by – but Rosie and Jake were insistent that they go to see him.

'Wow,' she said, aware that her voice was breaking a little. 'That's beautiful. He'd really like that, guys.'

Rosie and Jake looked at each other, happy that their hard work on the card had met with her approval.

'Rosie did most of it,' Jake admitted.

'Hey, that's not true.' Rosie gave him a playful shove. 'You did all the drawing.'

'It doesn't matter.' Laura smiled at them. 'It's really beautiful.'

Chapter 45

6.49 p.m.

As the rain lashed down, Laura peered along the length of the Menai Bridge towards the white BMW, which remained motionless at the far end. She and Gareth had walked to the south side of the bridge ten minutes earlier to check in with Warlow, who was monitoring proceedings from the warmth of a car.

The raindrops bounced and splashed off the nearby pavement and dripped noisily from the steel structure above.

Laura shivered as she watched the helicopter circle again, its beam swathing the car in a brilliant white light, before it ascended into the darkness and disappeared into the cover of the low, black clouds. There was a storm, and the distant rumble of thunder was getting closer.

The shadowy figures of two AROs, with Glock machine guns at the ready, hurried into position about fifty yards from the stationary BMW, training their weapons on the target vehicle. An ARV had already pulled across to block the road at the side of the bridge. Its rotating blue light illuminated the painted steel barricades and enormous chains that swung in a giant U-shape from the limestone towers, giving the scene an eerie atmosphere.

Although it was difficult to see from where she stood, Laura knew that there were several patrol cars parked up about a hundred yards behind the static car.

Jake and Beth were inside.

What are they doing now? Laura wondered. Her mouth was dry and her breathing shallow.

Pulling the collar up on his coat, Gareth jogged over. His hair was matted from the rain and his face was wet. 'Nice night for it. What's going on?'

'I don't know. They've been sitting there for about five minutes now. I was expecting them to come out, but now I'm not so sure.'

Gareth shrugged as he wiped water from his face. 'They can't stay in there for ever.'

'No. And there's nowhere for them to go.'

'The chopper had to leave because of the storm. Northbound traffic is being diverted over to Britannia Bridge.' Gareth squinted through the rain at the stationary car and pointed to the high steel barricades that partially obscured their view. 'I can't really see what's going on.'

'Yeah, I know. I'm going to wander down there and get closer. I don't want some trigger-happy ARO making a bloody mistake.'

There was a flash of lightning that lit up the entire sky, illuminating the Snowdonia mountains in the distance behind her. Then, a second or two later, the deep grumble of thunder.

Suddenly, the BMW headlights went out. The car was now just a dark shape, barely visible in the driving rain and darkness.

What did they do that for?

Laura and Gareth moved quickly and got halfway across

the bridge. Splashing through puddles, Laura felt the cold water against her ankles. She stared down. The 200-foot drop into the churning black water below made her stomach lurch with vertigo again.

There was another flash of lightning, which seemed a lot closer than the last.

How safe is it to be on a metal bridge, over water, in a thunderstorm?

The car was about 75 yards away, but the darkness and tinted windows meant it was impossible to see inside.

There was another flash of lightning.

The doors of the BMW opened and five figures got out.

Red pulled Beth so that she was in front of him. He had a machine gun in his other hand and the Puma back over his shoulder.

Callum walked around from the other side of the car. He had Jake in front of him with a handgun in his right hand and the rucksack full of money over his left shoulder.

Laura gasped. Jake looked so tiny and helpless at this distance.

'Listen up!' Red shouted. 'We're walking over the bridge nice and slowly. If you stay back, no one will get hurt. By the time we get to the other side, we want a car waiting with its engine running. Is that clear?'

Laura walked towards them. She wanted to see Jake and let him know she was there and that everything was going to be all right.

'Where are you going?' hissed Gareth.

'I can't just stand here and do nothing,' she snapped.

As the group moved out to the centre of the bridge, Gareth walked out so that he was in line with them. His hands slightly raised. 'We can get a car for you. We just need a few more minutes,' he shouted.

Red shook his head as he continued walking forward with

Beth in front of him. 'Don't try to stall us or I'm going to shoot her. And that will be your fault.'

Laura edged closer down the pavement on the bridge. Her hair was wet from the rain and matted to her forehead. She couldn't take her eyes off Jake. She wanted to call out to him. To let him know she was there.

Gareth held up his Tetra radio and gestured to it. 'I've just had confirmation. There's a car coming. I promise it'll be here in five minutes.'

'If for one second I think you're lying to us, there's gonna be a bloodbath here, copper,' Red yelled.

Gareth nodded. 'I understand that. I'm just asking for five minutes.'

The group continued to edge forward along the centre of the bridge.

Out of the corner of her eye, Laura spotted two dark figures moving on top of the huge stone archway that stood at the centre of the suspension bridge. Then she saw the tell-tale glint of a red laser. They were police marksmen getting into position.

Gareth was now only about 25 yards in front of them. 'Everyone take it nice and easy.'

Without warning, Jake looked across and saw Laura looking at him.

'Mummy!' he cried.

She smiled at him. 'It's okay, Jake. I'm here. Don't worry, okay?'

The feeling of wanting to protect him was unbearable.

Red turned to look at her and in that moment, Beth wriggled free from his grasp and ran towards Jake. Red raised the gun and took aim.

Michael stepped in front of him and the gun. 'Don't even think about it!'

Red narrowed his eyes in fury. 'Out the way, dickhead, or I'll shoot you!'

Michael shook his head. 'Go ahead. Do it!'

For a few seconds, Red seemed rattled and uncertain of what to do. Then suddenly, he turned and marched straight for Laura.

Before she had time to turn and get away, he had grabbed her by the hair, spun her around and put her in a choke hold. He then jammed the muzzle hard into the side of her head.

Oh my God!

'In that case, you're coming with us instead,' Red said angrily.

Gareth put up his hand. 'Hey, take it easy, mate.'

Red dragged Laura forward, his forearm hard against her throat. 'Right, me and her are walking out of here, got it?'

Gareth held up his hands. 'Fine. I just need you to stay calm.'

'Don't get any funny ideas, pal,' Red hissed through gritted teeth. 'Otherwise I'm gonna blow her brains out!'

I can't breathe.

They staggered over to where Callum was standing with Jake and Beth. Laura's head was starting to swim from lack of oxygen. She tried to pull his forearm away from her throat.

'You're strangling me!' she gasped.

'Shut the fuck up!' he growled, pulling her forward. 'It will be nice for you. Mother and son in the car with us.'

For a second, she thought she was going to lose her balance and fall.

At this rate, he's going to break my neck.

Then something caught her eye. It was the red laser sight glimmering from the top of the stone archway. It was trained in their direction.

'You do know there's no way that I'm letting you or your son go when we get where we're going,' Red whispered.

This is it. Now or never.

FUCK YOU!

This move had worked before and she prayed to whatever Higher Power existed that it would save her a second time. Raising her foot, she stamped with all of her strength down onto Red's instep. In the split second Red loosened his grip on her throat, she bit as hard as she could into the flesh of his forearm.

'AARRRGGHH!'

Red yelled in pain and released her from the choke hold.

In that moment, she dropped to the ground as fast as she could.

The police marksmen now had a clear shot.

CRACK! CRACK! CRACK!

Three bullets hammered into Red's chest and he crumpled into a heap, dead.

Sucking in air, Laura tried to get her breath.

Callum's eyes were roaming around in terror. He pulled Jake closer to him.

'Let him go,' Beth growled.

'Mummy!' Jake shouted.

'It's all right, darling,' Laura croaked. 'I'm here, okay?'

'Shut up! All of you!' Callum growled.

Michael approached Red's dead body and took the machine gun that was still in his hand. He turned, marched towards his brother and aimed the gun at him.

'Put down the gun and let him go!' Michael shouted.

Callum's eyes widened. 'What the fuck are you doing?'

'Put down the gun, Callum.' Michael shook his head. 'It's over.'

Callum frowned. 'What, you're going to shoot me, are you?'

Michael shrugged. 'If I have to.'

A voice came from further down the bridge. 'Callum, Michael's right. It's over. Please put down the gun.'

It was Neil Cole. He walked slowly up the bridge towards his two sons.

'Dad?' Callum asked disbelievingly.

Michael frowned, as though he couldn't believe his own ears.

Neil got to about ten yards away, looked over at Callum and gestured to Jake. 'Look at him, Callum. He's ten years old and you've got a gun to his head. How is that all right?'

Laura looked over at him. 'Please, Callum. You don't need to do this. Just let him go.'

Jake looked at her. He was shaking.

Callum took a deep breath and blinked. He had tears in his eyes as he stared at his father. 'I don't care what you've got to say. You fucking left us!'

'I'm sorry,' Neil said. 'But this isn't the way, is it?'

Michael let the gun drop down to his side. 'Please, Callum. Come on. Just put the gun down, mate. It's over.'

'Do the right thing, Callum,' Neil said.

Callum closed his eyes for a few seconds. He nodded slowly, then took the gun away from Jake's head and dropped it to the ground. He sank to his knees and began to weep.

Jake sprinted over into Laura's arms and she picked him up. 'Oh my God, are you all right?'

'Mummy,' Jake said in a shaky voice.

She kissed his face and then held him to her tightly. 'I'm so so sorry. Are you okay?'

Jake nodded and buried his face in her chest.

Gareth and several uniformed officers moved in, handcuffing Callum and Michael.

Laura lowered Jake to the ground, crouched to face him and held both his hands. She looked into his bright blue eyes. There was a distance to them. She wondered how or if Jake would ever recover from what had happened today.

'I want you to know how proud I am of you. You've been

so, so incredibly brave. And, you know, Daddy would have been so proud of you today too.'

Jake looked at her blankly. 'Can we go home?'

'Of course we can, darling,' she said, pulling him into her arms once more.

Chapter 46

It was midnight. Jake was tucked up in Rosie's double bed next to her and she stroked his head and smiled. Elvis was sprawled on a thick rug nearby.

Laura sat at the end of the bed against the wall, hugging her knees and looking at Jake. She had come so close to losing her son. It was too terrifying to think about the what ifs or the what could have beens. All she knew was that Jake had been through a terrifying, harrowing ordeal and she worried if he would ever come out the other side. The only thing she could do for now was support him with all the love and patience she possessed.

'Can we keep the little light on tonight?' Jake whispered, pointing to a small lamp with a pink shade that stood on Rosie's bedside table.

'Of course,' Rosie replied.

Jake yawned and squinted over at Laura. He gave her a half-smile.

'Are you tired, sleepyhead?' she asked, smiling at him. She was afraid of what he might dream about. Nightmares of men with guns. He had witnessed Red being shot and killed.

Jake turned his head sideways onto the pillow. His eyes

started to droop. He was falling asleep. Rosie put her arm gently around him and interlaced her fingers with his.

Laura gestured to Rosie that she was going to let them sleep as she edged slowly off the bed and went over to the door.

As she padded along the landing, she felt the utter emotional and physical exhaustion of the day. Her legs felt like lead.

Putting her hand on the wooden bannister to steady herself, she blew out her cheeks.

I never want to experience a day like that for as long as I live, she thought.

She went gingerly down the stairs, into the kitchen, and spun the top off a bottle of Merlot. Pouring herself an enormous glass of wine, she made her way into the living room.

Gazing out of the window, she saw the moon was full and buttery in colour. It looked as if it was actually sitting on top of the Snowdonia mountains across the water. She remembered something on the morning news about there being a special Mead Moon or Honey Moon that night. From what she could remember, mead was some medieval alcoholic drink made from honey, water and hops. As she recalled sitting on the sofa and watching the telly that morning, it truly felt like a million years ago.

Taking a long gulp of wine, she felt the alcohol hit her empty stomach and radiate warmth. She put the glass down and flopped onto the sofa.

'You got him back,' a voice whispered. 'I knew you could do it.'

Sam sat on the leather armchair opposite.

'Did you?' she asked.

'Of course,' he said. 'Never a doubt in my mind.'

'I don't know if we're ever going to get him back,' she admitted with a lump in her throat. 'Not properly.'

'Come on,' Sam said. 'He's a tough little man.'

'He is.' She blinked away a tear. 'But he's only ten. And I'm scared it's all going to scar him for life.'

'Hey, it's going to be fine,' Sam said as he walked over, sat down and put his arms around her. 'He just needs lots of TLC.'

Chapter 47

By the time Gareth walked into the CID office the next morning, there was an expectant buzz in the room. Officers broke into a round of applause and cheered.

Getting to the front of the room, he looked suitably humbled by their reaction. Having had three hours' sleep, he was now running on adrenaline and caffeine.

'Right, settle down,' he said, holding up his hands good-naturedly. 'We got a result yesterday, and that's down to every single person in this room. We're a team and we showed that beautifully yesterday.'

Andrea grinned and held up a tabloid newspaper. Along with a photo of the *Anglesey Princess* and the headline of ANGLESEY SIEGE!, there was a smaller photo of Gareth captioned: 'Gang hunted down by DCI Williams'.

'Yeah, but it's your ugly mug that's in the papers, boss!' she joked. 'You're famous.'

'Can I have your autograph, boss?' Ben teased him.

'Piss off, the lot of you,' he returned good-humouredly. 'There's plenty for us to be getting on with.'

There were some ironic groans as the CID offices settled themselves in for the morning briefing.

'But if anyone happens to be in The Bull around six, the first few rounds are on me,' Gareth added.

There were cheers and high-fives all around.

He went over to the scene boards and pointed to the photos of the gang. 'This is Paul Griffin, more often known as "Red". A police marksman shot him and he was pronounced dead at the scene.'

'Not a great loss to the world,' Declan muttered.

Even though he agreed, Gareth ignored him. 'Obviously that officer is now upstairs with the post incident manager. He'll also be with me later today so we can give our statements to the IOPC.'

'They should give him a bloody medal,' Ben said.

Gareth went over to the scene board again. 'Callum Cole is being held at HMP Rhoswen in North Wales. According to our Duty Solicitor, he is pleading not guilty to all charges. He gave us a "no comment" interview, so we are going to trial. He'll be up in front of a judge at Mold this afternoon.'

There were grumbles and sighs. Preparation for a trial like that was going to take huge amounts of manpower and a mountain of paperwork. It was time and money that could be spent on other investigations.

'On the other hand, Michael Cole has pleaded guilty to all charges and is helping us with our enquiries. We've had a call from Merseyside Police who informed us that Michael has been working as a CHIS within the Croxteth Crew for the past six months, passing vital intel to the NCA,' Gareth explained. 'He is facing some lesser charges, and he's in the Vulnerable Prisoners Wing at HMP Rhoswen.'

'I don't get it, boss.' Declan said with a surprised expression. 'Michael Cole tipped us off about the drop in Beaumaris, knowing that his brother was going to get nicked?'

Gareth shrugged. 'Your guess as to his motivation is as good as mine.'

'Glad he's not my brother,' Declan snorted. 'Callum Cole must have seriously screwed his brother over on something to piss him off that much.'

'Okay, the Crown Prosecution Service are going to be in and out for the next few weeks as they build up the case against Callum Cole. I'll need all witness statements and interviews typed up in full asap,' Gareth explained. 'Declan, I need you to liaise with Merseyside Police. We need all the intel they have on the Croxteth Crew sent over here as a matter of urgency.'

'Yes, boss.'

'Andrea?' Gareth said. 'Talk to forensics and ballistics. We recovered two firearms yesterday on Menai Bridge. We're going to need the cartridges and bullets analysed for DNA, prints, rifling and any specific tool marks. If these weapons have been used during any other crimes, the CPS are going to want to know before, not after, we get to trial.'

'Yes, boss,' Andrea said as she headed over to her desk. She then looked back at him. 'Oh, and boss?'

'Yes, Andrea?' Gareth replied as he grabbed his files from a nearby table. It was time to wrap the briefing up and get on with some work.

'Who *is* Laura Hart?' she asked.

He frowned. 'How do you mean?'

'Well, she told everyone she's not a copper, but she was incredible.'

'No, she used to be though,' Gareth explained. 'After what I saw yesterday, and what she went through, I can tell you she's a big loss to the force. We could do with someone like that here. And yes, she was incredible.'

Andrea raised her eyebrow and gave him a knowing grin. 'Anything you want to tell us, boss?'

'Get on with your work,' Gareth said with a rueful smile as he headed over to his office.

There was no denying to himself though that he was finding it difficult to get Laura out of his mind.

Chapter 48

One month later

Laura scanned the room, surveying the dozen or so clients who were starting the final day of her *Tough Negotiating in Business* course. She was starting to wonder how many more of these courses she would run. It wasn't that they weren't successful. It was the nagging thought she'd had in recent weeks about returning to her former career. Maybe it was a crazy idea? She didn't know. However, it was a thought that now excited her more than she ever thought it would. She would need a full medical and psychological evaluation before anything could be put in place, but then she could slot back in at the same rank.

'Morning, everyone,' Laura said brightly as she perched herself on the table at the front of the room. She was going to start off with something a bit different as it was their last day. Walking over to her laptop, she clicked a button and projected a slide onto the wall. The title read: *The Theory of the Black Swan.*

'Until the seventeenth century, the world had only ever seen white swans. As far as anyone was concerned, all swans were white. So, if you were a betting man, or woman, you could have staked your life that the next swan you saw would be white. But then Dutch explorer Willem de Vlamingh went to western Australia, and lo and behold, he saw black swans. What do you think we can learn from this?'

A keen young man with glasses put up his hand. 'I'm guessing that you can't know everything? That some things are going to be unpredictable.'

'Great. Good answer, Chris,' she said, looking at his name sticker. 'The unknown unknowns. Things we couldn't have predicted. And these *unknowns* are the Black Swans.

'There is a case used by the FBI to highlight this. In 1981, a man in his mid-thirties named William Griffin shot his mother, stepfather and a handyman in their home in Rochester. He proceeded to a local bank, shot two police officers and took nine people hostage. During the negotiations, Griffin said that all he wanted was for police officers to come to the car park outside and have a shoot-out with him. FBI officers were confused. They'd never had such a bizarre request. It was normally a helicopter or money, or both. Griffin gave them an hour before he would start shooting hostages. Now, never in the history of the FBI up until this point had a hostage-taker killed a hostage on the deadline they'd given. This meant they saw it as a way for the hostage-taker to show that he was serious, but it was only ever seen as an empty threat – a bargaining tool in the negotiations. Based on decades of experience, that was the truth. But after an hour, Griffin came through on his promise and emptied both barrels of his shotgun into a junior bank clerk. He then walked out of the bank waving around the shotgun and was killed by a sniper. Suddenly, the truth had been changed. Something they had never predicted had happened.

'The Black Swan theory tells us that things we thought

were impossible actually do happen. The question is, how can you be prepared for this?'

The man in glasses put up his hand. 'Are you suggesting that there are some people who can't be negotiated with?'

Laura thought for a few seconds. It was a good question. 'There are some people who are damaged, vindictive or, in Griffin's case, suicidal. In those instances I would say yes, those types of people who, at first glance, seem impossible to negotiate with. Their motives are warped and therefore unpredictable.'

'What can you do in a situation like that?' the man asked.

'Remain flexible. You might think that someone you're dealing with is irrational to the point of being crazy, but 99 per cent of the time they aren't. Use the leverage that we talked about. What does that person want? What is their worldview? Find common ground wherever you can. And most of all, treat them with empathy, however hard that might be.' Laura looked out at the students. 'Listen to others without prejudice, be honest, act with dignity and respect. I'm hoping that the skills you've learned on this course can be taken and used for your lives in general, not just the boardroom. Our lives are a series of negotiations, compromises, disputes and settlements. Handled correctly, they can lead to peace of mind. And essentially, that's what I think we're all looking for – if we're honest.'

Michael came out into the visiting area of HMP Rhoswen, a brand-new, state-of-the art prison in North Wales. Having passed information onto Merseyside Police, Michael was worried about how much coverage the case was getting in the media. It wouldn't be long before everyone in the prison knew who he was. Some violent prisoners would love the notoriety of having attacked or even killed him.

Before he had even sat down in his cell, Michael had found

a razor blade carefully positioned on his pillow. A kind of welcome gift from a guard or a fellow inmate – an invitation for him to commit suicide.

Walking into the visiting area, he saw a young woman he recognised sitting in. the far corner. She gave him a half wave as he approached.

'Beth,' he murmured uncertainly as he sat down opposite her on a blue plastic chair that was secured to the floor.

'Hello, Michael,' she said. He'd forgotten how attractive she was.

He frowned. 'If I'm honest, I was really surprised to see your name on my visiting register today.'

She took a breath and looked at him. 'I wanted to talk to you. I think it's part of me trying to get over what happened that day.'

'Of course.' Michael nodded.

'Why didn't you didn't tell me you were a police informant?' she asked.

'I think I was too scared someone would hear me if I said it out loud.'

'You wanted to let me and Jake go,' Beth said as she raised an eyebrow. 'Weren't you scared you would get shot?'

'I don't think so,' Michael said, and shook his head. 'The day had just got so out of hand. But I could see how scared Jake was. How is he now?'

'He's getting there,' Beth stated thoughtfully. 'But I'm not going to pretend what happened hasn't had a significant effect on him.'

Michael found her words difficult to hear. The thought of that little boy being permanently scarred by what he and the others had done that day was distressing.

'I keep playing it back in my mind,' he admitted. 'I wonder what I could have done differently. If I could have done something that could have stopped all that happening.'

She looked at him. 'I'm not making excuses, but you're seventeen. And they were two grown men with firearms. I'm not sure what you could have done. Would I be right in assuming that when you got on the boat that morning, you thought the police were going to pick you up on Beaumaris Beach with a minimum of fuss?'

'Yeah, that's exactly it,' Michael said with a sense of relief that Beth understood what had been going on in his head. 'I didn't know they had guns until we were halfway there.'

'But you were willing to see your own brother go to jail?'

Michael thought for a few seconds and then leaned forward in his seat.

'He didn't leave me much choice. He and Red were taking more chances, getting more violent. I thought he was going to end up dead sooner or later. I tried to talk to him about it but he wasn't interested.'

'You thought he was safer in prison than out?'

'Yeah. And I know that sounds mad,' he mumbled.

'No, it doesn't,' Beth said as she looked at him. 'And what about you? What happens to you now?'

'I've got some minor charges to face,' Michael explained. 'My solicitor reckons I'll still get six or seven years, but serve two, if I'm lucky.'

'And then what?'

'I've signed up to do my GCSEs,' he informed her with a sense of pride. 'And I want to get myself a trade or work with kids like me. But I don't know if my criminal record will allow me to do that?'

'Are you being charged with a violent offence or anything to do with children?' she asked.

Michael shook his head. 'No. Intent to supply and robbery.'

'Then it is possible that you could work with kids or teenagers in the future,' Beth explained. 'I trained with a teacher who had been to prison.'

Michael's face lit up. It was exactly what he wanted to hear. 'Really? I didn't know that.'

'You know what?' Beth said to him. 'After what you've been through, what you've done and where you've been, you're exactly the kind of person who could make a real difference to kids or teenagers facing the same kinds of trouble and temptation you faced. Do you want me to look into it for you?'

He furrowed his brow. 'Why would you do that?'

'To help you,' she explained. 'I'll come back here, this time next week, with some info. And we can go through it together.'

'Really?'

She smiled. 'Really.'

'What's the catch?' he asked with a bemused smile.

She laughed. 'There is no catch, Michael. I want to help you do something with your life. That's why I became a teacher.'

Chapter 49

Friday 22 July

The last day of the summer term at St Mary's Primary School had finally arrived. Crouching down in her kitchen, Laura clicked the lead onto Elvis's collar. She sometimes wondered why they bothered having a lead. If Elvis decided he was going in a certain direction, it was pretty difficult to persuade him otherwise. He weighed nearly 120 pounds, which Rosie and Jake had worked out to be a whopping eight stone!

As the sun beat down, she popped her sunglasses on, went out of the front door and began to walk over to the school. She couldn't believe that it was Jake's last day. Where had the time gone? The idea of him joining Year 7 at Beaumaris High School was terrifying. He would have to wear a proper blazer and tie. There would be a different teacher and classroom for every lesson. She wondered how he would deal with the change.

Aware that the pavement was hot, she allowed Elvis to roam onto the grass verges as they walked down the hill from their home towards the centre of Beaumaris. The Menai

Strait was alive with sailboats, canoes and jet skis. The beach and seafront teemed with tourists.

In the distance, she could see a long white cruise boat – the *Anglesey Princess*. The sight of it made her uneasy. She wondered if she would ever look out over the Menai Strait in the same way again after the hijacking.

Her thoughts turned to Gareth, as they did with increasing regularity. And the thought of him was accompanied by a flutter of electricity and excitement. Since the hijacking, she had come to the decision that it was time to move on in her life. She wasn't even fifty. She had no desire to spend the rest of her life alone. And she suspected that Gareth felt the same way about her.

Getting to the centre of Beaumaris, she strolled past the disused Victorian gaol, which was now a museum and tourist attraction. It was a dark, forbidding building, even in the summer sunshine. She had read how the prisoners had been tortured in the nineteenth century with whips, the treadmill or even a stretching rack. When she had been a police officer, she had always found the function of prisons a difficult concept. Depending on the case she was working, she would sometimes decide that punishment and deterrent were a prison's primary role. Yet, on some cases, especially when she learned about the horrendous childhoods the offender had suffered, she fully considered rehabilitation into society to be a prison's most important function.

She crossed the road to the shadowy side to make sure that Elvis's paws didn't burn on the hot pavement. A couple of locals gave her a cheery wave as they cycled past. Beaumaris was definitely a place where everyone knew everyone. It was such a lovely contrast to life in a city.

Stopping outside the school gates, Laura looked out over the enormous playing field where most of the children from St Mary's Primary School were involved in fun activities for their last day. There was a bouncy castle, face painting and an ice-cream van.

She saw a figure approaching. Beth. 'How are you doing?' she called to Jake's teacher.

Beth smiled. 'I'm fine, thanks.'

'Six weeks' holiday,' Laura said. 'After what you've been through, no one can say you don't deserve it.'

'I know.' Beth raised her eyebrows. She then gestured over to Jake, who was running with his friends and blowing soapy bubbles up into the air. 'He's doing so well.'

'I've never really thanked you for what you did that day,' Laura admitted. 'Not properly.'

Beth frowned. 'You sent me flowers and wine to say thank you.'

'I don't think Jake would have survived it, if you hadn't been with him,' Laura explained. 'I don't mean physically. I mean mentally. He's told me what you did for him and it was incredible.'

Beth shook her head. 'Anyone else would have done the same.'

'No,' she said as she looked directly at her. 'They wouldn't have. We're all incredibly grateful for what you did that day.'

'I knew that Jake had been through so much already. My instinct was to protect him. He's such a lovely boy.'

'Thank you,' Laura said, and then couldn't help but crack a joke to lighten the suddenly heavy mood between them. 'He's not so lovely when United lose.'

'I'm going to miss him next year,' Beth admitted.

'Listen. We're both in Beaumaris,' Laura said. 'You'll have to come over in the summer. We'll sit in the garden, drink rosé and put the world to rights.'

Beth beamed at her. 'I'd really like that. Thank you.'

* * *

346

The remand wing at HMP Rhoswen wasn't busy. Many of the prisoners who were awaiting trial were watching television, playing pool or in the prison gym. There was the odd shout from the games room, but otherwise it was quiet.

Callum came down the green steel stairs and onto the area of the second floor. There was a strip of light-green right through the middle of the floor all the way along the wing. Everything else was various shades of grey – the doors, the walls, the ceilings. The air smelt of prison food and cigarette smoke from outside.

Gazing up, he saw a figure looking down from the fourth-floor staircase. It was Michael. Their eyes met for a moment, and then Callum looked away. He couldn't bear to look at his brother after what he'd done.

A few minutes later, Callum returned to the small, neat cell that he shared with a young man who had been convicted of assaulting a police officer in Llandudno.

His cellmate looked up from his tabloid newspaper. 'There's some stuff in here about you and your brother, if you want a read?'

'Not really,' Callum mumbled.

The cell was basic. A single bed with a blue blanket and green pillowcase against each of the opposing walls, with a table in between where there was a television, a blue plastic knife, fork, spoon and bowl.

'Fish and chip Friday today, mate,' the man said with a smile. 'Highlight of the bloody week.'

Callum looked over at him and then saw his expression completely change.

Shadows loomed across the doorway. Turning back to the cell entrance Callum saw two large men in their early twenties. One was mixed race and covered in tattoos. The other man had a flat nose and blond hair.

The tattooed man clicked his fingers at Callum's cellmate and pointed to the door. 'Get out!' he snarled.

Callum felt his stomach twist in fear.

Shit! Who are they?

The young man scuttled out like his life depended on it.

'Callum Cole?' the tattooed man asked in a thick Scouse accent.

Callum's heart was beating so fast that all he could do was nod.

They're Scousers. This isn't good.

'Your brother's upstairs, isn't he?' the blond man asked, gesturing to the ceiling.

Callum felt like his throat was closing. 'Yeah,' he mumbled.

'And he's a fucking grass, isn't he?' the tattooed man asked.

'Yeah,' Callum stammered. 'But I didn't know that.'

The tattooed man shrugged. 'We're not interested in that. But a couple of our friends from Croxteth are worried that your brother is going to testify against them.'

'And they're not happy at the thought of going back to prison,' the blond man explained.

'I can't stop him talking. He's on the VP wing.' Callum was shaking as he babbled.

'The thing is, Callum, our friends in Croxteth want to send a message to your brother to keep his mouth shut,' the tattooed man said with an apologetic expression on this face. 'And the way to do that is to get to you.'

Callum moved back on the bed and put his hands up defensively. 'Please—'

In a flash, the men were on him.

The tattooed man punched Callum on the jaw. It sent him reeling back onto the bed. He produced a clear plastic bag from his pocket, pulled it over Callum's head and pulled it tight.

Callum gasped for breath, kicking his legs frantically.

The blond man pulled out a knife with a serrated blade

348

and swiftly stabbed Callum in the stomach and chest five times.

The pain was excruciating.

He put his hands to his torso and felt the blood soaking his shirt.

He tried to suck in air, but it was no use. His head was swimming.

Then everything went black.

Chapter 50

It was nearly eleven p.m. by the time Gareth pulled up outside the address on the outskirts of Llangefni. He stared up at the large, detached house. It was a mission to appease his curiosity. He felt he owed it to himself to see where his wife Nell was now living. She had moved out two weeks earlier, although she still had some of her possessions to collect.

Gareth wondered why a man in his mid-forties was still single and had never married. He consoled himself that it was evidence there was something wrong with Leith. There had to be some kind of darkness hidden away in his past, didn't there?

The double doors to the garage were open and he could see two familiar shapes on a trailer under black tarpaulin covers. He knew exactly what they were. Jet skis. No doubt that twat Leith and Nell had been taking romantic trips off the Anglesey coast on them. The thought gnawed at his stomach.

The house itself was a modern executive build and had at least four or five bedrooms. The wooden window frames and front door had been painted a fashionable olive green – although it probably had some terribly pretentious name like Duck Green or Card Room Green. Parked on the circular gravel drive was an enormous white Audi Q8 SUV with a personalised plate: AL 1000.

Prick!

Leith had cut a treeless patch of immaculate grass into neat lines like the turf at Wembley Stadium. It was separated from the neighbour's land by a chain-link fence. Closer to the house, on the edge of the patio at the back, was a dark blue box about ten feet square. It had a black, padlocked lid and a coil of a hosepipe.

Are you kidding me? He's got a hot tub!

Gareth didn't think he could feel more inadequate or humiliated. His feelings of self-pity and self-loathing had reached an all-time high. Looking down at the new bottle of Black Label whisky he had bought from the off-licence an hour earlier, he wondered if he should just unscrew the top and have a good, hard drink. It would numb the pain temporarily, wouldn't it? It would help make the anguish go away.

Pull yourself together! She's gone. The marriage had been over for years, so deal with it, he tried to tell himself.

He decided not to open the whisky. Instead, he turned on the ignition and headed home. What he needed was a different perspective.

There was no guilt on his part. Nell had moved in with a man who had everything. And if he was honest, what would he do if Nell suddenly turned around tomorrow, told him she had made a big mistake and she wanted to move back in? That turn of events wouldn't make him happy either. He didn't want her back. He wasn't in love with her anymore. So, why had he reacted so badly while sitting outside Leith's impossibly perfect home? He knew it was male vanity. Was he really so childish as to know that he didn't want to be with his wife, but not want her to have a new life with someone else? Did that make him pathetic? Probably.

By the time he reached the outskirts of Beaumaris, he remembered what a sense of relief he had felt in recent weeks, being in their house alone. He no longer had to suffer watching her intolerable happiness as she left the house in new clothes, full make-up and designer perfume. And he would no longer have to listen for the door to see when – or if – she decided to come home. She was gone.

He was a single man. And to his surprise, that felt more than all right. It felt liberating.

Parking on his drive, he got out and took a deep lungful of the summer air. Even though it was nearly midnight, it was balmy.

He went in, tossed the car keys on the kitchen counter and went to pour himself a drink. His mobile phone lit up and flashed. Someone had sent him a text.

It was from Laura Hart!

Hi Gareth, I know, like me, you're not a great sleeper. And all coppers love true crime! Thought I'd let you know that I'm currently watching a true crime doc on Netflix called The Hillside Strangler. It's definitely worth a watch. I love the opening line which stated, 'The 1970s was the Golden Age of serial killers in the US!' Hilarious. Hope you're okay and see you soon. Laura x

Gareth smiled. She had finished her message with a *x*! Wow.

He didn't know if there was a Higher Power up there, but he wondered if there was some strange kismet at work that had made Laura text him?

Then he had a thought.

He grabbed his phone.

Hi Laura, Yeah, I can't sleep either! Fancy a midnight swim instead? Usual place? Gareth x

As he watched the little signal on his phone that indicated Laura was typing back, he held his breath.

Oh God, was that way too pushy? Does a midnight swim sound weird?

His phone pinged with a reply.

Brilliant idea! See you there in 15 mins! X

Gareth's face broke into a beaming smile as he went to go and get his swimming gear ready.

Chapter 51

The Crown Pub on the outskirts of Beaumaris was having a lock-in. The landlord had gone around closing the curtains and locking the doors. There were about twenty regulars inside, drinking and laughing.

In the far corner, Geoff and Steve sat together, nursing their pints. Geoff was still wearing a sling, even though Steve was convinced it was just to get sympathy from the punters whom they had started to take to Puffin Island again on the *Anglesey Princess*. There had been fears that after the hijacking, the tourist trade for the boat tours would die a death. Ironically, the media coverage of the incident had seemed to boost demand. Geoff assumed that people thought it was a one-off and were fascinated to go on the boat that had been at the centre of such a dramatic story.

'One for the road?' Steve asked as he pointed to Geoff's empty pint glass.

'Are you trying to get me drunk?' he laughed.

'Yes.'

'You know why they say "one for the road", don't you?' Geoff asked.

Steve shrugged. 'No idea, mate.'

'In the old days in London, when the prisoners were taken from Newgate Prison to be hanged at Tyburn, they were allowed to stop at the taverns along the way to have one last drink. So they could have *one for the road*.'

'Well, you learn something every day,' Steve said. He pulled out a scratch card from his pocket and tossed it over to Geoff. 'I forgot I bought that earlier. Have a look and if we've won half a million, you can take me to that place in America you keep banging on about.'

'Hampton Roads?'

'That's the one,' Steve said as he went over to the bar.

Taking out a coin, Geoff put on his reading glasses and scratched away at the card. After four lines, he realised they had won £10. *Oh well, next time.*

Steve came back, plonked the two pints down on the table and raised his eyebrow. 'So, are we off to America?'

Geoff chortled. 'Not on ten quid.'

Steve smiled and shrugged. 'Looks like we're stuck in Beaumaris together then.'

As they looked at each other, Geoff felt Steve reach under the table and take his hand. He held it and gave it a reassuring squeeze.

Geoff smiled as he lifted his pint. 'As my cockney mate used to say, "One for the frog"!'

Steve frowned. 'The frog?'

'Frog and toad, road. Cockney rhyming slang,' Geoff explained. 'Cheers!'

'Cheers!' Steve laughed.

They clinked their pints and Geoff squeezed Steve's hand back.

Chapter 52

As Laura got to the deserted sweep of Beaumaris Beach, she let Elvis off the lead and he bounded away across the wet sand. She narrowed her eyes and looked over at the horizon. Even though it was just before midnight, there still seemed to be some kind of blue hue at the edge of the sky. She remembered that the area of the sea before the horizon was called 'the offing'. In the old days, ships that were about to arrive were said to be 'in the offing'. Nowadays, the phrase had become part of everyday language.

As she took off her thick hoodie and trackies, she felt a little self-conscious. There was no doubt that there was a strong attraction between her and Gareth. However, she wasn't sure whether the invite for a midnight swim had been the friendly suggestion of a fellow cold-water swimmer – or something else. If she was honest with herself, she secretly hoped it was the something else.

The wind picked up, and she decided it was going to be warmer getting into the water than waiting for Gareth on the beach. As she took the first tentative steps, an inch of water washed over her feet. Gazing across at the Welsh mainland, there was enough moonlight and residual light from the day to see the dark, uneven line of the Snowdonia Mountains cutting their way through the night sky.

When Laura was a child, it was the myths surrounding King Arthur and Snowdonia that fascinated her the most. She remembered her taid telling her off for being so obsessed with the history of 'an English king', as he said. He told her she should be proud of her own Welsh history.

Despite her taid's reprimand, Laura was still drawn to the Arthurian legends. The stunning lakes in Snowdonia that claimed to be the location of the Lady of the Lake, and the resting place of the mystical sword Excalibur. The hoof mark discovered on the banks of Lake Barfog, near Betws-y-Coed, which is said to have been made by King Arthur's horse when he pulled an evil creature from its depths. And Bardsey Island, off the coast of the Llyn Peninsula, the final resting place of both King Arthur and the mighty wizard Merlin.

An enormous wave splashed against her stomach, breaking her train of thought. August was the perfect time for night swimming. It was the one time of year where the air temperature was lower than the water's.

Taking a breath, she leapt with her arms forward and dived. For a few seconds, she was in that wonderful silence under the sea's surface. And it was in the depth of the sea that she could find herself through the lovely, calm connection with the natural world. The sounds, the light, the textures were all different. Her body had no weight. She could glide in any direction as the briny water held her limbs. It was a special place – wonderland of dreams, freedom and of meditation – and she knew that when she returned to the real world above, this time spent in utter tranquillity and peace would allow her to be the best version of herself.

She broke the surface and took a deep breath, then smoothed the water from her face and hair.

A figure emerged out of the darkness and walked into the sea.

Gareth.

'Room for one more?' he joked.

'I'm not sure,' she quipped. 'It's a bit of a squeeze.'

He laughed.

In the moonlight, she could see his smooth chest and chiselled arms. He was in good shape and clearly looked after himself. She wondered what it would be like to run her hands over them.

'Have you had a good evening?' she asked as she bobbed down into the water and let the sea come reassuringly over her shoulders.

Gareth gave an ironic laugh. 'I might tell you about it later, if I'm feeling brave.'

'Oh dear. Like that, was it?'

'I'm afraid so.'

'You know what the best cure for that is, don't you?'

'I do,' he said as he launched himself in a superb dive into the water.

That was impressive, she thought. It had been difficult to appreciate through his clothes just how physically powerful he was.

For a few seconds, he disappeared.

I really think he likes me, she thought.

The momentary silence added to her sense of excitement and anticipation.

Then his head surfaced, and he blew water from his top lip.

'Better?' she asked.

'Much,' he replied with a broad, sexy grin.

Twenty minutes later, Laura and Gareth sat on top of a dune, huddled in warm clothing. Elvis sat on the next dune, surveying the beach.

'When I feel like this, I just want to stay here for ever,' Laura admitted as the sea breeze flicked at her wet hair.

'And then life gets in the way.' Gareth shrugged.

'Life, the past, the future, everything,' she reflected.

Gareth reached into his swim bag, pulled out a silver hip flask and held it up. 'I brought this with me.'

She raised her eyebrow. 'It had better not have water in it!'

'Fire water,' he said and handed it to her.

She took a long swig. It hit the back of her throat, burned and made her cough. 'God, sorry. You weren't joking about the fire water, were you?'

He smiled as she handed it to him.

'You must miss him,' he said softly.

'Sorry?'

'Your husband. You must miss him.'

She nodded. 'Yeah, I do.'

'Every day?'

She nodded slowly. 'Yes.'

'I can't imagine how you get through that.'

'It gets a bit easier. Just very, very slowly,' she said quietly. 'But I don't think the missing bit ever goes.'

'No. And I guess it doesn't feel fair either?'

She turned and looked at him. He was more perceptive than she had given him credit for. 'No, it feels like some cruel trick. And it makes you very angry.'

There were a few seconds of silence, and he handed her back the flask.

'What about the job?' he asked.

'How do you mean?'

'Do you miss it?'

'Of course. All the time,' she said, surprising herself at the depth of passion she felt as she answered. 'Being a detective was all I ever wanted to be.'

'What about now?'

'Yeah, that's a funny one,' she said with a wry smile.

He raised an eyebrow. 'Why's that?'

She took a few seconds to think and then said, 'Because up until a month ago, I would have told you that there was no possibility of me ever being a police officer again.'

He gave her an inquisitive look. 'But now you can?'

'Yeah,' she admitted with a nod. She couldn't believe that she was saying it, but it had been nagging away at her ever since the hijacking.

'Wow,' he said under his breath. 'From what I saw on that one day, you're an incredible copper.'

She pulled an embarrassed face. 'Oh God!'

'Seriously,' he said. 'You would be an amazing addition to the North Wales Police.'

'I need to run it past my kids first.'

'What do you think they'll say?'

'Rosie will be supportive and tell me I should do whatever makes me happy,' she said. 'And Jake – I'm not sure. He lost his father in the line of duty, so I don't know how he'll react.'

'Either way, you sound like you've made your mind up.'

She gave a little laugh. 'I guess I have. I just haven't told anyone. Apart from you, I suppose.'

'Well, I'm flattered.'

'You never know,' she joked. 'It might not be long before I have to call you "boss".'

Gareth laughed.

Keen to move the conversation away from her, Laura remembered that night when she'd run into him outside the pub. 'Enough about all my stuff. How are things with you? The last time I saw you before the hijacking—'

'I was very drunk,' he interrupted and gave her a rueful smile.

360

'Yes, you were very drunk.' She laughed. 'And you probably told me more than you intended. It didn't sound good.'

Gareth took the flask back, took a long swig and sat forward. 'You asked me how my evening was. Well, I was sitting outside the house of the bloke that Nell's moved in with.'

'Oh God!' she said, pulling a face. 'She moved out?'

'Don't worry. I wasn't intending on breaking in and killing them in bed with a hammer,' he admitted with a wry smile.

Laura laughed. 'Oh good. I'm glad. What with you being a DI and everything.'

He chuckled. 'Yeah, I suppose that wouldn't look good.'

'So, why were you there?'

'I wanted to see where she's living now,' he conceded. 'And then it dawned on me that if she turned around tomorrow and told me she had made a big mistake, I wouldn't be relieved.'

Laura raised an eyebrow. 'You wouldn't?'

'No.' He shook his head. 'Our marriage was over years ago. She doesn't love me and I don't love her. And for some reason, tonight that feels okay.'

Laura laughed as she took the flask and raised it. 'Hey, here's to us. A pair of slightly pathetic, sad, middle-aged losers, sitting on a beach in Wales.'

'I don't think you know how funny you are,' Gareth said as he smiled at her. 'Or attractive.'

Wow. Okay, I wasn't expecting that.

She felt her pulse quicken.

'Yeah, well, it's dark and you've had whisky,' she replied awkwardly.

He shook his head. 'No. I've always thought you were attractive. And I think you know that I really like you.'

This feels a little awkward.

'I guess,' she admitted.

361

He leaned forward and looked at her.

Oh my God, is he going to kiss me?

He pointed to her eye. 'I think you've got something on your eye. It might be something from the sea.'

Reaching up, she wiped her right eye.

'Sorry, it's still there,' he said, shaking his head. 'Close your eyes for a second, and I'll get it for you.'

Closing her eyes, she waited for him to brush whatever was on her eye away.

Instead, she felt his warm lips push against hers.

You cheeky bugger!

She couldn't help responding as she kissed him back.

Nice move.

They kissed each other, softly at first and then more passionately.

Chapter 53

It was one a.m. by the time Laura got back from the beach with Elvis. Going into her bedroom, she took off her clothes and wandered into the en-suite bathroom. She turned on the shower and waited for it to warm up. Then she looked at herself in the mirror. With no make-up and straggly wet hair, she looked an utter mess.

Oh my God! How on earth did you let him kiss you looking like that?

As she stepped into the shower, she let the jets of hot water wash over her face and hair. She couldn't help but think of the twenty minutes she had just spent kissing Gareth on the beach. And it gave her a thrill. She felt like a giddy teenager. In fact, she hadn't sat on Beaumaris Beach *snogging* a boy since 1988. She had gone for a walk after school with Johnathan Clarke and kissed in the dunes until it had started to rain. Then she had skipped home, listened to her Kylie Minogue and Tiffany cassettes on her Amstrad tape-to-tape player, dreaming of the life she and Jonathan Clarke were going to live in the future. A week after that, she found out that Jonathan had been seen snogging Suzie Watkins – and that was that.

Taking her white robe from the back of the door, she went and brushed her tangled hair and put moisturiser on her face. She had to stop herself projecting some kind of future for her and Gareth.

It was just a kiss, you silly woman! she told herself.

Walking over to the bed, she folded down the thin summer duvet and stepped out of the robe.

'You're late coming to bed, aren't you?' said a voice.

It was Sam. Not only had he startled her, the sound of his voice made her heart sink. She felt a terrible guilt.

What if he knows what happened with Gareth?

'I couldn't sleep,' she explained. 'So I went for a swim.'

'On your own?' Sam asked with a smile.

It was only now that she felt she could look at him. 'Yes, of course!' she said with an expression to suggest it was an absurd question.

'Just asking,' he said.

Getting into bed, she looked at him. 'Well, budge over. I'm exhausted and I need to go to sleep.'

'Aren't we going to cuddle?' he asked with a mock sad face.

'Of course we are, silly,' she said with a forced smile.

Rolling over, she put her head on the pillow. Sam moved behind her and wrapped his arms around her.

'Night,' she whispered.

'Yeah, night,' he whispered.

She closed her eyes and wondered how she was ever going to sleep. Even though she was bone-tired, her brain was ticking away like an unexploded bomb.

Chapter 54

Laura woke to the sound of knocking. Glancing over at her clock, she could see it was only seven a.m.

Seven a.m. on a Sunday! Are you kidding me?

With a loud groan, she threw back the duvet and then made her way downstairs to the front door.

If this is some bloody delivery I've got to sign for, I'm going to kill them!

As she opened the door, she saw a familiar face looking back at her.

Pete Marsons.

'Sorry. I've got you out of bed, haven't I?' he asked with an apologetic smile.

'Erm . . . yes. But it doesn't matter.' She smiled as she squinted at him. 'It's just lovely to see you.'

She ushered him through the door and then gave him a big hug.

'I felt so guilty that I haven't got down to see Jake, or any of you, after what happened,' Pete explained. 'And so when I woke up this morning I just jumped in the car.'

'Come on in,' she said. 'I'll put some coffee on.'

'How's Jake doing?' Peter asked as they made their way

through to the enormous kitchen area. They had spoken on the phone several times since the hijacking, and Laura had kept him up to date with how things were.

'He's all right,' Laura said. 'Better than I thought he'd be. But he can still get very anxious around certain situations.'

'It'll take time,' Pete said. 'I can't wait to see him.'

Laura glanced down at her watch. 'You've got another couple of hours before he surfaces. And as for Rosie . . .'

'Midday?' Pete asked with a wry smile.

'Not far off,' Laura said as she set up the coffee machine.

'So, I'm stuck with you for a bit,' Pete teased her.

'I guess so,' she said as she put ground coffee into the machine's filter. 'How's Anusha?'

'She's spending the day out in Wythenshawe, horse riding,' he explained.

Laura nodded. 'I remember she loves riding. Why don't you ever go with her?'

'Are you joking?' He snorted in laughter. 'Me on a horse? No, thanks.'

Clicking the button on the machine, she closed the lid, and the coffeepot filled.

After a few seconds, she looked over at him. 'I've got a strong feeling there's another reason for you visiting today.'

Pete shrugged. 'Why?'

'Because I've known you for over twenty years,' she said. 'And you just get this look.'

Pete made a face. 'There is something. But I didn't want to launch into it before we'd sat.' He pulled a memory stick from his pocket. 'Got a laptop to hand?'

She nodded, went over to the table and came to the breakfast bar with her laptop. Opening it, she logged in and then slid it in front of him.

'Is this to do with Butterfield?' she asked. She was now feeling uneasy.

'Sort of,' Peter said as he pushed in the memory stick and tapped on some keys. 'I thought I should show you, rather than tell you over the phone.'

'Tell me what, Pete?' she asked. 'You're worrying me.'

He turned to look at her. 'You remember we traced a burner phone that was used to make the emergency call on 12 August 2018?'

She nodded. 'You said it had originated in Trafford Police Station.'

'Exactly,' he said. 'I've checked the log. The phone call was made at 9.12 a.m. So, that would mean the uniformed officers were still in Trafford Police Station in briefing. They didn't head out on patrol until just after 9.20 a.m.'

She frowned. 'Sorry, I don't understand the significance of that.'

'You will in a minute,' he said. 'That means that Sam and Louise McDonald's first shout for the day was to go over to Brannings Warehouse. That's confirmed by CAD records.'

'Okay,' she said, but she was none the wiser as to what point he might be driving at.

Pete clicked a button and a mobile phone record came onto the screen. 'This is the record for the mobile phone that made that call from Trafford Police Station at 9.12 a.m. I looked at other calls that burner phone had made in the following few days and I got the tech boys to triangulate any calls they could find data for.' He pointed to a phone call that was made on 14 August 2018. 'Whoever it was made this phone call two days after Sam and Louise died in Brannings Warehouse.'

Laura nodded. 'Yes. I can see that.'

Pete clicked to a map of Manchester. 'And the phone call was made from Gorton Cemetery here—' he pointed at the map '—at 2.17 p.m.'

She remembered Gorton was a suburb about six or seven miles to the south-east of Manchester.

Pete pointed to the map again. 'There's an ASDA store right opposite the cemetery so I pulled the CCTV from their hard-drive from 2 p.m. onwards on 14 August. At 2.11 p.m., a car drives into the ASDA car park and a man gets out and heads for the cemetery.'

He pulled up the footage and started playing it. Laura could clearly see a tall man in a baseball cap and sunglasses crossing the road and going through the wrought-iron gates.

She frowned. 'You can't see who it is.'

'Wait until he comes back,' Pete explained as he played the CCTV footage forward to 2.23 p.m. 'This is him again. Except now he's not wearing sunglasses.'

Laura squinted at the CCTV footage as the man crossed the road and walked towards his car.

It was then that she could see his face.

It was Superintendent Ian Butterfield.

'Butterfield?' she whispered. 'So the burner phone was definitely his?'

Pete pointed to the screen with a dark expression. 'Yeah, that's not even the shocking part. Look at this woman who follows him out of the cemetery one minute later.'

Laura peered intently at the screen as a young woman crossed the road outside the cemetery, walked into the ASDA car park and headed in the opposite direction to where Butterfield had parked his car.

It was only as she turned to look at a man walking past with a trolley that Laura saw a face that she instantly recognised.

I don't understand . . .

The blood drained from her face as she reeled in horror. She gasped. 'That's Louise McDonald.'

How can Sam's partner still be alive?

368

'Yes,' Pete said grimly.

'But she died with Sam in Brannings Warehouse!' she whispered. 'What's going on?'

'Louise was only identified by her jewellery after the fire,' Pete gently reminded Laura. 'We were never able to obtain DNA evidence to undoubtedly prove the identity of the body.'

'But we went to her funeral,' Laura exclaimed in utter bewilderment.

'I know, Laura,' he said and then pointed to the frozen image on the screen. 'But whoever is in that grave, it's not Louise McDonald.'

DCI Laura Hart returns in the next thrilling instalment of
Simon McCleave's Anglesey Series

In Too Deep

Available to pre-order now

Your **FREE** book is
waiting for you now!

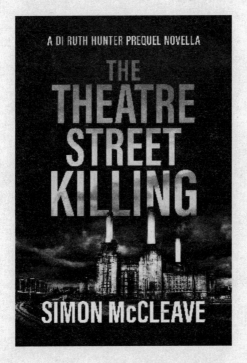

Get your FREE copy of the prequel to the
DI Ruth Hunter Series NOW!

Visit:
http://www.simonmccleave.com/vip-email-club
and join Simon's VIP Email Club.